THE WAR MACHINE

The War Machine

by
Barry W. Levy

DOUBLE ‡ DAGGER

© 2024, Barry W. Levy

All rights reserved. No part of this publication may be reproduced, stored in a retrieval system, or transmitted in any form by any process—electronic, mechanical, photocopying, recording, or otherwise—without the prior written permission of the copyright owner. The scanning, uploading, and distribution of this book via the Internet or via any other means without permission of the copyright owner is illegal and punishable by law.

> Library and Archives Canada Cataloguing in Publication
> Levy, Barry W. author
> The War Machine / Barry W. Levy

Issued in print and electronic formats.
ISBN:978-1-990644-93-1(paperback)
ISBN: 978-1-990644-94-8 (ebook)

Cover Design: Paul Hewitt
Interior Design: Winston A. Prescott
Author photo credit: Helenna Santos

> Double Dagger Books Ltd.
> Toronto, Ontario, Canada
> www.doubledagger.ca

"Let your plans be dark and as impenetrable as night, and when you move, fall like a thunderbolt."

Sun Tzu, from *The Art of War*

For Dale and the heroic boys of MACV-SOG.

Author's Note

"In my dreams I hear again the crash of guns, the rattle of musketry, the strange mournful mutter of the battlefield."
General Douglas MacArthur

I'VE NEVER SERVED IN THE MILITARY or seen any kind of combat other than schoolyard fights and two attempts at almost getting my orange belt in karate. None of my immediate family members on either side have military backgrounds. I did have severe trauma when I was a small child that haunts me, and I deal with the PTSD that has followed me since, but my scars have nothing on the men and women who have found themselves in combat situations. Like the front-liners in medicine who fought in hospitals and clinics all over the world during the COVID Pandemic, the trauma of combat soldiers was compacted by layers of trauma heaped upon each other, day after day, and I give them all my most profound respect.

    I clearly recall being in the grade twelve and hearing that the Russians had invaded Afghanistan, and the world was half expecting another world war. My friends and I didn't want to die in a war, but we also couldn't deny that we had a strong urge to volunteer to fight.

    Between 30,000 and 40,000 Canadian men felt the same way during America's war in Vietnam. They crossed the border and volunteered. In doing so, they pretty much replaced all of Uncle Sam's draft dodgers. A similar number of Americans had also crossed into Canada during WWII and volunteered to fight in Europe before America got into that war. This ingrained right of passage intrigued me, so when I met my first Canadian Vietnam veteran and got to know his story, questions came up that got under my skin.

Why the hell did he go? And how can he even function with the massive amount of trauma and loss he experienced? Why did Canada quietly make $3B in war materials for the US during the war, and another $10B in non-military materials that went mostly to South Vietnam, while making a big public show of trying to negotiate peace? What kind of country am I actually living in? How does the world actually work, and what is my place in it?

The more I dug, the more skullduggery I found. I have to admit I started this investigation from the point of view of someone who agrees with war only as the very last stage of diplomacy. There's not a shred of John Bolton in me, but I also understand that the world is a dangerous place with a lot of dangerous people and some very sharp edges. I've seen it with my own eyes. I don't think anyone can reasonably disagree with fighting Hitler's forces, but what I found in my research was that a similar authoritarian hand left its fingerprints all over this period of Canadian history.

I don't like it when my government lies to me, and I don't like it when it takes its marching orders from another country and then prances around like it's saving the world from tyranny. It was especially astounding to find out that America didn't ask Canada to help. Our politicians and business leaders volunteered us, without bothering to ask its citizens. That's not doing the people's work.

When the thin edge of fascism makes its way under a democracy, it's important that citizens make a lot of noise and the press reports on it. In this case some people tried, but it took nearly a decade for anything to come of it and by that time the war was over, and all the money was in the bank. The press in Canada was asleep at the wheel, and frankly, so were the citizens.

I can't say what was in the hearts of the Canadians whose companies made things like napalm, bullets, and agent orange for the US, but we have all seen the horrifying results in newsreel footage and movies.

It surprised me at first that a lot of Canadians were mad at me for digging up all this dirt on the land of my birth, and have asked me, "What's your point? Don't you love your country?" The best way I can answer that was to let them know that loving my country is exactly why I'm doing this. A democracy can only function when its citizens insist on the truth. Canada is one of the last bastions of democracy on Earth, and acting like a fan all the time is not the way to protect it. You have to participate, or it all falls apart. Constantly holding your government's feet to the fire is our duty.

There were four dark years in America that ended in an attempted overthrow of the government in 2021, and that is what the end game looks like when elected officials ignore the rules of democracy and work from the fascist playbook. The press was again late to that party, and in some cases participated. In this case it happened to the most powerful, well-armed, democracy the world has ever known, so don't think it can't happen anywhere else at any time. It can and it did, and it could happen in Canada.

The War Machine is set in a more comfortable time, 1988, when we weren't being spied on by our phones, electronics, and appliances. It was near the birth of the cashless society, and nearing the end of newspapers as we knew them. Although the story is loosely based on my late friend's story of signing up for a tour in Vietnam and ending up in a never-ending nightmare, it is a work of fiction that is peppered with real facts about what Canada tried to hide about its involvement in the Vietnam War. At its core, it's a spy thriller about ordinary people thrown into extraordinary circumstances, and then dealing with the resulting scar tissue. It's a story about tragic loss, but more importantly, The War Machine is about moving forward with hope and healing. I hope you enjoy it.

Elephant Grass
Vietnam, 1968, somewhere near the Laotian border

THE IROQUOIS' BLADES POUND like a war drum as Kick looks past his combat boots at the grassy hilltop coming up fast. Hand signs. Jumping. Crouching. Running low for the tree line. Huey sounds fading and North Vietnam invading his senses. The reek of damp rot. Heat like a furnace. Babbler birds chattering all at once. Ears straining for clicks of metal, foreign voices, or shifting feet. Fuck it's hot.

If the jungle's not trying to kill him with weather, it's sending snakes, rock apes, tigers, or the Viet Cong. Kick looks at the other camouflaged faces, panting in the heat. His boys are focused. He tells them with his hands to lay dog for thirty minutes. See if Charlie comes calling. Near the end of basic training his drill sergeant used to softly drop nuggets of military wisdom into their ears. "Be swift as the wind, gentle as the forest, fierce as fire, unshakable as the mountain."

Kick and his five boys keep this in mind as they wind through the elephant grass like snakes, slow and quiet. Pivot right, slide leg and shoulder through the blades. Pivot left, slide through. Pivot. Slide. Pivot. Slide. They're whispers on the sticky breeze. Not seeing much, but not being seen. Their other senses compensate. All the M16 muzzles are down, the safeties off. The wet hairs on Kick's arms stand straight up, desperately trying to wick away the heat. A cluster of sweat hangs on his face for a moment, before racing down into his open tiger-striped camo shirt. His spartan body is soaking wet. He looks much older than his twenty young years. At only five-foot-seven he's strong like steel cable, flexible like rubber, and completely fat free. He's a Canadian-born, American-made killing machine on his second tour, and he's leading a crack team of soldiers. He's living his dream.

The air is still. Kick listens hard for anything to give away his prey. The Cong and the North Vietnamese Army. Armed, trained, and supplied by China and Russia. They're out there in the grass. Above in the hills. Dug deep into tunnels. Waiting. Squatting. Listening. Ready.

Kick catches a glimpse of Hollywood McCormick's muscular form on point. The Crazy Canuck loves point. Seeping adrenaline and heart-thumping rhythm are recreation to him. He's a spring loaded, six-foot-two beast. But he's silent. Hollywood's gear doesn't make a sound as he slides along. Not a tinkle. Not the smoke grenades, or the regulars. Not his knife, his M16, or the unconventional sawed-off shotgun. Not even the cheap sunglasses stowed in his shirt pocket that gave him his nickname. Hollywood's shit is tight. He varies the time between steps to something close to random, and everyone follows with broken cadence. Simpson, the Black kid from Chicago, calls it white boy rhythm.

Before they left this morning, Hollywood said what he always says for good luck. "Looks like a badass mother of a day." He's sweating profusely as he looks back at Kick, and smiles before popping a salt pill. Kick and the rest follow suit. Running low on salt can really fuck up your day in 'Nam.

Looking behind, Kick checks in with Simpson. He's still green, but solid in a fight. Next comes Frosty the Australian from Brisbane, who's cool under fire, and reliable. Watt is next with the radio. Kick likes the attitude on this smart-assed New Yorker, who takes pride in his job and makes sure no one forgets how important he is. In the rear is Beach, with seven kills now. He's West Texas to the core, from cattle country around Marfa, and he's a badass piece of work.

They haven't had an officer with them for weeks, since the last second lieutenant caught a round in his skull being John Wayne. The Lt sparked up a smoke on patrol which is like hoisting a flag that says, "Kill me." He was warned, but he knew everything, and it was only dumb luck he was the only casualty. Now Kick's the sarge in charge and everything's working great because his boys ain't broke. The team is dialed in like one animal. From any angle they *are* the jungle, hunting in perfect silence.

It takes thirty minutes of sliding through the elephant grass like this to get to a hilltop. They'll go to ground for the night and wait for signs of fires, movement, chatter, and Charlie's favorite, nuoc mam. Kick loves that nasty fermented fish sauce. It drifts through the jungle like death and has helped them notch more kills than anything else.

When they find a VC camp, they call the nearest firebase for an artillery strike. *Arty*. Hollywood calls it arty arty boom boom. Once they direct the fire mission, they call for an EVAC and *di di mao*. Local for run like a hell. They never want to meet the enemy face to face. Not in Chuck's back yard.

They are ghosts floating through the bush. A long range recon patrol. As Frosty puts it, "They fuckin' find it, fuck it up, and fuck the fuck off."

There's a pull in the pit of Kick's stomach. Shit. He stops cold. A second later Hollywood's arm shoots up at ninety degrees and forms a hard fist. They all freeze and their M16s quietly rise. He opens his mouth to breathe silently. After twenty seconds Vietnamese voices grow loud enough to hear.

A patrol is moving past on a high-speed trail at their three o'clock. There's the unmistakable metallic sound of weapons. Now yelling. Still frozen. More yelling. Hollywood slowly gets low, and the rest follow him down on one knee. He directs four of them to aim in a pattern toward the voices, with Beach looking 180 degrees the other way, watching their six. They kneel in silence, glistening in the grass.

Wet Yer Whistle
November, 1988 — Vancouver, BC, Canada

KICK HAS STARED AT THIS SAD OLD GIRL a hundred times wondering when they're going to put her down. A ruin of herself, she groans against her moorings, worn down by time, salt, and struggle, but still holds her rusted head high.

Flexing his cigarette hand, he watches the shrapnel scar on the back of it change shape, then turns it over for the exit scar on his palm. Should have worn gloves today. He feels old and looks the part. No one can ever guess his age. Most peg him at late fifties, even though he's only forty-three. Who would assume a five-foot-seven shrimp like him is a decorated war hero, trained assassin, occasional spy, and a highly paid mercenary? Cigarette smoke blows back into his eyes, and he pinches them closed. They're raccoon-dark and wrinkled to shit. The years have not been kind to his body. He's strong-armed it through well over twelve labors and come inches from death too many times to count. He touches his forehead.

He's messed up and it's fucking with his inner radar. He feels eyes on him constantly and people behind him, but no internal alarms have gone off. It's weird. Like his natural defenses are being jammed. His eyes feel strange.

There's a cruel waterfall pouring hard behind his face that drops into a deep chasm in his chest. He takes a drag on his smoke and the bite feels good. A little pain often snaps him out of these funks, but not today. The low tide reeks. He's lightheaded but trapped under a heavy blanket of gloom. Smoke curls seductively up to his face. The smell reminds him of childhood, baseball and freshly cut grass. Happier times with his parents.

He drops his smoke and the heel of his cowboy boot crushes the butt.

His boots need a polish. Months of this shaggy beard and long crazy hair are driving him nuts, but he can't bring himself to deal with it. Kick has never let himself go like this. Like a lot of vets, he prides himself on being clean-shaven and squared away. But he's not. The more he fills the chasm, the deeper it gets, the harder the water falls, and the heavier the blanket presses down. Last time he saw himself in the mirror he looked like darkness. He used to enjoy his badass appearance, but he's starting to look dead. Kick touches the Smith & Wesson M&P-45 holstered under his left arm, then taps on the silencer and spare mag. He feels a bit better.

Kick's been low before, but now he can't remember how he got out of it. An assignment? His mind's so foggy. He breathes deeply and catches a whiff of the ocean again. His breath dissolves in the putrid air. It smells like death. He's seeing things again. Strange things he can't think about, so he doesn't, and that makes it worse. The strange things get mad when they're ignored.

His mind goes soggy and limp as his boot touches his olive drab backpack. There are random newspaper clippings and bits of paper sticking out. What are they for? Why can't he remember? His mind used to be sharp. He picks up the rucksack and looks at it like a child. Right. The mission. For truth. He remembers that much. He's telling the fat cat story. That's what it is. Tell that story, no matter what. It's coming back to him. He knows where he is. Pier Number Three at the Versatile Pacific Shipyards in North Vancouver. What's left of it, at least. It's rotting away, collapsing, or getting smashed up to make way for shiny condos.

The sky is still drizzling and by the look of the darkening clouds it's going to rain hard soon. Hissing sounds spray from passing cars in the distance. People are scurrying with umbrellas, or running with heads down, hats on, and hoods up. The holiday lights are up, and it's good they burn day and night. He's clinging to the happy little lights, since the sun barely seems to rise this time of year. A salty tear rolls out of one eye. He's capsized with no way to right himself. The military didn't teach him that.

Across the harbor, set against Vancouver's wall of glassy buildings, a Helijet, crammed full of suits, all warm and cozy, takes off on its way to Victoria on Vancouver Island. Kick fought a war for the suits and they don't even know it. They'll know it before this is over. The suits said the war he fought was for freedom, but he knows it was really for tin, rubber, and rice. His war's mission was to protect trade with Southeast Asia from the commies. Fuckin' commies.

The mission he's on now will have to be his last though, because he's running out of juice. But he must Charlie Mike — complete the mission. His mind follows the sound of the Helijet rotors, and he gets lost in the thump of the blades.

The next thing he knows rain is pounding off him at the top of cement stairs. They lead down to a basement bar. Somehow, he made it to East Pender Street, in Vancouver's lower Eastside. An old country and western song drifts up from a door at the bottom of the stairs. 'Dusty's Wet Yer Whistle' has been newly painted in gold and black letters on its wired glass pane. His right foot's killing him today, and he shifts the weight off it. Waylon Jennings' 'I'm a Ramblin' Man' is playing as he limps on down the stairs. A deep voice cuts through the twang like a cannon, and Kick gets ready to face the music.

❖ ❖ ❖ ❖

Dusty, the bar owner, cocks his bald head as he hears the gimpy walk coming down the stairs. He mumbles to himself, "Motherfucker's got his fuckin' nerve." He's a six-foot-six barrel of a Black man, and his left bicep bulges as he pulls on the draft tap for Phil, an older heavy-set man of Malaysian descent. Probably won't charge him for this. Once upon a time Phil had a bunch of car dealerships, but he drank them all away.

The gimpy walk pauses outside the door. Dusty imagines he's lighting a smoke to get his nerve up, before he steps inside and drips all over his clean floor. Dusty looks down at his Merle Haggard 'Mama Tried' t-shirt, and sighs. "And if he tells that fuckin' joke again, I'll pop him."

"What's that, Dusty?" Phil asks.

The door opens and Kick walks in, cigarette in his mouth, dripping water everywhere. "Jesus, Mama should have *tried* harder!"

Phil laughs, but Dusty doesn't even look up. He strokes his Fu-Manchu mustache and murmurs, "Un-fucking-believable. Fair weather fucking asshole." Malaysian Phil can see he's about to be in the middle, so he salutes the tattered Marine Corps flag above the bar and thanks Dusty for kicking ass in Khe Sahn before scurrying back to his table, holding the pint like a sacrament.

Kick sniffs the air. "This place smells a bit less like failure today."

Dusty takes him in. His hair and beard are insanely long and shaggy, and his eyes have sunk back into his face. He's lost weight, which Dusty didn't think was possible, and looks crazed.

Dusty puts his hand on the draft tap. "You look like proof that no one here gets out alive." Kick says nothing. Dusty pours him a pint of the shitty stuff and plants it on a coaster. "Or like Che Guevara's illegitimate dead cousin. From the ugly side of the family."

"You look like Ho Chi Minh's legitimate daughter. Is it cultural appropriation for a Black man to have a Fu Manchu? And what happened to the Afro?"

Dusty scoffs. "This is a mustache with a soul patch. And I'm shaving my head like all the cool brothers."

"That beer for me?"

"I ain't drinking that shit." Dusty pours himself a whiskey neat. Kick dumps his pack on the bar and shakes the rain off his coat.

Dusty watches the water scatter on the floor. "You're so considerate. Maybe I should use your disgusting face to mop that up."

"Cool brother, my ass." Kick hangs his coat on a hook under the bar top. It's a small detail Dusty is proud of, along with the boot rail at the base and the original marble top. Kick settles on a stool and gulps his beer.

Dusty waits until he puts it down, then raises his glass to Kick. "Cheers."

"Oh yeah. Cheers."

"So?"

"So what?"

"Where you been for six weeks?"

"Working."

"Really? 'Cause your handlers have been trying to find you. Musta lost your number."

Kick finishes his beer and butts his smoke. "You know I don't have a phone."

"Right. In case the VC are still looking for you. Something tells me if they wanted to get to you, they wouldn't call first." Dusty looks at the backpack. "Still trying to put the country in jail?"

"I just have to get it organized and published."

"Is that all. You must be talking to a publisher then." There's a pause. "Look, take some friendly advice and hang up your fuckin' spurs, Tex. Just settle down and stop ... whatever the fuck it is you're doing."

Kick holds up his empty glass and looks at it with disgust. "You're still buying reject kegs from O'Keefe? I thought you'd have moved to an up-market brand by now. Like Aqua Velva." He belches.

"Guess you're not familiar with that whole gift horse thing, huh?"

"Why are you so snippy?" Kick snaps.

"Snippy? You walk in here looking like a homeless junkie, after I spent weeks wonderin' if you were alive or dead."

"Come on!"

"You *come on*! When 'Nam vets drop out of sight, what does it usually mean? Do I have to say it?"

Kick looks at the bar top. "I haven't been myself."

"Ya think?"

There's a strained pause. "I'm sorry."

"There it is." Dusty drains his whiskey. It's clear to Dusty that his friend's in trouble, but he knows he can only push so hard. Dusty pours himself another, grabs Kick's pack, and heads to a table to see what's in it. He stops short. "Nothing explosive in here, right?"

"Don't be stupid."

"That's a legit question. Don't think I've forgotten about what's in this bag sometimes." Dusty takes a seat. "Pretend you're normal and have a conversation with an old friend you haven't seen in weeks."

Kick does a half-assed job of pouring a fresh beer and walks over.

Dusty looks at the head on the beer and shakes his head. "Oh my god, you're a grown-ass man and you don't know how to pour a proper beer!" Kick ignores the remark as Dusty pulls out several newspaper clippings from the pack and examines them. "What ya got in here?" He reads the headlines. "From *The Telegraph*. 'Bazooka Barrels, Tank Parts, Bomb Sights - All Made in Canada for Vietnam'. All right, here's a good one, 'Death of Beheaded Canadian Official Ruled Suicide'. Now that one's funny 'cause he would have had to cut off his own head."

Kick snatches the clippings back and sits. He picks up a candle from the table. "What's this?"

"You like that? Every table's got a candle now. I'm classin' the place up."

"Are you going to start serving *cuisine*?"

"If by that you mean poutine, it's crossed my mind. I'm coming up on my ten-year anniversary."

Kick looks around. "No shit. We've known each other that long, huh?"

Dusty laughs. "Yeah, you dragged your arrogant ass in a few weeks after I opened. Hadn't heard lip like that since Danang."

"You're gonna need more than candles to gentrify this old dump."

"You let me worry about that." Dusty points at the articles. "This was all reported years ago, right? Can't you tell no one cares? Move on."

"Once I put it all together and give it some context, it'll get it done. You'll see. And you're right — I need an editor, and I'm ... working on that. Your problem is your tail's still between your legs. Hiding up here in the great white north. Don't you ever go back to Atlanta to visit?"

"Where they called me a baby killer? And all those white cops? No thanks." Dusty pours himself another whiskey. Phil is mumbling to himself at his table. "You still good, Phil?" Phil puts his head on the table.

Kick looks around. "Why's it so quiet in here?"

"Tomorrow's welfare Wednesday. Don't worry, it'll be packed by noon."

Dusty sits back down. "So, when Canada finds all this out, what do you expect will happen? You'll get a parade? A thank you? No one gives a shit."

"People deserve to know how the world really works. Is that wrong?"

"Stick your nose where it doesn't belong, you'll get your head chopped off."

"Sometimes that's the only way things change," Kick snaps back.

"I don't see a lot of headless people bragging how they changed the world, do you?"

Kick takes a long drag on his cigarette. "Seriously, candles?"

"I'm gonna bring in new customers."

Kick looks over at the snoring Phil. "Something wrong with your current clientele?"

"I like Phil. Know why?"

"His charm and personal hygiene?"

"You're one to talk. Phil grew up in Kuala Lumpur, during Vietnam," Dusty says. "We're two of his heroes 'cause we stopped communism in its path, so his family didn't have to fight them in Malaysia. When he moved to Vancouver, he was shocked to find out everyone thinks America *lost* the Vietnam War, 'cause in Malaysia, we won. Which is why, as you know, a lot of our buddies put down roots in Southeast Asia."

Kick's unusually quiet for a moment, and Dusty thinks he sees a tear in his eye. "Yeah," Kick says. "We did all right. To us."

Dusty touches his glass to Kick's and says, "Badass motherfuckin' commie-killin' sons-a-bitches, that's what we are." They drink. "You sure you're okay?"

"Fine," Kick answers. "Great. Just busy."

Dusty eases off. "Well good, 'cause I'm having an *event*. It's an anniversary party, and one of the local papers is giving me publicity. I've reached out to try and get some local military types drinking here on the regular. Happy hours, open mic nights, maybe some comedy."

Kick laughs, and Dusty says, "See? You're already entertained."

"Okay, I've never seen you as much of a comedy guy. And are you expecting a lot of mirth to come out of these *military types*?"

"Maybe! Sometimes comics need a place to try out new stuff. And you know what happens when they do that?"

Kick laughs. "Crickets?"

"No."

"Heckling?" Kick laughs harder.

"No, smartass. Other comics hang out, too. Bring friends and have drinks. And if they wanna smoke a joint in the bathroom, where I just put in a new exhaust fan, I won't give a shit, unlike some places around here. That's just some of the changes I got planned." Dusty pulls a flier out of his pocket and stuffs it in Kick's pocket. "My event is on Thursday, motherfucker, if you're not busy jacking off to newspaper clippings 'n' shit."

"That's Veterans Day."

"It's called *Remembrance Day* here. In case you forgot, Canadian. Try and dress presentable, and bathe. Jesus, you smell like a rock ape's asshole!"

"You need one rule," Kick demands.

Dusty sighs. "Don't go there."

"No draft dodgers. It should be on a sign at the door."

"Like they're going to make a bee-line for my bar. An after everything we went through over there, you can blame them for not going. Seriously?"

Kick raises his voice. "When you're called, you go!"

"You weren't called! No one called you! You didn't get drafted, motherfucker — you volunteered! What the fuck were you thinking anyway?"

Kick picks up his bag and coat and storms out the back.

Dusty stands up and yells, "Shit, that's all it takes to get rid of you? Wish I knew a decade ago! And use the front door like a normal person!" The back door slams and Dusty stares at it.

Kick's been spit-polished and clean-shaven for as long as he's known him. He's had other vet friends go to seed like this, and it hasn't ended well. There aren't many 'Nam buddies left in Dusty's world. Kick may be a pain in the ass, but he's still his best friend, and he's in trouble.

Dusty heads back to the bar. "Fuckin' asshole."

3
WHITE SOCKS

KICK MAKES HIS WAY HOME down East Hastings Street through a hard rain, past the junkies, dealers, hookers, neon signs, and noodle houses. He's rattled. The odd feeling he's been having still haunts him. There are blips just outside his radar.

He's approaching the police precinct at the corner of Main where they've resigned themselves to the whole sordid situation of the Lower Eastside. If they can keep the drugs, overdoses, and mayhem confined to this area, the thieves might stay out of tony places like Point Grey, Kits, or, heaven forbid, West Vancouver. One person's TV or VCR is another's way to pay for a fix.

A violent noise snaps his head around. A bare foot, strung-out guy in ripped jeans and no shirt, jaywalks across traffic making brake lights pop, and rubber squeal. He slams his hands down hard on the hood of a shiny new BMW, long wet hair flying in the rain, and screams bloody murder at the horrified driver. A schoolgirl in uniform cowers in the passenger seat, and when the man sees her, he stares. "I went to school! I was a kid!"

People stride into traffic here all the time, holding their own version of court. It's the last bit of power they have, after their lives have been swept away by drugs, booze, mental illness, or all of the above. Some are veterans, which Kick tries not to think about.

He stops at a red light as the rain comes down harder, so he pops up the hood of his coat. Vancouver rain amazes him. It's a living force that knows just how to fuck with you. Not like a nice predictable Asian monsoon you can set your watch by that pounds straight down. Vancouver rain is moody, sneaky, and shows up whenever it feels like it. It will defy gravity and come at you sideways, blow around in a mist and get in places it shouldn't go, or hit you from above like buckshot. It rains so hard here sometimes it bounces off the pavement and hits him square in the face. Right now, it's like AK-47 rounds.

Today is cold. And it's not just cold, it's *wet cold*. The kind Kick hates the most. One degree above freezing, so there's maximum dampness straight to the bone marrow. He still loves Van, though. It's as close to home as it gets.

Water runs off the curb, down the side of the road, then into a storm drain. From there it pours through a series of crisscrossing pipes under the crisscrossing roads, carrying every bad dose, drunken piss, shit, puke, dead rat, bug, and spent needle straight to the ocean. The refuse of the refuse. Kick stands at this crossroad of misery and pain, wondering how he got here. He had such promise, and so many dreams. Like coming home a hero, getting married, having kids, and teaching them what they need to know to thrive in the world. He tries to shake off the feelings, because feelings make you vulnerable, and vulnerable people get killed.

The wind picks up and carries a familiar voice to him. "Long time, no see."

Kick's head swings around, and he catches a large figure passing in tiger-striped fatigues. It's Hollywood. He's in the middle of the road like the crazy shirtless man. Traffic races past his char-scorched body and his bloody face with the broke-ass sunglasses hanging off it. A helicopter thumps overhead, and Kick feels the war creeping in. His heart starts to pound. Hollywood's smile drips with dark blood. He should run out there and save him. A passerby bumps Kick, and the vision vanishes.

Another guy clips him. "The light's fuckin' green, man!"

Kick's hands are shaking, but he collects himself and crosses the road, still looking for his old friend. He stops on the other side under an awning and lights a smoke, his hands still shaking. Hollywood? Why is he here? He pulls hard on his cigarette and exhales into the pounding rain.

A child's voice asks, "Shoeshine?" He looks, but there's no kid. Hard wires spark, and there's a hard pull deep in the pit of his stomach like his guts are being pulled down by a hook. A blip has entered his radar. His nostrils flare, senses heighten, and pupils expand as he looks across the street. An Asian man with a black umbrella is looking into the window of the Carnegie Centre, watching him in the reflection. An old trick. Fucked-up or not, Kick's training dials him right into combat mode. He searches the Asian man's face but can't place him. But he can tell the man knows him, and he's staring right back. Ballsy.

A chill creeps up Kick's spine, but it doesn't bother him. He takes another drag on his smoke and keeps eye contact. There's no shake in his hands now. Both men know it's decision time. Fight, flight, or freeze? This Asian guy doesn't look like the flight kind. He looks like the fight kind. Kick is trying to think of the writer who penned, "To live, is to be hunted." Motherfucker wasn't wrong.

If this was Danang, he'd head over and solve this with his Smith & Wesson, but he has different rules here. Rules Kick doesn't like, but in this case the protocol is to evade, so he turns, heads a few doors down the street, and slips into the front of the Empress, a skinny but elegant hotel from the early 1900s that's seen better days. He slows down at the bar and greets a bearded old white guy with an ink vine scar on his neck. "Hey, Robert! If ya looked any better, I'd be suspicious."

"Ha. You always have something funny."

"Mind if I cut out the back?" Kick asks.

"Sure. You don't have to ask."

"Thanks. Be good." Kick keeps moving.

"And if I can't be good, I'll be good at it!" Robert yells after him.

Kick forces a chuckle and waves as he heads past the bathrooms and exits into the back alley where he pauses and checks around. There's nothing but junkies, dumpsters, and a delivery truck that's always here around this time of day. He takes a right and hustles down the alley.

Two blocks away, past the old Patricia Hotel, he can't see a tail, so he cuts back up to East Hastings and grabs a city bus. He rides it for nine blocks, gets out, and then heads up one block and ducks into a seedy walk-up apartment building. Two and a half floors up he stands on the landing and looks down at the street from the edge of a dirty window. Less than a minute later, the same guy, with the same black umbrella and same coat, walks down the opposite side of the street. The figure slows, pretends to window shop while checking who's nearby in the reflection, then starts looking up. Kick allows one eye to stay on the mystery man. Anyone looking at his window will see little else but reflection, but they could see movement, so he stays perfectly still.

It's the same guy. He must have a driver, or his own car. Kick memorizes the details. Chinese, five-foot-eight, no scars, black gloves, smoking a cigarette in his right hand, umbrella in his left. Raincoat looks like London Fog, suit and tie underneath, and he's roughly thirty to thirty-five years old. Seems ex-military by the haircut and bearing. Nothing clicks, but something's distantly familiar. It's his eyes, but Kick can't place him. Finding no one in the upper windows, the stranger turns back to the shop window, then carries on up the street.

That's when Kick notices his feet. He's wearing white socks. Could be a Company man, but, if he's CIA, why not just make contact? Kick is kind of AWOL, but if that's the case his handlers could just get him a message. Unless they're trying to hit him? Not likely. But maybe someone else. Also, not likely.

Who wears white socks with a suit?

It'll be dark in less than an hour, but he chances walking the alleys back to his place. He repeats his upstairs trick two more times, but there are no more tails, no one suspicious. He carefully picks his way back to the elegant 1911 Edwardian-style Balmoral Hotel on East Hastings. Kick loves the big sign that was added later in the forties and became part of the neighborhood's neon era. Like the hotel, the sign's in sad shape. He watches the front door from an alley across the street for thirty minutes, then sneaks into the back door of the nearby Regent Hotel that looks right across the street at his place.

Kick lived at the Regent for a while when he first moved back to Vancouver. It's another grand old lady from the same era. Once inside, he heads to the front desk where a mouse-like man is working the large reception desk. Kick already has his coat off. He slips wordlessly to the other side of the desk and sits down on the floor bedside the man's feet, staying invisible to anyone else. The small man doesn't look up from his newspaper, but says in a thin voice, "Hey, Kick. Need a few minutes there?"

Kick takes out a pack of Marlboros and slides them onto a shelf beside Roger. "Sure do, brother, if that's okay?"

"You know it is."

"See anyone?" Kick asks.

"All clear. I'll keep you posted," Roger answers casually.

The front doors open and young voices chatter in German. Backpackers making their way down the West Coast to Mexico. They ask Roger about the history of the place, if it's haunted, was there a speakeasy here, and the rest of the usual questions. Kick is dying for a smoke, but the Germans are excited and take their time checking in.

While Roger records passport numbers and gets payment, he fills them in on the area. "The Regent's is an eight-story Chicago-style gem built in 1913 for tourists and business travelers arriving on the new Canadian Northern Railway and by boat via the new Panama Canal. Originally, it had its own barbershop, shoeshine stand, and cigar store. She's been spruced up and renovated for low-income social housing on the lower floors, and the rest is open to good folks like you out seeing the world."

Of all the friends Kick has in the neighborhood, Roger is his most steadfast. He served his tour in Vietnam as a Marine chopper mechanic in 1968, and figured he'd have a better chance of avoiding violence by keeping his head in the guts of a Jolly Green Giant. That worked out great until August 23rd when they were hit by the Tet Offensive, known among vets as Tet '68, or just Tet. His base was overrun and instead of overhauling a Sikorsky, Roger found himself fighting for his life. The only weapon Roger had was an oversized wrench, so he cracked open his enemy's skull, stole his AK-47, and picked off eleven NVA soldiers who had taken key positions. One had a satchel charge ready to throw into a hooch. Roger watched him get blown into tiny pieces and a spray of pink mist. Once a Marine, always a Marine. The event scarred him badly inside, and he was never the same.

For his exceptionally meritorious service, the Corps awarded him the Distinguished Service Medal. Once he rotated home that medal couldn't help him sleep, and he usually worked a double shift at the hotel to keep his mind occupied. Kick could tell he was a vet at first sight, and he's one of the few people Roger trusts with his story. Everyone else sees a meek little man who's easy to push around. He's uncomfortable with violence, mostly because he's afraid he'll go all the way once he starts. When he's been bullied in the past, Kick has taken care of things for him, and the neighborhood knows better now. No point in Roger waking up his ghosts, when Kick is fine with exorcising his own.

After an hour hiding at the front desk, Kick gets up and slips into the hotel proper, turns down a hallway, and steps into a large janitor's closet. Snapping on a penlight, he walks to the back of it, moves some boxes, opens a small door, and walks down some ancient creaky stairs into a dark void. It's a tunnel that runs under the street and connects with the basement of his hotel.

A few minutes later, Kick opens a door and appears on the basement level of his home at the Balmoral Hotel. He walks past the laundry, the furnace room, then stops in front of an unmarked black metal door. He checks the hinge side for a small piece of paper stuck between the door edge and the jamb, almost invisible below the lower hinge. It's exactly how he left it, and he's satisfied that no one has opened the door since he left. It's an old habit that's saved his life more than once over the years. He feels woozy as he pulls his gun, but steadies himself, then quietly slips inside.

He switches the lights on and checks the shabby but clean bathroom, kitchen area and living room, then the bedroom that contains a single bed that's perfectly made. The windowless place is more of a bunker than an apartment, but there are some homey touches and a few bookcases packed with everything from spy novels and science fiction to American classics and poetry.

He lays his gun on a beat-to-shit coffee table covered with empty beer cans, an overflowing ashtray, and newspapers. Under the newspapers he spies a full mickey of whiskey and pulls it out. From a shelf over the kitchen sink he grabs an exquisite cut-crystal tumbler with a chip in the base. Kick found it in the basement last year and cleaned it up. Who knows what rich prick drank out of it in the hotel during the roaring twenties. He pours the rotgut, takes a solid drink, and then another. He makes himself a peanut butter and strawberry jam sandwich and sits down in a beautifully beat-up leather armchair he stole from a vacated room. Kick is literally living in the past.

The jam squishes out of the bread as he bites it and catches his eye in an odd way. He feels strange. On the wall in front of him, there's a spider web of intersecting red strings that connect newspaper stories he has pinned to the wall. It looks like a hunt for a serial killer, and in a sense it is. There are articles with sections circled in red connected to other clippings, names scribbled on scraps of paper, all stuck to the wall and leading to other walls and the ceiling. Some of the papers just have dollar signs on them with question marks, and silhouettes of people.

Everything connects to one central piece of paper that has a big question mark on it. That question mark represents a hub of psychopathic organizations that create and support conflict to bump up their bottom lines. He's intrigued by the power they have. He takes another bite, and bright red jam drops onto his hand. He goes to lick it off his finger but stops. His eyes moisten. He looks at the red strings as they turn into jam and run down the walls.

His head fogs up as he drains the whiskey from the crystal glass and goes to pour another. He chugs from the bottle. There's jam on the side of the mickey. He puts it down. He's unbalanced, like when he was back on the pier. His mind is flaccid and runny like a painting by Dali. Jet-black thoughts scuttle in like spiders. The jam on the wall is now blood, and it pools at his feet. His gun is looking at him.

His mind is powerless to stop the dark churning in his head. An evil gravity pulls him through his chair, through the floor, and into a thick, soft darkness. He falls deeper and deeper and as he slips in, he feels the pain of his life and the things he's done. He won't find relief for another thirty years or more when he finally dies and finds peace.

Time stretches in front of him like a thin dark thread, but there's a bright glow at the end. It looks like a beautiful oasis. It looks like peace. The answer is simple. He'll make the thread shorter by pulling the brightness up to his face, and he'll live in there. In the peace. Kick sighs in relief as his jam-covered hand touches the gun. It feels like the right choice. The perfect choice. A peaceful choice.

There's a loud *bang* in the room followed by the sound of broken glass. He springs back up into the room, and his eyes snap over to his dresser. A framed picture has fallen face down. "I'll look before I go."

Something's moving. From behind the dresser a child's head peeks out. A tiny Vietnamese girl, no more than ten years old, steps out from behind the dresser. Then she's gone.

Kick stands and picks up the framed black-and-white photo. It's a group shot of him and his team walking away from a chopper. Through the cracked glass, he sees himself shirtless in camo pants and jump boots, with a wide bandage around his ribs plus one on his right hand. A reporter snapped it right as they got off the bird. He's being helped along by Beach and Simpson, still carrying their M16s. At the front of the pack, Frosty is helping Hollywood, who has one arm in a sling, and a big shit-eating grin on his face. Kick looks happy, or maybe it's pain. He touches a thick scar on one of his ribs. They became golden boys that day. He looks at his old friends in the photo and his heart swells. Tears run down his face and hit the floor. They're dropping like a hard rain. He looks down and wonders why the floor is spinning up at him so fast.

Go to Ground
Vietnam, 1968

KICK'S HEART IS POUNDING SO HARD he figures everyone can hear it through the elephant grass. Hollywood is smiling. Asshole. There could be a hundred reasons why Charlie is yelling. None of them means his team has been spotted.

The argument in Vietnamese gets closer and more heated but is soon interrupted by louder yelling from someone just arriving, obviously in charge. He barks what must be orders and things settle down. The patrol moves on.

Kick and the boys settle in and wait for thirty minutes. When the time is up, he nods at Hollywood, who points his index finger up, makes a quick circle, then pulls his fist down. *Form on me.* They head out slowly.

It's dusk when they reach their hilltop and set up for the night. Beach and Simpson each take two claymore mines out of their packs and start setting them up.

Each mine fires over seven hundred steel balls at four thousand feet per second and can take out multiple targets up to 165 feet away. Beach runs his fingers along the front of one of the mines to make sure it's pointed the correct way, just like Kick taught him. He does this every time without fail, even when he can read it in broad daylight. *Front Toward Enemy.*

Beach lies on his stomach and places each mine so it has a good line of fire. For safety, the unconnected hand detonators are in his pocket, and he spools the wires back to the center where they'll sleep. He really loves claymores, and anything else that blows up for that matter, but being in a position where they were forced to use these would be horrible. A firefight deep in enemy territory is tough to win, especially at night. Then there's the thorny issue of getting to an extraction point to meet a chopper. Long-range recon patrols stay alive by staying invisible.

Kick moves over to help Watt as he tosses a stick with a string tied to it, up and over a branch twenty feet in the air. Watt tapes a copper wire to the string then Kick pulls it up to the branch and secures it. The wire gets attached to the radio antennae. That, combined with being on top of a hill, gives them a clear signal back to the firebase.

Watt powers up the radio and Kick calls in the situation report. The enemy is always listening and there's no way they want to give them time to triangulate their position and pay a midnight visit. Kick speaks softly.

"Big Bud, this is Tiger Top, do you read?" There's a short static-filled pause.

"Tiger Top, this is Big Bud. We read you."

"Gone to ground. More info in three six zero mikes. Do you copy?"

"Copy, copy, copy, Tiger Top. We'll stand by."

"Tiger Top, out."

The entire exchange takes less than twenty seconds. Watt powers down the radio and grins as he opens his LRRP ration with a smile. He's got freeze-dried chili con carne, coffee with cream and sugar, and a round piece of chocolate for dessert. Kick remembers Watt's first time in the field, and how excited he was to finally get a LRRP ration. The meals originally showed up around '66 as a cousin of the dehydrated rations made for astronauts. Kick and his boys have to be nimble and quiet, so heavy canned food won't work in the field. They never have a fire out here, so Watt spoons the freeze-dried meal into his mouth, takes a swig of halazone-purified water, and swishes it around before swallowing. When he's done eating, he'll do the same with the coffee, cream, and sugar.

They lie in a five-pointed star formation so they each face a different direction. Darkness messes with your head, especially after a few nights of little sleep, so they memorize the landscape and mentally sketch out everything in their view. That way there's no confusion between a tree stump and a crouching VC.

Kick is beside Hollywood, looking at their progress on the map with a red-filtered flashlight. They check their compass and go over the three landing zones, or *LZs*. Pre-determined places where they'll be exfiltrated.

Kick digs into his dry chicken stew. The natural world around him settles in for the night. Then he notices movement to his right. It's Beach. He raises his head and swivels it around. This kid has the best fucking nose. He zeros in and points, then touches his nose with the other hand. He makes a wiggling motion with the non-pointing hand to indicate *fish sauce*. Death is riding on the breeze. Kick smiles as he gets a bearing with his compass and gives Beach a thumbs up. Tomorrow, they hunt.

Hail Mary, Joe, and the Company Men

IT'S THREE IN THE AFTERNOON as Kick heads down Powell Street in East Vancouver. The rain has held off and points of sunshine stab through the dark clouds as he moves from one side of the street to the other. He goes up one or two blocks to parallel streets, then doubles back, gets on a bus, goes back a few blocks, then turns and heads back the same way he started. All the time he's watching, without looking like he's watching. The encounter with the man in white socks is still fucking with his head. His pace is quicker than usual, and his limp barely slows him down. When he's sure there's no tail, he makes his way across Powell and into Mary's Diner.

Kick still calls it by its original name, Hail Mary's. Back in the day it was open after hours for hospitality workers, and you could tip extra for a special coffee or hot chocolate. In this part of town, it was not unheard of for shady deals to get done late at night. Those days are long gone, and the new Mary closes at four, which still gives her a twelve-hour day. Sundays are dark.

A small brass bell rings as the door opens and closes. Kick looks around the place, sees no threats, and takes a stool at the end of the counter that is as far from the door as possible, just to the right of a hooker wearing high black boots and a decent wig. Otherwise, the customers are all railway workers in dirty coveralls tucking into good greasy diner food. A small, framed poster on the wall reads, *Where Are We Going? And What Am I Doing in This Handbasket?*

There is a large mirror above the order window that's angled down at all the customers. From here Kick can watch everything without watching. A black coffee arrives a few seconds later served by Mary herself. She's the original Mary's daughter, Catherine Mary, but just Mary to everyone. In her mid-fifties, she's a good six inches taller than Kick. Her hair is up as usual, and Kick notices she's using a new hair dye.

"Hey, Mary. Like your hair."

"Nice of you to notice," she says. "What's new, McGoo?"

Kick looks up with a smile. "Not much here. How you livin'?"

Mary puts a hand on one hip and smiles. "Any better, I'd get arrested. Adam and Eve on a raft?"

"Yup, wreck 'em," answers Kick.

She yells through the kitchen window, "Scrambled on toast for the gentleman, Joe."

A low gruff voice from the kitchen shouts, "I don't see any goddamn gentleman." Joe pokes his head through and scowls at Kick.

Joe Montague is built like a brick shithouse and sports a flat-top. Kick checks out his stained Bob Marley t-shirt with the words *Stir It Up* under the Rastafarian's face.

"Have you considered buying t-shirts that are grease colored?"

Joe pulls it down over his gut and laughs. "You look like forty miles of logging road, buster!" He leans a well-muscled arm on the window ledge, showing off his Marine Corps tattoo with *Korea* inked underneath.

Kick looks back at him, straight-faced, and says, "You must be looking in the mirror then, jarhead."

If anyone else directed that word at Joe, there'd be fisticuffs, but he just laughs. "You're lucky I have my hands full, fancy pants, or I'd be out there adjusting your attitude."

"You and what army?" Kick asks.

"Hey, if I wanted to get something done, I sure as hell wouldn't call the army!" Joe likes this one the best. He flexes his Marine Corps tat, and howls with laughter.

"You been good?"

"Can't complain, and it wouldn't do any good. Where you been?"

"Livin' the dream, brother."

Joe heads back to the grill. "You might want to check the warrantee on that dream, friend, 'cause you look like a nightmare! You in disguise as evil Santa?" Joe's killing himself with his humor.

"I've got a Christmas present for you, wise ass."

"Ooooo…" The eggs and toast come up, and Joe rings the bell for show. "Adam and Eve, wrecked worse than my first marriage, and I hardly even spit in 'em."

Mary swoops by, grabs the plate and slides it in front of Kick, then tops up his coffee. "All part of the great service here, amigo." She sets the Heinz bottle in front of him.

"How long have you put up with that clown now, Mary?"

"Sixteen glorious years."

"God help you."

"God help us all, brother."

The bell over the door rings, and Kick checks the mirror. Out of the corner of his eye, he watches two men enter. One is older, large, late forties and balding, and the other is mid-thirties, a bit taller than Kick, trim and in solid shape. They both have on dark trenches, and the older one carries a tabloid newspaper and a paperback under his right arm. The shorter one has a hardcover. Kick notices it's the Greek classic, *The Iliad*, by Homer.

Mary greets them. "It must be Tuesday. The book club's here."

The larger guy smiles and waves. "Still trying to improve myself, Mary." The two take a booth. Kick deliberately moves his coffee over to the left of his plate, and then digs into his eggs.

An hour later Kick is working on his fourth coffee and picking through a crossword. The hooker is gone, the railway men are back at work, and the two members of the book club are paying their bill with cash. The bell rings as they walk out.

Kick lays down his cash. "It's been an experience, you two," he says to Mary and Joe. "I hope I survive."

Joe yells, "Yeah, 'cause it'd be a shame if you never came back!"

Mary gives a wave and says, with a touch of concern, "See you soon, Kick. Be well."

Kick opens the door then stops and turns back to them. "You should fix this door. It sounds like a fucking bell."

Joe fakes a laugh. "Hilarious. I've never heard that one before."

It's close to five as Kick snakes back down Powell. He hits the overpass at Clark, waits and checks around, then heads to an unlit area underneath where a white van sits with its lights off, engine running.

◆ ◆ ◆ ◆

Taylor fidgets in the driver's seat of the van, watching his boy take all precautions before approaching. "I don't know what's gonna happen here, so try not to piss him off, okay?"

A West coast surfer voice comes from the back of the van. "Hey, I'm easy. I just wanna get the cut of his jib, man."

Taylor looks unassuming to the untrained eye, but those who've worked with him know what a well-tuned CIA officer he is. He sighs and checks the gun in his holster. "He's never done this before. I'm concerned."

The passenger door opens and closes so fast Taylor almost doesn't get turned in time to see Kick take his seat in the dark van.

Taylor speaks first. "Glad you could make it, Princess."

"Taylor," Kick says curtly.

"Nine missed Tuesdays at the diner, and you haven't left a signal. I had work for you. Where you been?"

Kick turns to the back of the van, where he sees the younger guy on the floor with a penlight, reading his book. He doesn't look up. "Who's this?"

"Baker. He'll grow on you. Like mold. Look, we can catch up on your absence later. I saw the coffee signal, and you saw the paper under my right arm, so let's talk."

Kick sighs. "There's a tail on me. Asian, early thirties. Followed me down East Hastings a couple of days ago. He picked me up at the Carnegie Centre."

"Well, that's exciting."

Baker shuts his book. "Did he track you before that? Like during the nine weeks you've been on this bender?"

Taylor sighs as Kick shoots Baker a dagger. "I've been doing research."

"Really? Thinking of going for your masters?" asks Taylor. Kick doesn't laugh or take the bait.

Baker continues. "So psychologically you're okay, then? Not overindulging, sleep deprived, hallucinating, or anything like that?"

"Who the fuck are you to question me, Spicoli?"

Taylor lets the awkward moment settle. "You recognize the tail?"

Kick shakes his head. "No, and I got a good look at him. He was wearing white socks with a suit."

Taylor looks offended. "Why the fuck would anyone do that? Baker?"

"Sweaty foot problem? Could be fungal," Baker replies.

"You see, Kick. Like mold. You know, Baker was just telling me about the Greek writer he's reading, who wrote about shell shock way back at the siege of — what?"

"What the fuck do I care about Greeks?" Kick fires back.

Taylor feigns indignation, and then pulls out his pack of Marlboros. "Well, if you're going to get all testy, I'll just keep my early Christmas present." Kick tries to grab the smokes, but Taylor's too fast.

"You can't bribe me into thinking you're cool."

Taylor takes out a cigarette. "I already know I'm cool. I ride a Harley and everything. By the way, your pal Dusty's having a shindig in a few days." He lights his smoke.

Baker waves his hand around in protest. "Hey, you forgetting the whole second-hand smoke thing?"

"No one asked you, *dude*," Kick snarls. "Can we focus on the white socks guy?"

Taylor soft-sells him. "You should support your friend at his party, is all I'm saying."

"Look, when I need help with my social calendar, I'll ask. What do I do with this guy?"

Baker asks, "White Socks?"

"Yeah, fuckin' White Socks!"

Taylor ignores the outburst. "Well let's not kill him, for starters. We need to find out who he's working for, and what they're up to. He doesn't know where you live, right?"

"Right."

"And he didn't follow you today, right?" asks Baker.

"Right."

"So next time you lose him," Taylor suggests, "follow him back to where he came from, and report back."

Baker adds, "But don't kill him. And show some support for your friend, dude. Dusty's getting a nice write-up in *The Telegraph*."

"You know Dusty hates you, right?"

"He likes me fine. I tip well," says Taylor.

"No one wants the CIA at their bar," Kick snaps.

"Then show up for your meets, and we won't have to chase you down, will we?" Taylor takes a long drag on his smoke. "You miss my free American cigarettes?"

"Why are you being an asshole?" Kick asks.

"Me?" Taylor asks. "I didn't disappear, then show up looking like Grizzly Adams on smack."

Baker pipes up. "Yeah, you're not using, are you?"

"I've fuckin' near had enough of you, Baker!"

Baker turns back to his book with a shrug. "Just asking."

"All right." Taylor pulls out a carton of Marlboros and offers it to Kick. "Merry Christmas. I guess I should have bought you a razor too, 'cause you might want to shave."

"You're a fuckin' stylist now?"

Baker pipes up. "I like it."

"First thing you've said I *totally* agree with, valley boy. Anything else? And don't say go to Dusty's thing."

"If I was a guy trying to get something published and had a friend with a connection at a newspaper, meeting that connection might be good, that's all."

Kick stews for a moment. "Fine. See you Tuesday." He opens his door.

Baker raises his voice. "Troy."

"What?"

"The Greeks held the Spartans at Troy for ten years, and Achilles was broken by shell shock, after his best friend died. It's a really great book."

"I didn't ask."

"I hear you like to read, bro."

Kick slams the door, and they watch him walk away.

"Let's get info on this reporter," Taylor says.

"Yeah. Kelly O'Leary. I'll dig up what I can." Baker gets into the passenger seat. "You pushed all his buttons just right. He told you everything."

"You could've skipped the bender and heroin remarks. I thought he was going to derail. You wouldn't want that."

"I can see that now." Baker snaps on his seatbelt.

"I say we help him along with this thing he's trying to write," says Taylor. "Might put some demons to rest. I'll check my sources up top and see what they think."

"Does he get like this a lot?"

"This time's different."

"Should one of us watch him?"

Taylor shakes his head. "That'll just make him mad. Now that he's got Dusty's thing to look forward to, I think he'll make it to the next meet. Probably. Odds are he'll come to satisfy his curiosity. Then we can see what's what."

"Is he gonna make it, boss?"

Taylor looks worried. "You know what they say: 'When you get to the end of your rope, tie a knot and hang on.'"

"Washington?"

"Close. It was Lincoln."

Taylor puts the van in gear. "All we can do is try to be there when he hits the bottom. And if this isn't the bottom, it'll fucking well do till the bottom shows up."

6

What Are Friends For?

A SOFT RAIN IS FALLING, and the air is cold and damp. Kick's right foot stabs with pain at every step, but he's had a couple of stiff whiskeys, so it hurts a bit less. He throws a look over his shoulder as he crosses to the other side of the street. Is he just getting paranoid, or is someone watching him? The whole white socks thing has him on edge. Just to be safe he grabs a bus going the opposite way. By the time he gets to Dusty's bar several young men are standing outside at the top of the stairs smoking a joint. Every one of them is wearing a red plastic poppy to mark Remembrance Day.

His dad would start seeing those blood-red poppies every year around the first of November, and his mood would darken. He'd drink more, snarl more, and start screaming in his sleep. The poppies never let his father move on. Kick can't decide if things like poppies, holidays and parades were created to show respect for those who served, or if it's all some sort of marketing ploy for the military industrial complex. Fucking suits.

One thing he has decided is these tall, beefy fuckers outside Dusty's have never seen combat, and it gets right under his skin. He snatches the jay out of one guy's hand, takes a couple of sharp, deep hits, then tosses it over his shoulder without looking back. The group is speechless as he hobbles down the stairs, blowing smoke out at the bottom. Then they laugh. Kick doesn't like that either.

He opens the door and stops. "Jesus H. Christ on the fucking cross."

Dusty's bar is full of balloons and streamers, and country music is playing. A microphone has been set up, and there's an old slate blackboard on the wall with drink specials written in chalk. The place is packed, the air thick with cigarette smoke, and Dusty is pouring pints, one after another, and setting them up on the bar. He's all spiffed up in a decent shirt, a tie, and a jacket. A fucking *jacket.* Even his shoes are new and shiny. Shit. He's wearing a poppy. Everyone is. Kick sets his jaw and limps inside.

Dusty doesn't notice him, so he works his way through tables of Canadian military types and hangs his coat on his usual hook under the bar. His regular stool is occupied by some string-bean kid, so Kick smacks him on the shoulder. The kid takes one look at his scary hair and beard, and bolts. Kick grabs a draft and settles in.

Dusty looks up. "You decided to grace me with your presence, El Diablo."

"Balloons? What are you, ten?" Kick lifts his glass.

Dusty leans in. "Look, it's gonna be different today. This reporter's gonna speak, there's a photographer coming, and I already told them not everyone wants to be photographed, but you're gonna be nice. Right?"

"Why are you even asking that?"

"You know exactly fuckin' why."

"I'm just here to support you. Even though you're starting to look too clean to be mean."

Dusty is suspicious but satisfied for now. "Yeah. I do look good."

The storeroom door opens, and Taylor and Baker walk in. Dusty mumbles, "I told them not to use that door."

They maintain their cover and ignore Kick, wave hello to Dusty, and take a couple of empty stools at the far end of the bar. Dusty holds up a bottle of Kettle vodka, gets a tepid okay from Taylor, and shakes up four ounces of it with ice. He delivers the shaker and two glasses with fancy olives impaled on toothpicks.

Taylor remarks, "Jesus, the service is good here." Baker pours, and they clink and drink.

Dusty mutters as he walks past Kick. "No vermouth in my bar. That shit's for fuckin' pussies." Kick smiles and lights a smoke.

Kick's on his second beer when he catches sight of a striking woman walking in. She's very pretty, petite with long blonde hair, and she wears a red wet-look raincoat with a matching umbrella. There's a scruffy guy with a big camera tagging along with her. Dusty waves them over, and they pick their way through the crowd.

The only open stool is right beside Kick, so Dusty comes out and moves it as far away from him as possible. The photographer gets an action shot of Dusty smiling with the bar stool in one hand and the full bar behind him. Kick turns his face away as the shutter clicks.

"Nice. I'm Sam, *The Telegraph's* photographer. I'll be out of your hair as soon as I get what I need."

"Great. Thanks." Dusty points at Kick. "Don't sit too close to him, Kelly.

He's dangerous, although I'm pretty sure he brushed his teeth today. Jury's still out on his hair."

Kick watches as Dusty takes her things and puts them behind the bar. Kelly keeps a file folder with her. She smells amazing, and he tries to place the scent. It's like honeysuckle. He's surprised by a wave of sadness that crashes over him. His mother used to wear something like that. He tamps down the emotion and lights another smoke.

Dusty takes out a bottle of Michael David Petite Petit, yanks the foil off, and pulls the cork out with a loud pop. Sam the photographer captures the image. Dusty pours a splash of the dark red into a proper long-stemmed glass and offers it to Kelly to sample.

"It's okay. You can just pour."

Dusty proceeds, and Kick looks confused. "You have wine that's not in a box?"

"For very special guests I do," Dusty replies. "And keep your hands off."

Kick knows he's not just talking about the wine.

"Great party, Dust!" a happy Malaysian Phil interjects as he waddles up to the bar. "I'm making new friends!"

Dusty hands him a fresh pint. "That's great, Phil. You enjoy yourself."

Phil takes a sip and strikes a serious drunken pose. "As a former business owner, can I give you a piece of advice?"

"Okay, Phil, lay it on me."

"No matter what happens, don't live in the past," he states solemnly. "Just move it on forward, bud. Just move it on forward. Like you're doing here."

Dusty hides a smile. "I'll remember that."

Kick is about to tap Kelly on the shoulder, but Dusty steps in. "Kelly this is … an old military friend who decided to crawl out of his cave today. This is Kelly from *The Vancouver Telegraph*."

Kelly shakes his hand and notices the scars snaking up under his sleeve.

"Nice to meet you, Kelly."

"You too. I didn't get your name."

"No, you didn't." Kick shoots a look at Dusty. "There's a story about that, but it's … not for public consumption."

"Oh. Well, I'll just have to live in suspense for now, I guess."

Satisfied everything is fine for the moment, Dusty moves to another customer.

Kelly hands Kick a business card. He reads, "'Kelly O'Leary.' Irish. I like you already."

They toast. "To the Irish."

A thin old man with a long gray beard and a ponytail sets a tray of empty glasses on the bar. He has a faded Screaming Eagles tattoo on his forearm. "Hey, man," he says to Kick.

They shake hands. "Robbie, good to see you again. Didn't you work at *The American*?"

"Still do. Just helping out today for a bit."

"Good to see you again, brother." Kick turns to Kelly, "Robbie was one of the Battered Bastards of Bastogne."

"Wow, that's amazing! Maybe I could talk to you about it some day?"

"Nope." Robbie picks up a fresh tray of pints and leaves.

Dusty comes back. "Some vets just don't, Kelly. It's nothing personal."

"I understand." She takes a sip. "Dusty this wine is great."

Kick jokes, "Yeah, Dust, you're a regular Somalian." Kelly laughs, and Kick's shell cracks open a bit.

"Ten thousand comedians out of work, and you're makin' bad jokes," Dusty quips. He starts pouring five double rye and ginger ales, and Kick steals one when he's not looking, drains it, and holds the glass under the bar top. Dusty thinks he miscounted and pours another. Kelly's not saying a word. Kick hands the empty glass off to Robbie as he comes back. Kick downs his beer. The double whammy hits him nicely.

"So, were you in the 82nd or 101st Airborne?" Kelly asks.

"For my first tour I was 101st. Screamin' Eagles, just like Robbie."

"Wow, that must have been something."

"It was definitely *something*."

One of the rye and ginger boys, skinny but well-muscled, walks up to the microphone, taps it a couple of times, then asks, "Can you hear me?"

His friends shout back. "Unfortunately!" The laughter grows after each response.

"No! Shut up!"

Kelly laughs harder at each insult.

"Yeah, and you sound like an asshole!"

"Go home. No one likes you!"

Ginger Boy smiles weakly. "Okay, thanks."

"You're welcome, dickhead!"

"You givin' a speech, glamour boy?" Kick asks Dusty.

Kelly answers, "I'll be saying a few words."

A twinge of jealousy sparks through Kick. He looks across the room at the rye and ginger boys again, and really hopes one of them looks at him, just once. Down at the end of the bar, to his right, Taylor and Baker are getting to know Malaysian Phil.

Phil asks, "What line of work you guys in?"

Taylor takes it. "Sales for a US plastics company. Pretty dull, but it pays all right."

"Well, I took early retirement, but if you ever need a good deal on a used car, I still have some connections," Phil confides. "Just let me know."

"Good to know, Phil. Thanks," Taylor says with a smile.

Baker says earnestly, "When we need a used car in a hurry, we usually just steal it."

Phil stares at Baker, then laughs. "Ah, that's a good one right there. Oh, that is good!"

Kick sees Kelly looking his way and leans toward her. "You know, it's one thing to be an American and get drafted into Vietnam, but I'm a Canadian who *volunteered*."

Kelly looks surprised. "Sorry, what?"

"A lot of Canadians fought in 'Nam."

"No. Really?"

"Really."

"How is that possible?"

Just as Kick is about to answer, Ginger Boy, with his highball in hand, comes back to the microphone, looks over to check with Kelly, then says, "So, uh, keep it down for a minute guys. We've got a special guest who's going to say a few words here." No one pays any attention, and the room carries on. "Come on, you guys …"

Kick stands quickly, avoids Dusty's arm shooting out to stop him, limps to the mic, and shouts. "TEN-SHUN!" The room falls silent, a few guys fly to their feet, and all eyes turn to Kick. He stares them down, then makes a grand gesture for Kelly to come on up, which she does. Kick takes the highball from Ginger, drains the glass on the way back to his stool, and sets the empty glass on the bar.

Dusty whispers, "Classy. But I thought we had an understanding about you and whiskey in my bar."

"Won't happen again."

Kelly lowers the mic to her level. "Can we get another ginger ale and …?"

"Rye," Ginger Boy squeaks.

"Another rye and ginger for this gentleman, please?" Dusty pours it and hands it to Ginger as he walks by, carefully avoiding Kick.

Kelly reads from a typed sheet of paper. "Thank you for coming today, and welcome to Dusty's Wet Yer Whistle, which I hope will become a regular watering hole for all of you."

"As long as there's a happy hour, we'll be here!" yells Phil from the back,

30 | THE WAR MACHINE

followed by laughter.

Kick knows he shouldn't drink whiskey, but every time he tells himself he won't, a dark part of him convinces him he really should. It's like a spark meeting gasoline. He takes a beer to level himself off. Dusty eyes him as he wipes a highball glass.

Kelly continues. "Patrick 'Dusty' Tucker was born in Atlanta, Georgia. He and his two sisters were raised mostly by their mother, since his dad traveled a lot as a sales rep. Dusty was drafted into the Marine Corps late in 1967, went through boot camp at Parris Island, and arrived in Vietnam just a month before the The Tet Offensive in 1968. 'As bad luck would have it,' to quote Dusty, he was stationed at Khe Sanh, and managed to survive the long siege there, although many of his fellow Marines and ARVN soldiers did not."

The room falls silent as Kelly continues. "After his tour, Dusty rotated back and decided to take a trip to Vancouver, where, to quote him again, 'No one spit on him or made comments about his military service. And he couldn't help but notice, the city had some of the most beautiful women he'd ever seen.'" Cheers and clapping erupt from the room.

"He managed to buy and renovate this establishment using his Marine Corps savings as a down payment. Everything in here, from the shine on the floor to the paint on the walls is the result of good old-fashioned elbow grease, and I know that he is proud to have you all here today to celebrate his upcoming twenty-year anniversary."

There are more cheers and clapping from the crowd and a chant of, "Dusty! Dusty! Dusty!" and "Speech, speech, speech".

Kick is jealous, but also proud of his friend, and joins in the chant. "Speech, Dusty. Come on!" Dusty throws his towel on the bar and picks up his whiskey, and Kelly steps aside as he walks up to the microphone.

"All right, you good for nothin' freeloaders, I have two rules here: drink lots, and pay your tab!" The photographer snaps off a bunch of pics of Dusty and Kelly, all smiles. "Thanks for coming. Thanks to Kelly here for getting the word out about my little place, and ... and ..."

Kick gets to his feet, pours some of his beer on the floor, and says, "And here's to those who can't be with us today, because they goddamn well gave it all."

Dusty, close to tears, looks at Kick and drinks. Everyone raises their glasses and says soberly, "The fallen." Kick turns his head away as he sees Sam the photographer pointing the camera his way. Taylor and Baker look down at the bar as the flash goes off. The room drinks as Dusty returns to the bar.

Sam shakes Dusty's hand, waves to Kelly, and then, camera in hand, heads out the door.

Kelly steps back up to the mic and starts to wrap it up. "You'll find the whole article in Saturday's edition of *The Vancouver Telegraph*, which I hope you all subscribe to since we have a new expanded sports section. Now I suggest getting back to the music. What do you think of that?" There's another burst of cheering.

Johnny Cash's *I Walk the Line* blares and the party is back on.

Kelly comes back to her stool, and people come up and congratulate her. Phil gives Dusty a big sloppy hug and smacks him on the back. "I'm so happy to know you, Dusty. Thanks for being my friend."

Dusty hugs him back. "You're always welcome here, Phil. Now go have a good time."

The good times continue. An hour later, a few women have wandered in, and Baker is chatting one up. Dusty seems quite happy with his party. The crowd has thinned out a bit. Phil has already gone home, and some of the older military types have moved on. About half the crowd is still enjoying themselves, and everyone but Kelly seems drunk. She sips her wine slowly and keeps her head on straight.

A wave of dizziness washes over Kick, and he decides a good piss in the men's room will straighten him out. He feels worse once he gets there, takes a stall, and shuts the door. "Fuck it." He sits down to pee, puts his head in his hands, and closes his eyes.

◆ ◆ ◆ ◆

When Kick opens his eyes, he's looking down at his cowboy boots, and notices they need a good shine. But there's something weird about the floor. It looks *runny*. On the other side of the stall door, he sees the tiny bare feet of a child. He opens the door and finds the young Vietnamese girl he saw a few days ago. He's been seeing her off and on for years.

One of his boots is on her shoeshine box. "What are you doing here?" he asks.

The girl looks at him. "Shoeshine?"

She's very calm as she shines his boot, which is melting into the box.

"Big jungle, soldiers fight," the girl says softly. "Huge tiger picks me up. Meet your ancestors. Shoeshine?"

She can't be here. He's dizzy. His boot is fused to the shine box.

The bathroom wall behind the girl is now covered with the articles from Kick's wall, connected by bloody strings that drip their way to the question mark in the center.

The girl is gone. Kick is now frozen in a black-and-white picture his dad once showed him of a wide canal in the little town of Damme in Belgium. Nothing and no one is moving. The shoeshine box is stuck to the boot he's wearing. This part of Belgium must have been beautiful before the Nazis, he thinks. Kick's dad is standing beside him, but he's barely twenty, has short buzzed off hair, and is just skin and bones in his oversized Canadian uniform, coat, and helmet.

Boom! The scene explodes into color, and the sounds of combat are deafening. His dad yells, "The Krauts were on one side of the canal; we were on the other." Clumps of Canadian soldiers are huddled close by, popping off small arms fire over the canal at a large concrete pillbox, where a machine gun fires back at them.

"They were in thick pillboxes along the canal, but eventually we rooted 'em out. Flamethrowers, then hand-to-hand. God, the *smell* ..." Kick recognizes a stench like burning pork.

Another explosion. He's now eight years old, wearing his cowboy pajamas, and his dad stands by him completely naked. Thick blood gushes from a bayonet wound in his dad's gut. The combat continues.

Kick asks, "Why is there war?"

"Law of the jungle," his dad answers. "Old men send their children to kill each other. It's a tradition."

"Are you cold, Dad?"

"I'm dead, son. I don't get cold."

"Why did you go and fight?"

Blood is pooling at his dad's feet. "My country called, Europe called, the King called, and since I was invincible, I answered. Thirty thousand American boys snuck into Canada to fight with us before the US joined World War Two. They heard the siren's call. That was way before D-Day. The day the sea turned red like jam. Newsreels promised a better life when we got back. They promised thick juicy steaks with mushrooms and onions, a hero's welcome, and real home cookin'. They didn't promise I'd be half crazy, or my wound would never heal, or that I'd be a boozer and hurt my wife and son, or ..."

Kick's dad kneels in his puddle of blood and grabs Kick by the shoulders. "Son, I want you to promise me something."

"What?"

"If they call you to war — *RUN!*"

A satchel bomb sails into the German pillbox, and a massive explosion engulfs it. Young Kick hits the deck, and as the smoke clears, his dad is still there, but he's now forty-four. The age when Kick last saw him, before he shipped out to Vietnam.

Kick is crying. "I thought it'd be a great adventure."

His dad laughs. "Some old priest once said, 'War makes thieves, and peace hangs 'em.'"

"I thought war would be exciting," Kick says. "Like robbing a bank." Burning men pour out of the pillbox and start melting, then get shot. They sizzle as they hit the cold canal water.

Kick cries harder. "I didn't think I'd get caught."

The landscape changes to Vietnam, right after a napalm strike. The bodies on fire are not just soldiers.

His dad fires his rifle at the melting people, then turns back to Kick. "I told you to run."

7

The Bottom

KICK'S LEGS AREN'T NUMB YET, so he knows he hasn't been unconscious too long. He gets up from the floor slowly, does up his pants, and wipes tears from his face. He figures the only remedy is another drink, so he washes his hands and face and weaves a path back out.

There's a table where he can have his back to the wall and keep his eye on both doors, so he sits there. Appearing sober while drunk is one of Kick's superpowers. If he doesn't have to stand up or walk, it'll be hard for most people to tell how plastered he is. Taylor has been keeping one eye on him while he and Baker continue drinking those annoying vodka things. Other people are getting them too now, and Dusty's having a good time overcharging for martinis that are just vodka and olives. Kick motions to him for a beer, which he reluctantly pours.

Dusty asks Kelly to deliver the beer to Kick. As she makes her way over, she notices some of the red poppies have fallen off people's coats and are scattered on the floor. Kick notices too and finds it irritating. He sits up straighter as she sits down across the table from him.

"So, you volunteered to fight in the Vietnam War, but you said your dad was Canadian. Are you?"

"Yup. Born and raised in supernatural British Columbia."

"Then how could you volunteer?"

Kick takes a drink. "As you probably know, Canada took in a lot of draft dodgers and deserters, so the US military wasn't exactly turning away volunteers."

"Really? Okay. So how did it work once you crossed the border?"

"Pretty simple. My friend and I went to an army recruiting office."

"Which one?"

"Blaine, in Washington State."

"Then what?"

"I said I'm from Canada, and I want to volunteer for Vietnam. They wrote down my home address as General Delivery, Blaine, Washington, and gave me a social security number, and a haircut." Kick downs the rest of his beer.

Kelly is stunned. "And it happened that day?"

"It most definitely happened that day. They didn't want anyone going home and thinking it over."

Kick offers Kelly a cigarette, which she accepts, and he lights hers then his. "Because the US military thought all Canadians spoke French, they directed us into special forces."

"Because Vietnam was a French colony, and they thought you could connect with the locals. Do you speak French?" she asks.

Kick snorts. "The only French I knew was on the back of the Corn Flakes box. I learned what I had to know in country."

Robbie the waiter is cleaning glasses, and while Dusty's not looking, Kick waves at him to bring them another round. "I did basic training, advanced infantry, jump training, and they shipped me out with the same buddy who volunteered with me. We flew to Hawaii on Pan Am and the movie they showed was *Herbie the Love Bug*. It's about a car that thinks it's a person. We changed planes and headed right to Saigon, and guess what the movie was?"

"*Herbie the Love Bug?*"

Kick points his cigarette hand at her. "You got it. Just when it was feeling like a pretty cool vacation, the pilot tells us, 'We're coming into Cam Ranh Bay, and it's a hot LZ.' That means a landing zone under fire. The plane came in fast and steep. There were no stairs, and we all jumped. Mortars were exploding all over. Three men broke their legs jumping. We found cover until the shelling stopped, and that was our 'Welcome to Vietnam'. From that point on, it was a long waking nightmare."

Kelly cocks her head. "When did it stop?" Kick is confused by the question but is saved by Robbie showing up with the drinks. "Dusty says to slow down."

Dusty has his hands on his hips and is giving Kick the stare-down.

Kick ignores him and takes a wistful drag on his smoke. "You know, if you're looking for stories about 'Nam, I can fill a whole book. Maybe two."

"I don't know. The paper keeps me pretty busy."

"You newspaper types put out books, right? You get to be an expert on something, put it all together, and make a bunch of extra cash, right? I'll bet a book like that would make a lot of money."

Kelly's saved by Ginger Boy, who comes up and says nervously, "Excuse me, sir, but I heard you were long range recon and I'd like to buy you a drink." Kick gives him a death stare. Ginger squirms. "If that's okay?"

Kick doesn't even look at him. "Crown Royal. Neat." Ginger hustles over to the bar. Somewhere deep inside, good Kick knows he should get a cab home, but bad Kick is just getting started. He whispers to Kelly, "You know I did four tours? The last two were off the books."

Kelly is genuinely impressed. "Oh. You mean …?"

"*Covert* is the word you're looking for."

"Sure. Got it."

Ginger returns with the whiskey and presents it to Kick, who just looks at him, so he puts it on the table. Kelly stifles a grin.

Ginger Boy goes to leave. "Whoa there, ginger, you can't just *didi mau*." Ginger looks confused. Kick shakes his head. "*Didi mau* means leave, run, or fuck off. In other words, get the lady what she's having, get yourself one, then come back and sit down." Off goes Ginger Boy with some level of either excitement or dread. Dusty's caught on to what's happening.

Kick waves him off. "I'm all right, jarhead," he calls.

"Don't you dare, asshole," Dusty warns from the bar. Kick waves him off again. Dusty shakes his head and starts removing breakables from the top of the bar. Taylor notices but does nothing.

Kelly asks. "Don't you dare what?"

"He's just mad I called him jarhead. Most people can't say that to a Marine and live."

"Why? What does it mean?"

Kick takes a drink of his whiskey. "If you unscrew the head of a Marine, and look inside you know what you'll see?" Kelly shrugs. "Nothing. Like an empty jar. The Corps likes it that way, so when they point at a hill and say, 'Take it!' there's nothing inside to stop them."

"What does he call you?"

"Oh, he's got a list. *Grunt*. *Chicken Man* and *Puking Buzzard* for the 101st Screaming Eagle emblem. That was my first tour. He calls me *Airhead*, and, of course, *Screaming Asshole*. Pardon my French." Kelly laughs.

Dusty gets a plastic bin and starts clearing tables. "Motherfucker," he mutters. Baker notices what's happening now, but he and Taylor are chatting up women and appear not to care.

Ginger is back, the three of them raise their drinks and Kick toasts loudly. "To Dusty, my best friend in the whole world!"

Everyone says, "Dusty!" Dusty keeps picking up breakables from tables.

Kick points his cigarette hand at Ginger. "For being so God damn nice, and buyin' me this drink, Ginger Boy, you get to ask me one question."

Ginger is scared. "Anything?"

"Anything at all." Dusty gets the last of the ashtrays, candles, and anything else that might be used as a projectile or weapon into the bin and heads back to the bar.

Ginger sips his drink, chokes on it a bit, then asks, "I heard you were a ghost jumper in Vietnam and took out classified targets. Is that true?" Dusty looks like he's getting ready to move. Taylor and Baker stop talking and watch.

Kick curls his index finger in a *come closer* gesture. Ginger reluctantly does, and Kick whispers, "Fuck yeah." Without warning he head-butts Ginger. Dusty is already there, pulling Kelly out of her chair, before any blood sprays her way. Ginger screams in pain as blood pours out of his nose.

Kick is on his feet. He drains his whiskey, smashes the glass on the floor and yells, "Any you candy-ass motherfuckers got a problem with that?" Two of Ginger's pals rush over and take swings at Kick, who blocks the first few strikes. Taylor and Baker keep watching, seemingly unconcerned.

Dusty places Kelly behind the bar. "He won't make it this far," he says to her. "Probably."

Kick takes surprisingly quick punches at Ginger's pals, and one buckles and drops after a devastating shot to the head. Kick ducks the second one's jab, and while he's low, sacks him, then breaks one of his teeth with an uppercut. "Three down!" Kick declares loudly as a chair hits him from the side.

Two guys grab Kick while the biggest soldier in the room steps up. Kick tries to boot him in the nuts but misses. "You cunt-faced shit-eating fuck!" Kick yells.

Cunt Face doesn't like his new nickname and hits Kick hard in the belly. A bad choice since everything Kick ate that day projects all over his t-shirt and pants.

Kick looks at his puke and says flatly, "I don't remember eating that ..."

The two guys holding Kick check themselves for spray as Cunt Face runs for the men's room.

"Amateur." Kick heaves again all over the floor.

Dusty steps in to calm the situation. "Okay, let's take it down a few degrees and get you boys some drinks on the ..." The slate chalkboard with party specials crashes over Dusty's head and cracks in two. Baker's girl is holding one piece of it, not knowing what to do next. Dusty cocks his fist at her, and she drops the piece of chalkboard, grabs her coat and purse, and bolts out the door. Her friend kisses Taylor on the cheek and exits nonchalantly. Kick's on his knees trying to catch his breath. Taylor and Baker sit back and take in the rest of the show.

Kick is about to stand up when a boot comes in. Right in the ribs. He looks up to see Ginger Boy, and he's crying. "I was trying to show respect!" He goes to boot him again, but Dusty's huge fist flies in, just a bit too hard, and adds a shiner to Ginger's messed-up nose. The donnybrook escalates as someone yells, "General quarters!" Everyone heads toward Kick and Dusty.

Taylor takes out a coin and flips it. Baker calls, "Heads." Taylor reveals that it's tails.

Baker shakes his head. "Shit."

Ginger is trying to pull Kick up to punch him, so Baker grabs Ginger by the hair and slams his face into the floor a few times. He crumples. That's *one*.

Cunt Face emerges shirtless from the bathroom, muscles rippling. He looks at Baker and goes to boot to him in the nuts. Baker catches his foot with both hands and twists it until there is a hideous crunch. Cunt Face falls to the floor screaming in pain. Baker says, "Two."

Another guy turns on Baker, so he extends his fingers out flat on one hand and delivers a *sword hand* horizontally to the guy's throat. It's a move designed to collapse the windpipe, but Baker delivers it with a lighter touch. This is just enough impact on the windpipe to give him something to gag about for the rest of the day. Baker knows there's no point killing anyone. It's supposed to be a party after all. Three down.

Another guy jumps on Kick and takes a wild swing that connects hard on his jaw. Kick drops like a sack of potatoes, while Baker cold-cocks the guy on the chin, knocking him out. Kick is trying in vain to get up, but he's too weak.

Taylor holds up four fingers to Baker. Baker has only one move left to clear the floor.

Dusty has put down two guys and is wearily on top of a third delivering a punch here and there. Another guy literally jumps on Dusty's back and wails away on him.

Baker yells, "Hey!" The guy on top jumps off and steps toward Baker like a redneck Dirty Harry. Dusty finishes the one underneath him with an elbow to the face, then collapses on top of him. Kick has nothing left and drags himself up against the wall.

Baker and Dirty Harry regard each other for a moment. "What're ya waiting for, little boy?" Harry barks. Baker says nothing. "Maybe yer waitin' for yer balls to come down, ya martini-drinkin' pussy-ass piece of shit!" Baker smiles. He likes that one. Dirty Harry comes in hot with one arm swinging. Baker calmly deflects it to the outside and brings his other elbow up under his chin. Dirty Harry doesn't feel lucky as the shockwave goes right to his brain stem. He's out like a light.

Baker looks at Taylor who holds up five fingers but jerks his thumb to the other end of the room. Standing with his mouth wide open, and half a beer in his hand, is one last soldier. Baker is out of moves, and Taylor is grinning. Baker looks at the guy and says ominously, "You have thirty seconds to get out of here before I fucking kill you." The guy drops his beer and runs like the wind.

Taylor laughs hard and applauds. "That was one of your best, man! Drinks are on me today, kid. That was fucking outstanding." Kelly claps too, and Baker takes a bow. He grabs what's left of his drink and drains it. Taylor pulls a US hundred from his wallet, smacks it on the bar, reconsiders, then takes out another and slaps it on top. Dusty moans from the floor. "Keep the change, Dusty. Looks like y'all are gonna need it. Better get your bearded friend there a stretcher. He doesn't look so good."

Kick tries to stand. "I'm fine. No one asked for your help …"

The two CIA boys get their coats on and start walking out.

Taylor says, "Too bad about those girls. They were really getting to like us."

"I think so too," Baker agrees.

Taylor takes a look at the busted-up bodies and furniture, and pretends to notice Kelly for the first time. "You need a ride anywhere?" She has her coat and purse and is stepping around bodies, heading for the door. "No, thanks. I have a cab coming."

Taylor and Baker wait at the door for her. "I really like the new sports section in *The Telegraph*, by the way," Taylor comments.

"Thanks. I'll pass that along. Hey, did you guys know Canadians fought in Vietnam?"

Taylor looks surprised. "Really? You hear about that, pal?" he asks Baker.

"No, but that's interesting. You think you'll write something about it?"

"Not sure yet."

"I'd like to read that," Baker says. "Hey, I'm starved."

Taylor holds the door open. "Let's hit Bob's for some Thai. I worked up an appetite watching you fight." Taylor laughs his big booming laugh, as they head up the stairs. "Hey, it's Kelly, right."

"Yes."

"You hungry?"

"Nope. I'm heading home. Nice to meet you guys."

"Take care."

The conversation fades away as Dusty gets up slowly and looks at the carnage. There are red plastic poppies all over the floor. "Great. Just fuckin' great! You boned me again."

Kick just gets to his feet and then falls back down. "Too bad the photographer already left." He reaches into his pocket, smiles as he feels Kelly's business card, then passes out in his own vomit.

8

THE TELEGRAPH

THE NEWSROOM SOUNDS LIKE A MULTI-CAR PILE-UP. Phones ring, reporters pound typewriters and explode at each other, and the air is thick with cigarette smoke and profanity, but somehow this process will build tomorrow's paper. Sitting on the edge of Kelly's desk is Val, a beautiful woman of Pakistani heritage in her early thirties. "So, the whole place just started fighting?"

"Yeah, it was everyone," Kelly answers. "This crazy guy started it all by head-butting some kid in the face, then inviting everyone to fight him!"

"That is awesome! And he said he went to Vietnam even though he's Canadian?"

A few desks over, Sam the photographer yells, "The sports guy did the same thing. It was some sort of hush-hush deal we had with the Yanks. There's stuff in the archives, but it's in the Evil Room. Ask Stewart. But, uh, don't tell him I told you."

Val asks, "Do you have a number for the sports guy?"

Sam lowers his voice. "No. He killed himself. He was a great guy. More Vietnam vets have died by their own hand than were killed in the war itself."

There's a heavy silence. "That's terrible," Kelly finally says.

"My dad calls it the invisible price," Val offers. "You're going to do something on this, right?"

Kelly hesitates then says, "I don't know, Val. It's a rich subject, and this guy is compelling, but he is a fucking mess. And if *Canada in Vietnam* is such a big deal why hasn't anyone else done it by now?"

Sam answers, "Maybe they got scared off, or it got buried. Who knows? In war, truth is the first casualty. The boss did stuff on this when *The Pentagon*

Papers broke. Everyone else here was too scared. He'll love this, if you pitch it right."

Val says, "Stewart likes big, deep topics, but if you want him to do something for you, it's got to be his idea."

"I've noticed. Why is that?" Kelly asks.

"He's a guy." Val laughs. "By the way, I know it was your father's anniversary the other day. You doing okay?"

"Yeah. I'm heading there after work to change the flowers. Thanks."

An arm waves from Stewart's office. "O'Leary!"

Val jumps off the desk. "Oh shit. He's calling you in, Kelly. Have fun."

Kelly hustles toward Stewart's office. A rumpled sentry named Penny sits at her desk out front. She squints her ancient eyes at Kelly over her reading glasses and frowns. Kelly smiles back. Penny watches her like she's heading to the gallows, then spits into her trash can. Kelly passes through the open door with a brass placard that reads *Malcolm Stewart — Editor in Chief*.

Stewart stands behind his huge desk, which is completely covered with newspapers, stacks of file folders, and books. His voice booms as he wraps up a call, and Kelly can smell the half-eaten tuna sandwich sitting by his black coffee.

"Get it done!" The phone slams down on its cradle and Stewart plants himself in his huge well-worn office chair with a thud. He's tall, fairly slim, and still has most of his gray hair. Kelly knows he is well past sixty-five, and there's no mistaking that he runs the show here.

"This is pretty damn good, Kelly, this Dusty story, but now you need to dig into something meaty, while you carry on with the fluffy stuff. Anyone who's stayed on at this paper has made a point of going the extra mile. You understand what I'm saying?"

"I do, and I'm great with that."

"Good. But there's no overtime pay or any of that shit, right?"

"No problem. None of that ... What do you suggest I look at?"

"Anything local that can expand internationally is golden."

"Okay." Kelly shifts in her seat. "There is something, but I can't tell if it's half-baked or what."

"Spit it out. I'm getting old over here."

"I heard at Dusty's bar that a lot of Canadians fought in Vietnam, in a very unofficial way, but I'm not sure if it's true. The vet I was talking to is one, but a bit of a wild man."

"Well, that's got the right appeal, plus I did my own take on that back in the day when *The Pentagon Papers* broke."

"I heard you were the only one here who had the guts to do anything."

"You goddamn well heard right! War is deception, and there was definitely a cover-up here, but nobody's done a deep dive. Maybe it's been long enough they'll have let their guard down."

Kelly brightens. "Sure."

"Reporting, *good* reporting, is a combat sport, kid. You need to get in there and fight. But you'll have to fight sneaky. Have the battle won before they even know it's started."

"Right."

"Weren't you looking into Canadian arms sales last year?"

"Yeah, but I don't know if there's a connection."

"Let me know what you find out next week." Stewart returns to editing some notes.

"Oh. So, I'm doing that?"

"Get out."

"It's just ..." Kelly waits.

"Christ, it's just what?" He looks up impatiently.

"I'll probably need access to the Evil Room for the arms stuff."

Stewart sits back in his chair and studies her. "Who told you it was called that?"

Kelly shrugs. Stewart points out at his sentinel. "See Penny for the key and give it right back to her after every goddamn visit, and anything you sign in or out, you have to write it all in the log. Don't forget. And now ..."

"Get out?"

"I was going to say fuck off, but you're catching on, O'Leary."

◆ ◆ ◆ ◆

Taylor sips his coffee behind the wheel of the van, parked behind some laurel bushes at Mountain View Cemetery. Baker has the binoculars on Kelly, who is bundled in her raincoat and hat, as she stands in the pelting rain. Her umbrella is lying beside an old grave marker. A small mound of dead flowers and a worn-out wreath lie close by. Kelly lays out a new set of flowers and a wreath in front of the headstone.

"How does she look?" he asks Baker.

"Sad. Angry. She's crying."

Taylor takes out his notepad. "Ready when you are."

Baker refocuses. "Thomas O'Leary, born January 3, 1921. Died, November 14, 1970. It's a huge headstone. He had some dough."

"And her mother?"

"Born, September 25, 1929, and died June 15, 1962."

Taylor writes that down. "Wait. That's O'Leary's birthday, right?" He flips back a page. "Yeah. It is. Died in childbirth. So, she had no mother growing up."

"That's rough. And she lost her dad young too." Baker takes the notepad from him. "I'll start running this down as soon as we get back."

Taylor takes the binoculars and looks. "She does look sad."

"You're such a softy," Baker teases.

"I do have a soft spot for the press. You know, when it suits me."

GIVE ME A PLACE TO STAND, AND I WILL MOVE THE EARTH
Vietnam, 1968

KICK DOESN'T REALLY SLEEP. The boys seldom do in the field. They lie in their star formation with two on watch at a time, allowing the others to at least close their eyes for an hour or two. Smells drift into their position all night, with bits of noise here and there from the same general direction. At one point they hear a distant helicopter that quickly fades. It's definitely not American. Whatever's in that valley, it's important.

The birds ramp up their morning songs, even while it's still dark. Kick doesn't have to tell anyone what to do. Gear gets quietly packed, and dry meals, coffee, and sugar are washed down with water. The shithole is filled and covered. It's the start of day three, and they all know it's going to be a bitch, one way or the other.

Beach gives the claymore mines to Frosty, who puts together one of his masterpieces under Beach's red-filtered flashlight. Frosty is a mad genius, and he's rigging the claymores with a trip mechanism. They are all connected so when one goes, they all go. He adds his special treat too. Using heavy tape, he secures a white phosphorus grenade to the front of each mine. He calls it Frosty's frosting. His philosophy is if they've made the effort to hump these heavy bastards all this way, why not leave as many presents for Charlie as possible.

Frosty leaves a map of Saigon and a boonie hat in the center. The hope is whoever happens upon the camp will step in to pick up the bait and trigger the explosions. This should take down a few men and draw the enemy here, instead of to their extraction point.

Hollywood crawls over and whispers in Kick's ear. "Looks like a badass mother of a day." Kick could punch him for breaking protocol by speaking, but he gives him a tense nod back.

Frosty finishes just as the sky is light enough to move out. Simpson looks nervous, and Kick gives him a squeeze on the shoulder. Hollywood moves hyper-focused along the ridge. He looks into the valley for hints of a camp, but there are none, until half an hour later.

Out of nowhere, and with no visible trails connecting to it, an encampment appears in the valley, hopping with activity. There is a small river running beside it, and it looks like equipment is being moved into the camp on it. Soldiers, gear, and equipment are moving quickly along the riverbed, which is confusing. Kick trains his binoculars on it. It's like they're walking on water, even though the river is clearly too deep. Something to speak to HQ about. There is enough activity for at least a brigade, and Kick knows what they do here today could make a real difference. Not to mention being a feather in their caps, assuming they survive.

Hollywood pulls everyone down with a hand sign and brings out his map. They have good cover here. As the men lie flat on their stomachs, Kick marks their position. Hollywood uses a range finder, their location, and elevation to estimate the target. Thankfully, there's no wind to factor in. He puts an X on the map.

Kick has chosen LZ One as their extraction point, based on its proximity and, he hopes, their ability to get there fast. He checks in with everyone to make sure they're ready and gets nods back. Watt powers up the radio and Kick takes the handset.

Kick speaks in the same controlled voice. "Big Bud, this is Tiger Top, Big Bud this is Tiger Top, over." There's a static-filled pause that seems to last forever.

"Tiger Top, Big Bud, we have you, over," comes the response.

"Fire mission."

"Roger that, Tiger Top, send it."

Kick steels himself. "Grid Kilo Zulu seven four three-three niner five eight seven, enemy encampment, battalion strength, troops in open."

"Roger that Tiger Top, Kilo Zulu seven four three-three niner five eight seven, enemy encampment, battalion strength, troops in open, one battery, three guns, two rounds ICM, two five seconds, over." There is a short pause. "Shot over." The team listens for the incoming artillery rounds.

Kick's stomach ties up in knots. "Shot out," he says back.

"Splash out."

Kick counts backwards from ten in his head. All eyes go to the encampment as a high whistling sound approaches. Someone in the camp yells, but it's too late. Three shells land within split seconds of each other around the camp, one hundred and fifty feet apart. Men scream and scatter as bodies go flying. Smoke and debris fill the air.

Hollywood has the binoculars on the scene. "Adjust fire. Add two hundred, right forty to two hundred. Fire for effect."

Kick repeats this, and gets the same back in reply, and then hears, "Shot out."

Kick spits out, "Big Bud, EVAC LZ one immediate, repeat EVAC LZ one immediate."

"Tiger Top, EVAC LZ one in one five mikes. Repeat EVAC LZ one, one five mikes. Tiger Top, splash out!"

Kick says quickly, "Splash Out. *Bookoo* thanks, Big Bud. We are *didi mau*."

Watt doesn't wait for the reply as he snaps the handset into place, and powers down. Hollywood gives the *form on me* hand signal, and the boys make their way after him at double time, as hell descends upon the encampment in the form of 105 mm shells. The explosions are massive and continuous.

Hollywood does the unthinkable and switches to a high-speed trail and steps up the pace. They are right out in the open. If they meet anyone on this trail they will have to shoot and hope the element of surprise gives them enough edge. They're all doing their best to watch for trip wires and traps. Kick looks at his boys. The strain on their faces makes them look a hundred years old, as they run for their lives. The ground heaves with shockwaves, and Kick's heart pounds like a jackhammer. They might just pull this shit off.

10

Trust Me

THERE'S BEEN NO MORE SIGN OF THE MAN in white socks and Kick's inner radar has calmed down since the brawl at Dusty's. He's placed himself in a booth at the back facing the front window so he can see the entire diner and everyone who goes by. He winces in pain. Parts of him are bruised and sore as hell from the beating he took, but he's cleaned himself up. He runs a hand through his clean shaggy hair and checks his watch. She should have been here ten minutes ago.

The bell over the door rings, and Kick looks up from his corner booth to see Kelly in her red raincoat, and a clear plastic umbrella. She looks up at the bell and smiles. Mary is adjusting Christmas decorations and checks her out while Joe peeks around the kitchen window. Mary shoos him back to his grill, and Joe blows her a kiss.

Kick gives a small wave. "Good afternoon, Kelly," he says politely as he rises and offers his hand.

Kelly shakes it with a surprising firmness. "I'm glad you called. We didn't get a chance to finish our conversation a couple of weeks ago. You look like you're still in one piece. Sort of." Kelly takes off her coat, hangs it on a nearby hook, shakes her umbrella, snaps it closed, and puts her purse on the seat beside her.

He's impressed with her confidence. "It'll take more than a bit of recreational fighting to stop me. Still raining out there?"

"Not as hard." She sighs. "You know, I used to see a lot of fights at this dive bar across the river from Ottawa when I studied at Carleton. It was an unpredictable place."

"Sounds like the Chez Henri in Hull." Kick says. "It had a good jukebox."

"That's right, it did. Anyway, not the first brawl I've seen, but I have to say yours was the most entertaining."

Mary arrives with coffee pot in hand. "Who's your friend?"

"This is Kelly O'Leary from *The Telegraph*. She wants to hear a couple of war stories. Kelly, this is Mary. She owns the joint and lets her husband, Joe, work in the kitchen."

Kelly smiles. "Nice to meet you, Mary. I really love your place."

Mary pours coffee without being asked. "Thanks. It gets the job done. What can I get you to start?"

"Best coffee you'll ever have," Kick offers. "Joe makes it Army style. It'll kick your ass."

Mary puts a menu in front of Kelly. "You don't need one of these, do you, Kick?"

He takes one. "I'm full of surprises today."

"What else is new." Mary heads over to a couple of big guys who just sat down at the counter. "Hey, guys, wet enough for ya?"

"Okay, what is army style coffee?" Kelly asks.

"Thought you'd never ask. Heat ten gallons of water in a big vat, add a giant can of Maxwell House, and when it boils shut off the heat, and add the magic touch." Kelly waits. "Starting from the center, you slowly pour in cold water in a spiral pattern. It settles out the grounds. Then ladle the coffee into the big urns. Perfect every time. Try it."

Kelly tries hers. "Wow. Perfect. So, I'm intrigued by what you told me at Dusty's. Do you have any idea how many Canadians volunteered for Vietnam, like you did?"

"It varies. Canada admits to three thousand who were legally allowed, and the US won't release any numbers. It's anywhere between thirty and forty, and I'd say closer to forty."

Kelly is shocked. "Thousand?"

"Yeah. Forty thousand."

"That's about how many Americans came here to escape the war."

Kick looks disgusted. "Ironic. So why is this interesting to you?"

"Well, it's obviously secret Canadian history, and secret US history for that matter, plus I've already written something kind of related to this."

"What does *kind of related* mean?"

"I wrote some articles about Canadian arms manufacturing last year. How we brand ourselves as a country that promotes peace, while we make and sell instruments of war."

"That's called a dichotomy."

"Or talking out of both sides of your ass."

Kick laughs. He likes her.

"And what's your angle? Do you just want recognition, or something else?"

And she's direct. "What else could it be?"

"I don't know, but I need a story that's based on solid provable facts. Something regular people can connect to that ties into something universal."

Kick puts more sugar in his coffee. "So those two railway spikes at the counter could relate to it, but it could also sell to the fat cats in ivory towers."

"Exactly. By the way, where'd you go to school?"

He laughs. "Danang U."

Kelly smiles. "Hm. You seem well educated; that's why I asked."

"I'm naturally curious and I read a lot."

"It shows." Kick's not exactly immune to flattery, and a hint of a smile crosses his face. Kelly continues. "My point is, the broader the appeal, the better it'll sell. A parent could relate to it, a kid thinking of a military career, a peace activist, a veteran, or just a taxpayer."

"Sounds like a Hallmark card."

"No, but you get what I mean, right?"

"I'm catchin' your Frisbee," Kick says, as he waves Mary over. "Before we go any further, did your dad serve?"

Kelly's looks confused. "Why?"

"'Cause it matters."

"My father worked for a company that makes footwear."

"Oh. What did he do for them?"

"He dealt with large corporate accounts and spent a lot of time on the road. I didn't know him that well."

"Sounds like he's no longer with us. I'm sorry."

"Thanks. Yeah, he died when I was young. I was raised by an aunt and uncle mostly. My mother passed away when I was born." She looks down.

The conversation skids to a stop as Mary comes to the table. "What'll it be, Kelly?"

"Oh, you go first."

"Monte Cristo, please Mary," Kick says with a smirk.

"Oh my, Joe! He's getting a Monte Cristo!" yells Mary.

Joe sticks his head out. "What? Did he win the lottery or something?"

Kick calls back, "Just keepin' you on your toes, Julia Child."

"Now I'm intrigued," Kelly says. "The same for me."

"Whoa, it's a run on Monte's! Hope you can handle it!"

Joe pretends to panic in the kitchen. "Aaahhh!"

"Coming right up, *mes amis*." Mary heads off.

Kelly says, "I think there is a great angle with you and Dusty. You know, two friends who served, one special forces, one a Marine, but from different countries."

"I think there's a better angle with greed," Kick sneers. "You know, two countries who fought the same war, one out in the open, the other sneaking around like a little bitch."

"Do you have hard proof of that?"

"Sure. We sold three-point-three-four billion dollars in Canadian nickel that was used in war planes, missiles, and armored personnel carriers. We pushed Canadian-made bazooka barrels, radar and sonar equipment, bomb sights, explosives, and aircraft engines. And we sold them good Canadian whiskey. Plus, we sent humanitarian aid and ran hospitals, but gave it all to the South. North Vietnam got sweet fuck all. That's just the tip of the iceberg. I'll get you documents if that's what you need." Kick leans back. "But we don't involve Dusty. He's not built for this kind of thing."

Kelly smiles. "He looks built to me." Kick doesn't bite. "So, you can handle it, but he can't?"

"I'm uniquely qualified to handle *whatever*. That's how I was trained."

"I've got to say this all sounds a bit shady. Will you be breaking any laws?"

Kick shrugs. "*You* won't be, and that's all you need to know. There's a fair amount of info that's public if you know where to look. Canadians did a shitty job of holding the government accountable. So did the press, by the way. I have sources for all the classified material you'll need."

"So, you know a guy who knows a guy?"

"No. I'm the guy. Can you trust your editor?"

Kelly isn't ready for this. "I can. He broke similar stories in his day. He calls himself a hippie capitalist and says democracy can't work without us all knowing the truth. 'Keep the pricks honest; otherwise, fascism is just around the corner,' he always says. "I think he's rooting for me."

Kick studies her. "Where'd you grow up?"

"Me? Montreal. My dad's company was headquartered there. And I went to Carleton U, like I mentioned." Kelly pivots, and Kick lets her. "I'm thinking we start with a human-interest story, tease out some juicy arms deal morsels, and keep digging until someone stops us."

They bounce ideas back and forth, and the conversation eventually comes back to food. Kick tells her about an army favorite known as shit on a shingle. Kelly can't tell if he's making it up, but he's adamant. "I'm telling you, it's delicious."

Mary arrives with the Monte Cristos and tops up their coffees. "Enjoy. Joe doesn't get to make too many of these, so he put a little extra love into them." Mary touches a hand to Kick's shoulder. He gives her a nod to let her know everything's good.

"You're gonna love this food," says Kick, and digs in.

"I hope so, but I've never had one. What exactly is it?"

"Two slices of French toast with ham, turkey, and Swiss cheese inside. Mayo and mustard of course."

Kelly isn't sure but takes a bite. "Wow, that's really good."

"See? You'll be ready for shit on a shingle in no time." Kelly laughs, and Kick smiles. "You know there'll be people who'll want to keep this quiet, right?"

"I sure hope so."

Kick likes her, and not just for her interest in him. He feels the same connection he would with a soldier but can't understand why. She's definitely never seen combat.

Kelly tells him more about her earlier years at school, while Kick inhales his food. Mary is back to entice them. "Interest anyone in pie? Peach, blueberry, and cherry, all fresh today. The crust'll melt in your mouth."

Kelly is only half-finished, and starts to protest, but Kick pipes up, "One blueberry and one cherry. Mary will give you a doggie bag if you can't finish it."

Kelly finally says, "Fine. But the blueberry's for me."

"Yeah, you don't strike me as the cherry type," Mary says as she's leaving.

A small laugh escapes from Kelly. "She's fun."

"Yeah, she and Joe are like family. Tell me more about your father."

"I don't have many memories of him, but I do remember standing on a chair at the kitchen counter, doing some baking with him."

"You know, I've made pie."

Kelly laughs. "You have not."

"Have so. I used to help in the mess when we'd be grounded by weather or whatever. Sitting around used to drive us nuts."

"I don't see it."

"The military is an amazing machine, Kelly. Anything it sets its mind to gets done. Hell, they set up three Coca-Cola plants in North Africa during World War Two just to fight Rommel."

"I'm sure it was thirsty work."

Mary is back with the pie. Before Kelly can stop her, she buries each piece in dollops of thick freshly whipped cream. Then she's gone before Kelly can say anything.

Kick laughs and digs in. "You'll get used to the hospitality."

"And the calories." She tastes it. "This must be really bad for me, because it is *so* good."

"Told ya." Kick grins. For the first time in a long time, he feels like a regular person. Just sharing a meal with someone in a little diner. It's the first really good time he's had in ages, and Kelly's enjoying herself too. He wishes he'd taken the time to at least shave, but it may have come off like he was trying too hard.

He takes her in. "When I was training soldiers, I came to understand that the best way to make someone trustworthy was to trust them."

"Mmm. Hemingway."

"What?"

"That's a quote from Ernest Hemmingway."

This is news to Kick, but he continues. "Right. Well, what I'm trying to say is I'm going to trust you. But understand I'm way out on a limb. Get it?"

Kelly knows she's landing a whale. "I'm flattered. I trust you too."

"Yeah. I guess it's a two-way street."

"So, what's the story about your name?" she asks.

"My father was a sergeant major in the Canadian Army and when I volunteered to go to Vietnam, I made it a goal to make first sergeant. The US Army term for that is *Top Kick*."

"Did you make it?"

"Well, one of my old buddies had been calling me *Kick* since I was a kid, so it would've been embarrassing if I didn't. But yeah, I made sarge and a few notches past that, I guess."

"And is it all right if I call you Kick?"

"Just don't tell anyone else. That name's a bit of a secret. I mean it."

"I can tell you do. And I'll keep it between us."

Kick checks her for bullshit and is satisfied. "I have something for you before you go."

"Thanks. What is it?"

"Not yet. Listen carefully. Don't open it till you're home or in your office. It's … just *don't*."

"You have my word."

Kick waves Mary over.

"I did my best, Mary," says Kelly.

"I'll pack that up for you, sweetheart," Mary says with a smile, and heads off.

"So, I meant to ask you earlier," Kelly says. "Why did you decide to go to Vietnam?"

Kick lights a cigarette. "I wanted to be like my old man. He had his war, and this was mine. And I was going to take care of the bad guys."

"So not for medals, or honor?"

"At first. That faded pretty quick. I got lots of hardware, but I left it all at the Wall."

"But why would anyone stay for four tours?"

Kick's face darkens, and he looks down. Then he quickly grabs his coat, slides a thick manila envelope into Kelly's purse, and walks out the door without a word. Joe and Mary look out from the kitchen as the bell rings. Kelly tries to say something, but he's gone.

♦ ♦ ♦ ♦

Kelly stands by the booth looking confused as Mary comes over. She lays down the bill and the takeaway bag. "Don't worry. That's just him. He likes you, though. Usually, he's just scrambled eggs on toast."

Kelly lays down some cash and says, "No change, thanks. It was very nice to meet you and Joe. I hope to see you again."

Joe yells, "You come back any time you want, Kelly. *Any* time."

"Thanks, Joe. Would you mind calling me a cab, Mary?"

"Of course."

"I think I'll wait outside and get some fresh air."

"Before you go, Kelly, take some advice. He's more fragile than he lets on. And it's best not to ask too many questions about what happened over there. You don't want to wake the beast, if you know what I mean."

"You're a good friend, to say something like that. I'll tread carefully."

"You're a peach. Good night!" Mary waves.

Kelly steps outside and feels the cold fresh air. She looks both ways, but there's no sign of Kick. Not that she expects to see him. Her head is swimming with conflicting thoughts. Kick is kind of way out there, but he's very charismatic. She can see why men would follow him into battle. And the facts he threw out, just off the cuff like that. She can't wait to see what this envelope holds. The cab pulls up, and Kelly waves at Mary and Joe inside, who are closing for the day. They're such a nice couple. Maybe there's a chance for her someday. To find someone who understands her. Kelly gets into the cab, hopeful all this will lead somewhere great and take her where she wants to go.

11

IT'S ON

KELLY CLOSES THE DOOR, hands Stewart the envelope, and then sits down while he finishes up a loud phone call. He's at a full boil. "We can't give away that much ad space just because we misspelled *surreptitious*! No one should use a word with that many syllables in a newspaper anyway! A quarter page, same location, and tell them I'm personally fuckin sorry, that's all they get. And check the goddamn spelling this time!" The person at the other end of the phone is still talking as Stewart slams it down. "O'Leary, got something good?"

Kelly lays out lunch at the diner, while Stewart reads the contents of the envelope. He looks at her from time to time, until she finishes with "So, we've agreed to meet again."

Stewart drops the documents on his desk. "Goddamn it, this is good. Where'd he get it?"

Kelly tries to tamp down her excitement. "I decided not to ask on the first meeting. Does it look legit?"

"Legit? It implicates the Canadian military in allowing harm to come to soldiers at CFB Gagetown when they tested Agents Orange, Purple, and White. Toxic herbicides known to cause cancer. They let them spray it all over the place with no protection! Then they just dug a hole and buried the leftovers!"

"Now what? Do I call them?"

"No! They'll get spooked and start hiding things. Let me think." Stewart yells out his door, "Penny, who's that guy who's always calling about tennis?"

"Squash!" Penny yells back. "And it's Bill What's-his-ass. He's army or something and his daddy was a general."

"Fuck, that's right." He strums through his rolodex, then picks up the phone and dials. "Bill, it's Malcolm at *The Telegraph*. I hear you suck balls at squash."

Stewart smiles at Bill being sassy on the other end. "Yeah? I will kick your chunky-soup army butt." He takes out his appointment book. "Thursday at four is fine. It'll be good to see you again, especially while you're gasping for air." Stewart laughs. "Sure, I'll put a hundred on it. Hey Bill, while I've got you, can you get me a list of military personnel in Gagetown from," he flips a page. "sixty-two to sixty-six, with contact info, and I need to keep it quiet. No, it's just some budget discrepancy, and I'm crossing my t's here, that's all. Okay, I'll keep out of it. Can you bring it on Thursday? Great. Looking forward to smashing you into a fat little grease spot!"

Stewart slams down the phone before Bill can launch a retort, puts the documents back in the envelope, and hands it to her. "Write this down. Once I get these names, call the lowest ranks first. Ask if they tested herbicides there and if they were any good. Do *not* mention the words *agent*, *orange*, *purple*, or any other colors. Call it weed killer. Ask how it was applied, how and where it was stored, how much was used, if they wore protection, if there's any left, and how it may have been disposed of. Got it?"

"Got it." Kelly keeps scribbling.

"If anyone asks, you're writing an article on the advancement of weed prevention for the garden section. Make working photocopies of these documents, then file the originals, including this envelop, under my initials in the Evil Room. Do it all yourself and show this to no one. Talk to no one. Tell no one. The only way to keep a secret is to tell absolutely no one. *No one*. Not even your friend what's-her-name out there. Stick your head in and give me a nod when it's done. Got all that?"

"Yes, sir, I've got it."

"And Kelly."

"Yes?"

"Set up another meeting in about a week with this Kick guy, but don't look too excited, and try and get more stuff like this."

"Okay. Will do. He's interesting, but he makes me nervous."

"I bet he does. Be cautious. If he was special ops, he has seen some real shit." Stewart gets up and looks out the window. "This kind of crap by our government is not fucking okay. Citizens run democracies, not bureaucrats, and especially not foreign ones. It's rumored Canadian power companies are spraying Agent Orange under high-tension lines, but we've never been able to prove it. Park rangers have complained they keep getting sprayed by overhead planes in some of the parks, and some trees are mysteriously dying, but there's no hard proof. Parks! Where people go camping with their kids, for God's sake!

Fuckin' criminals. Okay, get back to work."

Stewart picks up the phone again and hits a button. "Penny, block off late Thursday afternoon, and get me all the stuff I need to play squash. Yeah, I know how long it's been. And make sure O'Leary here gets whatever she needs from now on, including from *that room*. Yeah, we should figure out a better name for it. Yes, very much too *on the nose*." He hangs up, looks at Kelly, then points to the door.

"But how do I tie all this together? I mean …?"

Stewart smiles. "Kid, don't get ahead of yourself. In the words of Honest Abe, 'Give me six hours to chop down a tree, and I'll spend the first four sharpening the axe.' Gather up all the facts, and then see what the story is. The truth is already written, and you just have to uncover what's hidden, or *surreptitious*, as some fucking idiots here might say. Paint by the numbers. Fill in the blanks. Those are all the metaphors I have. And now?"

"I get out." She grabs the envelope and heads for the door.

"O'Leary."

"Yes."

"Tell no one."

◆ ◆ ◆ ◆

Kelly closes the unmarked door of the Evil Room, and double-checks it's locked. She heads down the dim basement hallway, back upstairs, then settles in at her desk and tries to focus on a local story. It's about a fish and chip place called Moby Dick's that's getting heat from fussy locals for having the word *dick* in its name. Kelly shakes her head.

"Still running down that dick story?" Val asks.

Kelly looks up. "Yeah, we can't have people naming businesses after literary classics."

"What's next? Catcher in the Rye leads to alcohol abuse? Coriolanus is pro butt sex?"

"It's a slippery slope, Val."

"Nice one. So?" asks Val.

"So what?"

"How did all that go? What'd he say?"

"I'm not being weird here, but I can't talk to anyone about this story."

Val's excited. "What? Oh! Okay, but are you tying this into that whole thing from last year? About the arms industry, you know, the history of all that?"

"That I can talk about." Stewart is in his doorway staring at her. "Shit. Be right back."

"Had lunch yet?" Val yells after her.

"No."

"Meet you at Moby Dick's. You can call it research."

"Be there in ten," Kelly confirms, then pokes her head into Stewart's office.

"All done down there?" he asks. Kelly nods yes. "It's the small details that make the difference, O'Leary. Don't forget to confirm with me afterwards next time."

"Yes, sir. Won't happen again." Kelly heads back to her desk and dials her phone.

"Moby Dick's. Our seafood is a classic," a guy on the other end greets her.

"Tony? It's Kelly from *The Telegraph*. Can I swing by with a photographer?"

"Totally. I'd love that!"

"Be there in a few." Kelly hangs up.

"Hey Sam, got time for an easy one?"

Sam the photographer grabs his camera. "*Easy* is my middle name, Kelly O."

"You know the fish place near Coal Harbor?"

"The *dick* one?" he asks.

"They're getting some heat about it."

Sam laughs. "Getting heat about their dick? We should all have this problem. What's next? The Three Musketeers are pro-NRA?"

Kelly and Sam find Val outside chatting up Tony. They get a shot of him in his apron holding a massive cod with the Moby Dick's sign above him.

Tony says, "Thanks for the exposure. These clowns don't realize how much they're helping my business. Please don't print that."

"Don't worry, that's off the record," Kelly says. Sam has to run, so Tony gives him some two-for-one vouchers before he takes off.

"You two have time for a late lunch?" Tony asks. "It's on the house."

"You read our minds, sir. Two fish and chips, and we'll rough it at a table outside."

"True Vancouverites. Comin' up."

They sit down, and Val says, "So tell me that theory again about the arms financing?"

"Okay, in its simplest form, it probably started with Napoleon."

"If I remember, he had a butt-load of cash, and wanted to conquer Europe, right?"

"Yeah. France had just sold Louisiana to the US for fifteen million dollars, so he was rolling in dough. But the rest of the countries in Europe didn't have the cash to fight the fights they wanted to have. As Napoleon said, 'an army marches on its stomach.' So, these countries got loans from big bankers, who made money on the interest."

"Naturally. Like my Visa card."

"Exactly, Val. After a long war, peace is restored, and the bankers rake it in."

"Right. It's a lucrative model. War is good for banks."

"That's right, and banks never stop working, especially during wars. Credit cards from any country will work in any war zone, even the enemy's. It's called a *cha-ordic* transaction — order even in chaos. So today, let's say there's a country on the edge of ruin. A bunch of agitators stir up a sensitive part of the country to start a war."

"Like Sudan, or Sri Lanka?" Val suggests.

"Right again. Some state wants to separate, an ethnic or religious group wants their own country or language, some country has a food shortage, or a poor economy is blamed on an ethnic group. Banks loan money to both sides, and the longer the war goes on, the better it is for banks. The war ends eventually, and the countries have to rebuild. The loser is usually broke, so they borrow even more money, but have nothing left to put up for collateral except things like timber, oil, and mineral rights, and the financiers are happy to use them as collateral. Plus, unemployment's high, so there's cheap labor. This pattern gets repeated, and the beat goes on."

"But don't they eventually pay back the loans and get their resources rights back?"

Kelly shakes her head. "No. Usually there's a ruler or dictator who takes a bunch of the money for himself, his family, and his friends, or his wife buys half a million dollars in shoes. The country never gets rebuilt and is always at the mercy of the lenders. The people get screwed."

"So, banks are one of the reasons why wars never end?" Kelly nods in agreement. "In your article you have a name for them like… the industry, gray men… what was it?"

"I call them The Machine. The cold-hearted financiers who run it all."

Tony drops off their food. "Two fish and chips, cider vinegar, tartar on the side. Enjoy!"

He heads back in. "Thanks, Tony!" Kelly takes a bankcard from her purse. "You know how you can now get cash from bank machines with a bank card?"

"Yeah."

Kelly holds her card up. "They're already starting to use them at stores to pay for things, the same way you use your credit card. Know what that means?"

"I'll be broke forever?"

Kelly leans in. "It's the beginning of a society where everything you buy, and everywhere you've been, is documented. Someone could figure out we had lunch here today, and what time."

"But if you're not doing anything wrong, what's the harm?"

"What happens when another Joe McCarthy shows up? Or someone comes into power, and they happen to like white supremacists and Nazis? Or they think liberals are Antichrists? Or the Jews get blamed for everything again?"

"I get it. But what's the end game? If The Machine gobbles up every territory, they'll just end up owning every country. They'd own …"

"Everything. Everything and *everyone*. The aim of fascists is power, simply for the sake of power. They want total control, and they'll say and do anything to get it."

Val shakes her head in horror, as a handsome Asian man comes up beside her and asks flirtatiously, "Do you have a light, by any chance?"

Val is immediately smitten by what sounds a bit like a British accent and holds out her hand to Kelly, who hands her the lighter from her purse. Val lights the man's cigarette and smiles sweetly at him.

"Thank you. That's very kind," the man says with a big smile. "Have a wonderful lunch."

Val watches him walk away. "He's cute."

Kelly leans toward Val. "Look at that. He's wearing white socks."

12

Dust Off
Vietnam, 1968

THERE IS NO FEELING THAT COMPARES to being hunted by men. The air is electric as the boys run like demons along a tree line by a large grassy area. Hollywood veers into dense cover and drops to his belly. Everyone else does the same. Senses and nerves are lit. Chests heave, nostrils flare, and eyes bulge as they lie flat and wait, soaked in sweat. The shelling finally stops back in the valley.

Hollywood taps Kick and points out into the grass. There's a patrol sprinting right at them. The LZ is a five-minute run down the tree line, but these seven Viet Cong soldiers complicate things. It doesn't look like they've been seen yet, but everyone knows what to do.

The VC slow down as they come under the trees. Their eyes haven't had time to adjust from bright sun to shade, so the boys are invisible. The patrol moves right past them not twenty feet away. Kick and his men each follow a different combatant with their rifles. Just when it looks like they are free and clear, the last soldier stops, sniffs the air, and looks in their direction. He can smell them. The soldier asks a question, and points toward where they are hidden. Kick can hear his own sweat hitting the ground. The entire patrol turns their way.

Kick carefully pulls the pin from the grenade he's holding and waits for a chance. And then it happens. There's a distant explosion, and the patrol looks away. Frosty's claymores just went off. Kick lobs the grenade in a perfect arc, while everyone opens fire with single shots. It's over in a matter of seconds. Simpson and Beach hustle over to finish off any survivors with headshots, while everyone else bolts along the trees to the extraction point. With any luck the claymores will draw all the attention.

They arrive at the LZ, and Watt has the radio headset ready for Kick as he slides in beside him and calls the chopper. It's an eternity until he hears that beautiful squawk.

"Tiger Top this is *Jolly Jack*. We are two mikes out. Pop smoke," comes the voice of the pilot. Hollywood lobs a smoke grenade into the grassy area, as Simpson and Beach rejoin the team. Yellow smoke builds and rises as the repetitive thump of an HH-3E approaches. It sounds like freedom.

"Jolly Jack, yellow smoke is Tiger Top."

"Roger that. Sit tight." Thirty seconds later the big green bird drops on the smoke, and Kick sends everyone running low at it while he brings up the rear.

Hollywood is the only one that hears the *zip zip zip* of the AK rounds. A bullet tears through Kick's shirt, burns through his skin, and glances off his seventh rib with just enough force to fracture it. His breathing becomes excruciating, and he falls to the ground as blood soaks his shirt.

Hollywood boosts Simpson into the bird, then turns for Kick. All he sees is a hand poking up through yellow smoke. He runs toward him, slinging back his M16 and pulling out the sawed-off shotgun. Kick often wonders what got sprinkled into Hollywood's genes to make him the way he is. Was it from some wild Irish warrior generations ago, or from his mother's German side? Back in the world, people might call him cold-blooded, or a psycho. But when you're in a jam like this, he's the cold-blooded psycho you want coming to save your ass.

Hollywood lobs a grenade well past Kick's position. "Fire in the hole!" he screams, then tosses red smoke right beside Kick to help cover their escape. Hollywood stoops to grab Kick just as his grenade explodes in the middle of four Viet Cong. Two of them go down.

Hollywood comes up with Kick in a fireman's carry, fires both barrels of the sawed-off into the smoke, then runs for the chopper. There's screaming in Vietnamese from the other side. Kick slips out of his grasp a couple of times from all the blood, but Hollywood manages to hold on. AK-47 fire rips through the red and yellow smoke, as Kick pulls his Colt pistol and returns fire from his slung-over position. Hollywood keeps charging hell-bent-for-leather at the chopper.

The VC soldiers are close enough for Kick to see their fiery eyes through the smoke. No one has to tell him there's a hefty bounty for a LLRP's head, and he can tell these guys want every goddamn one of them. Kick fires a third time, and the result is pure luck. He catches one of them in the pelvis. He goes down, but it's not a serious wound and Kick knows he'll be back soon. Hollywood is starting to slow. Kick fires at the second soldier as he comes out of the smoke. There are nasty buckshot wounds on his face.

◆ ◆ ◆ ◆

Bihn sees the flash of the shotgun and feels a spray of hot buckshot hit his face and chest. Running hard in his tire-tread sandals and half-rotted pants and shirt, he knows he must keep going. When his brother Hien takes a shot to his right hip a few seconds later and buckles into the grass, he knows what to do. The pact they have means he keeps charging no matter what, so Bihn runs headlong into the red smoke. Both brothers are skin and bones from extended time in the jungle, eating bad rice and the odd rat or reptile, but they're fast, agile, and fierce. Bihn can smell the American's fear, and tastes revenge.

He and Hien joined Ho Chi Minh in the North six months ago. Their parents were killed by an Arc Light bombing raid while they were tending the family rice fields. They wouldn't have even heard the B-52 planes overhead they were so high. There would have been just the last-minute whistle of the five-hundred pound bombs.

The brothers know they may die for their efforts, but it's an honorable way to go. Their communist leaders have told them that South Vietnam is starving and falling apart. Unlike the Americans they're chasing, this is their home. They won't rotate home after a year. Their tour ends when the people who killed their parents are burning to death in their helicopters, or choking on their own blood. For these brothers, there's only do or die.

His brother Hien screams at him to kill them all. The pain in his voice cuts him to his core, but he keeps shooting at the big one running with the small one on his shoulder. He has to slow them down, so that the other patrols can join the fight and finish them off.

The smaller man is shooting at him with his pistol, so Binh trains his fire on him. He knows Americans don't leave injured men behind. If he can take them down for a minute or two, they can take out the whole team, and the helicopter.

Bihn hits the smaller one's pistol, knocking it from his hand. Blood spurts from both Americans, and they fall close to the helicopter. He has them cold. Hien screams at him to throw a grenade into the helicopter and finish them off. The large American is trying to help the small one back up. Bihn has the grenade in his hand when he sees a large flash from the helicopter door.

◆ ◆ ◆ ◆

Kick's hand explodes in pain as the Colt flies apart, shattered by a bullet. Pieces of the gun burn into his hand. A fragment hits Hollywood's right shoulder and blood sprays out of his back into Kick's face. They both go down in the grass, ten feet from the chopper. Kick can't get up, but Hollywood struggles to his feet. Even above the thumping chopper blades and rotor wash, he hears the screaming in Vietnamese behind him. Kick looks at the door of the chopper.

Simpson is laser focused on something behind him, so he turns. The VC soldier has a grenade and is about to pull the pin. Simpson's round hits Bihn's left cheek, shattering the upper section of his head. His skull explodes, and blood, brains, and pink mist blow out behind him. The other wounded VC soldier is still screaming, and has managed to get to one knee and raise his rifle.

As Kick is close enough to read the inscription of the side of the Jolly Green that reads, 'So Others May Live' when he hears "DOWN!" Hollywood's full weight flops on top of him. The door gunner unleashes a burst from his GE GAU-2/a mini-gun. The salvo lasts only a second, but more than a hundred 51-millimeter rounds slam into Hien, animating his body into a horrific dance. He flies apart in a chaotic burst. For these brothers and their family, the war is over.

Two more VC patrols scream into the LZ. Frosty and Beach jump from the Huey and help Hollywood, while Watt grabs Kick. They all scramble inside the bird as it heaves itself off the ground with Hollywood's legs still dangling out the door. The on-board gunners open fire from both sides at the approaching Viet Cong. AK-47 rounds ping off the bottom of the Huey for a few seconds until they are lifted out of range. Kick strains his ears for the hiss of a rocket-propelled grenade, but it never comes.

He looks around at his boys, panting, bleeding, and shaking on the chopper floor. Hollywood pulls his legs inside, and Simpson tends to his wound. Beach does the same with Kick, and both get a shot of morphine.

The Huey pilot radios in, "Big Bud, this is Jolly Jack. We have Tiger Top and are en route. ETA two-zero mikes. Have medical stand by. We have one chest, one hand, and one shoulder wound, all gunshots, over."

Hollywood lets out a fierce war cry and starts laughing. The pilot looks back with a big grin. Hollywood yells, "Charlie Mike! Call it in!"

"Big Bud, Big Bud, Jolly Jack here. We have a very happy Tiger Top. They are Charlie Mike, repeat Charlie Mike, completed mission. Have beer on ice for these hardcore mothers."

"Jolly Jack, this is Big Bud. Outstanding, outstanding! Drinks are on the goddamn house!"

Kick grabs Hollywood by the neck and pulls him close. God, he loves this man.

13

THE FATHER

KICK IS IN THE PASSENGER'S SEAT of the white van with Taylor and Baker, parked under a big moody cedar near Pandora Park, where there are no streetlights. It's another rainy night, and Taylor keeps the engine running to stop the windows from fogging up. The headlights are off, and there's just the glow from the dashboard and the occasional passing car for light.

"They said no rain for two days. How can they be that wrong?" Taylor asks.

Baker is sitting on the floor in the back reading with his penlight. "Dude, adjust your perspective. Expect it'll rain every day until the middle of April, and when it doesn't, it'll be like a bonus."

Taylor shakes his head. "Irritating at times, isn't he?"

"Like mold." Kick lights a smoke and blows it back at Baker. "What are you reading now? Playdough?"

"Yeah, it's Plato. I finished *The Iliad*, so you can have my copy." It lands with a thud beside Kick's seat. The cover has a bronze statue of Achilles, with his elegant plumed helmet, shield, sword, and lance.

"That's the only picture in it, so maybe you should stick to cowboys," says Taylor.

"It is a cowboy book, if you think about it," Baker suggests.

"Just curious, but in between coffee klatches, what did you find out about her dad?"

Baker tosses an envelope on top of *The Iliad*. "I prefer tea."

"Shocking." Kick holds a penlight in his teeth while he goes through each page in order.

Taylor explains. "He worked for a company called Martech, and he did sell boots. In fact, you probably wore them in 'Nam. Probably shot his bullets and tossed his grenades too."

"The guy got around, huh?"

"He did," answers Baker. "And what Canada didn't make, he found elsewhere for Uncle Sam, and wrapped it all up with a nice little maple leaf they could legally defend. Under the 1956 Defense Production Sharing Agreement, Canadian companies got the same consideration on defense contracts as US companies. That included raw materials. By 1960 Canadian companies could also do research and development for the Pentagon."

Taylor adds, "It gets better. Something called the CCC, the Canadian Commercial Corporation, helped secure contracts for Canadian companies at the Pentagon. All legal."

"So why did they work so hard to cover it up?" Kick asks.

Baker shrugs. "Politics. 'Propaganda is to democracy what the bludgeon is to a totalitarian state.'"

Taylor sighs. "In other words, they pounded us with bullshit."

Kick is annoyed. "Is this the part where someone guesses who the fuck said that?"

"Chomsky," Taylor snaps.

Baker smiles. "Excellent!"

Kick is not entertained. "Back to the point at hand, Shakespeare. Kelly's dad was an international arms dealer?"

Taylor lights a cigarette. "Yup. A big one."

Baker smiles. "'The sins of the father are visited upon the children.'"

"This is getting annoying. Homer?" Kick whines.

"Euripides, but yeah, another old Greek," Baker answers calmly.

It's Taylor's turn to bring them back on topic. "All we know is something went wrong. Her dad just disappeared."

"Voluntarily?"

Baker sighs. "Unknown. We can't find anyone to confirm what went down. We know his family is originally from Montreal, but he worked out of Vancouver. That's it."

"But you think they offed him, right?" Kick asks.

Taylor shrugs. "Or he killed himself. It happens." He looks right at Kick.

Kick looks away. "All right, does she know all this? I got the impression from her she has an idea. And how does this affect things?"

"There's no proof that she knows," Taylor replies. "She was a kid, and went off to live with relatives back east, who appear to have been normal. We haven't sent anyone around asking questions. It might make things weird at this point."

Baker says, "If you're worried about getting more material like the Agent Orange stuff, these particular friends of ours share your feelings about Canada getting away with murder, for lack of a better term."

"No, murder sounds about right," Kick says.

"It drives them batty these guys made so much money," says Taylor. "And Canada came away looking like a bunch of peace-mongers. Make no mistake: this is very, very off the books. I'm sticking my neck way out for you, and if anyone up the food chain finds out we leaked this stuff, we're toast. They'll probably know anyway, but they don't want to *know*. Get it? They're going to look the other way, unless we give them a reason not to. So, we keep this tight, and our sources will be happy, plus you'll be happy. And if we are lucky enough to get this shit published, I'll make sure there's no way to trace how it got out. Understood?"

"Understood. Why are you doing this?" Kick asks.

Taylor smiles. "Obviously this is very important to you, which is why I made the inquiries, but I didn't expect this level of commitment from the folks on my end. They're pissed off, and they want this exposed almost as much as you do."

"I've got to admit, I admire the con job," says Baker. "Uncle Sam took all the heat, and Canada exploded their GDP for the ten years of the war, birthed their arms industry and somehow sold themselves as the voice of humanitarian aid and peace."

Taylor laughs harder. "Yeah, Pearson was polishing his Nobel Peace Prize while he pulled all the strings, and Trudeau just kept it rolling along, and even squeezed in time for a photo op with John and Yoko. I don't know if it was planned that way or not, but con job indeed."

Baker smiles. "You might even call it a *snow job*."

"Now you're just trying too hard. So, how do we move forward?" Kick asks.

"Steady as she goes," replies Taylor. "Our friends will keep feeding you classified goodies, and you keep moving this article, book, or whatever it is along. Meanwhile we'll try to track down our boy in the white socks. We brought in a friend from Hong Kong to help." Taylor takes out a still from a security camera, and a couple of photos from a low-resolution camera.

Baker speaks up. "These are from one of our favorite gangland restaurants downtown two nights ago. You know the place."

"The beef and ginger hotpot is outstanding."

The photos show White Socks at a table with one other person of Chinese descent. The pics are too far away, but the socks are evident, and his dining partner looks familiar.

Kick asks, "Is that our old friend Mr. Chung?"

"Yeah," Baker answers. "So White Socks is looking for weapons, or worse."

"You want me to pay him a visit?"

"Our Hong Kong friend is on that," replies Taylor.

"Who is it?"

"You'll find out soon enough." Taylor laughs.

Baker adds, "If we can get this socks guy's name, that'll help."

"The Chinese consulate haven't declared him as staff there or anything?"

"Nope," Baker says. "So that makes him a free radical. We're on it, but stay frosty."

"*Stay frosty*? Is that a term from your book club? Sounds fuckin' stupid."

Baker laughs. "I'm really starting to like you."

Kick's not laughing.

"That's all we've got so far." says Taylor. "Keep that info on her dad secure."

"Will do." Kick says. "I'm gonna set up another meet with her and confirm the ground rules."

"Keep us posted." says Taylor.

Kick tucks the envelope inside his raincoat. Taylor sneaks a look and notices the butt of his gun.

"Can you get me something on bombing runs in North Vietnam?"

"What do you mean?" Taylor asks.

"There were rumors when I was in country that International Control Commission officials from Canada were trotted up to North Vietnam by the NVA and shown the results of Operation Rolling Thunder."

"Yeah, so?" asks Taylor.

"So, when they got back to Saigon, they met with certain people and told them what hit, what missed, and by how much. Apparently, they had photos."

Taylor laughs. "Canadians on the ICC did bomb damage assessments? Canadians really are nice and that's a great con! Why have spies in North Vietnam when a bunch of Canucks get invited up to see the results firsthand? Very well played, right?"

Baker smiles. "That shit's tight."

"I'll reach out to my friends in high places and see what we can find out," Taylor says. "We need to take a page from that playbook, Baker. I mean, that's fucking brilliant."

"Okay, I'm good. Got any Marlies?" Kick asks.

"You're breakin' my bank account here, Kick."

"You expense it. Don't give me that shit."

Taylor hands over a carton. "Okay, but once you have your little book deal, or article, we need to get back to business as usual. Higher-ups want to know who White Socks is, sooner rather than later, and you owe me a little something for all this."

"For smokes?"

"For helping you with this newspaper thing."

"Like what?"

"I don't know," Taylor muses. "I haven't been fishing up here yet."

Kick puts up his hood and opens his door. "You can buy salmon at a store. Why bob around in the cold to get one?" Just before Kick steps out, he grabs *The Iliad*.

Once the door has slammed, Baker puts his hand out toward Taylor, who sighs, reaches into his pocket, and holds out a twenty.

Baker snatches it. "I knew he'd take it. Even if it's only to tell me how much it sucks." Baker sniffs the bill. "Ah, the sweet smell of success."

"I've got another twenty says he won't get past page fifty."

Baker gets into the passenger's seat. "I'll take that action. He seems better. This newspaper thing must be helping, huh?"

"I hope it works. I've got big plans for him if he can pull himself out of this dive."

"Maybe that reporter woman will nudge him in the right direction. Seems like he could use a little romance."

"I was thinking the same thing." Taylor hits the lights, stabs the van into drive, and takes off into the dark wet night. "Fucking rain."

14

BROWN EYES

IT'S SIX A.M. AND KICK CAN TELL in his bones it's a nasty, cold day out there. His cowboy boots stand on the coffee table; he's finally given them a good coat of polish. He likes to let it set for a day before the spit shine, so he pulls on an old pair of black rubber shoes, popular in the Pacific Northwest. The arthritis in his hands is bad, so he also slips on his black leather gloves. He puts up the hood on his coat, and then takes a disgusting stained gray blanket that he found in the alley and wraps it over his head. It covers him down to his knees. Since the White Socks incident, he takes no chances.

Kick heads to the back exit of his building that opens into the alley. He stoops over like an old man, then gingerly steps outside into an ice-cold fog that's clinging to the city. He turns left and shuffles along the alley, then turns left two streets up and huddles on the bench at a covered bus stop on East Hastings. Similar looking homeless people are wrapped in whatever they can find, curled up on cardboard in doorways, trying to stay warm and get some sleep. To anyone watching, he's just another one of them.

Kick watches without watching. Most of these people are locals he knows to some extent. It's hard for outsiders to blend in here, which he likes. It takes ten minutes for the next bus, but Kick lets it pass. He keeps watching until he is sure of every person on both sides of the street and sees no one in the upper windows. When the next bus pulls up, he stands and lets the blanket fall to the ground. He hobbles onto the bus, looking down while he flashes his bus pass to the driver on the way in.

He looks out the bus window to see if anyone is following. All he sees is a skin-and-bones white woman, high on something. She picks up the blanket and shouts, "Mine!"

Kick covertly checks the occupants of the bus, decides he's good, and sits at the very back where he can see everyone come and go. He hops off downtown near BC Place and walks for six blocks, changing sides of the street twice. There's a coffee shop with a big corner window, so he ducks in, gets a small drip with double sugar, and watches outside. Nothing, and no one.

The number four bus that crosses the Burrard Street Bridge into Kitsilano is uneventful too, so he jumps off and walks up to Broadway. All clear. On Broadway he gets the number ten back downtown and gets off in Gastown. It's the oddly named part of town where skid row meets the cobblestoned tourist area. Morning traffic is still inching up Water Street as he steps down from the bus. By this time, it's getting packed with sightseers waiting for the Steam Clock to do its loud steamy thing. Crowds can be your best friend if you need to lose a tail, but they can also make it hard to spot one. As he crosses the street and heads up Water Street, he feels it. The pull in the pit of his stomach.

Then, as clear as a bell, he hears Hollywood's voice. *"Two o'clock."* He turns to his right and sees the threat. But it isn't White Socks. Her stillness in a sea of activity is the first red flag. She's a completely different temperature than everyone else. Like a cold spot in an old house. A better spy would keep moving while keeping an eye on him, but she is stock still, staring at his reflection in the window of a business that's been closed. Same old trick. The pull in his stomach increases, but it isn't panic. It's information.

Hollywood's voice says, *"Gun."*

Peripherally, he sees that the woman is bundled up in dark rain gear. A black scarf is across her nose and mouth, her hair is under her hood, and she is wearing brown gloves.

This isn't the time for Kick to care about hearing voices, or why his stomach does what it does. There were guys in country that said they had a sixth sense, which meant they had no sense. They took risks based on hunches, and eventually died, usually with all their men.

Kick doesn't like the idea of the supernatural, even though his dead friend seems to speak to him sometimes. He doesn't want to think about that at all. If it's true that his friend's ghost is real, it might mean he'll end up being trapped wherever Hollywood is right now. He was trained to solve problems with reason, based on years of training and experience, and in his experience, dead is dead. Even just considering he might be wrong about that, makes his head swim. If there are threats he can't put his hands on and kill, he doesn't want to know them.

To his thinking, this warning mechanism of his is something warriors naturally develop if they live long enough. Maybe his senses are more developed now, or he has more senses available to him after years of hyper-vigilance. Maybe combat opens something dormant in people. At this moment, he could care less; he's just grateful for the gift. For a split second he wonders if Homer covers this in The Iliad.

Kick can't tell her ethnicity yet, but she has a low back injury, or a bad left knee or hip, that gives her an odd hitch. How did she follow him? She wasn't on his bus. Kick looks down the street at the bus that dropped him off. Shit. There is another number ten bus right behind it. He missed it. She probably saw him in Kits, kept her distance, and got on the bus right behind his. At this time of day, they tend to bunch up and get right behind each other. Excellent tradecraft to use a bus to follow a bus.

Kick calmly slips into a store selling tourist knick-knacks, and watches her through the front window, from the corner of his eye. She's still on the other side of the cars that are inching forward in traffic, pretending to look at a tourist map. As Kick makes a loop around the inside of the store, a tour bus slowly starts to crawl across her view, and she has to keep moving to stay ahead of it. She's about to lose sight of him, so she runs a few steps forward and keeps an eye on him.

The words of Kick's drill sergeant come back to him. "The god of war hates those who hesitate." He was quoting Patton, and Kick took those words to heart many times. When they got jumped a few times in 'Nam, they chose to charge the ambush and fire on automatic. The enemy never saw it coming, and each time they had a split-second *Oh shit* moment where they had to decide between a defensive posture, or not. That moment of indecision was enough to turn the tide every time — except for one.

That's what Kick does now. He gauges the progress of the bus. At the right time he heads out the front of the store, turns, and makes direct eye contact with her. What beautiful brown eyes she has. She's Asian, and there's a scar above her left eyebrow.

Just like he expected, there's a moment of indecision, and she turns away to regroup. Kick knows that once you've called the game, it can't be played anymore. She's now exposed, and knows it, so she'll have to either pursue, or retreat. Kick walks back the other way and is blocked by the bus. He then makes a break for an alley to his left, as fast as his limp will take him.

He keeps his hood up and head down, and hustles to the end of the alley where it dead-ends in a T at the railway tracks. To the right and left, is a wide-open alley. All the buildings have flush jimmy-proof security doors with no alcoves or places to hide. A block down to the right a couple of guys are smoking crack; otherwise the area is empty. It's foggy, but not enough to hide him. There's nowhere to escape. He ducks left around the corner to think.

He covers his face with his hands and looks up for security cameras. One is bent over and obviously broken, and the other faces up the way Kick came. His habit of keeping his head down pays off again. His face would not have been seen. There are no cameras that he can see covering the back alley running along the train tracks. A chain link fence separates the alley from the tracks and provides no cover. The railway yard will have their own cameras in there, but they probably won't cover this far, and if they do, they won't pick up much detail at this distance.

There's no way she won't follow him down here. He would, in her place, but for Kick right now it's fight, flight, or hide. There's a dumpster a few feet to the left that's not visible until you get partway down the alley. It might be bulletproof, depending on the caliber. The lid on one half is propped part way open. No point being the nail when you can be the hammer.

Kick moves quickly and slips inside the dumpster. As he crouches down, he opens his winter raincoat, unzips the thick fleece jacket underneath, and pulls his Smith & Wesson from its holster. While still looking up the alley, he screws on the silencer and racks a round.

There's no one coming yet, so he pulls the dumpster lid down quietly until it clicks at the lowest catch, giving him a six-inch gap. He's just given himself a very smelly suit of armor. He leans against the back of the dumpster and braces himself with a wide stance. His hood is pulled down to his brow, and his grip is a comfortable two-hander sighting up the alley, with the muzzle resting on the edge of the bin. He's glad he wore his thin gloves.

At this angle, Kick has the last third of the alley in his line of sight. He watches and listens. The rain gets heavier on the metal lid. Instinctively, he controls his breath. Slow in, hold, slow out. He counts each breath. Listening. Watching. Breathing. Counting.

For what seems like an age there is no one. No sound of footsteps, and nobody at all in the alley. The crackheads have moved off. And then he sees her. Brown Eyes walks carefully but steadily down the alley, with that unusual hitch to her step.

◆ ◆ ◆ ◆

Her right hand is in her coat pocket, holding her gun. She knows it could be a trap, but there's nowhere for anyone to hide. She sees the dumpster and stops. It sits innocently in the fog, covered in graffiti, with bits of garbage scattered around it. One lid is open a bit, and she catches a whiff of its disgusting odor.

It looks undisturbed, and it's more likely he either fled left or right down this alley or jumped the fence into the railway yard. But you never know. She keeps the revolver in her pocket and pulls back the hammer.

She takes a few more steps forward. He's likely in one of those boxcars or running between parked trains. How did he spot her? They warned her that he's paranoid, but she's never had a target stare her down like that. This will not go over well with her bosses, if she loses him. She can't afford another fuckup. She takes one more step forward, then another, and freezes. Fuck. Without taking her gun out of her pocket, she raises it to fire.

◆ ◆ ◆ ◆

Even through the metallic rain on top of him, Kick hears her pull the hammer back. It's a wheel gun, probably a snub-nose .38. Small, won't jam, and packs a good punch. Not great at a distance though, so she must've been planning something close. Maybe brush past him and put a few slugs in his side. One in the head once he's down.

Kick wonders if he left any signs outside the dumpster that might give him away. A boot scuff, disturbed gravel, anything that could make her suspicious. He could fire now, but a few steps closer would be more accurate. Good. She's looking at the rail yard and stepping closer.

Kick sees her eyes widen. She's seen the silencer. The hand inside her pocket is coming up. He fires twice. *Plink, plink.* At the same time there's a loud bang from outside.

Her gun has fired from inside her coat pocket, as Kick's first shot penetrated the base of her throat, probably shattering the C-6 or C-7 vertebrae and severing her spinal cord. His second round gets her below the chin, exits, and ricochets off a brick wall further up the alley.

She's down. Kick looks left and right carefully, then all the way up the alley, at the rooftops and windows. There's no one, and there are no screams, so he removes the silencer and holsters it and the gun. His hands are shaking as his penlight comes out of his pocket and he looks down. Both shell casings are side by side on a dark green garbage bag. He pockets them, then takes an old t-shirt that's in the bin and wipes off where the muzzle was resting, getting rid of any gunshot residue as best he can. He checks the time on his watch. Every second counts.

Checking his surroundings once more, he pushes open the lid, hauls himself out of the dumpster, and closes it all the way. With nothing more than a quick glance at her corpse, Kick limps away from her with his head lowered, down the alley that parallels the railway tracks, at a steady but unhurried pace. The limp is the only thing that concerns him. If he's on a camera somewhere, that will narrow things down for the cops. Three blocks later, he still hasn't heard any yells or sirens, so he takes a deep breath to steady his nerves and heads back up to Water Street. He turns right and mixes in with the crowd heading toward the SeaBus terminal.

Then he hears them. Sirens. The first is police, followed by ambulance, then more and more police. If she was embassy staff, all hell will break loose. Cops will check cameras in the area, so he continues to keep his hood up and his head down. So far, so good.

Kick walks past the First World War bronze statue by Coeur de Lion MacCarthy, and glances at the majesty of the winged angel lifting a soldier to heaven. He's come close to meeting that angel so many times, and he could practically hear her wings today. The Sea Bus terminal is packed, and a few people look his way. Must be the dumpster smell. He heads into the public bathroom.

In a stall, he closes and locks the door, drops the shell casings into the toilet, and flushes it six times to push them far enough into the sewage system to make them non-retrievable. In all the excitement he didn't realize he had to pee, so he takes care of that too. With his gloves still on, he removes his raincoat and rolls it into a ball. Then he checks to see if the gun is visible under his fleece jacket. It's not, so he zips it up all the way and exits the stall.

One guy is washing his hands at the sink, while two other guys are taking a piss at the urinals. He stuffs the coat into the garbage bin when no one's looking and puts some paper towels on top of it. Two more men enter the bathroom. Kick washes his hands with his gloves on, to remove some gunshot residue. No one notices. He pulls them off and washes his bare hands, dries them, then wipes off the taps he touched. Outside the bathroom, Kick walks toward a smoke shop in the huge lobby. He drops his wet gloves into another garbage bin, just outside.

Kick enters the smoke shop and buys a pack of Dunhill cigarettes which are not his brand, some sunglasses, a cheap pair of black knit gloves, and a blue baseball cap with a Blue Jays logo on it.

The cashier says, "Go Jays."

Kick keeps his head down and nods, then steps out, and removes the tags on the hat and shades. He put them on, plus the gloves, and starts walking. He touched nothing in the store that he didn't take with him, and he said nothing. So far, none of his fingerprints should be anywhere.

Next, he heads to the escalator heading down to the SeaBus departure area.

At the bottom is a bank of pay phones, and he goes to one. His hands are still shaking as he dials a sixteen-digit number and waits for a series of tones and buzzes. When they stop, there is a five-second pause, and Kick hits six zero four. There is a loud click, and a deep mechanical-sounding voice comes on and says, "Pilgrim."

"Tiger."

The voice responds, "Proceed."

Kick checks his watch. "Hometown. Water. Abbott. Foxtrot. Confirmed. One-five. Dirty. LZ Five. Two days. Zero dark sixty."

The voice comes back with, "Hometown. Water. Abbott. Foxtrot. Confirmed. One-five. Dirty. LZ Five. Two days. Zero dark sixty."

"Confirmed." The line goes dead.

Kick hangs up, takes a deep breath, and exhales. He has just informed the CIA watchers that cover the Vancouver 604 area code, of the cross-streets and gender of his kill, that it happened fifteen minutes ago, and that it is not possible for the scene to be cleaned up. He also called for a meeting with Taylor and Baker in two days, one hour after sunset at preset location five. Kick takes stock of how he's doing. So far, he's still running like a well-oiled, but shaky as fuck, machine. A swell of stress pours through him as he breaks out in flop sweat. It's like he's back in the jungle. Kick walks over and joins the end of the ferry line as rivers of perspiration run down his back and chest. He mops his brow with a hanky and lets out a long, quiet sigh. The SeaBus has just docked, and he waits quietly to escape.

15

Doc, Cookie, and the The Dough Boys
Vietnam, 1968

KICK AND HOLLYWOOD GET HUSTLED into the dispensary, and the medical staff go to work. Both of them are still riding adrenaline highs as Doc gives them the once-over. "You boys look familiar, and judging by the scars, not your first rodeo?" Because the medical teams usually work under incredible pressure, they move at lightning speed. Today is no exception, even though there's a lull right now, but that can change in a heartbeat. A nurse swabs the blood off Kick's hand with alcohol, before she even says hello. He yells from the sting.

"Pussy!" Hollywood laughs, until the same happens to his fragged shoulder.

Kick manages a laugh. "At least you didn't shit yourself this time."

"I can tell stories too if you want," Hollywood fires back. Both men could embarrass each other with tales of firefights where they ended up wet and sticky.

The doctor preps some instruments. "Aren't you the guys who charged an ambush a few weeks ago? Kick and …"

"Hollywood is that asshole's name," Kick says.

"Now I remember. How's that calf muscle, Kick?"

"It was just a nick." They both know it was an AK-47 round that went through and through. Kick likes this guy. He's one of the good doctors who keeps you talking, even if it's painful.

"You know it's normal to lose control of your bowels and urinary bladder when someone's trying to kill you, right?" the doctor asks. "Gets the unnecessary tasks out of the way. For most people getting shot at is rare. I've been there too. Not fun, in the middle of surgery, getting shelled and shot at. I've had to close a chest wound with my pants full of crap. The amazing thing is my body's become used to it now and doesn't react that way anymore."

The doctor gently pulls a fragment of the Colt from Kick's hand. He holds it up for them to see. "There's a bit of John Browning's handiwork right there. Somehow it slipped right between everything important. Bit of a habit with you, I've noticed. No severed tendons, but it is going to hurt like hell once the nerves grow back."

The nurse sterilizes it again, and Kick shouts. "Jesus H. Christ!"

"That was the worst of it," says the nurse, completely unruffled. "I'm going to stitch you up now. Try not to cry like a small baby."

Hollywood laughs. "Yeah, crybaby, try and relax!"

"You're in deep shit when I get out of here, punk."

Hollywood laughs harder. "Come on, you got me beat, Kick. My frags were all puny."

Doc interrupts. "You had a piece of the trigger and a fragmented AK round in there, Mr. Hollywood." Hollywood smiles. "Are you guys the team that makes the latest guy who shits his pants do laundry for everyone?"

"That's us."

"How meritorious of you," Doc says to more laughter. "You are both incredibly lucky. And today, luck was enough. You're both going to be catching up on some reading. Hollywood, you can do that in your hootch, if you promise to behave, but Kick, you'll be hanging out somewhere very very dull. Better start scrounging for books. It's nice to see you again, boys, but let's not make a habit of it, all right?"

"It's a deal, Doc," Hollywood says with a wave..

❖ ❖ ❖ ❖

Hollywood has his arm in a sling when he comes up to Simpson, who's washing clothes. "It's a shitty job, but someone's gotta do it!"

Simpson wrings out a t-shirt. "Funny. How long's the sling on for?"

"Till Doc tells me. You almost done?"

"My last one, H. You heading to see Cookie?"

"Let's do it. I'm fuckin' near starved!" Hollywood exclaims.

They find Beach, Watt, and Frosty drinking coffee in the mess tent. Hollywood's still buzzing from the morphine. The boys love hearing the gruesome medical details, and that Kick's ribs will be tricky, and he'll be laid up for a while.

"I couldn't get all the crusties out of your camo pants, Beach," says Simpson, "so they'll be a bit stiff next time you put 'em on."

"If my pants can't stand up on their own, I don't want 'em." The boys are all smiles since Cookie, the mess sergeant, has heated up their favorite meal. He calls them all the 'dough boys' since they go through so many biscuits. It's also a callback to the soldiers of WW One. Watt says, "Go see Cookie. He's got *SOS*,"

"Fuck off!" Hollywood shouts, and he and Simpson take off. Everyone loves Cookie's take on this time-honored military tradition, commonly known as shit on a shingle.

"You're the best fuckin' man in the whole fuckin' army, Cookie!" Hollywood tells him when they get there.

Cookie sports a high and tight flat-top, and grins as he serves up generous portions for both men. He loves his boys and makes sure they get fed like kings. "I found mushrooms and sherry on the black market, so there's a little somethin'-somethin' in there. Coffee's extra special today too. There's some VIP on base."

The two head back with steaming trays and dig in. "By the way, nobody tell Kick any jokes," Hollywood says. "He has to baby his ribs, and laughing's the worst, I'm told. You can tell jokes, though, Beach, 'cause yours are never funny."

Beach flicks coffee at him. "So, Kick's gonna be all right?"

"That fucker was born lucky. It's like bullets go around him. By the way, we have to get an After-Action Report ready for some colonel at sixteen hundred. They're out there right now doing a mop-up, and body count. They hit it with snake and nape after we got out, and they're checkin' out that river trail situation. It's like they walked on water."

"Brass is gonna like this a lot, I think," speculates Watt.

"What's the chatter?" Beach asks.

Hollywood grins widely. "Keep this to yourselves for now, but we not only took out a battalion, we might have hit someone big. Charlie's all over the air waves freakin' out, man. I heard it from one of the nurses while I was gettin' stitched up."

"How big?" Beach asks.

"Could've been a colonel, or a fuckin' *general*."

"Holy shit! What's the story with your shoulder?" asks Watt.

Hollywood shrugs. "Frags. Sling stays on for a while. They pulled a beauty outta Kick's hand. He'll have a wicked scar."

"Nice." Simpson sips some of coffee. "Oh, that is good. Now, I don't know about you white boys, but I plan on drinkin' like a fuckin' asshole!" Everyone laughs, as Cookie comes out with blueberry tarts fresh out of the oven.

"Shit, Cookie, I might marry you," kids Frosty.

Cookie laughs and heads back.

"We're lucky to have you!" Hollywood yells after him. "Lets gets some beer and do this AA report. We're gonna get fuckin' medals!"

16

An Agreement

KICK'S HANDS ARE STILL SHAKING as he walks calmly off the SeaBus in North Vancouver. He has them stuffed deep in his pockets as he follows the crowd up the ramp, through Lonsdale Quay, and up to the third story of the Market Building. He stands outside against a large post like he's just having a smoke and watches the next three SeaBus arrivals. No one appears suspicious. He checks his watch and confirms he still has two hours before his rendezvous. He needs a drink.

After paying cash for a mickey of Royal Reserve rye at the liquor store on Esplanade, he walks a winding pattern to the bus stop on Lonsdale, checking for a tail, without looking like he is. He waits half a block away until he sees the bus, then limps up quickly just in time to get in through the back door, flashing his transit pass from a safe distance.

He goes for five stops, then gets off at a camping store near Thirteenth. There he picks up a dark blue Helly Hansen raincoat with an insulated liner, new black leather gloves, and a black wool watchman's cap. Rubber rain shoes are on sale, so he gets a pair of those and picks up a new Zippo and some fluid, paying cash for it all.

Kick tosses his baseball cap and his old rubber shoes in a trash can outside a convenience store, where he buys an extra-large coffee loaded with sugar. Outside, he pours two thirds of it out and fills the rest with whiskey. The adrenaline and cortisol are still working their way out of his body, and his hands still shake. The gun and silencer are still with him, but he has a plan for those. He drinks half the whiskey and coffee mix. It's amazing. While he's stopped, he fills up the lighter.

It's been a year since he's had to eliminate a target. He feels completely off balance, and it worries him. He drinks again, puts his new gloves on, and heads down the hill, carefully detouring, and watching for tails. He tosses his empty cup in a bin at a bus stop.

Kick knows most of the security guards along the Vancouver waterfront. He did overnight guard work after he got back from overseas contractor work. It helped him collect his thoughts and avoid people. It was also convenient for the CIA to have someone they could drop into harbor locations from time to time.

A lot of security guards are veterans. Some are from 'Nam or Korea, and some are former cops who got booted out. They all like him because he's one of them. Plus, he gives out cigarettes freely and always has time for a chat. It's good tradecraft. Below Esplanade he approaches the guard shack for the Versatile Shipyard, and waves at the stocky man inside. It's *Buck*, a Korean War vet, who's inspecting the paperwork from a one-ton truck on its way out.

He waves as Kick walks by and tosses a fresh pack of Marlies on his table.

"Are you on a diet, Buck?" he asks.

"Yeah, I only gained five pounds last week." Buck laughs as he buzzes him in through the small door in the gate.

Inside the shipyard Kick avoids his usual haunts like the pier and finds a storage building instead. He shuts himself inside, lights the Zippo and puts it on some crates to illuminate the room, then checks his watch. There's forty minutes before his meeting. In five or ten minutes the shipyard will be empty, except for Buck. Since it's slowly being torn down, there's not much to guard, so there aren't any cameras. That's one of the reasons Kick loves this place. The other reason is that it's secured by a high wooden fence on three sides, and the fourth is facing the water. He lights a smoke with the lighter and takes out what's left of the mickey.

A lot of things bother him about this kill, so he goes back over the past ten years in Vancouver. He's taken out eleven targets and grabbed up three more who were secretly taken out of the country. None of that bothered him. This is different. Kick has a hard time getting at his feelings, due to his lifelong habit of pushing them down.

He cycles through his targets, one by one, until he gets to the eleventh. Brown Eyes makes twelve. It dawns on him. "Shit. I've always been the hunter."

The cap comes off the mickey and he puts the rest down his throat. It's been so hectic, just getting here, that he hasn't had time to realize this probably has to have something to do with that White Socks guy.

Kick is now the prey. "Poor bastards. They don't know what they're in for." He feels better and enjoys the rest of his smoke.

With five minutes to spare Kick goes to a rarely used door on the western side and waits. The ten-foot wooden slat wall is accessible only by the main gate on the north side where Buck is, plus another double door for smaller vehicles on the same side. The door at the west was originally just for workers to come and go on foot, and that's the one he's using today.

When Kick's not feeling right, the shipyard is where he comes to get his head on straight. He's helped Buck pass the night playing gin rummy or crazy eights many times. Other guards too. He can tell tonight will be another all-nighter.

A couple of minutes later, he hears the knocks. Three, then two, then one. He puts his hand on his gun, and then knocks back twice. Three knocks come from the other side. Kick pulls back the top and bottom locks and pulls open the door with a creak. Kelly stands on the other side.

"Quick."

Kelly steps inside. Kick closes the door and locks it. "How did you get here?"

"What?"

"Don't fuck around. Tell me exactly how you got here."

"Oh, yeah," Kelly answers, a bit shakily. "I took the SeaBus over, then a cab to the mall in West Van. Had lunch in the corner of the food court and watched everyone, just like you said. No one following."

"Then?" Kick asks.

"Okay, I went outside to the upper level and crossed over the bridge thing to the mall on the other side, then walked back and caught a bus back to the Quay. There was still no one following. I walked over to Chesterfield, then down First Street, changing sides of the street twice. Once I got here, I walked past and waited in a doorway across the street out of the rain until it was time. I still saw no one following or watching, so I came here and knocked."

"What about the SeaBus?" Kick asks. "Anyone staring at you? Corner of their eye?"

"Just one guy," she answers. "White guy, about thirty. Heavy build, bad mustache."

"What did you do?"

"What you told me. Stared back at him and gave him the finger. He looked embarrassed, and never looked again. He didn't follow me either."

Kick is satisfied. "Okay. Let's talk.

"What's with the cloak-and-dagger? I mean, I get it, but did something happen?"

"I'm just following procedure. Believe it or not, I do this all the time."

"Jesus. Even to buy groceries?"

"Lately."

BARRY W. LEVY | 83

"Well, you sure know how to show a girl a good time."

Kick isn't in the mood. They head into a giant old dry dock building with the end of it completely open to the water. The sun is squeezing through the clouds as it drops in the winter sky. The building has a two-hundred-foot ceiling, and they look like miniature people in the land of giants.

"This is really beautiful," Kelly says. "Almost romantic."

Kick is annoyed. "Enjoy it while you can. It's burned now and we can't come back here. Every meeting will have a different location."

"What's going on?"

"I have people following me. Bad people. I don't know what it's about, but they may follow you to find me, and I need you to always do what I say. To the letter. If I don't show up to one of these meets after an hour, don't worry. It means there was a tail and I had to shake it."

It finally sinks in for Kelly. "Sorry. It's just, uh, really unusual for a civilian like me."

"That's okay. How did it go with your editor? Did he like the Agent Orange stuff?"

"That's definitely on the right track. Got anything else like that?"

Kick takes a moment, then focuses on Kelly's eyes in a very uncomfortable way. "Who did you tell?"

"What?"

"You heard me. Who did you tell?"

"My editor, but that's it."

"Does he know my name?"

"No. I don't even know your name."

Kick takes her by one shoulder. "Kick. Did you tell anyone that I'm known as Kick?"

"No. Jesus, you're scaring me. You told me not to, and I didn't." Kelly keeps his gaze.

Kick breaks contact, lights another smoke and walks on.

Kelly does her best to catch up. "What is this place anyway?"

"Used to be the Wallace Shipyard, but it's called Versatile now. They started building fishing boats here in 1894."

"Do they still do that?"

"They use the big dry dock on the other side for repairs sometimes, but it's all getting torn down." They walk toward the water. "Sorry about all that. I'm just being careful. And frankly I've been a bit sloppy lately. That's on me. Come on down here. It's a nice view."

"It has a real charm to it."

"A lot of history. They built armed cargo ships here for the Second World

War called Victory ships. The Battle of the Atlantic was pretty much over by the time they rolled out, so they were mostly used to carry troops home as part of the US's Operation Magic Carpet." Kick points at the old freighter. "My old man could have come back on something like this. Could have been that one." They sit on a huge old wooden tool chest. "This is the *St. Jude*. She used to be called *The Haiti*."

"I thought it was bad luck to rename a ship?"

"Not this one. It made it through World War Two, Korea, and Vietnam. After that it recovered the three-hundred-pound nose cone from *Discoverer 13* for the CIA's *Corona* spy satellite project."

"How do you know all this?" Kelly asks.

"I like history. Plus, the guards here like to keep the story of this place alive."

"You know what they say, 'those who don't know history are destined to repeat it.'"

"Those who don't know the *mistakes* of history," Kick corrects her, "But I get your point."

"So, they'll just cut it up for scrap?"

"Yeah. Here it was born, and here it will die." They look at the *St. Jude*, patron saint of lost causes, waiting sadly for her end.

Kick checks his watch and helps Kelly up. They walk in silence for a while, back to the western door, then Kick says, "I have to go, but I need to tell you something. It's about how things go from here." He butts his cigarette and is surprised how nervous he is. "I'll give you everything you need for your story — classified documents, whatever."

"Great!"

"In exchange, you tell everyone about the forty thousand Canadians who served in Vietnam, and all the greedy suits who got rich arming America."

"As long as you can back it up, I'll get it printed. Do you want compensation?"

"No. I may not look like it, but I'm good for money. As for Dusty …"

"Come on …"

"No! Keep Dusty out of this."

"Why? War buddies from different countries is great human interest," Kelly pleads.

"I mean it. Let him be."

"Why?"

"Some people shouldn't relive this kind of stuff. It's hard to handle."

"Okay, okay, I get it. No Dusty."

They're at the western door. Kick unlocks it but doesn't pull it open yet. He looks her dead in the eye.

"I'm anonymous, and I stay that way. If you name me, even as just Kick, I'll kill you. I'll kill you, and you'll never be found." He lets it sink in.

Kelly is stunned. "What?"

"You heard me. My identity remains a secret, or you're dead. And if I don't kill you, someone else will, you can be sure of that."

"Let me get this straight. You want your story told, but you want no credit for it, no payment, and I'll die if I tell anyone who you are?"

"Sounds like you've got it straight."

Kelly regains her balance. "You're quite the charmer."

Kick looks at her quizzically.

"Why?" she asks.

"None of your business why. I don't exist. You tell the story, then we say goodbye. Deal?"

Kelly takes a moment. "Can I have a cigarette?"

Kick is irritated, but he pulls out his Marlies, gives her one, and takes one for himself. Kick goes for his lighter, but Kelly sparks hers first. She doesn't light his. Kick finds her strength attractive and feels the pull of a physical connection, but it's also a confusing moment for him. She takes a long drag and gives him a seductive look. "It's a deal on one condition."

"What?"

Kelly exhales and puts a hand softly on his chest. "Bake me a pie." Kick is now really confused. "Bake me a pie, or I will kill *you*, and you'll never be found." She walks out and shuts the door.

Kick stands with his mouth open. Who the fuck is this woman? He slowly locks the door. He's never met anyone like her. His chest feels warm where she touched him. She just asked him out.

The sun is down by the time he walks back to the water. Beyond the end of Pier Number Three, Vancouver's lights dance off the dark water in front of Kick. The silencer comes out of his holster, and he tosses it out to the left with a splash. The Smith & Wesson goes to the right, and the extra magazine right up the middle. Silt and salt water will take care of them, and he'll dump the holster later.

Kick turns back to see the guard shack lit up with Christmas lights. Maybe Buck's ready for a game of cards. He walks back down the pier toward it.

"A fucking pie?"

17

THE RECIPE

KICK STANDS DRIPPING INSIDE THE DOOR like a wet, whipped dog. It's just past closing, and Dusty's Wet Yer Whistle is empty except for Dusty himself, his hulking frame leaning on a mop. The broken furniture from the fight has already been replaced or repaired. One of the tables has a different colored leg that's been frankensteined onto it. Dusty stuffs his mop back in the bucket, puts his hands on his hips, and looks at the water pooling around Kick's feet.

"You better be here to apologize for wrecking my bar, and fuckin' up a very important day in my life!" Dusty booms. Kick says nothing, and Dusty lets him soak in his own shame. "Why're you here?"

Kick steps forward and holds out a soggy envelope. Dusty opens it and counts a fat wad of damp twenty-dollar bills. "That's a start. But I *know* you. You *want* somethin'." Kick says nothing, and Dusty explodes. "Tell me the truth!"

Kick drops his backpack on the table. Dusty peeks into it carefully and waits for an explanation. It doesn't come, so he carefully opens it, then slowly removes a one-pound box of lard and sniffs it. He puts it down with disdain. Next comes a dozen eggs, five of which are broken, a small bag of flour, a shaker of salt, a small container of vinegar, baking powder, a bag of brown sugar, a large plastic bowl, and a bunch of random and useless-looking utensils. "Least you ain't makin' a bomb this time."

"It's for pie."

Dusty stares. "Oh, you need to make a pie, do you? And who might said pie be for?" Kick doesn't answer. Dusty struts around. "You don't just need help; you need a *lot* of help. A man like you can't make a pie. Pie is an art form. Pie is delicate. Making pie is like … making love. You gotta be *gentle*."

Kick is defiant. "I'm fuckin' gentle."

Dusty holds up the lard like it's radioactive. "Who the fuck told you to buy this?"

"A lady at the grocery store."

"How old was she?"

Kick shrugs. "Older."

"Like a hundred and fifty? No one uses lard anymore! That's old-fashioned shit. That crust has gotta be all light and fluffy, and for that you need to do it French style, with *butter*. It's gotta melt in your mouth, fool!"

"Come on, you worked the mess. Help me do this!"

"Oh, it's like that, is it? I should change all my plans and help you woo the girl you met through *me*? The girl you met at *my* party? The party *you* ruined and got us beat up at? Remind me why I still even fuckin' talk to you." Kick starts towards the bar, but Dusty stops him. "Oh, no you fuckin' don't! No drink for you until I hear the magic fuckin' goddamn words, motherfucker!"

"I knew this was a stupid idea." Kick heads to the table to collect his baking supplies, but Dusty blocks him. He's so short that he's looking directly into Dusty's chest. Kick won't look up, but says quietly, "Sorry."

Dusty puts a hand up to his ear. "What? I heard you mumble somethin', but it was so quiet."

"If you can't be an asshole with your friend, where the hell can you be an asshole?"

"But you, my friend, have made being an asshole into an *art form*. I'm waiting."

Kick sighs hard, and then yells, "I'm sorry, I ruined your fucking party, jarhead!"

Dusty nods his head slowly. "From you, I will accept that as a sincere apology. Now please get us both a beer, and let's get at this pie."

Kick heads to the bar and starts pouring.

"Stop!" Dusty yells. "Tip the glass on its side and pour slowly so you don't get a big head on it. And take it from the red tap. That's my favorite, and you can have some too, if you pour it like a fuckin' grown-up."

Kick is not enjoying this, but he needs his pie. Plus, this is Dusty's good beer from the microbrewer. He pours an almost perfect beer, then starts another one for himself.

"It fascinates me how there are things you do to perfection, and others where you're a complete and utter fuck up," Dusty informs him. "By the way, I heard there was a nasty take-down in your neck of the woods, and the Chinese consulate is super pissed. They lost someone kind of... *affiliated*. In broad daylight. You hear about that?"

Kick brings the beers over but doesn't answer.

Dusty continues, "One of my cop friends told me it was two shots to the throat. Severed the spinal cord. Came right out of her shoes. Almost like a trained *sniper* did it."

They clink glasses, and Kick says, "*Chang shoo-ming*."

Dusty savors the taste of his special beer. "I don't speak Chinese, but I take it that means mind your own fuckin' business?"

"It means *long life*. Which comes to people who mind their own fucking business."

Dusty drinks again. "This is a damn good beer. So complex."

Kick regards his glass. "Yeah, I detect notes of fuck-nuts with a jarhead aftertaste." He goes to pick up the lard, but Dusty beats him to it. He turns the package around until he finds the recipe, then rips it off, and tosses the lard on the table. Dusty looks over the instructions.

"Well, this doesn't look too hard. Even for you, *grunt*. Because you're as much a grunt as I am a jarhead, motherfucker. Notes of me punchin' you upside the head. Fuckin' comedian."

Kick snickers, and they both clink and take solid drinks.

Kick takes out a smoke and Dusty pulls out a joint. "I'll take myself a *Kool*, if you don't mind. This time of night I mellow out." They light up.

"You go ahead and drift away, jarhead. I got this whole pie thing," Kick says confidently.

"Hey, what do they call a grunt with an IQ of one hundred and fifty?" Dusty asks.

"Don't start."

"A platoon!" Dusty laughs.

"Why did the Marine cross the road?"

"Why?"

"He was stuck in the chicken."

Dusty laughs hard. "So, a Marine asks a grunt if he wants to hear a joke about how dumb grunts are. The grunt says, sure but the guys on both sides of me are grunts too, you still wanna tell your joke? Marine says, 'Nah, I don't wanna have to explain it three times.'"

Kick clinks glasses with him again. "So, you never told me how you learned to bake in Force Recon."

"The truth is, I stuck my big dick where it shouldn't been stuck, that's how." Dusty takes another long haul on his joint. "We had leave in Panama City after the first month of recon training, and me and my boy Johnny found ourselves at a private party. One thing led to another, and we connected with two ladies, if you know what I mean. Mine was the daughter of a colonel, who shall remain nameless."

"So, they threw you in mess hall?"

"No. First they did that thing where they dump a mountain of fuckin' potatoes in front of you at dawn and tell you to peel them all. It crushes your soul, man. Me and Johnny had to stay there till they were all done."

"Shit."

"Well, me and Johnny got so good at it we'd be done in six or seven hours,"

"How?"

Dusty keeps talking as he walks to the main door and locks it. "We bribed the sarge in mess hall with two forty-pounders of bourbon for the secret. Step one is to not give a fuck how much potato gets wasted." Dusty sits back down. "It's like this. One guy cuts off the ends of the tater square with a cleaver. Boom, boom. The other guy peels off just the sides in four or five strokes. Hit 'em all with a hose later to wash 'em off, and bingo."

"That's genius. But that's not pie."

"We still had to put in the rest of the day. So, sarge taught us how to make pies, tarts, biscuits, bread, you fuckin' name it, and we started to kind of like it. The boys started lovin' our baked goods."

"I know what's comin'," Kick says.

"As soon as they found out we were enjoying ourselves, and getting' popular, they threw us right back into the Panamanian jungle." Dusty laughs. "I got nicknamed Dusty because I was always covered in flour."

"I'll be damned. Gimme a hit from that." Kick takes a couple of big hauls on it.

"Puff, puff, pass, man," Dusty reminds him. Kick hands it back. "Did you do the pack of Marlies, pack of Kools thing? You know, with your weed in the Kools pack." Dusty asks.

"I never smoked dope over there. I drank. A lot. But I wanted my head clear in the shit, so no drugs for me, or my boys. We'd get back from five or six days out there, debrief, get fuckin' loaded then sweat it out for a day and head back out. We had a good rhythm. Usually."

Dusty reads the recipe directions off the lard package. "Okay, put three cups of flour, one and a half teaspoons of salt, same amount of brown sugar, and half a teaspoon of baking powder in the bowl."

Kick looks on the table, then inside his pack. "I don't have a teaspoon."

"You don't even have a cup, man! Bet you don't have a tablespoon either, do you?" Dusty is disgusted. "I don't think this imaginary old lady of yours ever made a pie."

Kick gets a coffee cup and a set of measuring spoons from the bar, then fills the cup with flour.

"Level that off." Kick takes the Ka-Bar from his pack, uses the flat edge to level the flour with the top of the cup, and dumps it in the bowl.

"Do that two more times," Dusty orders. "We'll have to use ratios to try and get this done." Dusty finishes his joint, while Kick puts in the salt, brown sugar, and baking powder. Dusty's comfortably high and enjoying his beer. "Even you grunts like our Marine Ka-Bar. You can cut through a car roof with that baby. Okay, mix up those dry ingredients. Then get ready — for the *lard*." Dusty laughs hard. "I can't believe you got *lard*!"

Kick's getting flour all over himself, the table, and the floor. He lights another cigarette, just to complicate things. He's also getting flour all over Dusty, so Dusty moves to a stool at the bar and focuses on the baking instructions again. His buzz has him micro-focused on the details on the box, so Kick quietly takes the broom, and slowly inches the handle toward the cuff of Dusty's pant leg.

"Some good recipes on that?" Kick asks quietly.

Dusty doesn't notice what's happening and stays locked on the box. "Umhmm." Kick gently slips the end of the broom under Dusty's cuff and touches his skin. Dusty rockets off the stool, spills his beer, and yells, "AAAH!" He looks at Kick in shock. "What the fuck ...?"

Kick's laughing hard. "Too good to resist! You're still scared of snakes?"

"No! Seriously, asshole! Not funny! Thirty-seven venomous snakes in 'Nam, and I met thirty-eight of 'em! Jesus, that was *not* funny!"

"All right, sorry."

"You really harshed my buzz, man!" Dusty tries to collect himself. "Snakes can't be trusted. They can bite you even when they're dead!"

Kick lights another smoke. "They can not!"

"Can fuckin' so!" Dusty grabs a section of *The Telegraph* and reads. "'A severed snake head will strike at a mouse for over an hour after it's dead.' It's right there!" Dusty tosses the article at him.

"If it's in the paper it must be true." Kick continues reading out loud. "'I cut the head off to get it identified, and the rattlesnake head bit me through my pants.' Well, I'll be damned. I'm going to remember that next time I'm putting snake heads in my pants."

Dusty pours himself another beer. "You are *not* funny."

"All right, I'm not funny. Sorry. What's the next thing I do here Gordon Blue?"

Dusty takes a long drink of beer. "Cut up bits of that fuckin' lard, you fuckin' dick, and fuckin' blend it in." Kick looks confused and Dusty shakes his head.

"You don't have a pastry blender, do you? Yeah, don't answer that." Dusty sighs and heads behind the bar. "This ol' lady was from Hansel and fuckin' Gretel, wasn't she? You know she *played* you. *Lard* ..." Dusty gives Kick three forks for stabbing olives. "Put these together, and just get at it."

Kick cuts the lard into chunks, then pulverizes them into the flour with the forks. More flour goes flying. "Hey, I don't think I ever asked you. What'd you think? Your first day in country?"

"Me?" Dusty snorts. "Shit. Too many snakes, and too late to change my mind."

Kick keeps mixing the dough. "You think you'll ever move back to the US?"

"No. Why would I move away from all this? I love Canada!"

"Are you kidding?" Kick puts the bowl on the table and looks up at Dusty. "To live in the most powerful country the world has ever known, full of undying optimism and entrepreneurial spirit. No country has ever created more financial prosperity! And try and tell America they can't do something! There's a dune buggy on the fuckin' *moon*! Who else would do that? And all the social programs and handouts here make people slack off. This country is spoiled, full of complainers, and there's not enough competition. Monopolies all over the place. There's only one phone company, for the love of God, and it's owned by a US company, by the way."

"Well, I love living in Canada," Dusty crows. "It's an *alternate universe* version of America. Stingy with the health care sometimes, but I don't have to worry that I'll die if I can't pay. You can get a gun if you really need it, but not if you're fuckin' crazy. The taxes are high, but I have a Corps buddy who's an accountant, and he's got it figured for me. Plus ..." He holds up his draft, "...I really *love* the fuckin' beer! This one is over six point five percent! This place is *freedom*!"

"You're disgusting. But I'll drink to freedom every time." Kick holds up his beer. "Freedom." They drink.

"I get it. I wouldn't go back to Atlanta either if I was you. But you liked Seattle, right?"

"Sure, 'til I started hearing that fuckin' twang in people's voices." Dusty sighs. "Them southern crackers started showing up, and that was it. I took one weekend trip up here, and I fell in *love*. I loved the women, I loved the hippies and the weed, and then I saw this place for sale. Boom! I had a lawyer on that by Monday. My Corps back pay that was all stashed away I slapped down for a down payment on this beautiful old bar from 1913. Plus, I got an extra ten percent from the exchange rate."

"How'd you get it without having to buy the hotel? Don't they have to go together?"

"Pfff! They couldn't wait to get rid of this. It was legally partitioned, and the liquor license came with it. There'd been nasty shoot-outs here. Bunch of people died, junkies kept croakin' in here, and none of the fat cats or the banks would go near it. Everyone says it's haunted, but I ain't seen no ghosts."

"Right time, right place."

"Right Marine!" Dusty clinks with Kick. "And goddamn it, the people are so *fuckin'* polite in Canada I sometimes feel guilty. It's truly one of the last free countries left. Plus, Canada didn't fuck me into a war I didn't want to fight, and then take a giant shit on me. And excuse me, but I'm pretty sure you've never been pulled over for being *white*. Where I grew up, most of my friends didn't make it to twenty. They were shot for doin' things like walking or driving while Black. That's an everyday occurrence for Black people in *my* America."

"You're right. But name one successful company that's come out of Canada? Just *one*."

Dusty thinks for a few seconds. "Radio Shack."

"What?"

"Fuckin' Radio Shack. Do I win something?"

Kick heads to the bar and pours a fresh sloppy beer with a big head. "I'll keep that in mind when I need a shitty pack of triple-A batteries." He sits and starts kneading the dough.

"So, you're still seeing that girl?" Dusty asks.

Kick stiffens and throws Dusty a dark look. "There's nothing wrong with me and mind your own fucking business!"

Not the answer Dusty was expecting, but he puts it together. "I was talkin' about Kelly. Who did *you* mean?" Dusty sits back down at the table.

Kick looks at the dough for a few seconds, then starts kneading again.

"You gonna tell her the truth?" Dusty asks.

"Stay outta this, jarhead!"

"You gonna tell her about Hollywood?"

"Don't go there, pal, 'cause we can always talk about you."

Dusty sits back.

"To answer your question, the story at the paper's going well," Kick says. "She's nice, and says her editor wants the truth. We might get this published. Maybe break it wide open."

"Hmph. That's good. I hope it works out. I gotta say it'd be nice to see the pricks who made all that money get the heat they deserve. And I hope nobody gets hurt."

"No one's getting hurt. Now what?"

"Hmm?"

Kick holds up the bowl with the lump of dough in it. "What's next?"

"Yeah, right. Does it feel sandy?" Kick squishes some dough between his fingers, and shrugs. Dusty pulls a bit out and rubs it around. "I'll make a baker out of you yet, *airhead*. I'll shake up some ice water, and you put an egg and a teaspoon of vinegar in this glass."

Kick cracks an egg into a glass and adds a spoonful of vinegar, while Dusty goes to the bar and mixes ice and water in a martini shaker.

"Okay, now watch a pro." Dusty takes the tablespoon and expertly scoops out five tablespoons of ice-cold water from the shaker into the glass with the egg and vinegar, then stirs it.

"It's not gonna taste like vodka, is it?" Kick asks.

"If it does, it's on purpose." Dusty laughs. "Okay now, beat the fuck out of it."

Kick does. "You're not talking to Kelly, are you? About war stories and all that?"

Dusty starts rolling another joint. "What if I am?"

"Why don't you let me handle all that from here on?"

"You're worried I'll steal her."

"No. You're ugly as fuck."

"Now I know you're lyin', because *you* are the ugliest *pukin' buzzard* I ever seen. What's the real problem here? Huh?"

Kick mixes harder. "It's not something everyone can handle, that's all."

"Oh, you don't think I can handle it? I'm not the one havin' nightmares about little girls, and old missions, pal. Plus, if you're really going after the truth, you're gonna have to tell it all — Hollywood, that tiger stuff. *All* of it, man." Kick stops mixing, as Dusty continues. "Or you could let it all go and get on with your life."

"This is my life!"

Dusty stands. "No, this is what you replaced your life with. Literally. You're digging up the dead, man. Why? No one wants to know their government lied to them and helped kill a million people! That'll make 'em feel shitty. They want to talk about figure skating, the RCMP Musical Ride, fuzzy kittens, hockey, and what a great place to live this is. They just wanna be happy!"

"The truth's gotta be told! And if you need to talk, talk to me."

Dusty laughs. "If *I* need to talk? Okay, let's say I do. How do I let you know? You don't have a phone, so I can't call you. You never show for appointments, or vote, because that makes you predictable in case someone's trying to kill you. I don't even know where you live. Christ, you can't even walk down a street without doubling back and changing fuckin' sides like James Bond."

Kick sits quietly in the lonely world Dusty just painted for him.

"Let me feel that." Dusty grabs the bowl and pulls out some dough. He adds a bit more water and kneads it. "Okay, you're good." Dusty puts the bowl back on the table. "You're not getting any younger super spook. Those fuckin' new guys cleaned your clock pretty good at my party."

"Sure, but look how many it took!"

"That wouldn't've happened five years ago, or even two!"

Kick takes a moment. "It's eating me up, Dust, and I can't let it go. Maybe I have to balance the scales for the shit I did. Those fuckers involved need to be exposed for what they did. And I can either handle it or I can't, but I've gotta spit it out before it destroys me."

Dusty lights his joint and nods. "There it is, man. There it is. That was truth, and I respect that." He holds out his hand. Kick comes over to shake, but Dusty pulls him in and gives him a big hug. "Go complete your mission, you grunt-faced ugly-assed screamin' asshole motherfucker. You go ahead with your bad self, and balance the scales of fuckin' justice." Dusty growls.

Kick's uncomfortable with his face pressing into Dusty's chest. His voice is muffled. "I know you're just hugging me 'cause you're high, so I'm gonna let it slide."

Dusty laughs and lets him go, "Okay, chicken man, you do that."

Kick goes to the table and gathers up all his stuff. Dusty takes a good pull on his jay, and points to the dough. "Keep that cold. I assume you have a fridge, since you like beer. And get a pie plate, but don't ask any crazy old ladies for advice on that, and ... fuck. Get a rolling pin. Rub flour on it, then roll the dough on a cutting board that's lightly floured. I can tell by looking at you, you're good at coverin' things with flour. Then lay it into the plate. Oh, fuck... You'll figure it out. Use a fork to crinkle the edges and put the crisscross shit on the top. Like on the package here." Dusty tucks the lard package into Kick's bag. "God, I hope you don't kill her with this pie."

Kick heads for the back door, then stops. "Shit! What about the filling?"

"Damn. I don't know. I don't have time to show you how to make apple pie properly, so buy somethin' at the store. What's her favorite?"

Kick looks hopeful. "Blueberry?"

"Easy. Get a can or two of that," Dusty says.

Kick goes to the door.

"Wait! You gotta pre-bake the crust for ten minutes at 375, *before* you put the filling in. Remember that! You don't want to embarrass yourself with a soggy-ass crust. Then pour in the filling, do the crisscross shit, and bake until it smells great, but isn't burned to shit."

"Got it." Kick turns to leave again.

"So, you pre-bake at what temperature?" Dusty asks.

He puts his hand on the doorknob and says, without turning, "375."

"And how long do you bake the whole pie?"

"About *go fuck yourself* minutes."

Dusty's laugh booms. "You might actually pull off a miracle and get this done, *grunt*."

Kick opens the door and is halfway through.

"One more thing, and this is important."

"Jesus — what?"

"She'll like you better with a shave and a haircut. Even a flat-top'd be better than the Charles Manson shit you got goin' on." Kick flips him the bird and slams the door.

"Hippy!" Dusty shouts as he turns on some music. He sings along with Charlie Pride's "The Snakes Crawl at Night", and heads back to the bar. "I don't think there *was* no old lady." Dusty keeps laughing, pours another beer, and sings.

18

COLONEL CAMPBELL
Vietnam, 1968

THE MEDICAL TENT DOOR SWINGS OPEN, and a full-bird colonel walks in with a dossier in his hand. Kick is the only one conscious in his section and has propped himself up in bed reading the only book he could find. The colonel is accompanied by a young second lieutenant who gives Kick a curious look before stepping back outside.

Kick instinctively goes to salute, but the colonel stops him. "At ease. You shouldn't do that. I've had cracked ribs and it's no picnic. Keep the pain meds up so you can breathe deep. Shallow breathing can lead to pneumonia in cases like this, and that's the last thing you want."

"Yes, sir."

Colonel Campbell sits and looks at the book Kick is reading. "Some light reading? I found Marshall McLuhan fascinating. 'War is never anything less than accelerated technological change.'"

"It's a bit heavy, but it was the only thing handy. The boys will be by later to stock me up with something with a bit pulpier, I'm sure."

"That's good. Staying well-read is one of the things we look for in people we consider moving up." That gets Kick's attention. "I'm Colonel Campbell, and *you* are Sergeant David Tacker." He flips through Kick's file. "I understand everyone in your inner circle calls you *Kick*?"

"Yes, sir. My father was a sergeant major for Canada during the Second World War."

"Top Kick, huh? You're a Canadian volunteer, then?"

"Here to do my part." Kick figures he's kissed enough butt and drops the *sir*.

"You're not the first one I've met. And you're without an officer?"

"The last one didn't work out."

"And why was that?"

Kick squirms a bit. "He didn't listen. Smokin' and jokin' while taking a dump. Charlie took him out. We almost didn't make it back."

Campbell studies Kick. "I'm glad you did. You have an interesting profile." He closes Kick's file. "Congratulations on what you and your team accomplished, and before you give me a lot of *Aw shucks* modesty, let me fill you in. Taking out a battalion is already a big deal, but this was no ordinary battalion. We know this one was hosting a show-and-tell with three NVA colonels and a general ... from China."

"Shit."

"Shit, indeed. The general humped out overnight to an LZ five klicks away, where he was choppered out. He missed all the fireworks, but the NVA colonels weren't so lucky. I want to tell you about this general if you have a minute." The colonel doesn't wait for an answer. He opens a dossier, and hands Kick a photo. "We are not sure of his real name, but he's referred to as the White Tiger. According to legend, once a tiger is five hundred years old it turns white and becomes a kind of magical guardian of the West. Whoever he is, that's how they see him, and it looks like he's running North Vietnam's military operations."

"We did hear a chopper the night before. That's never happened before."

"Yeah. An NVA chopper is rare down here. A Chinese one would be something else completely. Whoever he is, we came damn close to pulling his card. And being on the battlefield makes him fair game, Chinese or not." Colonel Campbell takes a solemn moment. "What I have to tell you from this point on is classified, and I need you to keep it in the vault."

Kick winces as he sits up straighter. "I understand, sir."

"I work out of *MACV-SOG*. Heard of it?"

"Sure have, Sir." Kick has an idea where this is going. *The Military Assistance Command, Vietnam — Studies and Observations Group* sounds like some kind of after-school club. But it's a highly classified special ops program that carries out covert missions. They're the hardcore badass tip of the spear and they're making a real difference.

"I head up the Phoenix Program. We meet guerilla tactics on their own level."

"I've heard a few rumors."

"Like what?"

"POW and pilot rescues, kidnappings, assassinations, and some crazy psy-ops."

Campbell's expression doesn't waver. "Extractions, renditions, terminations, and psychological military operations, but psy-ops for short. Correct."

It never ceases to amaze Kick the way the military can sanitize some of the most brutal actions on Earth with fancy words. Like changing *search and destroy* into *sweep and clear*.

Kick almost can't believe what's happening. Campbell pulls out more documents on the White Tiger, and hands them over. "I've heard great things about you and your team, and I'd like you to carefully consider what I have to say. I'm putting together a new unit in the next few months. It's new and off the books. I mean, really off the books. I know you're short, and you're out of here in nine weeks, but start giving it some thought." Campbell stands and adjusts his uniform. "I hear the CO has pretty good air conditioning, and a reasonable taste in scotch, so I'll be back in about an hour. Look over all this White Tiger material." Campbell looks around at the unconscious wounded soldiers in the room. The stress he is under becomes clear for just a few seconds before he looks down and heads for the door. "When I get back, I'll want your thoughts. Lieutenant Jakes will watch the door until then, so you're not disturbed." Campbell walks out the door.

◆ ◆ ◆ ◆

The files are back in the dossier when the colonel returns. This time the lieutenant stays inside, and watches Kick. Campbell sits down. "Well?"

Kick clears his throat. "Based on known sightings he's unpredictable, but his area of operations is restricted. There are only so many routes he can travel to get to and from these locations, even with the occasional helicopter. We'll still need to cast a wide net to have any chance of hitting him. If he's the only game we're hunting, it'd be a waste of resources. However, if you consider the other medium to big-game targets we will snag in the process, we could make a sizable dent in their command structure."

Campbell's intrigued. "Good. But why is he on the actual battlefield? Why take the risk? He could make officers meet him back in China, or anywhere he wants."

"That's true. I mean, we almost got him. Either there's something operational he's overseeing personally, or …"

"Or what?"

"He's vain. This guy may have started believing his own press. He may think he's invincible. I've met soldiers like that here and they're all dead now."

Campbell looks like he's heard exactly what he was hoping for. "I want to drop your team into Cambodia from now till the end of your tour, so you can watch some of these trails. No uniforms, rank, or dog tags. We'll give you a 'yard soldier. JJ is one of our best. All the teams use indigenous troops for navigating and interpreting."

Kick feels a thrill run through him. "There it is."

Campbell smiles. "After you're all back to full strength, that is. Your CO is okay with it. We had a good talk. You and your team will have to take a pretty serious oath to join SOG and sign a twenty-year non-disclosure agreement. Once you're in, you're in, and you're family."

This is music to Kick's ears and his CO is probably getting promoted, which is fine by Kick. "My CO's Canadian too, sir."

"Well. Must be something in the beer." Campbell laughs. "Naturally, this is all hush-hush. We're not officially in Cambodia. Right?"

"Right, sir."

"Get lots of rest. You're going to need it." Campbell takes his dossier and leaves with the lieutenant. Just as he's going through the door he turns. "I'm really glad I met you, Sergeant." The door shuts quietly.

Kick takes two painkillers and tries to contain his excitement. Hollywood was right. It has turned into a badass mother of a day.

19
Preparation

KICK FINISHES FIFTEEN MINUTES OF JUMP ROPE in his underwear, then snaps off forty push-ups. He does the same number of sit-ups, burpees, and chins. After that he stretches his hamstrings, calves, shoulders, arms, lower back, and neck. He repeats the entire process two more times and finishes it all with a finger dexterity exercise where he touches his thumb to each finger in order at maximum speed. He repeats this in the reverse direction on one hand, while continuing in the original direction on the other, then switches back and forth from hand to hand, until he feels satisfied.

Kick washes his best black t-shirt and underwear in the bathroom sink and hangs them to dry near the heater. Standing naked in front of this bathroom mirror he gets what Dusty was talking about. He looks like a fucking serial killer. His scraggly hair and beard are one thing, but when he sees all his scars and wounds, they trigger dark memories. Each one represents people he treasured and lost, and events where he almost died. Not to mention the various levels of guilt he feels for the people he's killed. He can't look himself in the eye.

Kick cuts a distinctive figure. He's thin like a yoga master, with tightly coiled muscles packed around a spartan frame. He looks exactly like the part he's playing; a highly efficient killing machine.

There's a deep scar cut diagonally across his well defined abs, and a deep red one on his ribcage from the bullet that cracked his rib. Over his shoulder he catches a look at three large pucker wounds from AK-47 rounds. There are dozens of shrapnel scars and knife wounds, and a large ugly scar on the top of his right foot, plus the one on his hand from his Colt. There are several more random ones, including the bullet that went through his calf.

He gives his thick beard and crazy hair a good look in the mirror. "Manson wasn't half as handsome as I am." Kick covers the drain with paper towels and places scissors, an electric razor, and a straight razor nearby. The scissors go into his hair and chop it off to about an inch from his scalp. He sets the electric razor on the longest setting and takes off all the hair on his head and face. He shortens the setting and uses that on his face, around his ears, and on the sides of his head. Turning around, he uses a small mirror to help get the back. The third pass is on a medium setting, blending the short length at the bottom into the longer on top. He shapes it all into a classic flat-top.

After he left the military, he often had to be his own barber, and now it's a habit. Truth be told, he doesn't trust anyone near him with a sharp object. He cleans the bathroom, brushes his teeth, then lathers and shaves with the straight razor. He's shaved with his Ka-Bar before.

Standing back, he gives himself a look. He feels like a new man, and looks handsome enough, in his own way. With the facial hair gone his strong cheekbones stand out and his blue eyes are more piercing. His hair has become salty over the years, and it's striking now that it's short. He could step into his old uniform and stand tall and proud.

Kick hasn't been with a woman for several years, and he's nervous. The memory of the last woman he was with still haunts him. He was sleeping with her and had a nightmare. When he woke up, his hands were around her throat, and she was punching him in the face. She packed and left, and he didn't blame her. In the years since, he's woken up outside his apartment several times, poised in a crouch, ready for hand-to-hand. That's the only reason he started wearing underwear to bed.

Pulling on his pants he heads into the tiny kitchen that adjoins the living area and pre-heats his small stove to 375. His whole living space has been scrubbed down and everything's squared away, except for some random grocery bags and his backpack. Kick takes a white ceramic pie plate out of the fridge. It holds the sacred dough he and Dusty made. One of the best times he's had with Dusty for years.

A wooden cutting board sits on the counter, and he tosses flour onto it and spreads it around. The blob of cold dough plops onto it. Kick looks around. There's a paper grocery bag with a rolling pin sticking out of it. He takes it out, removes the price sticker, and rubs his floury hands all over it, then adds more flour for good measure. He looks at his watch. There's no time to fuck anything up.

Rolling the dough goes fine, until it sticks to the rolling pin. Kick adds more flour, which helps, and he gets the thickness fairly even. When he tries to get it into the pie dish, though, it tears, so he spoons in some water, kneads it again, then rolls it out, and adds more flour. Mocking Dusty he says, "Ya gotta be gentle …"

This time he finds a way to peel off the dough and slide it in. He trims off the excess neatly with his Ka-Bar, then crinkles the edge with a fork. He lights a smoke and turns on the fan over the stove. The oven is at temperature, so he pops the crust in and looks at his watch. He cracks a beer and enjoys his cigarette. There's leftover dough on the counter.

"Shit. Crisscross," he mumbles. Kick flattens out the dough and roughs it into a square, then cuts it into thick strips. Satisfied, he pulls out the can of blueberry filling, then stops. He looks everywhere for a can opener, but can't find one, so he stabs the side of the can near one end with his Ka-Bar and slices off the top. The blueberry mixture goes in the crust, and he hides the cans in the garbage. Time to start the main course.

Kick takes out a pound of fatty-looking ground beef, onions, butter, milk, a bad-looking bottle of port, and a loaf of white bread. He checks his watch and lights a new cigarette. He hauls out a huge cast-iron skillet, turns on an element, and starts to heat it up. He tosses in onions with butter, then the beef, and stirs it all. The fat gets drained into an empty coffee can, and all the beef goes on a big plate. Half the fat goes back into the pan, plus milk, water, and flour. Kick adds salt and pepper and tastes it.

"Nope." Kick finds two cloves of garlic in the fridge and smashes them with the side of his Ka-Bar. They get added, along with a generous slug of the port, more fat, more salt, some pepper, then more flour until the gravy has a good thickness to it. Kick gives it a taste. "There it is."

There is movement outside his door. Kick freezes. It's not time for her yet. He turns off the stove and silently moves toward his door. As he walks past his fleece jacket, he reaches underneath and pulls out a Glock P80 9mm and slides it into the back of his pants. His black t-shirt is dry, so he pulls it on. Silently, he limps to the door in bare feet and listens.

◆ ◆ ◆ ◆

Kelly's footsteps click lightly along, as a thin needle of light cuts the jet-black darkness in front of her. The guy who gave her the penlight was awkward, but very nice. When he swore her to secrecy, though, he made it clear he wasn't fucking around.

"What the fuck am I doing?" Kelly says out loud, damn sure no one can hear her voice since she's at least six feet underground. She knows she's doing the right thing to follow her story, even if it does lead through a stinky disgusting old tunnel. On one hand, this could be leading her to a terrible death; on the other, it could net her an award for great journalism.

And then, right in front of her, is an ancient-looking door. She turns the old doorknob and slowly pushes it open. It creaks like it's from an old Hammer film. "Jesus, it's like I'm visiting Vincent Price." She steps carefully into a dimly lit basement from the early 1900's.

"This guy is a fucking trip," she says quietly. Walking forward, she sees exactly what she was told she would see, and follows the rest of the directions until she comes to an unmarked black metal door. She knows she's early, but there's no fucking way she's hanging around out here by herself, so she knocks exactly the way she was told. All this cloak-and-dagger shit had better be worth it, because it's all a bit much.

20

DATE NIGHT

KICK RESTS HIS HAND ON THE BUTT of his Glock and looks through the peephole. There's a four-inch blade in a sheath fixed to the inside of the door beside it. A sequence of knocks take place, and he knocks in return. Kick opens the door quickly and checks around before looking at Kelly. She smiles nervously and then steps inside as he closes the door.

She notices the knife. "Oh! Nice touch. Every home needs a deadly weapon at the front door." Kick just stands there, trying to decide if it was a joke.

Kelly is wearing form-fitting casual jeans and a light blue sweater that brings out her eyes. Her winter jacket is a dark blue all-weather raincoat with a hood, worn down. On her head is an off-white cotton winter hat with a dark blue pompom on the top, and she has an oversized purse. But it's her footwear that grabs his attention: a pair of two-tone men's-style brogues. All he can think about is how impractical they are for wet weather, and how she must draw a lot of attention to herself. Odd. He stares at them.

"They're from a local guy named Fluevog." Kick just nods. "Wow," she says, looking at his haircut and shave. "There *is* a face under there. I wasn't expecting the makeover. Especially after my little underground adventure back there."

There's another awkward pause before Kick speaks. "Yeah. Dusty's been giving me a hard time about my appearance. A Marine could be out of water in the desert, and still find a way to get a clean shave every day."

Kelly forces a smile. "Can I come in?"

"Shit. Of course. I mean, please." Kick steps back to let her in and takes her things.

"Shoes on or off?"

"Better off, I guess. That tunnel's a bit nasty."

"Yeah, I may never be the same." Kelly pops off her shoes, then surprises Kick by heading right for the kitchen. "What's cookin'?"

Kick quickly dumps her things on the coatrack and follows. "I know it's not the nicest walk, but the tunnel's secure. Not many people know about it. I use it too, sometimes. And Roger may not look it, but he's been to hell and back, and he's trustworthy."

"He was very nice, and he gave me this." She holds up her penlight.

"Keep it. I've got a few other things for you too."

"I've gotta ask, why is there a tunnel between these two hotels?"

"They were dug during Prohibition, and helped the city's upper crust maintain discretion," Kick answers. "Both hotels were built in the early 1910s. When things were dry, the movement of booze, hookers, and the fancy people who enjoyed both had to be hush-hush. Vancouver has tunnels connecting the whole downtown. I can show you around them sometime. Might make a fun article. One goes right to English Bay."

"That's really interesting," Kelly says. "You know Charlie Chaplin had a tunnel under Sunset Boulevard in Los Angeles that connected to the Chateau Marmont for bringing girls back to his place. But your tunnel wins for sheer creepiness."

Kick takes that as a compliment. "Told you I was hard to find." He takes his backpack off a 1950s leather club chair and offers it to her. "Please, have a seat."

Kelly does, and sinks right in. "Comfy." There are two elegant standing lamps from the 30s, and a mica table lamp from around 1920. Kelly looks around approvingly. "You know, this place is really homey. It's like a private club car with no windows."

"I've managed to collect a few things from this neighborhood over the years."

She notices the spiderweb of news clippings, and photocopies on the wall, and Kick stiffens. Kelly gets back up and looks at two articles. 'Blood on Canada's Hands — $300M a Year in Vietnam Arms Sales.' Another reads 'Nearly 150,000 Canadian Arms Jobs for Vietnam War.' She steps back and points. "Both of these were written for *The Telegraph* in '72, by my boss, Malcolm Stewart. I'm impressed. You've been doing some homework."

"You don't think that makes me look crazy?"

Kelly laughs as she picks up a thick copy of The Pentagon Papers from a table and flips through it. "It makes you look like a reporter." Kelly zeros in on the big question mark that all the strings lead to. "The Machine."

"What?"

"Nothing. It's a theory I've been working on for a while about how wars are financed."

Kick goes back to the stove and puts the frying pan on low. "By the fat cats.

Hey, you'll never guess what we're having." He pops two pieces of white bread into the toaster.

"I don't know, but I can tell right now that it's not low calorie."

Kick looks crestfallen. "I didn't consider that. Sorry."

"I'm just kidding. It smells amazing. What is it?"

"A surprise."

"As long as I don't have to go back in the tunnel." Kelly reaches into her bag. "I don't even know if you drink wine, but ..." She pulls out a bottle.

"If it goes with beef, it'll work great."

"It's the same one Dusty had. I thought it was pretty good, although I'm not a sommelier. Or a Somalian, for that matter."

"Oh, you got that one," Kick says with a smile. It's the first time she's seen him smile, and that, coupled with the shave and haircut, gives her a different perspective on him. Another of Kick's little miracles is that he's managed to keep all his teeth, which is not bad for a guy who clearly likes to fight. Kick looks around. "Okay. Somewhere around here is a corkscrew."

Kelly jingles her keys. "I've got an emergency one on my keychain. Not that I drink a lot of wine or anything." She laughs, and Kick once again savors the sound of it. Kelly has trouble with the cork. "Could you?"

"Oh, yeah." He yanks it right out with a loud pop. "Do you want me to pour some?"

"Maybe let it breathe for twenty minutes or so."

Kick has never heard of this. "Sure. You want a beer in the meantime?"

Kelly considers it. "Sure. Why not?" He grabs two cans of Molson Export from the fridge and a couple of frosted glasses from the freezer. He looks over to see if she's impressed, but she's not looking. Kick pours two perfect beers, and hands one to Kelly. "No breathing for this."

"Absolutely not."

"Good health." They both drink.

"You said you have some stuff for me?"

Kick heads over to his fleece and takes out two items. Kelly notices his limp again and sees the scar on his bare foot. While he is partially covered by the coat rack, Kick slips the Glock back in its holster under his fleece. He asks for Kelly's penlight and places it on a small table. He adds a bobby pin and what looks like a pair of black shoelaces.

Kelly looks puzzled. "Okay, what's all this?"

"First of all, you need to know about your secret weapon."

"Really? What's that?"

"You."

"Okay." Kelly looks skeptical. "And how does that work?"

"All the bodyguards and security firms hired to protect politicians and celebrities teach this, and it's simple." Kelly waits. "We all have an inner voice that lets us know when things aren't right. Right?"

Kelly smiles. "Like in a movie when you know it's a bad idea to check the basement while your friend heads up to the attic?"

Kick is distracted for a moment by how beautiful she is. "Yeah. It's the voice that says 'danger.'"

"Like listening to your gut."

"That's it. And the more you listen, the louder and clearer it gets."

"So, why does that work so well?"

Kick shrugs. "Evolution? It's something you cultivate, like any skill. And when it goes off, you listen."

"If this is so important, why don't we know it already?"

"We don't live in the savanna or jungle anymore. We've been socialized, taught manners and the 'proper' way to interact. That's how predators manipulate a target to do something stupid, like get in their car or walk to a secluded area. People tend to respond politely in the way they've been raised. An animal in the wild would never do that. Follow?"

"I do. So, if I find myself captured by someone like that, I'll need a bobby pin?"

Kick takes the bobby pin and removes the plastic tips with a paring knife. He takes pliers from a drawer and bends the straight end to 45 degrees, then puts it back on the table. "If you don't have pliers to do that, use your teeth."

Kelly looks at it. "I don't get it."

"Take the laces out of your shoes and replace them with these." Kelly looks suspicious. Kick asks, "What is your little voice saying?" Kelly nods and does what he says, while Kick gives his concoction a stir on the stove. The toast pops. Kick takes it out and puts in two more slices. He downs his beer.

"The penlight looks dangerous," Kelly says.

"All of that stuff can make it through any security checkpoint, and you're right, the penlight is dangerous. But what do you think those laces are for?"

Kelly feels them and shakes her head. "No idea."

"It's paracord. Short for parachute cord. First used for parachutes in World War Two, and popular now with outdoorsy types. I've used it to cut through rope when my hands have been tied, to get out of shackles, and to defend myself."

"Really? And the bobby pin? Emergency up-do?"

Kick has no clue what that means. "If you ever get handcuffed, that will set you free." Kick lowers the heat under the frying pan and pulls open drawers until he finds handcuffs.

"Always in the last place you look, right?" Kelly jokes. Kick doesn't get it.

"Most people don't have handcuffs lying around is what I mean."

"Oh." He cuffs himself in the front. "If this doesn't work, you'll have to serve dinner."

"Really — there's no need, I believe you."

"Time me." Kick picks up the bobby pin and inserts it into the top of the lock on one side, bends it back, and turns it. The cuff releases. He repeats the process on the other side and drops the cuffs on the table. "Felt like five seconds to me."

"Oh! That's good." Before Kick knows what's happening, Kelly snaps the cuffs on her own wrists. "Show me."

It's Kick's turn to be impressed. "I guess your little voice trusts me."

Kelly looks at him and smiles.

"Pick up the bobby pin," Kick tells her. "You're going to use it like a little shovel. Insert the bent piece into the straight part at the top. The circular bit at the bottom doesn't concern us." Kelly does this. "No, on the left side." Kelly corrects her mistake. "Now pull it back so it bends a little and turn counterclockwise."

The handcuffs click open. "I did it! Yeah. That is so cool." Kelly frees her other hand.

"Well done." Kick smiles and shakes her hand, as she beams. "Keep one of those in a front pocket, and one in the back, or in the waistband. 'Cause you never know." He tries not to show it, but just touching her hand sends a shiver through him. The toast pops.

Kick bolts back to the cupboard. "All right, let's eat." He grabs plates, and utensils, and puts them on the table. The oven is still on, keeping the place nice and warm. Kelly peels off her sweater, revealing a white blouse underneath. Kick notices without noticing.

♦ ♦ ♦ ♦

Kelly watches Kick as she finishes her beer. She knew coming here was crossing a line but took the chance anyway. He's definitely a dangerous person, but there's such a sweet side to him, and she can't deny a strong attraction. It's been a long time since she's been with anyone, and the element of danger excites her in a way that borders on arousal. What's happening is more than just physical, although that part is palpable. It's a kind of recognition. Like she knows him, and she's known him for a long time.

Kelly is drawn to Kick's bookshelves. It looks like he's been trying to figure things out through books, and his tastes are eclectic. "Have you read all these?"

Kick looks over and nods. "Pretty much. There are a few I still have to get to."

"You're better read than a lot of the people I work with."

"Sure, but *The Telegraph* is written for, what, a fifth-grade education?"

Kelly laughs. "Guilty as charged."

She looks at him at the stove and admires his incredibly fit body. His *guyness* and strength are magnetic, and she's surprised how soft-spoken he is. He's not modest, but his brags come off as legitimate. She knows he's seen and done things that most people can't imagine, and she's read that Special Forces soldiers have a self-confidence that is often mistaken for arrogance. Kelly's been around long enough to know that it's the fakers who make the most noise. This man seems to err on the side of humble. Whatever he's got going on, it's working for her.

◆ ◆ ◆ ◆

Kick feels something odd while he stirs the contents of the frying pan. He gets the same kind of feeling he gets with his vet buddies, or cops who've been in the shit. Like pieces of a puzzle fitting together, he feels comfortable with her, and he can feel his guard dropping. On the one hand it's nice, but on the other he's suspicious.

Kelly breaks the spell. "If I didn't know better, I'd say this is ragoût de boeuf."

Kick laughs. "Maybe in France, but in the US Army, it goes by something less fancy." As Kelly sits down, he puts a slice of white toast on her plate and covers it with the beef and gravy mixture. "Remember when I told you about SOS?"

"Oh, my god!" Kelly claps her hands. "I am so looking forward to this. We should pour the wine!" She goes to the cupboard to get wine glasses. Kick tries to stop her as she opens a cupboard door, but it's too late. There's a .38 Special sitting right in front of her, beside a can of baked beans. "Oh!"

"That's for home defense. Sorry. Probably doesn't go well with beef."

Kelly laughs. "Okay, *you* get the glasses. In case I set off a booby trap."

Kick pulls out two crystal tumblers and pours the wine into them. "Hope these will do."

"They look very nice, and European style will be great."

"Right." Kick makes a mental note on European style.

She raises her glass. "To self-defense." She takes a sip.

"I will definitely drink to that." Kick swallows half of his. "That's pretty good. Thanks."

Kelly smiles and takes another sip. "All right, I am starving, and I can't wait to try this." She digs in, cutting off a square of toast covered with maximum gravy and beef. "Whoa! That is ... a lot is going on there, and it's *great*. I mean it, that is really good!" She drinks more wine. "Oh, yeah. And it really brings the pepper out in this wine. I'm impressed. The Michael David winery probably has no idea that *Petite Petit* pairs so well with *shit on a shingle*." She laughs.

Kick takes in the bright bubbly sound and tries to memorize it. "It's even better once the gravy soaks into the toast." He takes some wine. "You're right. The wine really makes it. I may have outdone myself." He eats much more slowly than usual.

Kelly asks about where Kick grew up, and he lies and tells her it was up the coast near Bella Coola, where he learned how to hunt, fish, and live off the land. The last part is true. She tells him stories about school, and Kick tells her how he learned bad French from the Montagnard tribes in Vietnam, who learned it from French colonialists. Kick switches back to beer, and lets Kelly have the rest of the wine.

She can't finish her plate but pours herself a third tumbler. "I have to say I am almost impressed with this meal. But we made a deal, didn't we?"

Kick looks at the sink. Damn. "You got here before I got the top on." Kick takes the pie out of the sink and puts it beside the strips of dough.

Kelly gives it a look. "Did you brown the crust?"

"Of course."

"It actually looks all right. Let's do the top and get it into the oven, and while it bakes, you can show me how to use my new shoelaces."

They help each other weave the strips on top of the pie. Both are having fun, and Kick's feeling things he hasn't for felt for ages. Kelly's not drunk, but she has a good buzz on.

When the top is done, she stands back and says, "All right, Graham Kerr, let's bake it up!" Kick pops open the oven, and Kelly slides the pie inside. As Kick shuts the door she looks down at his right foot. "So, what happened there?"

Kick notices he's still in bare feet, and he's embarrassed. "Sorry, I meant to have at least socks on before you got here." He hustles into the bathroom, puts on some socks, and comes back out. "All right, take out those laces, and I'll find some rope."

Kelly smiles. "Rope? Okay, but first, what happened to your foot?"

"Right. Almost forgot you're a reporter." Kick looks down at it. "When things explode, shrapnel flies all over. On this particular day, a frag went right through that foot."

"Does it hurt?"

"Nope. Now, laces."

"Okay, Houdini, I am ready!" Kelly pulls out her new paracord laces, and

Kick shows her how to make a loop on the ends to put each foot through. Kick ties her wrists.

"You didn't tell me it was this kind of dinner." Kelly laughs again.

"All right, concentrate on a push-and-pull action with your feet to sever the rope. Like you're riding a bike. You'll see the paracord start to cut through the rope."

Kelly takes a few minutes, but she manages to cut through and free herself. "That's amazing!"

"Well done. Now, this might feel weird, but here's how you use that pen. He hands her the penlight, steps quickly behind her and, before she knows what's happening, brings one arm around her neck in a very gentle chokehold. "That's not too tight?" Kelly is surprised, but impressed with how strong he is for his size. He's not that much bigger than she is, and his body feels good against hers. Kick notices too. He can feel her pulse and respiration increase.

"No, not too tight." She struggles against him, but he tightens his grip.

"Best to make your opponent think you're submitting."

"Okay," she says. "So now I stick you with this pen, right?"

Kick uses his other hand to grab her hand with the pen in it. "Unless I do this."

Kelly adjusts by grabbing the pen with her free hand.

"Good. Remember, you can use any pen; it doesn't have to be one of these. You want to target the legs, crotch, but it's even better to focus on places you can do severe damage, like the carotid arteries on either side of the neck. I'll show you those later. But when you're held like this, you can disable one of your attacker's arms by hitting the inside of the elbow." Kelly does that at half speed.

"Now flip the end of the pen so the point is pointing up." Kelly does. Her warm body against his is forcing him to really concentrate. "Bring it straight up and over your shoulder, and you're going to hit me in the face, preferably the eye, but penetrating the cheek will also hurt like hell. If the bad guy moves his head away, take him in the neck or throat. You hit the carotid artery, and it's lights out."

Kelly half-speeds all that and does well. "Great. So, let's say I've done that, and I'm free." She turns to face him. "Can I just run?" He can feel her breasts pressing against him.

He clears his throat. "You could. But you want to complete the mission. We say Charlie Mike for that."

"Right. Charlie for complete, and Mike mission." Her voice is getting softer.

Kick is having trouble focusing. "Right. Focus on the line from the crotch to the eyes: solar plexus, throat, upper lip, and … nose. Stab, kick, cut, or punch any of those. If someone's trying to kill you, don't leave him there alive." Kick's heart is pounding. "Finish the job."

Kelly puts one hand on his cheek. He flinches, and she puts her other hand on his waist. He feels like he's falling into her beautiful blue eyes. Before he knows what's happening, she's kissing him, and he's kissing back. Her hand grabs his ass and pulls him in close. There's no point hiding how hard he is. Kick slides one hand under her sweater, feels the small of her back, then moves his hand down inside her jeans.

She unbuckles his pants, and he lets them drop. Kick stands there raw, having left his underwear drying in the bathroom. Kelly pulls off his t-shirt, while he undoes her pants and slides them down. She tosses his shirt on the floor and runs her hands over his back, feeling his scars. Her sweater and bra come off, and Kick feels her hard nipples against him.

Kelly jumps up and wraps her legs around his waist as they move into the bedroom. Kick lowers her to the bed, and she pushes her underwear down and kicks it off. Kick touches her, and then pushes inside. Their sex is primal, almost violent. At some point he finds Kelly on top of him. Their climaxes are so explosive he can't see for a few seconds.

Kelly collapses on him. They're both panting and glistening with sweat.

Kelly speaks first. "Holy shit ..." She rolls off. "That was intense. I mean *really* intense. You okay?"

Kick just lies there. "I don't know." Kelly curls herself around him, putting her head on his heaving chest. They lie there for a few moments, sweating and catching their breath.

Suddenly Kick lifts his head and sniffs the air. "I smell pie." Kelly jumps up and heads to the stove. Kick stops in the bathroom on the way and puts on his underwear. By the time he gets to the oven, Kelly is wearing his t-shirt and peeking inside the oven.

"You're the expert, but it might need another five or ten minutes."

Kick slides in beside her and looks. He doesn't have a clue. "That sounds about right. As long as the top isn't burnt." Kick grabs his cigarettes and offers one to Kelly.

"I think the occasion calls for one." Kelly pours herself more wine, and grabs a beer for Kick, who has his pants back on. He lights two cigarettes and hands one to Kelly.

They smoke and drink silently, until Kelly says, "Gotta say, that was pretty amazing."

Kick holds up his beer can and toasts her. He's trying to understand why he feels so great and so bad at the same time. For the first time in many years, he has let someone into his life who isn't a fellow soldier. He feels elated, yet vulnerable, and vulnerable is a red flag for him. But there's something kindred about her, and it's not just because she fits his body perfectly. He can't put his finger on it. Kelly puts her cigarette into the ashtray beside his, and Kick watches as their smoke intertwines.

He goes over and peeks at the pie. "This is pretty much perfect."

Kelly crowds beside him and looks. She kisses his cheek, and he smiles. He takes the pie out of the oven and sets it on top of the stove, then takes his Ka-Bar and cuts the pie into eight pieces.

"If I get two plates out of the cupboard, will I find a grenade?"

Kick laughs. "More likely a sawed-off shotgun. The grenades are all in the bedroom."

"Where they belong." They laugh.

"No, really. I'll show you later."

She goes into the bedroom. "I want my grenade with a side of blueberry pie, please. And two thousand calories of whipped cream." Kick serves up two slices, and heads in after her.

The pie is great, and they enjoy it together on the bed. "I can teach you some more self-defense stuff if you're interested, Kelly."

She nods in agreement. "Yeah, I'll take all you have of that."

"I've never had a guest here before, so I hope this isn't too… I don't know… unusual."

Kelly looks over at him. "I'm having a great time. Don't worry about it. And I'm not all that normal myself, believe it or not."

"Do you think this thing we're doing is going to work?"

"My editor seems to think so, and he's a tough nut," she answers. "The big question is whether or not the public has an appetite for it. This is Canada after all, and we're supposed to be *nice*. Anyone who gets too big for their britches moves to the US." She pauses. "You meant the stuff for the newspaper, right?"

Kick smiles. "That *is* what I meant, but since you brought it up?"

Kelly gives him a shove. "All right, speedy, let's take it one day at a time for now."

"Okay." Kick takes an envelope out of his bedside table and gives it to her.

She pulls out some documents and reads. There are sales receipts for TNT, copies of government grants and loans to arms companies, and more. "Thanks. I'll take a look at this later. We can expect pushback. The Liberals were in charge, so they don't want to be exposed, and the Tories will want to embarrass them, but won't want to anger their base by criticizing the arms industry. Then there's the NDP, and this is right up their alley — they'll love it. Hopefully, while everyone's figuring it out, we keep hitting them, and hopefully that'll keep them off balance."

"There's a lot in there about us negotiating peace while spying for Uncle Sam."

Kelly picks up Kick's copy of The Iliad. "Like a Trojan horse."

"Yeah, someone recommended that. It's pretty fuckin' wordy, but I like it."

Kelly opens it, and a business card falls out. Kick grabs it out of the air before she gets a look. "Bookmark."

She looks at Achilles on the front cover. "A Trojan horse that made a killing on their investment. Do you think that's all this is about?"

"If you're asking if Wall Street benefits from war, then my answer is 'Hell, yeah.'"

"How much did they pay you as a soldier?"

Kick puts down his pie. "In the army, my best year was five thousand bucks. Not that there was much chance to spend it over there, other than poker."

"I think if we can make the case, there's going to be a lot of shocked Canadians."

"Yeah. It'll be like finding out your parent's a crook." He feels Kelly stiffen, and realizes he's hit a nerve. "I don't know your story, and even if I did, I'm hardly one to judge. I can tell you, though, I'm grateful you're sticking your neck out like this. You're brave." He kisses her. "Especially going through that tunnel."

"I'm honored you trust me with this. Thank you." She smiles and kisses him back, then wipes blueberry off his mouth and kisses him again.

"Hold that thought." He takes the plates out to the kitchen. Underneath them is the business card that fell out, and he reads it on the way. It has the contact info for a shrink. "Fucking Baker."

Kick grabs his head. He feels like he's floating and looks down at his feet. The floor seems like it's moving. There's a sound to his left, and he looks over at the framed picture of him and his boys getting off the chopper in 'Nam. Hollywood's head turns and stares right back at him and says, "You should do it." Kick looks at the business card.

"You all right out there, cowboy?" Kelly yells from the bedroom.

Kick shakes his head and slips the business card onto the top shelf of the cupboard. He grabs a fresh beer and hustles back into bed. "Where were we?" Kelly kisses him, and they slide into the warm darkness of the covers.

21

HOLLYWOOD
Vietnam, 1968

THE BOYS HUSTLE OUT OF THE CHOPPER and into the tree line in seconds. As the chopper fades, they settle in. The jungle in Cambodia is not much different than Vietnam's. The camo on Kick's face is already running from the heat. Simpson broke his ankle last week, so he just has Hollywood, Watt, Beach, and Frosty. For SOG, this is a very small team, and they chose to bring just one indigenous Montagnard soldier for now. His nickname is JJ, and Kick can tell he's the real deal.

"JJ hate VC!" he told Kick.

They've done some intense SOG training together and a quick version of what's called One Zero school. It's special forces leadership training designed specifically for this type of work. Their mission is taking out a spy on a section of the Ho Chi Minh Trail.

This is their first time across the Cambodian border, and as far as the US Congress is concerned, they are way out of bounds. Colonel Campbell laid down the law regarding cover stories should they be captured. They are officially on patrol near the border. If caught, they simply report they got lost and accidentally strayed over. All their weapons have been swapped out for less conventional ones too. They are not in uniform, show no rank, and are not wearing dog-tags. This is strictly to protect the US government. It won't save them from the horrors of the Hanoi Hilton, and they all know the kind of treatment they're in for in a POW camp, so everyone's shit is tight.

After thirty minutes they head toward the Ho Chi Minh Trail with Hollywood on point. Their mission is to bring in artillery or air strikes on any targets near a specific fork in the trail, then call for extraction. If they see anyone on their hit list of officers, spies, or snitches, they become priority targets for kill or capture.

They snake their way forward without incident and find a good spot to rest overnight. The objective is within easy striking distance. Watt has already fired off a quick situation report from some high ground a few miles back. Bad weather has moved in, so they no longer have air support until it clears. Everyone seems confident, but Hollywood has been extra cautious on point. After freeze-dried dinners everyone settles into the usual star formation, and the night passes quietly.

At sunrise the weather is still bad, but they move out at a good pace and stop to check the map in a large patch of elephant grass. Except for Watt's sit rep last night, no one has spoken a word since they were dropped off. The place where the trail splits should be just over the next ridge. Kick looks up sharply. There's a hard pull in his stomach. The men notice, and everyone stops. There is no way they can be seen here. Elephant grass surrounds them on all sides, and they've been dead slow and quiet.

JJ motions to Kick. He hears movement to his left. Kick's heart starts to pound as he slowly raises his CAR-15 and turns back the way they came. The rest of the men do the same, getting on-line so they form a 180-degree curve. Kick is in the middle with Beach behind him. There's rustling in front. Thick sweat meanders down Kick's face, as he breathes slowly. He can smell his enemy now and holds two fingers up and points. Hollywood has one on the left, Watt is sure of one, and Frosty reports two on the right. Kick is pretty sure there are at least three behind him.

They are surrounded, but the enemy has foolishly created their own circular firing squad, instead of setting up a deadly L-shape. They can't shoot without risking hitting their own men. The boys have trained for a situation like this. This will be their impromptu variation on charging an ambush.

Everyone gets on their bellies, except Beach, who stays on one knee, aiming over Kick's head. Birds are still singing, and a gentle breeze blows through the grass as Kick signals to switch firing to automatic. Kick gets a fresh whiff of his hunters. Sweat and fish sauce. After a long moment, there it is. A snap. He raises his hand and shifts his aim a bit to the left. A flash of movement. Kick drops his hand.

All five unleash fully automatic fire covering one hundred and eighty degrees in front of them. There are screams and the sounds of bodies falling. They reload and switch to single fire, and everyone charges straight ahead with Hollywood leading, followed by Watt. Once they're away, Kick pops up and becomes the rearguard. They're running back the way they came so they know where some cover is.

Kick clears the tall grass, his face ripped with fear, and sprints through a large open space towards the downed trees. He can see all his boys in front of him as he turns back and fires at several NVA who are chasing. He hits one and the rest hit the deck. Kick fires again, hits another, tosses a grenade, then explodes into a sprint. If the boys can get behind those trees, call in arty, and get an EVAC, they could make it. Gunfire erupts behind Kick, and bullets zip past. Hollywood and Watt dive over a big log to the left, and Beach, JJ, and Frosty peel off to the right. That's when it happens.

Hollywood's feet leave the ground, and he sails over a log. It looks like he's home free, until pink spray bursts from his chest and he lands with a scream. Watt is also mid-air. His bullet enters the side of his head. He goes limp and lands face down on the other side of the log. Kick sees it all happen just as he is about to dive behind a log with Beach, JJ, and Frosty. From where he lands, he can just see Hollywood on the ground. The incoming gunfire pounds the logs in front of them.

"Hollywood!"

"Fuck! Watt is dead! Fuck!" His friend's voice is thick. "I'm hit bad. You?"

Hollywood's voice sounds like his lungs are filling up. The situation is grim, but Kick must get them out. He knows that they still don't have covey air support. The forward air controller plane and gunships are still grounded due to the weather. All they have is artillery, and maybe a crazy Jolly Green Giant will come out to get them. God bless those boys.

"We're good here, Hollywood. If you were gonna die, you'd be dead already, asshole! We'll have you in the air in ten mikes. Call in arty!"

Kick knows how fucked they are. No matter how much arty they drop, the enemy may be too spread out and too numerous to get them all. It only takes one RPG to take down a chopper.

"On it!" He turns on Watt's radio, still strapped to his corpse, pulls out the map, and figures it out.

Hollywood's position is being approached, so Kick fires his sawed-off M-79 grenade launcher. With the barrel and stock sawed off it's a virtual hand cannon. The shot takes out three NVA and stops the advance for a moment. They're starting to gather in on their position. Kick adjusts so he can see Hollywood better. There is blood running from his mouth. He probably has only minutes to live. Kick doesn't want to think about that right now. He's afraid he might freeze and get everyone killed.

As green tracers fly overhead, he hears Hollywood yell. "Fire Mission!" The coordinates follow and get repeated back. "Shot out." Hollywood tosses all the grenades that he and Watt have at the NVA. "Arty arty boom boom. EVAC LZ TWO!"

Kick knows what he's done is the only call but can't stop himself. Before he knows what he's doing, he's up on his knees. "NO! DON'T!"

"It's *done*. Go NOW!" Hollywood screams.

Bullets hit the log just below Kick, and a thick splinter flies off and stabs into his neck. Kick drops screaming, but it's not just from the pain. A rage builds inside him to a level that he's never felt. In his head, something sparks and splits, and he's filled with uncontrollable fury. He jumps to his feet so he can run toward Hollywood, but Beach, JJ, and Frosty grab him by his shirt, pull him down, and get on top. Kick screams, "I'll die with him! LET ME GO!"

Hollywood screams. "Splash out! Run, you assholes! RUN!"

The NVA charge Hollywood's position. JJ is off at a sprint. Beach lifts Kick by the back of his pants, Frosty grabs his collar, and they drag him as fast as they can away from the approaching shells.

Like howling demons, the artillery whistles close in, but the NVA keep charging at Hollywood. The first three 105mm rounds hit like the end of the world. The ground is shattered, and everything goes skyward. Kick, Beach, and Frosty are blown backwards off their feet. The deafening bombardment continues, debris explodes into the sky, then rains down hard on everything.

Kick shakes his head, trying to get the high-pitched whine out of his ears. He can see Hollywood's still there, still moving and caked in dirt. Blood pours out his mouth and down his filthy neck. The enemy regroups as Hollywood yells back into the radio. "Adjust Fire! Add 200, right 50 to 250. Fire for effect."

"NO! That's too close!" Kick yells as he struggles against Beach, JJ, and Frosty. Beach punches Kick hard in the face, and it still takes all of them to pull him away.

Blood sprays from Hollywood's mouth as he screams. "LZ TWO. NOW!"

Hollywood puts on his cracked John Lennon glasses, and waves goodbye to his lifelong friend. A bullet rips through his palm. It doesn't look like he felt it.

"Tiger Top, shot out," the radio squawks.

Frosty and Beach keep pulling Kick away, but he's lost his fight. He reaches out to Hollywood with both hands and tries to speak, but no sound comes out.

JJ screams at them, "*Didi mau! Didi mau!*"

The radio comes back with, "Tiger Top, splash out. Duck and cover, motherfuckers!"

Seconds later, the first concussions lift them all off the ground again and slam them back down. Just as they slam down the next set starts pounding until they don't know which way is up.

It continues for an eternity, then it's over. Dirt, splintered wood, body parts, and debris rain down. There's rushing water in Kick's ears. He looks around and sees Beach, who shakes him. Kick chokes, and coughs up the shit in his lungs. They look to where Watt and Hollywood should be, but there's just a crater. Enemy bodies stick out from the impact areas like the points of a star. Hollywood dropped everything right on top of his position and took the enemy with him. The air is thick with stench, and there's nothing to see but complete carnage.

An NVA soldier wobbles to his feet. JJ stands and shoots him in the head. A few more are moving further away. Frosty grabs Kick's M-79, loads it, and takes them all out. There's a chopper approaching. Kick is frozen in place. Frosty, JJ, and Beach grab him, and head to the LZ. Tears soak into the dirt on Kick's shocked face.

Hollywood is dead.

22
Visitors

TAYLOR HAS HAD ENOUGH OF THE RAIN. It's pounding a torrent in North Vancouver as his van pulls into an old shed in a junkyard. The door closes and the engine shuts off, but the lights stay on. He catches a vibe and looks around. He pulls his piece and steps out. The place smells of rot, and the rain is deafening on the metal roof. Something doesn't feel right.

Taylor whistles a quick ditty and listens. There's no response after half a minute, so he does it again, and eventually gets the whistle response he's expecting. Kick steps out of the shadows. He looks better than the last time he saw him.

Taylor and Kick have a few call and responses, and today Taylor chose the theme from *The Friendly Giant*. It's a Canadian kids' TV show about a giant who lives in a castle with a rooster, a giraffe, and some bizarre musical cats, and it's one of Taylor's favorites. He found it so hilarious that he had VHS copies sent to the embassy. Shows like this were staples for kids in Canada who couldn't get US channels, so they come in handy for times when only a Canuck like Kick should know the response. And so it is today with the giant's whistle.

"That you, Friendly?" Taylor asks.

Kick puts a finger to his lips. Taylor nods and opens the van's sliding door. Kick gets in and sits on the floor in the back as they drive out into the rain.

◆ ◆ ◆ ◆

Kick knows what's coming, but he's decided he's going to be truthful. Hopefully, that will do the trick since he can't see how he did anything wrong regarding Brown Eyes.

"I get a bad feeling from that place," Kick says as he climbs into the passenger seat.

"Me too. Let's consider it burned."

There's a carton of Marlboros behind Taylor's seat, so Kick puts them into his backpack. "Thanks for the Christmas present."

"For the man who has everything. By the way, Baker's busy running something down. You're making a new friend tonight."

"Wong?"

"Yeah. They're an acquired taste, but give it a chance."

"As long as there's no book club." Taylor laughs.

Kick is dying to light a smoke, but Taylor gets right to it. "It's hot as fuck since you took out that shooter. What happened?"

Kick lets out a deep sigh. "Most likely she picked me up around BC Place or in Kits, then eventually got on the bus behind me. I spotted her in Gastown, tried to evade, got boxed in, and had to take her out. I made it to this side of the water clean. Is it connected to the newspaper stuff? 'Cause it doesn't feel like it fits." Kick lights a smoke and takes a big drag on it.

"Wong's got intel on that."

"The gun, clips, and suppressor are at the bottom of the harbor, the brass got thoroughly flushed, and everything I wore is gone. I'm clean. Did you hear anything?"

"Plenty. No evidence was left by you. Nice job. They eventually put together you were in the dumpster. Good choice."

"Only choice." This is going better than he expected.

"I know. The shot from her coat pocket went so wide they haven't found it yet. There's muddy security footage of some guy in a hooded raincoat with a limp, but no one can make anything of it. Nice tradecraft. The crackheads in the alley have no clue. No camera's caught you getting in or out of the dumpster. Your response was textbook. You'll probably get paid out on it. She was a target of opportunity, and you did the world a favor. A few years ago, a bus full of kids went up in flames on one of her European ops. Didn't matter who got in her way, she was the kind of operative who'd plow through and get the job done. But one of the kids killed was the granddaughter of a US senator. I'm sure you can figure out the rest."

That couldn't have gone better, and Kick smiles as he enjoys the rest of his smoke. There's a slight figure in a dark hooded raincoat at a bus stop ahead, and Taylor pulls over and opens the sliding door. As usual, the interior light is off, and the figure gets in and sits on the floor.

"What up, homies?" The hood comes down, and there's a woman with thick blue hair, cropped at her shoulders. She has high, elegant cheekbones and dark brown eyes, and looks like a model. Kick wonders if it's a joke. Taylor's grinning like the Cheshire Cat.

"Alice Wong, this is Kick, as he's known to all his very special friends." Kick is at a loss, so he just sticks out his hand. Wong slaps it and holds out hers for a response. There's nothing. Taylor laughs.

"I thought you 'Nam boys had those slappy handshakes and shit. Guess not. Here you go." She pulls three fat waterproof envelopes from the back of her pants and tosses them at Kick. He catches a glimpse of her Glock 19, and a Navy Seal bowie knife on her belt. He picks up the envelopes.

"Who's got the smokes? Mine are soaked, and I brought them all the way from Hong Kong. How do you guys live in all this rain? It's like a frozen monsoon!"

Taylor tosses a pack of Marlboros over his shoulder, and Wong plucks them out of the air left-handed. "I'm keeping this pack. You fucking owe me."

Taylor laughs again. "Glad you could make it, Alice."

Wong quietly chain smokes, as Taylor takes them down a dead-end gravel road, where he does a three-point turn and aims back the way they came, ready for a quick getaway. Kick gives Taylor an envelope, then opens one for himself.

Wong doesn't bother. "I'll summarize while you read. Her real name was Winnie Soong, mid-level op for China until about five years ago, when she took up with a crime family that's connected to your old pal, Mr. Chung. I snapped a few shitty pics of him and the weird guy with the socks. You'll see them in there somewhere. Soong had twenty-seven kills we know of and took a bullet through her thigh a couple years ago during an infamous op in Greece. Taylor probably told you. She's been a ghost ever since."

"That explains her limp," Kick says. "What was she packing, a thirty-eight?"

Wong points to a crime scene photo of a .38 Special. "Nice! Taylor, do we have a prize for him?"

Taylor lights a smoke and smiles. "Yeah. You get to live."

"Who hates me so much I'm getting hunted in my own backyard?" Kick asks.

"We've got analysts poring through the family tree, but it's going to take a while," answers Wong. "Once we get a list and backgrounds, I'll let you know... Kick. How'd you get that name? It's pretty cool." Kick doesn't answer, so Wong keeps going. "They sent someone good enough to do the job, but expendable. She was probably trying get back in their good graces. Let's face it, she was a messy loose end."

Taylor says, "We have to consider that the newspaper story is the cause of this, but keep an open mind. You've had a storied career, my friend. Just so you

BARRY W. LEVY | 123

know, Ms. Wong, we've got a very, very off-the-books thing going on with a newspaper reporter here. It's an exposé on Canadian companies and the rich fucks who made bank selling Uncle Sam war material for Vietnam. We don't know if all this attention is because of that, or payback for something Kick did in his illustrious past."

Wong adds, "Okay. I didn't hear that off-the-books part, nor do I have any knowledge of any such operation, etcetera. As far as I'm concerned, feel free to let the fat asses in the suits have it all you want. Brandy-sipping fucking assholes. So, I get it — it could be a lot of things. Like this fucking socks guy. What a douche. Who wears shit like that? It's like he's never heard the word *covert*."

Kick looks back at her. "Have you seen your hair?"

"Hey man, that's how I roll."

"Look, Kick," Taylor says, "you're not going to like this, but we may have to squirrel you away for a few months if we can't get our arms around this soon. It has the potential to bring down our whole op here. We don't want Johnny Canuck catching wind."

Kick butts his smoke and lights another one. "Let's hope it doesn't come to that. Last time I ended up in Buttfuck, Alaska, for six months in *winter*. Not fun."

Wong laughs. "I don't know. Have you tried butt-fucking, Kick?" Kick glares at her. "Ha! Just checking you're still awake. Lighten up!"

Taylor's enjoying this. "All right, relax. We'll run down these crime family connections against all your kills, and anyone connected to Canadian companies, and Vietnam. If it's in there, we'll find it."

"I tailed Chung for a couple of days before you made your hit," Wong reports. "There's nothing *overtly* out of the ordinary — I mean, for a low life piece of shit like him. We're watching the port. He's got something sneaky going on, but it's hard to get a fix." She turns to Kick. "Hey, Baker asked me if you like the book. He keeps bugging me to read stuff."

Kick sighs. "It's fine but tell him he left his bookmark in it. And maybe we could just stick to the mission at hand?"

"You mean the card for Thomas?" asks Taylor.

"Yeah. Was that a hint?"

Taylor shrugs. "Hey, Tom is badass. He was in Chile in seventy-three. That guy has stories."

"Who's Tom?" Wong asks.

Kick ignores her. "He's CIA?"

Taylor laughs. "Of course. I talk to him on a regular basis."

Kick tries to process that Taylor just told him he's been seeing a shrink. He lights another smoke, puts his papers back in the pack, and hands them to

124 | THE WAR MACHINE

Wong. "What did White Socks buy from Chung?" he asks.

"Guns, ammo, and a bunch of C4 explosive," she answers. "You guys aren't going to tell me who Tom is, are you?"

"No," Kick answers. "Any idea what Chung has in mind?"

Wong shakes her head. "No. The socks guy is in the wind. He must know you made him that day, so they sent Soong to hit you. Whatever the deal is, they're committed. We may have to call in an extra body or two, boss."

Taylor sighs. "Yeah, it's looking that way, isn't it?" He butts his cigarette.

"Hopefully they're as charming as you," Kick says sarcastically.

"See?" Taylor says. "I knew you two would hit it off."

Kick looks away and shakes his head. Suddenly, he swivels fast to the front of the van. "Twelve o'clock!" Three seconds later a figure walks into view.

"Hello ..." Taylor says.

Wong moves into the middle and stares. "It's fucking spooky you just did that." The man is medium build, in a black raincoat, and appears to be looking right at them.

Kick turns to tell Wong to take the right side, but the back door is open and she's already gone.

"I'm telling you she's good. Guess you'd better take the left flank."

Kick racks his Glock and slips out the back door. He creeps up the left side of the van, crouching under the low branches of giant cypress. He has a good firing position, and can see Taylor in the van, checking his mirrors. Wong is nowhere to be seen.

There's a sound like something hitting the ground, and the attacker looks to Kick's left and levels his gun. Wong must have tossed a rock. Kick tracks the guy walking toward the spot. He's fifty feet away when Kick feels his gut pull. He scans right as a second man emerges behind Wong. He fires, but his target darts behind a tree. Wong wheels and fires too, but the second man retreats into the woods. They spin back to the first attacker and fire as he runs down the road they came in on. Taylor hits the headlights and speeds the van down toward the runner, as Wong and Kick give chase, firing repeatedly. Wong wings him. He staggers, then veers off into the woods.

"Get in." Kick and Wong hustle in the back door of the van. "We don't have the luxury of giving chase. Cops are likely on the way."

"Winged him. Right arm," Wong reports as she slams the door.

"Okay. We have to assume the van is compromised too, so let's switch that up now. Odd choice confronting us like that. Who are these clowns?"

"A couple of Chung's boys?" Wong postulates.

Taylor's pissed. "No one in their right mind would pull that shit on us."

"Unless they don't know who we are," Kick says.

"Didn't think of that." Taylor races down the muddy road. "Anyone else hungry?"

"I'm fuckin' starved. You kidding?" Wong replies. "You can buy Taylor, since you didn't get wet."

"Kick, you should dig into this material on Chung right now. You never know what might pop out of that photographic noodle of yours."

"Yeah, I could eat," Kick says. "Let's take a closer look at this over some Bob's Thai food."

Taylor smiles. "Excellent choice. Especially since you missed out the last time."

Wong perks up. "Why? What happened last time?"

◆ ◆ ◆ ◆

Kick, Wong, and Taylor dig into pad thai and spring rolls. Wong is inhaling her food. Taylor has a different van, black this time, parked nose first in a secluded area of a public parking structure. The three of them are in the back of the van with the interior lights on, and a light-tight black curtain across the cab and back windows.

Wong sniffs. "This van smells better than the other one."

Kick sighs as he comes to the end of a long document, tosses it onto a pile, and picks up a new bunch of papers and photos. He stops. He's holding a black-and-white photo of a large Chinese family. None of the faces jump out at him. The next is a black-and-white of a woman holding a boy up to look at a caged tiger in a zoo. Kick looks at the back of the photo, but there's nothing except *Beijing 1974*. He stares at the tiger.

Wong looks up from her stack. "What?"

Kick shakes his head and asks, "Why is this shot of a tiger in here?" Taylor looks at it and shrugs. "Never mind. I've gone through this pile twice," Kick says, and starts putting the documents back into their envelopes. He stops again at the photo of the crime family. "This family — do they deal arms?"

Wong laughs. "Does the pope shit in the woods? They arm the kinds of folks we don't like. What are you thinking?"

"I don't know," he says wearily. "How's the banking squeeze going on these guys?"

"Just getting started," Taylor answers. "Let's see what pops up. Kelly's not going to chicken out on getting this stuff published, is she?"

"Who's Kelly? Is that your girlfriend?" asks Wong.

"She's the reporter," Kick answers. "And she's totally committed. Her editor was the first to criticize Prime Minister Pearson when he was exposed in *The Pentagon Papers*."

"Just checking. We keep applying financial pressure to our favorite gun-running family, and maybe this pushes them into a mistake. Great work. Okay, I'm calling it. Take the rest of this pad thai, Kick. You could stand to gain a few pounds."

"Sure. Drop me in West Van. I haven't taken the bus over the bridge for ages."

"Dibs on the spring rolls," Wong chimes in.

"We got this, Kick," Taylor says. "It's just a matter of time till we connect the dots and shut out their lights." He turns off the interior, takes down the curtains, and gets into the driver's seat.

"And we'll do it fast, so you don't get sent to Buttfuck." Wong laughs, as she gets into the passenger's side. Kick stuffs the documents into his backpack and stays in the back of the van.

"You might want to stop sleeping at home, Kick," Taylor says.

"Yeah. I've been there too long, anyway. Too bad I really like it. One way in and out, secret tunnel; no one ever bothered me. Can you ship out my books?"

Taylor starts driving. "I'm telling Baker you said that. And yeah, we'll have someone come by after you're out of there."

The rain has let up, and they head down into North Vancouver proper. They crest a hill, and Taylor pulls over in front of a large, parked truck and turns off the lights. He watches his mirrors for a tail.

"We've got a safe house near Commercial Drive," Taylor says.

Kick considers the possibility. "I know it. I'll head there tomorrow night. I need to collect some things I'm working on with Kelly. Plus, I'll leave a standard surprise for anyone who might get snoopy."

Wong giggles at that. "Okay, now I know where I've heard about you …" Kick ignores her.

"I'll warn the guys picking up the books," Taylor says with a smile.

"I need to give Roger a heads-up, and make sure he knows what's going on. He's been a good friend. Can we get him a nice bonus for all his support? Maybe send him on a vacation?"

Taylor sees no one tailing them, snaps the lights back on, and takes off again. "That sounds like a nice gesture. The sooner the better for that. And, it goes without saying, don't leave anything that could lead to you, or us. Wipe down your prints, and if you leave a surprise, nothing *loud*," Taylor reminds him with a smile.

"Who do you think you're talking to?" Kick snaps.

"I'm thinking about Cairo," Taylor shoots back.

Wong starts laughing. "I knew it! That *was* you? Oh, man, that made me fucking laugh!"

Kick looks at Taylor. "How many people know about that?"

"Just a handfull. Sadat was pissed. It was almost an international incident."

Wong is ecstatic. "That op is so famous at training. You must be some kind of legend."

Taylor gives her a look. "The kind of legend that no one ever knows about. Right?"

"Of course," Wong snaps. "But take a bow for that one, pal. You blew up a Holiday Inn in Cairo! That's a fuckin' classic! Kick, we're gonna be *good* friends!"

"It was mostly empty," Kick says defensively. "Except for bad guys."

"Yeah, you Charlie Miked that one." Wong keeps laughing.

"Okay. In the meantime, Kick," Taylor requests, "consider why China wants you dead."

Kick's mind is in overdrive, piecing things together. The van stops at the bus loop in West Vancouver. He opens the sliding door a crack and peeks out.

Before he can leave, Wong says, "Hey, I wanna read that *Iliad* book when you're done. Baker won't shut up. He says it's a warrior's tale." Kick says nothing, puts his hood up, and steps into the darkness.

Taylor watches him leave. "Watch your six, spook."

Kick slams the door and can just hear Wong saying, "I like him. He's weird."

23

MAKE ME CARE

THE NEWSROOM IS ROARING, and Kelly's Olympic SG3 typewriter pounds like an M16. Everything has to get in before the Christmas holidays, and today's the deadline. A giggling Val hovers behind her with a bundle of articles in her hands, reading over Kelly's shoulder while she finishes the last few sentences about Vancouver's bitterly fought fish and chips war.

Kelly reads aloud. "'The White Rock location will keep the name *Moby Dick's*, while the downtown space will now be known simply as *Moby's*. To celebrate, lunch specials come with an extra piece of fish, until January 1st. Now that the dust has settled, it looks like the real winner is anyone who loves great seafood. The owner of the establishment decided against the popular idea of renaming his restaurant simply, Dick's.'" Kelly's still laughing as she rips the final page out, staples it with the rest, and heads over with Val to Stewart's office.

"Come on, I want some details," Val smirks. "Do you have time for lunch?"

"I don't know. I have to see how this goes," Kelly answers. "He wants to see me before I head out. He hates holidays."

"I noticed," says Val. "I'm heading to the Georgia for a real drink. It's all brokers in there, so no one will know us. Meet me when you're done?"

"It's a deal," Kelly replies.

Stewart's on the phone when they come in, so Val drops her pages into his inbox, and Kelly does likewise. Val waves on the way out. Kelly sits down just as he hangs up, then goes to his door and shuts it. He picks up a glass of scotch from his desk and drinks.

"O'Leary." He paws through his inbox, looking at the material that's been dropped off. "'Fish and Dick's' — excellent headline. 'Winter Cabbage Tips' and 'Holiday Decorating Ideas' from Val. Okay. And 'Pagan Origins of

Christmas' — an annual favorite. Good. 'Christmas Lights and Safety,' blah, blah. Lots of syrupy crap for holiday reading. Nice pictures; good. So, let's talk about where we are with this whole Vietnam situation."

"Well, he's not a fan of fascism, and has two of your stories on his wall, by the way."

Stewart is surprised. "Really? Well, I admire his taste. Pearson used that Nobel Prize like a top hat and cape, pulling off his little magic tricks. And you've been to this guy's home now, which is impressive, and I trust there were no issues." Kelly shakes her head as Stewart keeps going. "I've known some of these guys. They're suspicious of everything, and that's not a criticism. It's what kept them alive. Nothing to worry about with him, is there?"

"Nothing I can't handle. But he tells me he's being followed by some bad people. Should I be worried about that?"

Stewart weighs this information. "I don't have to tell you to be careful. He's obviously the real deal, based on the info he's getting us, but it's hard to say if he's just being paranoid, for the reasons I just stated. It's best to take it seriously, though."

"My bullshit radar is pretty good. The paranoia could just be from all his years of stress."

He looks her dead in the eye. "I don't know your background, Kelly, but I can tell you that most people breaking a story like this, would not be this cool-headed."

Kelly knows it's a compliment, but also a probe. "Ignorance is bliss, I guess. He's very motivated to get recognition for his Canadian Vietnam buddies. They were cogs in the money machine, and he claims it was commerce that started the war in the first place."

"He's right. That war was fought to help Japan, a valuable new US trading partner. It's hard for capitalism to function with communism getting in the way. But they were so afraid of a big war with China, there was never really a plan to win. The body count was ten to one in America's favor, and how do you fight an enemy that literally keeps throwing people at you? They were well-trained, hardcore fighters, and totally committed. The political plan was to stalemate, to stop communism right there, and they did. But the cost was enormous. People can debate the whole domino theory till the cows come home, but America stopped the commies in their tracks." Stewart leans forward. "You know how rough this could get, right?"

"I'm being careful, and I'm not backing down. There was no one of consequence to push me forward growing up, so I learned how to do it myself. I'm tough."

"Right. I forgot about what happened to your parents. That must have been very difficult. Do you want a scotch?"

Kelly shakes her head no, but Stewart pours her one anyway, and gives it to her. He picks up a letter opener and turns it in his hands. "If he's being followed, the sooner we secure this information, the better. Who knows what might happen."

"I agree."

"By the way, that material on TNT sales, tank stuff, forgivable government loans and grants is great, and it all checks out. I had no idea we manufactured the actual green berets, for the love of Christ! Talk about being America's bitch." Stewart laughs. "I would love to read *that* headline."

Kelly laughs too and takes a drink. This is one of the very few times in her life that she hasn't felt like an outsider. Despite her good looks, she has always felt like a bit of a freak since she had no parents. No one ever talked about it. No one ever talked about anything. Shit just kind of hung in the air. Now, she has a chance to do something that really means something. Not just to her, but to everyone. It could help set things right. And if she's not mistaken, she's just been let into the boys' club.

"Did you see the section where we sent doctors, nurses, and field hospitals to treat the victims of our own napalm?" she asks.

"We helped burn people, then gave them a Band-aid! It's a Joseph Heller novel, for Christ's sake. Plus, any medical support Canada gave freed up money in the US budget to spend on war materials. And humanitarian aid went only to South Vietnam, not the North. It's great, but it needs more. Unless Canadians get pissed off and scared, no one will give a shit. We've got company names, people in charge, and that Trojan horse angle, but unless the enemy is coming for *us*, we'll get no traction. Why is this important in 1988? Why tell it right now?"

"Because if this is allowed today, then what's okay tomorrow? Fascism starts with the thin edge of a wedge. Will they track what we're doing and where we're doing it with cashless bank card purchases? You're replacing typewriters with word processors next month. What happens if they find a way to access them and see what we're reporting on? Or modify a story? What if the wrong people end up owning the news media? The big question is, if they got away with *this* in the sixties and seventies, what are they getting away with *now*? And what's in store for us in ten years? Or in 2008, or 2028? Democracy functions on truth, accuracy, and participation, and the press is a guardian and bulwark there to safeguard it."

"Great!" Stewart slams his hand down on his desk. "Put all of that in, but use smaller words, and be ready for the other side to ask, 'If you're not breaking the law, what do you have to hide?'"

Kelly considers this. "Good one. I'll work on that."

"Okay. Keep digging on the angle with his friend, the guy with the bar — what's his name ..."

Kelly shifts in her chair. "Dusty? Oh, I don't think there's anything there."

Stewart takes her in for a moment. "Why are you uncomfortable with this?"

"What? I'm not. It's just that he made me promise to leave him alone."

"Kelly, you need more, and this Dusty guy could really fill in some blanks, especially about your source. You can apologize later."

"I don't know..."

"Look at this as a war against fascism. And all war is deception, right?"

Kelly takes a moment. "Okay, but I'll have to take it easy. Kick says he's a bit fragile."

"Of course. Go easy, but get as much as you can. You never know what's just under the surface sometimes." Kelly says nothing and takes another drink. Stewart looks at her wistfully. "God, I used to be like you. Back when I had a full tank of gas, a lot more hair, and not much to lose." Stewart pounds back his scotch. "Well, you won't be burdened by fish and chips crap for a couple of weeks, so write all this up, and don't worry about how long it is. I don't have too many years left in this chair, and I would *love* to go out with a giant shit-storm behind me. Ha! Go find me more smoking guns!" He sets his glass down and looks at her.

Kelly stands to leave, but stops at in the doorway. "Oh, and Mr. Stewart?"

"It's Malcolm."

"Right, Malcolm. I was just going to wish you a Merry Christmas, and happy holidays."

"What? Oh, right. Same to you. Some solid work this year, kid." He picks up his phone. "Do me a favor, though. Write all this up on that Olympic, even if those fancy computers show up. And use old ribbons so no one can spool them out and figure out what you wrote. Most of what the US embassy shredded in the last days of Saigon was taped back together by the North." He looks out the window, playing with the letter opener again. "And you're getting a pay bump in the New Year. You've been here long enough, and you've earned it. Congrats. You're now tied with the highest-paid journalist on my payroll."

Kelly smiles. "Oh! Thank you, sir. I mean Malcolm. Thanks."

Malcolm whispers, "Don't tell anyone, though. Got it?"

"Got it." She shuts the door on the way out.

She heads over to her desk and grabs her coat and umbrella. "I need a drink."

❖ ❖ ❖ ❖

Val is nestled in a corner booth in the old-school bar of the Georgia Hotel with a glass of scotch when Kelly walks in. She knows Val loves this place because newspaper people never drink here, and it has some cool old Hollywood history. Errol Flynn was a guest here in 1959, and died a few blocks away at a friend's place, plus everyone from Elvis to Nat King Cole to the Beatles and Queen Elizabeth II stayed here, and possibly sat where Val is sitting right now. The history and the deep rich interior of the place always makes Kelly feel more at ease. She gives Val a big hug.

"Happy holidays, girlfriend! Finally, we get some girl time!"

"Merry whatever! I'm going to miss you over the break. How was your meeting?"

"Pretty good. We're on the right track, but it's getting complicated."

"But what's the whole story? Who is this guy? Did you and him, you know…?"

Kelly smiles. "Calm down. I can't talk about the story at all."

Val is crestfallen. "Okay. I get it."

Kelly orders a Glenlivet 12-year-old, neat, and another on the rocks for Val. "Really, it's just me and Stewart on this and no one else. It's that sensitive. Sorry."

"But the other stuff, is … not as sensitive, maybe?"

Kelly blushes. "Okay, but keep it just between us girls."

"Oh God, yes! Start at the beginning. Where does he live?"

"All I can tell you is it's very hard to find."

"You said before that he's got this kind of *charisma*. What do you mean? Is he like super hot, or more rough around the edges?"

"Definitely rough, and the genuine article. Doesn't give a shit if anyone likes him or not, like not even a little."

The scotches arrive and, in a few minutes, they are laughing up a storm, talking about boys, work, and office gossip. When the bill comes, Kelly grabs it. "This is my Christmas present to both of us, Val. I don't have a lot of friends, and I'm grateful that I can call you one."

They get teary-eyed, and Val hugs her. "I'm so lucky to have you, Kelly O."

They get their coats on and head into the crisp winter night. The temperature has dropped, and snow is falling lightly on the city. Holiday lights are everywhere and there's a bounce in everyone's step. It's a moment so simple and beautiful, they just stand in it for a while.

"Have a great holiday, Val," Kelly says as she hugs her again.

"You too. I'm going to miss your face," Val says back. She points to a taxi headed toward them. "Take that cab. It's so festive I'm going to walk home."

They hug again, then walk their separate ways into the lights. Despite her deal with Kick, Kelly decides to take Stewart's advice and pay Dusty a visit. She heads toward the cab.

As Kelly watches her walk off into the snowy night, she doesn't realize that Val won't make it home.

24

Ghost Jump
Cambodia, 1969

THE BLACKED-OUT CHOPPER BLASTS across the sparkling Cambodian sky, just five hundred feet off the deck. It's in full dark mode, and they can see as well as humans can be expected to in the dark. There's a half moon rising in the open door. Kick loves night jumps. Crawford, his new spotter and radioman, is straight redneck from a small town in Oregon, and barely nineteen, but he's good.

Some guys were there when they left to wish them good luck and good hunting. Both were looking hard in full badass, with doo-rags, boonies and camo paint, and Kick with his Remington rifle. They call them *ghost jumpers* since they can't be seen at night, and their chutes are whisper quiet. The NVA have names for them too, but they're the kind that trigger nightmares.

Campbell set up some simple two-man missions for he and Crawford and they're going well. Crawford has a good handle on things, and Kick is okay with him. All he has to do is keep an eye out, get the range, occasionally shoot someone, and not get killed on the way home. This is their seventh jump together. Ten high-ranking officials have met their ends at the hands of these two, three taken by Crawford when Kick offered him the chance. He's taking fast to the training and should be ready to lead his own team soon. They're hoping for more kills today, and maybe even the main objective — the White Tiger.

The drop zone is close enough to the Vietnamese border that they can walk back in several days, if need be. These parts of the Ho Chi Minh Trail, just inside the Cambodian border, have good odds of officer traffic. Since they focused their ops here, it has really stirred things up.

Since Hollywood's death, Kick has been sullen, but effective. He took a severe emotional nosedive, then pulled out of it and pleaded to get back in the field. He feels cold inside, but that icy layer is hiding a white-hot ember of rage. He just wants revenge. His superiors can't say no, even though they know his mental condition. They have objectives to meet, and Kick is one of their deadliest weapons. He has become a nearly perfect soldier.

Kick watches Crawford fidget with his watch. Low-altitude jumps still make him nervous. There's no time for a backup chute at this altitude. The low altitude keeps them under the radar, helps with accuracy, but leaves no margin for error. If your chute malfunctions, your chopper gets hit, or you're shot in mid-air, you're dead. Break an ankle, you'll wish you were dead. Being on the run in Cambodia is a job no soldier wants, and no one wants to be captured. Kick would rather die than be an animal in a cage.

If he's going to die, he'd rather it was quick. His drunken father told him the only way a soldier can be truly effective, is to act like he's already dead. If you're already dead, there's nothing to fear, and Kick feels absolutely and totally dead.

He's had no time to truly process the loss of Hollywood, not to mention Watt. The Army in Vietnam doesn't do that. You suck it up, or you're a pussy. He hasn't talked to Frosty or Beach much since it happened. They all got drunk for a couple of days, then Colonel Campbell decided it was best to split them up. Frosty and Beach were both promoted to sergeant and have new teams now.

Behind Kick's back, guys are saying things. Like he can't be killed, or he has some kind of *force* around him. Soldiers want to hang out with him, wear their gear like he does, walk like he does. Some shake his hand hoping the mojo will rub off. It's stupid. He gives them tips and pointers to help them survive. Not all of them do and he doesn't get attached.

Kick knows the odds just haven't caught up to him yet. Odds can't be outrun forever, and deep inside he's okay to go when his time comes. In a lot of ways, it'll be a relief. Until then, he makes them pay for Hollywood, and then he makes them pay some more. He inflicts as much pain as he can and tries to fill the bottomless pit carved out by the death of his brother.

The NVA and Cong have superstitions about him. The psy-ops guys at Phoenix tell him Charlie calls him the Ghost. US patrols leave Kick's personalized skull-head cards in easy-to-find places. More gruesome reminders include leaving human eyeballs hanging from branches to let them know that *he sees all*. They chop off ears and nail them to doorways and trees to show *he hears all*. The psy-ops boys like messing with Charlie's head, and Kick is one of their best mind-fucks. He's an evil legend. A god tossing lightning from the sky. As far as Kick is concerned, "It don't mean nothin.'"

They get a one-minute warning from the co-pilot. Kick follows his breathing until he gets the signal, then jumps first. His chute snaps open, and he floats quickly toward a grassy hillside. Crawford is right behind him. As Kick gets closer to the ground the tree line comes in fast, and he wonders if he's going to overshoot and get hung up. In the end he rolls through perfectly. At this point though, he knows Crawford is in trouble. He quickly collects his chute.

The chopper fades, and he sees there are two problems. The first is that the jump signal was late, narrowing the landing zone. The second issue is that Crawford's chute didn't fully deploy, so he's moving too fast and heading for the trees. So far, Crawford's training is holding, and he hasn't made a sound. He still looks confident despite the fucked-up situation. Kick plants his rucksack on his chute bundle, just as Crawford hits the banyan tree.

He avoids plowing into the first branch by locking his feet together and using them to bounce off it. The branch snaps. This swings him sideways, and that's when a patch of large broken branches rips into his guts. With a sickening sound, his intestines pour out the other side. His mouth opens wide, but no sound comes out. The pain must be intense. His arms flail around in vain for something to grab onto. The chute still has momentum, and it yanks him into the branch harder, then pulls him sideways, tearing open the wound. He loses consciousness, and the chute goes limp. Crawford's full weight collapses onto the branch, and his back breaks. Blood and guts empty onto the grass.

Kick crouches quietly and thinks. He has few options. Panicking is not one of them. He listens carefully for any indication that someone might be close by. The breaking branches were the only sound that would carry. He could try and cut Crawford down with his rope saw and call for an exfiltration at first light. Kick looks around, runs through the options one more time, and makes up his mind.

There is a fire in his belly. He wants blood and he feels confident he can get it. Then for the first time he hears Hollywood's disembodied voice say, "Charlie Mike." Shit. He looks around. Nothing. There's just the sound of the jungle. Kick takes a deep breath and lets it out.

"Don't mean nothin'."

He pulls his ruck and chute into the tree line, then takes off his boots and socks. With just his sidearm, he monkeys up the tree to the body. After dropping Crawford's chow, weapons, and maps to the ground, he considers the radio. There's no way he can take it, but he can't leave it intact for Charlie.

Kick would usually carry a small emergency radio called an Erk-10 but they travel so light on these two-man missions he hasn't carried it for a while. If he destroys Crawford's radio, he'll be completely without communications and past the point of no return.

As he's drinking the water from Crawford's canteen like a camel, he decides. Fuck it. The dead man's doo-rag gets stuffed inside the canteen. The cap stays off, and he places the bottom of the canteen where most of the radio's electronics are located. He puts his .45 in the open end, wraps his own doo-rag around the muzzle, and fires a round.

It's pretty well muffled. He'd heard barroom stories about guys using a flashlight housing, or oil filter to make a crude suppressor, but a canteen might be a first. He puts a second round into the battery, then scurries to the ground and collects what he needs. The rest he buries in a hole and covers with brush. He buries Crawford's bloody guts where they landed, washes his hands as best he can, then covers them with gun oil to kill the smell. There's already blood in the air, and all he needs right now is a run-in with pissed off rock apes or something worse that might want to eat him.

Kick gets his gear back on, puts on his tire-tread sandals, and checks his map. He'll head into the breeze for two klicks before he hunkers down. Tomorrow at dawn, he's back on the hunt. He's going to Charlie Mike.

25

SPEAK OF THE DEVIL

KICK FINDS DUSTY DUMPING ASHTRAYS. "Speak of the devil. You must be the only person not out holiday shopping 'n' shit. I been dead all night."

Kick looks confused. "You just said *speak of the devil*. Who was here speaking about me?" He puts it together. "I told her to stop talking to you about that stuff."

"Really? Did I give away my rights or somethin'? I speak to whoever the hell I want!"

It's the wrong time to fight this battle. "Yeah, well, she is a reporter. Shoulda seen that coming. So, she just left?"

"Twenty minutes ago. Said she was heading home. Wanna beer?"

Kick sits at a table and puts his bag down. "Sure, thanks."

"*Thanks*? Now that's a step in the right direction. And very Canadian of you." He lets out a big laugh as he pours. "I heard your pie was a hit."

"Came off without a hitch. Thanks for that too."

"Another thanks? Who are you, and what have you done with my grunt friend? It is a Christmas miracle, all these manners! And you've seen each other a few times, huh? Seems like it's goin' all right." Dusty sits down with Kick's beer and a whiskey for himself.

Kick hoists his beer. "To Christmas fuckin' miracles." They drink. Kick looks like he's about to say something but can't.

"Uh-oh. I've seen that look before."

"I've got to lay out some shit, Dust, and I need you to listen."

Dusty sobers and sits back. "Okay."

"I've had a few tails on me recently, and so have my company boys."

Dusty's demeanor shifts. "So that *was* your bit of handiwork in Gastown."

Kick doesn't have to answer. "Who are they and what do they want?"

"We can't figure that out. I don't think it's the newspaper thing, but it could be. Could also be any one of a bunch of people in Southeast Asia, the Mediterranean, parts of Africa, or something to do with a Chinese crime family."

Dusty sips his whiskey. "You have covered some ground out there. But who'd know all that shit was you? You got a leak?"

"I hadn't considered that. Most likely it's coming out of China, since two of the tails were from there. They're brazen. I'm about to get Kelly somewhere safe, and I'm hoping to convince you to do the same."

Dusty looks offended.

"Don't fucking look like that," Kick says. "I know you can handle your shit. You have nothing to prove in that way. But if I were you, and I had the option, I might enjoy a couple of weeks on a beach somewhere during the holidays." Kick takes some vacation fliers out of his coat and puts them on the table. "There are some great last-minute deals." He circles one with his pen. "I hear this one's good. The women are hot; the beer is not."

Dusty clears his throat and rubs his fingers together. "I'm getting to that," Kick says. "I came into some money." He drops a bundle of US hundreds on the table. "I hear the Hilton there is great."

Dusty picks up the cash, and flips through it. It's ten thousand dollars. He smacks it into his palm a couple of times, downs his whiskey, and walks behind the bar with it. "I have been working pretty hard." He hits the music and cranks the volume. It's the Rolling Stones' 'Sympathy for the Devil' and Dusty jams with it. "Yeeow!" While he's singing, he writes something out with a black marker, then holds it up for Kick to read. *Closed for the holidays – See you next year!* Dusty lets out a big, booming laugh, and dances to the door. He tapes the sign on the glass, then pulls the shade down.

Kick pounds half his beer. "Thanks, Dust. It puts my mind at ease. And if you can, get a cab to the airport right now. Buy your vacation clothes when you get there, 'cause shit is moving fast."

Mick Jagger starts singing. Dusty is about to lock the door, but turns and yells over the music, "I am getting some buckets of Pacifico, and sittin' in my deck chair in the ocean, my brother! And I will be happy to spend some of Uncle Sam's dirty blood money while …"

Suddenly, the door is flung open, and three armed men burst in with handguns raised. A short, thin white guy with Buddy Holly glasses points a gun at Dusty's heart. Kick's Glock is halfway out, but the other two have him cold. Jagger sings the part about guessing his name.

The gunman on his left is tall and lanky, with jet-black hair, and Hispanic. His partner on the right is stocky with red hair and wears a stupid shit-eating grin like he just bagged the white whale. Red Hair keeps Kick covered, while his buddy goes back and locks the door.

"That's it for you two," he says with a grin. Kick pegs the accent from the Sonora part of Mexico.

Buddy Holly is slim but muscular, with a cocky attitude, and he appears to be the leader. They're all mercs. Takes one to know one. Looks like they work as a team since they're so familiar with each other. Probably think a comfy payday is coming their way for capturing or killing him.

Dusty looks mad enough to hunt grizzly with a jackknife, and Buddy Holly is savoring the confrontation. Like he's a featherweight holding off George Foreman. Kick and Dusty have been in some barroom scraps here and there, but nothing quite like this. Like most soldiers, though, they love to talk hypotheticals, which are always followed by arguments about Rangers versus Recon. 'Dusty gets jumped in his bar' is one of their favorite scenarios.

Dusty laughs. "Jumped in my own bar …" Mick's at the part where he held a general's rank and the bodies stank. Kick smiles at Red Hair.

Buddy Holly quips, "Not how you expected your day to end, huh?"

"This day's still got some punch left in it. It might surprise you," Dusty says.

"Oh, I can predict exactly how this will go, homie," chides the Mexican.

"Stay frosty, man," Kick says softly. Dusty spits on Buddy's face. There's a short moment where it looks like Buddy is going to shoot Dusty, but it passes. He and Dusty stare each other down.

Kick can't think about how he managed to miss another tail right now, let alone leading these cowboys right to Dusty. His training has kicked in, and all there is in the world right now, is this mission. He looks at Mexico and says calmly, "Your move, *cholo*."

Mexico isn't happy with that word. "Gun on the table. Face the floor, bitch." Using two fingers, Kick places his gun on the table with the vacation fliers and his tactical pen. He then lies face down on the floor. Mexico gets behind Kick and jams his gun into the base of his skull. "Left hand."

Kick puts his left hand behind his back. He is hoping for zip ties or tape, but he hears the handcuffs coming before he feels the cold steel. "Can I get these in fur-lined?"

Mexico tightens the cuffs. "Right hand!" Kick is cuffed. This confirms they need him alive. Mexico pulls off Kick's boots and takes his Ka-Bar. "Oooo, nice," he coos.

In his peripheral, Kick sees Dusty getting the same treatment. They're both cuffed at the ankles too and slammed into chairs at the table. Mexico and Red cover the boys, while Buddy looks at the fliers.

"Vacation?" He laughs. "There's no vacation for you!"

Jagger's at the part of the song about the nature of his game.

Kick coughs loudly, and Dusty grins. "No sympathy for the devil, huh?"

"Shut up!" Buddy walks around. "This is simple. Give us information, then you can go. Okay?"

Kick smiles. "Tell that fuckhead Chung we send our best for the holidays." Buddy stops walking. Kick has to crane his neck around to see him, so he hops his chair around to face him.

Buddy laughs at him. "You look like a bouncing idiot."

"Yeah, you work for Chung for sure. He likes to hire sloppy, cut-rate shit artists like you."

Dusty rattles his hand cuffs and makes a fuss, while Kick quietly does something behind his back.

Buddy grabs Dusty's cuffs. "What are you doing?"

"I can't feel my hands."

"I don't care!" Buddy yells. "Who are you, and who do you work for?"

"I'm Dusty, the sole proprietor of this bar. I work for myself. My full name's on the liquor license on the wall, which you could have just read instead of all this shit!"

Buddy smiles and nods. "Thank you, Mr. Dusty." Keith Richards is laying into his blistering solo.

"Shut off that music!" Buddy screams. "I can't hear myself think!" Red looks around for the stereo.

Dusty laughs. He hid it so drunk customers wouldn't fuck with his tunes. "Come on man, everyone loves the Stones!"

"And you, little white man. What's your name, big shooter? Who do you work for?"

Kick looks at the men guarding them. "Tell your goons to stop pointing those guns. They make me nervous."

Buddy gets right in Kick's face. "I was warned you are paranoid, and very irritating. So, I'm going to speed things up and cut off your hand. Get you motivated!" Buddy holds up the Ka-Bar. "And I am *not* sloppy."

"You don't have the cojones, four-eyes!" Kick shouts back.

"Oh, I will enjoy this..." Buddy croons.

"You'll have to uncuff me for that, but start with my left hand, please," Kick says. "My right'll be busy for a minute." In a flash, with a clink of handcuffs, Kick's right hand scoops up the tactical pen and pounds it into Buddy Holly's right temple. His eyes go blank.

At the same instant, Dusty clicks one cuff open, grabs Kick's Glock, and falls to the floor. His first shot goes wide of Mexico's head; Mexico fires back way too high.

Buddy's dead weight slumps on top of Kick, but he manages to yank out the dead man's gun. He fires at Red, who is no longer grinning, and takes off most of his left ear. He screams in pain but gets a shot off that hits his dead boss in the gut. Kick fires again and hits Red in the chest. He slumps down at the bar.

Dusty fires three quick ones into Mexico's gut. It backs the poor bastard up right to the bar, where he falls beside Red. Kick rolls Buddy off and struggles in the ankle cuffs to stand over the sputtering Red. He raises his gun and says loudly over the Stones, "My name's Kick. I'm a sole proprietor too." He puts a bullet in his head. There's just Mexico left, moaning on the floor. Kick takes out his bent bobby pin again and unlocks his other hand, then his ankle cuffs. Dusty does the same, while Nicky Hopkins takes his piano solo.

Kick slides Mexico's gun away, then gives Dusty a hand up.

"Mind if I finish him off?" Dusty asks. Kick nods in agreement.

Sweat drips off his brow, and his eyes are cold. "Don't mean nothin'." Dusty shoots Mexico between the eyes. Dusty looks shaky.

"Okay." Kick says softly. "You all right?"

"I'm good."

"Given the situation, can you make an exception on the whiskey?" Dusty doesn't answer, so Kick brings them a bottle of High West and two glasses. "Sit down and drink." Dusty turns down the music and puts his head in his hands.

Kick says, "I know, I know. Drink this right now." Dusty sits down, and drinks. Kick drinks half of his. "Jesus, that's tasty."

"Oh, my god that brought it all back," Dusty croaks.

Kick finishes his drink and goes back to the bar. "Sit tight. I have to make a call." He dials the sixteen-digit code, says all the magic words, and hangs up. "They'll call back in five. Let's get them all in the bathroom, and mop up this blood, in case the cops roll by."

"Nah, they never come here. A bar around here's not a priority."

"They'll have to if someone calls in hearing ten gunshots."

"Yeah, good point."

"Don't worry. By the time the cleaners leave, there won't be a trace. We do the big stuff now, that'll speed up the process."

"*Stay frosty?*" Dusty asks. "Where the hell'd you hear that?"

"Never mind. It's making the rounds with the younger crowd." Dusty grabs Mexico by the feet and drags him into the men's room, while 'Sympathy for the Devil' fades out with the *woo-woos*. Kick looks around for his knife. "You seen my Ka-Bar?"

"No. Hey, you tell those Mr. Cleans I need new tiles in my bathrooms," Dusty says. "You know, while they're at it." After Kick and Dusty get their footwear back on, Dusty rolls out the bucket and mop, adds extra bleach and soap, and cleans up the blood as best he can.

Kick finally finds what he's looking for. His Ka-Bar is sticking into the wall a foot from the dartboard. "He must have had a spasm when I stabbed him." Dusty looks over and whistles. Kick pours bleach all over the knife, wipes it down, and puts it back in his boot.

Kick grabs Buddy by his feet, then stops. His leg is twitching. "Shit!" Kick steps up to Buddy's head and rams his heel into the pen, jamming it all the way into the skull with a sickening sound. He touches the carotid artery. "Dead. Jesus, it's like your rattlesnake story." Kick checks the pulse of the other two. "All dead. I bet if I pulled that pen out it'd still write. Did I give you one of those?"

"Yeah. And it writes great. For a murder weapon." The tension breaks and they howl with laughter for a good two minutes. "Holy fuck, it has been a while since I've been in the middle of shit like that!" Dusty says, holding out his shaking hands for Kick to see. "That was fuckin' intense!"

The bar phone rings.

Kick answers. "Tiger." He listens for thirty seconds then says "Confirmed. It'll be locked up." He hangs up and pours two more drinks. "Whiskey's the only thing that calms the shakes." Kick downs his, pours himself another, and takes them over to Dusty. "Two hours until they can get here with everything. You're going to need a change of clothes before you go. Something to wear to the airport. And take a carry-on. They get suspicious if you show up with no luggage."

Dusty looks around. "Yeah, I've got my ruck here, and got my dress clothes from the party." He starts taking his clothes off.

"Throw all your clothes — shoes, socks, and everything, on top of the dead guys. Guns too. They'll get it all. And your tighties."

"I gotta go commando on vacation? You are *thorough*. You ever seen 'em do this stuff?"

"I had to do it myself once," Kick says. "They'll roll in barrels of nasty shit, and there's nothing left by the very end but sludge. The guns'll get melted down somewhere too. Your bar will be spic-and-span by morning. Oh, and don't bring your dress clothes back from vacation either. Just in case."

Dusty is buck naked now; he tosses his clothes into the men's bathroom. He washes his face and hands at the bar and throws Kick a soapy towel. Kick washes his hands and face and tosses the towel into the men's room. He then puts all the guns in too and shuts the bathroom door. Dusty asks, "What about you?"

"I'm going to have to risk it and change later. I've got to make a stop, then I'm off to a safe house." He gets up and grabs his pack. "You all right if I leave out the back?"

Dusty is buttoning his shirt. "Sure. I'll head out that way too. I need to square away some things, before I split. I assume your pals will let themselves in?"

"You know they will. Head to the airport within the hour."

"I'll be gone before that." Dusty still looks pretty unsteady. "I am going to get some beach time, get drunk, and fuck myself silly! And all on your dime, motherfucker!" He laughs uneasily. "'I'm a sole proprietor too!' That was good!" But Dusty isn't laughing.

Kick smiles but gives him a long look. He doesn't look good. "You sure you're all right?"

"Fuck off. I'm great. Get outta here." Dusty follows Kick to the back door. Kick checks in all directions, and then slips out. "Semper Fi, Dusty." The door locks behind him.

26

LOCKDOWN

IT'S SNOWING HARD NOW, and everyone is still out last-minute shopping or celebrating, but Kick doesn't have any holiday spirit. He moves like a shadow, slipping invisibly through the cold alleys and dark side streets of the West End, leading him to Kelly's apartment.

It's risky, but Chung probably isn't aware that Buddy and the boys have failed, and he wouldn't have another team ready anyway. He likely figures they're having fun working them over. By the time he realizes it's all gone wrong, there'll be nothing to find except a clean, empty bar, with no Dusty or Kick. At that point, Kelly will be his next stop.

He hates to admit it, but Kick can tell he is not one hundred percent. Probably not even fifty, and he has no one to blame but himself. His body and mind are the tools of his trade, and he's let them grow dull and rusty. Maybe Taylor's right, and he needs a good head-shrinking. His thoughts are swimming and focusing is hard, but he has to get through this crisis the best way he can, and he's convinced he will.

A couple is walking out the front of Kelly's building, and Kick slips in. He keeps his hood up and head down as usual, all the way to the empty elevator. His gloved finger hits the seventh-floor button. So far, so good.

After their series of knocks, Kelly opens the door wearing a blue bathrobe with her hair just nicely dried. "This is unexpected. Hi." She lets him in. "You look upset."

Once the door is closed, Kick says quietly, "I'm sorry to show up like this, but it's urgent. You need to pack some things and get your research together. I have to get you out of here quick."

"Wait a minute — why?"

"I can't tell you. Partially for your safety and because ... I've committed crimes you can't be privy to. Please trust me — your life is in danger." Once again, Kick forgets that Kelly is a journalist, not a soldier.

"What about your life?"

"I'm trained for this; you're not. Do what I say and you'll be fine."

"What does this have to do with me?"

Kick is frustrated, and his thoughts are getting jumbled. "Whoever is coming for me, will use you to get to me. The threat is coming from China."

"I have nothing to do with China!" Kelly snaps.

"No, but your dad did." He knows he's coming off the rails, but can't understand why she's not getting it. "We don't have much time, and I'm sorry to be blunt, but you need to pull your head out of your ass and move it!"

Kelly takes a moment. "Not until I know what's going on!"

"I can't tell you everything, but I know for sure they are coming for you!"

"Who says my father had anything to do with China? Don't show up at my door and start pushing me around! My Dad —"

"Your dad was a fucking arms dealer! He worked for the parent company of Martech, and if he sold any footwear at all it was worn by people like me! He had dealings all over the world and helped arm some of the worst people on the planet. Now move it!"

The blood drains out of Kelly's face, and she grabs the wall to stop herself from falling over. Kick tries to help her, but she pushes him off. "I'm sorry you had to hear it like that," he says. "I don't know what happened to him exactly, but chances are he was —"

Kelly pushes him away again and runs into her bedroom. She pulls out a big suitcase and starts violently throwing her things inside it. Her clothes, her research notes and material, her portable typewriter. "Fuck!"

"I'm sorry," Kick says. "I wish there was time to talk this out, but there isn't. I know you hate me right now, and …" He takes a deep breath. "If anyone asks, say you're taking a last-minute vacation."

"So far it sounds like it's going to be a super good time!"

"You didn't know there was something going on with him?" He knows how stupid the question is as it leaves his mouth.

"No! You know why? Because I was a fucking child! You get that? All I know is he got all weird one day, and, and …" Kelly starts to cry, and Kick goes to her. She slaps him hard across the face. Kick is stunned. "Don't fucking touch me! I was just a kid! And then he was gone, and I had no one, and no one told me anything."

Kick lets her cry, then says softly, "We'll figure it all out later, I promise. But right now, we need to move."

Kelly looks up at him and dries her eyes. "Only if you tell me everything that happened to you over there. And I mean everything."

"I can't. It's classified."

"Then fuck you! Get out and let me change."

He takes out two thick envelopes from inside his coat. "I know you're driven and want all the answers now, but I can't tell you everything. I can give you this, though." He tosses the envelopes into her suitcase. "The top one has details on all the companies that made things, who was in charge, who got grants, loans, favors, broke laws, and everyone involved. The other one is about your dad. You should know the whole truth." He leaves the room.

Kick heads into the living room. There he turns out the lights and peaks out the window. It looks clear. His heart feels like it's about to explode, his hands are sweaty, and he feels like he's falling. This is why he stays clear of relationships. They're messy and unpredictable. Kelly wheels her suitcase to the door.

He says softly, "Go out front and get a cab to the Sutton Hotel. I'll meet you in the lobby, and get you checked in. Don't speak to anyone, and don't check in without me."

"Getting involved with you was a mistake. You're a black fucking cloud, and I can't believe I thought this could ever work. It's just so sad." It's a knife through Kick's heart. His hand is shaking as he opens the door and lets her out. He hears the elevator doors close, and puts his head in his hands, but no tears will come. That couldn't have gone worse. After counting to sixty he clears his head and steps out of Kelly's apartment, closing the door quietly behind him. He walks down the stairs and out onto the street.

It's only five blocks to the Sutton on Burrard Street, and he moves like a dark mass shifting through the festive lights. No one gives him a second look as he double-times it. He's breaking his own protocols, but he just looks like someone getting last-minute holiday things wrapped up.

He finds Kelly on a courtesy bench in the Sutton lobby. Kick sits down beside her and slips a $10,000 bundle of mixed cash into her purse. His voice is surprisingly gentle. "That's for tipping staff, and whatever else you might need. Just *don't* deposit it into a bank." He puts a credit card into her hand. "This won't raise any eyebrows or lead back to you in case anyone checks. Your reservation is under Beth Lambert, staying for two weeks, visiting from Chicago. Sign that name on the back of the card right now." Kelly does what she's told. "Get room service for everything, so it's all charged to your bill. Don't leave your room, not even once, and don't let the cleaning staff in. Tell them you caught a bad flu on the plane. My place at the Balmoral Hotel is compromised, so don't ever go back there. I mean *ever*. It's not safe. Okay?"

Kelly gives him a cold look, but it's more sad than angry. "What will you be doing?"

"Trying to stop this from getting worse. Once I know more, I'll call your room. He slips her a blank card with a handwritten phone number on it. "You can reach me here or leave a secure message. If anyone tries to trace this number it'll show up as local to Chicago, so it'll make sense. Don't use your own bank or credit cards. They'll be watching those." Kick is trying to gauge her commitment, but his head is full of static. He can't tell if she's on board or not, but there's no time to hold her hand through this. There's too much to do.

Kelly says, "Got it."

"The security is good here. They handle celebrities, so if there's an immediate issue call hotel security. In an hour or two we'll have someone watching you here. You'll be very safe."

Kelly looks at him. There's real hurt in her eyes, not just because of her dad, but also because of what just shattered between them.

Kelly doesn't look at him as she speaks. "Until this story's done, let's keep our relationship strictly professional. Okay?"

She gets up and walks to the front desk. He's going to have to trust her; that's all there is to it. He moves to the exit and watches her check in. A friendly bellhop takes her bag, and leads her to the elevator, asking how her flight was. Kelly replies meekly, "All right, but it feels like I picked up a bug on the plane." So far, so good.

By the time the light goes on in Kelly's room, Kick's in the back alley looking up at her floor. Kick feels a bit more relieved. He heads down the alley and hops a series of buses and cabs that take him to Commercial Drive in East Vancouver.

◆ ◆ ◆ ◆

Once in her room, Kelly opens her suitcase and looks at the folders. "What a prick. What an arrogant fucking prick!"

She opens the envelope with the information on her dad and sobs softly as she looks through the pictures and documents. They're horrifying. As sad as she is, it's her pride, anger, and insatiable drive for the truth that push her to do what she does next. She considers her options, which are to stay put or dig deeper. She dries her eyes and pulls out a different coat and hat.

"Fuck it."

She walks out the door.

27

THE WHITE TIGER
Cambodia, 1969

KICK SLIPS THROUGH THE WET CAMBODIAN JUNGLE like a cobra. His sniper rifle is slung over his back on one side of his rucksack, his Ka-Bar in a sheath on his leg, and his sidearm is on the other side. He's making good time. It's an hour after daybreak, and he looks down a steep ravine onto a branch of the Ho Chi Minh Trail. He can still taste the coffee and hot chocolate mix in his mouth from breakfast. He doubled up on the calories this morning in case he has to run later. Maybe it's the smell of the jungle, or the adrenaline, or his big stupid smile, but he misses Hollywood right now. But he can feel him close by somehow.

Through his binoculars he sees an area that has been trampled down and shows evidence of old campfires. Taking out the range finder, he confirms it's just over half a mile away. He rechecks his position and likes everything he sees. If you have to pick a fight, you might as well take the high ground.

A few minutes later he's lying on his belly under a low jungle hunting blind he quickly put together out of vines, sticks, and vegetation. Kick blends completely into his surroundings. His face and hands have fresh camo. The enemy would have to walk right over him to know he was there. His Remington is set up on its bipod legs and ready to rock. The entire weapon and scope, is wrapped in burlap and plant material to eliminate reflection. He likes his chances.

Kick settles in and looks at his mark's picture and file lying beside him on the ground. He has studied it so many times it's embedded. If this target doesn't show up, he'll take the highest-ranking officers that cross his path. There are also targets of opportunity and known spies and traitors in the file. So, he waits.

Crawford's death was tragic, but it provided the first chance for Kick to work solo. He thinks about him hanging in the banyan tree, but it doesn't bother him. He doesn't know why, and he doesn't care. Kick hasn't slept much in the past few days, so he washes down more freeze-dried coffee with water. His eyes get droopy after a few hours, so he rubs a bit of tobacco on his fingers, then touches them to his eyes to sting them open.

After nearly eight hours the sun starts dropping behind him. It's all looking like there'll be nothing happening today, until he feels that sharp pull deep inside. A group of men walk into his kill zone. Holy shit. It's an enemy patrol with fourteen men. Two look very interesting and seem to be in command. Kick gets the binoculars on them. The taller of the two appears to be top dog, but his face isn't clear yet. A few things seem unusual. Kick gets a better look. Shit. Their gear is better than most, and there are long guns that look like Russian-made semi-automatic Dragunov rifles. This looks like a training mission for snipers. The only good news is that Dragunovs are half-assed for accuracy. If they were shooting from where Kick is, there's a fifty-fifty chance they'd miss a perfect shot.

Who the fuck are these two trainers? He follows them both through his scope for a bit, and then goes back to his list of targets. The short one looks familiar, but the taller one still hasn't shown his face. Kick takes a flick through the secondary targets and finds the short guy. He's a piece of shit known to have helped trick MACV-SOG into sending Americans into traps. His cover was blown a while ago, and he disappeared from South Vietnam. Taking him out will be a pleasure. Kick chambers a round.

He looks back through the scope. The light is falling behind his position when the tall man turns, and Kick can almost see him. There's a small patch on his shoulder he can make out now. It's the face of a tiger. The man turns a bit more, and his face is fully illuminated by the setting sun. The sight startles Kick, but he refocuses fast and sights the center of the man's head. He inhales, and then, on a whisper-soft exhale, he gently squeezes the trigger, and makes history.

28
Ripples

EVERYBODY AND EVERYTHING IS LOCKED in the men's room, and the bar almost looks normal. Dusty gets into the rest of his travel clothes, checks the time on the wall clock, then lights a blunt. After putting his pack by the back door, he shuts out all the lights. He takes a long, shaky haul on the joint and holds it. There's just enough time to make his redeye flight if he gets a cab in the next fifteen minutes. The pot will settle him out and help get him on the plane. It'll be good to get away and decompress.

There's a knock at the front door. Dusty freezes. The knock comes again, and then a woman's voice. "Dusty? It's Kelly."

Dusty exhales and shakes his head. "Girl, you are harshin' my buzz-buzz." He stubs out his joint, grabs a big knife from the bar, and walks over. Peeking under the blind, he sees Kelly on the other side. She's alone and has obviously been crying.

"I'm all closed up and heading to the airport. Last-minute vacation."

"A lot of that going around. Can I just get ten minutes? It's important."

Dusty looks back at the room and sighs. "I can only spare five if I'm going to catch my flight, so you've gotta make it quick." He lets her in, checks carefully behind her, and relocks the door. "Bathrooms are out of order. You do *not* want to go in there." He laughs uncomfortably.

"That friend of yours is fucked up, Dusty!"

"Ya think?" Dusty lights a couple of candles at a table.

Kelly takes a seat. "I mean, he's clearly an unusual guy, but he's been good to be around until tonight. He just went, you know, ice cold. Why?"

"I can't tell you anything personal."

"You've got to help me understand."

Dusty reaches over the bar and grabs a towel. "Okay." He searches for an example. "It was April 22nd, 1952, and lunchtime in Toronto. The weather was nice, and all these women working downtown are having lunch outside. From outta nowhere, like magic, all their nylons ripped. All of them. It was simultaneous."

"This is going to help?"

Dusty wipes up a bit of blood he missed on the wall, then tosses the towel in front of the men's room. "They had just tested the A-bomb in Nevada. The force traveled thousands of miles, and still had enough left to wreck all those nice panty hose."

Kelly isn't getting it. Dusty tries again.

"Okay. Two guys start fighting in a family restaurant. It's really violent, and they beat the shit outta each other. Those kids and parents watching are affected by what they witness. They head back into the world, and whether they mean to or not, it affects how they interact with people. Maybe they're irritable, or withdrawn, or they lash out. Maybe one of them hits someone else. No matter what, I guarantee you they pass some of that on. Violence is like that A-bomb. It ripples out."

"When does it stop?"

"What do ya mean, stop?"

Kelly thinks about that. "So, you can make positive ripples too, then? Or ripples of truth."

Dusty sighs. "Aw, shit. You're an optimist."

Kelly smiles weakly. "Guilty."

Dusty sits. "Have you spent a full night with him?"

"A few."

"And did he actually sleep?"

"He fell asleep once and woke up yelling. The other times I'm pretty sure he didn't sleep at all. I'd find him up reading. Look, I really like him, and not just because he's all dark and fascinating. I like being around him."

Dusty considers the situation. Maybe it's because his blood is still up from the fight, or he just feels for what Kelly's going through, but he takes a deep breath before speaking. "All right. Since you're makin' pie together, I'll give you some insight. But this isn't for your fuckin' paper."

"I promise. What about his dad? He hardly talks about him?"

Dusty checks the clock again, then continues. "That's a part of it. Kick got the letter while he was still in country."

"Did he come back for the funeral?"

"No. Some guys couldn't just come back to the world. When you're in country, there is no *over here*. Your mind gets ... You get off the plane, and suddenly everyone's trying to kill you. Life gets simple. If it moves, ya shoot it. It's like *Zen*."

Kelly doesn't get it. "What?"

"It's like this. At first, the end of your tour is a year away. That's a point of reference you understand. After a few weeks of combat, a day lasts forever, and the end of the year feels like it's a thousand years away. Then it feels like a million, so ya stop thinkin' about it. You see your friends dyin', and you get hard. Then your past starts to disappear."

"What?"

"Family, friends, school... yeah. Ya don't *wanna* remember. It makes everything harder. The past is like a planet you never lived on. So now your past and future are gone, and the only thing you have is your next meal, your next smoke, next breath, or what's right fuckin' in front of you. The enemy. Your life depends on you being in this very specific zone. *Zen*, man. You are right in the fuckin' moment. It's a dimension so unique only the people who've been there have the language to talk about it. There's no future, no past, no high school sweethearts, no dreams, no fishing trips with ..." Dusty's face clouds over and he takes a drink. "No one went to his dad's funeral except his mom."

"Kick's dad? Why?"

"His Legion buddies wouldn't go. Back then they didn't if it was ..."

"Suicide?"

"Then he lost Hollywood."

"His best friend with the sunglasses?"

"Yeah. They grew up on the same street. Enlisted together in Blaine." Dusty shakes his head. "That's all I can tell you, Kelly. Really. Just let it be."

"Just this part."

Dusty checks the clock again.

"Dusty, please!"

"Kick loved him, man! In a way only a soldier understands!" he yells. The outburst scares Kelly, and she sits back. "Being ready to die for someone else is a bond you can't even *imagine*! They'd been through everything together. He was his brother, his family, his priest, his savior, and Charlie took the *one thing* he still held dear. He snapped. I mean, he coulda gone the other way, and lost his will to fight. Just imploded. A lot did. Some had their hair go completely gray from shock, some went catatonic, incoherent. But Kick, he went all the way over."

"Why?"

Dusty's heart is pounding. He thinks about the friends he lost in Vietnam.

The best friends he ever had. "Revenge kept him from despair, and he committed himself to it. It's a job that never ends. A beast to be constantly fed."

"And that's when the CIA got him?"

"That's enough, Kelly. I have to catch my flight." Dusty gets up and walks to the door to let her out, but Kelly doesn't move.

"They put him into Phoenix, right?" she says. "The counter insurgency program? He told me," she lies.

"Why are you so interested? Why not let all this go? Have a normal life?"

"I care about him, and I can't be with him, unless I know exactly who he is."

Dusty is in a bad place. He shouldn't have answered the door. Shouldn't have started talking, because now he feels like a runaway freight train. Part of him wants to let it happen. Pick up speed and wipe out everything in his path. The other part is pulling on the screaming brakes as hard as he can.

The train continues. "They'd give Kick some asshole's picture and file, and drop him into Cambodia or Laos, right under the radar. He'd lie in the dirt half a mile away and wait for days if he had to. Roll over to piss or shit, then roll right back into position. Rain, heat, day, or night meant nothing to him. He was there 'til a man on his list died. There were a handful of these hardcore guys. All trained by him. Gifted snipers. It's not something anyone can just do. Breathing like a meditation master 'til that bullet takes their head apart."

Kelly is horrified. "And he never got caught?"

"He had a half-mile head start. Sometimes he'd lay traps and let 'em chase him to their deaths. If he couldn't get choppered out, he'd hide. Dig himself in or climb into the canopy. If they sent dogs, he'd sprinkle CS powder from his tear gas grenades on his trail and mess up their noses. There was a trick for everything with him. He'd walk back into Vietnam even if it took weeks, killing whatever he could for food. Bugs, worms, snakes, rats, whatever. He was a fuckin' legend."

"Who were his targets?"

Dusty's train rolls on. "NVA officers mainly, spies, or traitors. But he hunted a very specific prize. He never told me the guy's real name, and he still won't talk about him. They put a bounty on Kick. It was five years' wages for his head on a stick. Once he bagged this particular guy, though, the bounty went up to ten years' wages, and it was extended to his family."

"In Canada? How could they do that?"

"Bounties are as old as time, Kelly. Politicians pretend there are rules in a war, but when you get right down to it, it's a fuckin' free-for-all out there."

"Okay, but what happened? Did they get him out?"

"It was a genius move." Dusty shakes his head. "They killed him."

"They what?"

"He was listed killed in action, written up in *Stars and Stripes*. Coffin and flag sent home, all of it." Kelly can't find the words. Dusty continues. "The company did it all. Even the telegram to his mom."

◆ ◆ ◆ ◆

Port Hardy, British Columbia, Canada, 1969

Kick's mother stands in her front door in an old floral-patterned dress. She's looking at a Western Union envelope. Her hands shake as she opens it and reads.

DONT PHONE DONT DELIVER BETWEEN 10 PM & 6 AM STOP THE SECRETARY OF THE ARMY HAS ASKED ME TO EXPRESS HIS DEEP REGRET THAT YOUR SON, DAVID TACKER, DIED IN VIETNAM ON 17 MAY 1969 AS A RESULT OF WOUNDS RECEIVED DURING A COMBAT OPERATION STOP.

Her hand goes over her mouth, and her body convulses in deep, painful sobs. They're quiet at first, and get louder as she reads through her tears.

HE WAS STRUCK IN THE HEAD AND NECK BY EXPLODING FRAGMENTS AND BY BULLETS IN THE LEG AND CHEST AND DIED IMMEDIATELY STOP PLEASE ACCEPT MY DEEPEST SYMPATHY STOP THIS CONFIRMS PERSONAL NOTIFICATION MADE BY A REPRESENTATIVE OF THE SECRETARY OF THE ARMY STOP.

Kick's mother collapses on the threshold, the telegram gripped tightly in her hand.

◆ ◆ ◆ ◆

"How could they do that?" Kelly asks.

Dusty's laugh sounds like a child's. "They did whatever they wanted, man."

"And what about the girl? I hear him talking in his sleep. Who is she?"

"That's enough!" Dusty slams his big fist on the table, and Kelly jumps. "I am *done* with all this! I'm trying to have a nice life now, Kelly." Tears drop from his eyes.

"I'm sorry, Dusty. Please ..."

Dusty puts his head down and sobs. "I lost great friends there, Kelly! I still see them sometimes. My friend Tony trying to talk with no jaw while he bleeds out ..." Dusty's back heaves as he cries quietly on the table.

"I'm sorry. I'm so sorry I dragged all this up for you. Come on. Let's get you a cab, then I'll go."

Dusty sits back up. "You go. I'll get away in a couple minutes. 'Way you go."

"Are you sure?"

"Yeah," Dusty replies, wiping his eyes. "I needed to get that out, I guess." He laughs a bit as he walks to the door with her. "I'm better for it. Really. I'll see you when I get back."

"Okay, Dusty. I'm sorry again. Try and have a great vacation."

"Will do." Kelly leaves and he locks the door after her.

Dusty is frozen at the door. "Don't get any runs in yer nylons."

It takes a minute for Dusty to move. He picks up the bloody towel from earlier and opens the bathroom door. The bodies look weird. Kick's Glock is sitting on top of them, so he picks it up and looks at it. He chambers a round, turns it over, and looks at the other side. He notices the craftsmanship. Someone put a lot of effort into making this just so he could shoot that punk tonight. Does the guy who made it know how terrible it feels? Does he know what it takes out of a person to kill another human? He stares right into the pipe and wonders if he'll see the bullet coming.

29
Taken

KELLY WALKS UP TO EAST HASTINGS since no cabs are outside Dusty's. She feels terrible for putting Dusty through that, but Stewart was right. It's great material. She has a better idea who she's dealing with, and Kick's anonymous anyway. Plus technically, he's dead. All in all, she has misgivings, but feels like she did the right thing.

This part of Vancouver never changes character, Christmas or not. There's a man screaming at no one in particular, and a cop car has its cherries flashing with a pantless guy face down on the hood. The cabs are all still busy, so Kelly heads toward downtown.

It's not like she forgot she's in danger or didn't believe it. Rather, she discounted it because she desperately wants answers. Plus, she didn't like how Kick treated her. He was arrogant and pushy, and he acted like a prick. How could she have been so stupid to think they could build something together?

There are still no cabs, but Kelly notices a shiny black Mercedes half a block behind her. Probably a rich guy trolling for a hooker. A street person is trying to clean the windshield. The driver's window comes down, and a hand flies out with a fiver. The guy grabs it and runs.

A few blocks later at Burrard and Hastings, Kelly is still processing her feelings about Kick. How could she compromise her story by getting involved with her subject? But he's so comfortable to be around. Like they were made for each other. Her heart is saying yes, but her head is telling her no. As she tracks this inner conversation, a small voice inside her says something she can't quite hear, but it reminds her of Kick's lecture about everyone having a personal alarm system. Shit.

She looks behind her, and sees the Mercedes is still with her, and the reality of her situation lands hard. She has to get back to the Sutton fast. There's a short honk and she turns to see a yellow taxi beside her. The driver is smiling and waving, and Kelly jumps in.

She is about to tell him to take her to the Sutton, but reconsiders. "The Sylvia Hotel, please." Better to try and lose the Mercedes. The cheerful driver hits the meter and says into his radio, "Pharaoh to Sylvia, over," then starts chatting about holiday shopping, and his daughters. "I am Mustafa. Welcome to my cab!" Kelly soon finds out this bear-like man is from Cairo.

As Mustafa chats away, Kelly considers more of Kick's advice. She casually puts her arm on the back of the seat and looks slowly behind her. The black Mercedes is following.

"Would you mind if we take Nelson, boss?" she asks the driver.

"Yes, no problem." He signals to turn right, and Kelly notices that the Mercedes signals right too.

Just before Nelson Kelly tells the driver, "You know what? I'd like to see the lights on the water. Let's take Pacific instead."

"Great idea," Mustafa says. "The lights are beautiful!" He starts talking about all the boats that are decorated for the holidays out in English Bay. The black Mercedes also cancels its right turn and follows them down Pacific as Mustafa keeps conversing along his merry way.

When they're a block from the ivy-covered Sylvia Hotel, Kelly says, "This might be weird, but that Mercedes has been following me. Would you mind pulling over?"

The driver pulls into a parking spot immediately and watches his mirrors. "Yeah, that dog tailgate me, and this I hate more than anything. We will see what he does." The Mercedes goes by, and Mustafa keeps his gaze forward. "Son-of-bitches." He looks at Kelly. "Lady, I was driver for army, and I drive generals and VIP in my country. I will teach this dog something."

A block past the Sylvia the Mercedes turns right on Gilford and disappears, so Mustafa pulls out and speeds into the drop off zone for the hotel. He chuckles. "He is stupid. That street can only go back where he came in a circle." Kelly tips him well and wishes him a good night.

"I go behind him for a while, quick, so maybe he thinks you are still in my cab and they follow me some more." Mustafa laughs as he waves goodbye and Kelly heads into the lobby.

◆ ◆ ◆ ◆

Mustafa does follow the black Mercedes. The driver realizes his mistake and tries to back up the wrong way down Pendrell Street, but Mustafa blocks his way. There's no other traffic on the street, but the parked cars along one side make things tight.

The Mercedes double parks. Mustafa squeezes past it, as normal as can be, and carries on toward Denman. Before he can get there, a green Mercedes comes toward him, blocks the way, and turns on its brights. The black Mercedes snugs up right behind him.

Mustafa's not upset, though. He lowers his sun visor so he can read the diplomatic plates on the car in front of him. He says something to his radio dispatcher and prepares himself.

Mustafa rolls down his window and rests his arm on it, keeping the other one on the wheel. The Mercedes driver walks up beside him. She's a petite Chinese woman in her late twenties, with long black hair tied in a ponytail, dark sunglasses, and wearing a long black trench with the belt tied at the back. Mustafa notices there is a bulge under her right arm. "Yes?"

She lowers her shades, looks in the back seat, then shakes her head at the car in front of her. The green Mercedes maneuvers around Mustafa's cab and speeds toward the Sylvia.

"Do you need a ride?" Mustafa asks her. Her expression doesn't change but her knife moves toward Mustafa's throat in a blur. But Mustafa was an army driver, and he was a really good army driver. So good in fact, that he was recruited by the CIA during the Sadat regime. Taylor and Baker have worked with him on several occasions.

CIA agent Mustafa gets the driver's wrist on the first try with his left hand, bangs it against the edge of the door, and pins it there. He then quickly reaches into her jacket with his right and relieves her of her Type 54 Chinese pistol, with the nice black star on the grip. Before she knows what's going on, Mustafa racks the pistol one-handed between his knees, then yanks the driver's arm hard until her face is just inside the cab. He presses the gun into her gut.

His accent is thick like Egyptian honey. "Drop the knife. Your car must leave now."

The driver lets the knife drop, then yells in Cantonese to the remaining car, "Go to the hotel! I'll handle this. Go!" By her body language and lack of panic indicators, Mustafa can tell she actually believes she can take him. The second Mercedes takes off.

The two regard each other for a moment, and then the driver smiles at him. Mustafa smiles back, then pulls his new friend further into his cab and forcefully jams the gun deep into her mouth, pinning her skull against the doorframe. "Don't look to me like that," he says to her. "I know you speak English, so this is how it works, *habib*." Her head immobilized, the driver's eyes go wide, as she realizes just how fucked she really is. Mustafa frees his left hand, and quickly picks up a syringe with a yellowish liquid in it from his armrest. He jams it into the driver's neck; her scream is muffled by the gun. "The woman from my cab is somebody's daughter, and I will be rewarded for my good deed today, *inshallah*." The driver slumps unconscious into the cab like a rag doll.

Mustafa looks around and sees the closest people are over a block away. He reaches inside her overcoat, grabs the back of her pants and heaves her waif-like body across him into the passenger seat. He reclines it, straps her in, and rolls up his window.

"Pharaoh to Tinker," he says matter-of-factly.

Taylor comes back with, "Go Pharaoh."

"New sleepy passenger visiting from China. *DIP* friends dropped her off. They went back to see Sylvia. I will take her home, over."

"Roger that, Pharaoh," Taylor replies. "Outstanding, and Merry Christmas to me! Tinker, out."

• • • •

Kelly hustles through the Sylvia's lobby and gets into an elevator full of tourists. She exits on the first floor, and no one follows her. She looks out the windows at each end of the hallway and sees no tail. After taking the stairs down to the lobby she sees two cabs jockeying to get to her first. A familiar-looking guy gets out of his cab and waves at her, but she jumps into the first one since it's closer. Just in time too. The green Mercedes rounds the corner. She sees it, and the black one close behind, and slouches down. "The Sutton Place." The cabbie radios in.

The driver leaves immediately. Kelly carefully turns to look out the rear window but can't see anyone tailing them. She tries hard to think about her next steps, and what Kick would do right now. Her thoughts go back to what he said about security at the Sutton. She must get into the lobby.

The Sutton Place hotel comes into view, so she gets her cash ready, but notices that the driver is in the wrong lane to turn. "Wait, it's over there ..." Her cabbie suddenly makes a right into a public parking structure and starts heading down. Kelly shouts, "Hey!"

She tries both back doors, but they won't open, and she can't unlock them. Panic sets in and she searches her purse for the tactical pen, but she realizes she left it in her other coat. Kelly yells at the cabbie, "This won't work. I'm being watched." He's an older Asian man and he gives a thin laugh as he looks at her in the rearview. There's no divider between the back seat and the driver. Kelly takes a deep breath and quickly pulls a blue Bic pen from a pouch on the back of the driver's seat.

Without hesitation, she stabs it deep into the side of the driver's neck, right where Kick told her to put it. He jerks back in shock. Kelly feels like she's floating out of her body as she pulls his head back by the hair and shanks him again, and again, and again, until blood spurts freely from the wounds. The cabbie's foot jams down on the gas, and he gurgle as they slam into the sidewall of the circular ramp. The cab comes to a stop when it rams another parked car at the bottom of the ramp. A few shoppers returning to their cars with their arms full of bags stare in shock. While the driver tries in vain to stop the bleeding, Kelly scrambles up front. Blood sprays all over her as she forces her way out the passenger door. The green Mercedes appears and tears down the ramp. Kelly lets out piercing screams. "HELP! HELP!"

Before anyone in the parking structure can react, two Asian men jump out of the back of the green Mercedes and rush at Kelly. She screams again. Kelly is covered in blood, the bloody cabbie is slumped on the steering wheel, and two thugs muscle her into the waiting black Mercedes. The shoppers stare in horror, as it squeals up towards the exit, smashes through the wigwag, and screams onto the street in a tight turn, threading the needle between other cars. The stink of burning rubber fills the air as the black Mercedes side-winds its way down Burrard toward the bridge to Kits.

◆ ◆ ◆ ◆

Baker's cab roars up beside the Mercedes and clips its back fender. "Breadman to Tinker, package in black Mercedes southbound on Burrard passing Nelson, over," Baker yells into his radio.

He comes alongside and sees the blood-covered Kelly sandwiched between the two guys in the back seat, screaming. She gets a sharp elbow in the face and goes down. The sidewalks are packed with shoppers, so Baker can't force the car off the road. The driver is Asian, mid-twenties, with a scar on his cheekbone. He looks shaken by the pursuit, so Baker gives him a sharp nudge on the side of his car. The driver tries to nudge back, but he's distracted by the upcoming traffic light.

As they both speed into the yellow light at the Davie Street intersection, Baker's cab is clipped on the back fender by another Mercedes, this one blue, and he spins out of control. Doing his best to keep it on the road, he barely avoids a crowd of people by sliding into a streetlight pole, crushing the passenger door.

His car is dead, and both the black and the blue Mercedes are gone. So is Kelly.

"Fuck!" He picks up his radio. "Breadman to Tinker, I'm out of commission. Package is gone. Repeat package is *gone*." He looks around at the gathering crowd, puts on a baseball cap, and pulls up his hood. "Pick me up at LZ 1 in five mikes, over."

There's a pause, then Taylor responds, "Confirmed. See you in five."

Baker kicks open his door, and it opens with a sickening creak. He steps out, keeps his head down, and addresses the growing crowd. "Jesus, did you see that asshole?" Pretending to limp, he heads across the road. "I'm going to call my boss. Tell the cops I'll be right out." Baker heads into a falafel joint, walks out the back door, and disappears into the alley.

30
Returning
Vietnam, 1969

IT TAKES THIRTEEN GRUELING DAYS for Kick to walk out of Cambodia. He's dehydrated, sleep deprived, sore, and hungry, but otherwise has just a few bruises and festering cuts. His mission made ripples all the way to the top of the command structure, and not just in the US. In all the time he's been out of touch, no one knew if he was alive or dead. The sentries at the firebase grill him for a minute when he shows up. He has two weeks of beard growth, and no dog tags, but once he drops the magic word *Phoenix*, it all changes. A coded message goes out to MACV-SOG.

They burn his disgusting clothes at the firebase, get him some first aid, a shower, shave, and fill him with hot chow. He feels reborn. Rumors fly around the base, but the only one with the balls to ask him is a cherry private who issues him new fatigues. "How'd your mission go, sir?"

Kick shows no emotion. "What mission?"

He grabs two hours of rest, propped against some sandbags while he waits for the next chopper. Another bird after that gets him to Danang. He and Colonel Campbell have a brief face-to-face on the ride to a secure room, where he gets a haircut. His dress uniform is somehow there too.

Campbell fills him in, as he gets ready. There isn't time to coach him, or fancy up his mission report, let alone write it. The president is waiting. Kick tells Campbell that his spotter Crawford is dead, and that all the target photographs in his folder checked with a grease pencil have been neutralized. Campbell looks like he wants to kiss him. He warns him that everything he delivers to the brass today must be completely truthful. "Err on the side of humility and don't lie about anything," Campbell tells him.

Ten days ago, Campbell was concerned that Kick had not checked in since his drop. But when General Westmoreland summoned him to an urgent meeting, he knew something big was up. He just prayed his boys hadn't been captured. The general and his top aides tell him that all hell has broken loose in Washington. The Chinese are having a fit. The US embassy received a rare visit from an emissary who demanded answers about an officer assassination in Cambodia. No one had any knowledge of it, and even if they did, they wouldn't discuss it. They did suggest that if China didn't want their officers killed, perhaps they should keep them off active battlefields.

Kick knows this new sniper program is Campbell's baby, and not everyone is on board with it. Other colonels are jockeying for promotions, and sometimes it's not about what you've done to deserve it, but who has fucked up worse than you. Competitors can try to damage you so they look better. Kick's only objective is damaging the enemy, and he knows the higher up Campbell goes, the more damage Kick can unleash.

There is still some backwards thinking in command about snipers being less dignified because they kill from a distance. Some old dogs think it's cowardly. This completely ignores the distances involved in artillery attacks, or B-52 strikes, or the fact that a lot of these colonels fight the war in the rear.

If any of the regular army brass cared to ask, Kick would be happy to give them his opinion on why America isn't doing better. First, you can't bring a rulebook to a guerilla fight. Kick's rulebook is *Sun Tzu*. They're fighting an enemy that *are* the jungle. And the operations at MACV-SOG and Phoenix are making a real difference. It's the special forces boys that are kicking some serious ass.

The Cong and NVA don't defoliate with Agent Orange, or have starlight scopes, and Budweiser. They're using methods proven throughout history. Nomadic tribes used guerilla warfare against the Roman Empire, and the Huns kept the Romans, Visigoth's and Italians on their toes the same way. They became the enemy, so they could *know* the enemy. The only differences between Kick's overnight hunting trips back home and here, are that the weapons are bigger, and his game shoots back.

The President and Secretary of Defense John McNamara want Kick's report right away. Campbell tells him he'll be presenting to a room full of big muckity-mucks and what is known as the Country Team. The latter consists of the US Ambassador, the head of the CIA in Vietnam, and the head of Special Forces in Vietnam.

He also points out that not everyone in the room will be a fan. A lot of the top brass in the regular military hate that they have no control over what SOG is doing, and some think the special forces boys are playing fast and loose with the way they are conducting their part in the war. Not to mention they've done some pretty wild stuff after a few drinks.

Despite this, the President is a big fan of special forces, and Nixon has passed on that he wishes he could honor Kick personally and share the good news with America. God knows the administration needs some. But this is all top secret, and plausible deniability is paramount.

Kick listens to Campbell go on, but it's hard to focus. He feels like an empty shell. Danang is extra hot today, and wearing the full monkey suit just makes it worse. He misses the jungle. So many things are swimming around in his mind — violence, elation, loss, joy, and heartbreak. Hopefully, there'll be drinks at the end of this day. God, he's so hungry. Then they're outside a room with a young lieutenant by the door.

Campbell goes in first to do a pre-amble, while Kick waits for the lieutenant to show him in. Kick tries to remember the walk back to Vietnam, but his mind is hazy. He remembers making blinds to hide himself while he tried to sleep. A couple of nights he spent in trees. At sunup he was on the move again. On his last day, when he knew he was close, he felt the pull in his stomach, and turned to see his first tiger. It sized him up, sniffed the air, and casually walked away. By the fresh blood on its face, he assumed it had just fed. It never hurts to be lucky.

This morning he walked out of the jungle, and now he will perform in a surreal piece of theater so far from his reality, that he thinks this might all be a dream. They are all waiting for him with their bright ribbons and shiny boots. They're all on the other side of this nondescript door. He studies it. Looks like some bullshit hollow-core thing made of Asian mahogany. The wood was probably shipped to the US, made into a door, sold to the military, and then shipped all the way back here, just so he could walk through it. He's going crazy, but he takes a deep breath, and prepares himself. This is the last moment his story will be unwritten. The nervous lieutenant opens the door, and with a slow exhale and perfect posture, Kick steps smartly inside this wonderfully air-conditioned hallucination, and salutes.

He can't stop thinking about the tiger.

31

SAFE HOUSE

WHEN YOU'RE BANGED UP and on the run from the law, there's no better way to blend in than hanging with a bunch of bikers at a strip club. Baker's standing outside the Cecil Hotel like a scolded puppy.

He gets in the van. "Fuck."

"Don't be mad at yourself," Taylor says softly. "Once they had her, there was no way to get her back without a gun battle with hundreds of shoppers in the way. If they wanted her dead, they'd have shot her in the parking lot. She's bait. And we know who the fish is, don't we?"

Baker lights one of Taylor's smokes. "Jesus, easy does it on the smokes there." Taylor laughs. "Next you'll be giving up kale."

Baker shakes his head and coughs a little on the exhale. "I should have had her before she got in that cab, and I should have anticipated the switch in the parking structure. I dropped the ball."

"We were outnumbered and out played, but we have one piece of good news."

"What's that?"

"Mustafa grabbed up a henchman, and he's getting ready to work his magic on her at the house. Wong will help with the language issue."

"That is good news. It's great having Wong here." Baker butts his cigarette, which wasn't going that well for him anyway. "Okay, so we're still in business."

"We're still in business, so clear all that emotion out of your head. There's a hooded ski jacket behind your seat with a day pass on the zipper. I want you to clean out Kelly's room at the Sutton. The key card's in the right pocket. You'll find a beige van parked on lower level two at the hotel." Taylor hands him a set of keys. "I've put all your sniper gear, tactical, and radios in it, plus some other goodies. Head to the house when you've got all her stuff."

"Got it. All Kelly had to do was stay put. I waved right at her at the Sylvia!"

"Yeah, well, civilians," is all Taylor can say. "I'll bring food and everyone else's gear back with me to the house. As soon as we have a location, we can start planning. At this point it could be Chinatown, a warehouse in Richmond, or who knows. It'll be short notice, so be ready to roll."

◆ ◆ ◆ ◆

In a dark, secluded alley in East Vancouver, Mustafa has stripped the Mercedes driver naked. He's searched her clothes, bagged them up, and is getting her into a jumpsuit. He then binds her hand and foot with zip ties that he then covers with duct tape. Her mouth is gagged and taped over, and he blindfolds her blackout style. Mustafa is a stickler for the small details.

She had a pager on her that has several messages, meaning they know by now she's dead, or kidnapped. Her wallet has ID in it that might be real, and there's some cash. Her gun is Chinese government issue. He tosses all her things, except the ID, the pager, and the gun, into a dumpster.

The safe house is an old, thick-timbered two-story from the early 1900's. There's an attached two-car garage, installed by the CIA after they bought it. This allows Mustafa to park, then move his guest unseen into the basement. She's only eighty pounds if she's an ounce, so it isn't hard for him.

In the basement he sits her into a metal chair with armrests and secures her hand and foot to it with more tape. She'll be waking up soon. He turns his head, listening. It sounds like the garage door just went up.

◆ ◆ ◆ ◆

Taylor pulls in driving a green van, having swapped out the black one already, just in case. He buttons up the garage, brings eight large pizzas into the kitchen, then looks around and listens.

"Tinker?"

Taylor smiles. "Pharaoh?"

Mustafa comes around behind him and gives him a bear hug. "I am so happy to see you, Mr. Taylor, and so happy you brought all this food just for me!" They laugh.

"*As-salam alaikum*, Mustafa," says Taylor,

"*Wa-alaykumu s-salam*," responds Mustafa.

"Great work snagging that driver, old friend."

"My pleasure, *habibi*. Here is her gun, pager, and ID, but it could be fake.

We'll have to check with Wong. I look forward to seeing her!"

"Ok. Get some food. It's going to be a long night," says Taylor.

Mustafa slaps two slices of pizza together with the crust on the outside and eats it like a sandwich.

Taylor continues, "Once you're done eating, lay out all this gear in the living room."

Mustafa inhales his pizza like a pro and starts hauling duffle bags into the living room.

There's a knock. Taylor stands to the side of the back door. "Tinker."

"*The White Witch*?" says a voice on the other side. "Who comes up with this shit?"

Taylor checks the peephole. "Do you have to ask?" He opens the door for Wong.

"I'll brief everyone once the whole team's here. You hungry?" Wong follows Taylor into the kitchen, where Mustafa is chewing on another hank of pizza.

"What's up, big guy?" Wong moves in for a hug from Mustafa that takes her well off the floor.

Mustafa says with his mouth full, "My friend. Not since Berlin have I seen you! Welcome. Welcome. Come and see. We have beautiful, encrypted comms!"

Taylor interrupts. "Later for that. I need both of you downstairs."

Wong slaps two slices of pizza together like Mustafa. "Ground beef, feta, and onions, how did you know, Tinker?" They head to the basement.

The captive driver is still unconscious. Wong takes a good look at her. "This should be fun. You took no chances with the clothing, huh?"

"I don't want her fishing out a pill and dying on me."

"Or having one of those super-annoying trackers in the lining of a coat, or a shoe," Wong adds. She gives the driver a mild slap on the face, and she stirs a bit. Mustafa checks her pulse. "What'd you knock her out with?"

"M99," says Mustafa, as he preps another syringe. "She is so tiny, it was tricky. Especially with a gun in her mouth."

Wong giggles. "You are a *nasty* boy." Wong moves to stand behind their captive so she can't be seen, protecting her identity.

Mustafa pushes some of the contents out of the needle in a thin stream.

"Narcan?"

Mustafa nods as he administers the shot. The driver opens her eyes and looks around. She checks out Mustafa, sees her clothes are gone, and struggles to get free.

Wong speaks to her in Mandarin. "Don't waste your energy. We have you now. Answer our questions, and no harm will come to you."

The driver struggles even harder and screams under her gag. Mustafa takes out a new syringe.

"Scopolamine?" asks Wong.

"Sodium amytal," whispers Mustafa. "I have updated things." Mustafa injects her.

The driver's demeanor starts to change. When her head droops, Mustafa nods at Taylor. "Okay, Boss man."

The gag comes off, and Taylor comes over and starts a small tape recorder. The captive looks at him groggily, then looks back at Mustafa.

"I will warm her up with the softballs," Mustafa says. "Do you speak English well?"

The driver laughs. She's groggy but coherent. "I went to Princeton. My English is excellent."

Mustafa laughs with her and continues. "That is very impressive. What is your name?"

"Belle Chang. I'm not afraid." Wong's nod to Taylor indicates her ID looks legitimate.

Taylor asks, "Do you work at the Chinese consulate here in Vancouver?"

"Yes, I work at the consulate. People's Republic of China," she replies.

"Have you ever considered betraying your country?"

The driver snorts. "Oh, many times! They are cheap. I want money. I want nice things."

"And a better life? Living in America some day?"

"Oh, yes. I would love to live in America!"

"Good. Where are your friends that took the woman?"

"Hmmmm. We want the man, not the girl. We want the *ghost man*."

"Okay. If you tell me where the girl is, I will send the ghost man to meet with your people right now. That's what they want, right?"

"Yes! She is at the old harbor."

"In Vancouver?"

"North Vancouver. Old ship-making place. The ghost man likes it and will drop his guard. There will be lots of us. We are there now."

Mustafa looks at his watch and holds up two fingers. Two minutes left for the drug.

Taylor says, "Thank you. The old shipyard in North Vancouver. Which building?"

The driver coughs. "The old one with stacks of wood. Building Six."

"You have done us a great service and will be rewarded."

"How much?"

"How much would you like?" Taylor asks.

"You pay me fifty thousand. US dollars," she says back in Mandarin. She's getting sleepy.

Wong translates the amount, and Taylor nods in agreement. Wong says back in Mandarin, "We will set up your offshore account. Would you like more money all the time? Would you like to work for the CIA?"

"Yes! I will do that. More money. I want a good life," the driver replies. Wong nods a yes to Taylor who is already smiling. Wong writes down her addresses in Vancouver and China, and her phone numbers.

"How many men at the shipyard?"

"Very many." She's drifting off. Mustafa shakes his head.

"Okay. Sleep now, and when you wake, we will play a recording of this conversation to remind you. You work for us now. Understand?"

"Yes. I always want to work for CIA, live a good life … I want nice things …" She passes out.

Taylor stops the recording and says to Mustafa, "That's more than enough leverage. Once she's conscious, confirm what she's agreed to, and what will happen if her handlers get a copy of this tape. Show her a dead drop and some signals. Then take her to Shaughnessy, and make it look like she escaped from our van. She'll make her way to the consulate and give them the story. Give her some bruises."

"Okay, sure," says Mustafa. Wong backhands her across the face twice, kicks her in the shin, and punches her in the chest. Mustafa nods his approval.

"Congratulations, everyone," Taylor says. "We just created a mole."

Taylor shakes Mustafa's hand, as he beams with pride. "This is the reward of patience, preparation, and tradecraft. Pharaoh could have killed this target and moved on. But he played the long game, and created a gift for us that will keep on giving." Mustafa gives Taylor a big hug.

Wong slaps Mustafa on the ass. "Nice work, *Pharaoh*. How'd you get that handle? I'm a witch." Mustafa laughs, and Wong starts cleaning up.

Taylor heads upstairs and grabs a radio. "Breadman, this is Tinker, come back."

"Breadman, go," responds Baker.

"Sneak into Versatile Shipyard in North Van and establish Overwatch. Bad guys in Building Six. They're not expecting us yet. Meet you there at zero one hundred, over."

"Roger that. Out."

Taylor turns around and jumps out of his skin. Kick is standing inside the back door. "Shit! You're supposed to use the protocols, man."

"Just keeping my skills sharp."

"Showoff." Taylor takes him into the living room. "Get geared up. Put a vest on. These new RBA prototypes work well against rifle rounds. Did you hear all that downstairs, or is that a stupid question?"

"Yeah, I got it. That's nice work," says Kick. "But why didn't we get Kelly back?"

"Not possible without killing civilians, and you know it. Shake it off, and let's go make it right. I've got lots of fun toys here."

"It was my fault," says Kick. "I should have stayed with her till Mustafa showed up. My radar was off, and I read her wrong. It was sloppy."

Taylor slaps him on the shoulder. "Come on. We've got a lot to get done. We'll deconstruct this in the morning."

"Sure. I need to bag the clothes I'm wearing for burning. Dusty and I had some trouble."

"I heard. We'll talk about that later. Glad you're both all right."

"About that. Get someone to check on Dusty. He didn't handle it well."

"Oh?"

"Yeah. I sent him off to a beach, but I don't know if he … I need to confirm he left."

Taylor gets it. "I'll have someone check in with the cleaners. They know what's what. I'm sure he's fine."

"And how'd it go with Roger?"

"We couldn't find him, but the manager at the Regent Hotel said it's his regular day off, so don't start worrying yet."

"I don't like the feel of it."

"I've got someone on it, and I'll let you know. By the way, looks like Kelly was coming from Dusty's bar when Mustafa picked her up. He smelled booze on her too."

Kick shakes his head. "Yeah, that sounds about right."

Mustafa and Wong join Kick, and they get into their all-black clothing, gear, and thin black gloves. Taylor lays out the plan. When he's done, Wong and Mustafa go off and start setting up the comms.

"Congrats again on the spy," Kick says to Taylor. "I hope it works out. You're lucky Mustafa got her. My technique would have been drug free."

"Well, lucky for me and her. Look, we'll give you all the cover you need, but I need the leader alive, whether it's White Socks or whoever. *Alive and in one piece*. That's straight from Langley. Got it?"

"Langley? Isn't that the other side of Surrey?"

Taylor doesn't laugh.

172 | THE WAR MACHINE

Kick slips some extra clips into his vest. "Sure. Alive and in one piece."

"Put this in your ear." Taylor holds out a tiny device that looks like a miniature bullet.

"What the fuck is that?"

"If they find a mic and earpiece on you, they'll know you didn't come alone. This is a prototype from Langley. It uses electromagnetic induction so you can speak and hear with just this. Once it's in your ear, they'll never see it. It's pretty much invisible." Kick puts it in, and Taylor looks. "Sweet. You'd have to really be looking for it to see it. How's it feel?"

"Like it's not even there."

"Good. Give me a countdown from ten in a whisper."

Mustafa calls out from the other room, "Loud and clear, Boss." Kick's impressed.

"We'll try and get a mic placed separately, but this way you'll at least be able to hear us."

"I appreciate it."

"Okay. So, let's go get it done." Taylor smacks him on the back and heads to the kitchen. "Probably my last chance to eat for a while."

Wong comes back in. "Hey, stranger! Nice, comms, huh? I'm your wing girl, by the way."

"I work alone, but thanks."

"Can't do that, cowboy," Taylor yells from the other room.

"Why?"

"Too many bad guys. Wong doesn't take up much room. And you'll be hard pressed to keep up with her. She's notched almost as many kills as you."

Kick slips his Ka-Bar into a sheath on the side of his leg and snaps his Glock into the holster. "Don't slow me down."

"I was about to say the same thing," Wong says with a smile. "I'm the *White Witch*."

Taylor sighs. "You can shorten that to *Witchy*."

"Nice! Thanks, *Tinker*." Kick is still waiting.

Taylor's look is pretty much an apology. "*Achilles*. Baker said you'd like the reference, since he was a sacker of cities, and breaker of men." Wong starts laughing.

Kick leaves. "I'm getting some chow. Better not be anything with pineapple on it."

Taylor whispers to Wong, "I think he likes you."

"I heard that," Kick yells from the kitchen.

Wong smacks Taylor on the ass and quips back, "More than he likes you!"

Taylor tries to swat her back, but she's too quick.

Wong laughs all the way into the kitchen to get another slice. "I'm too fast for you, old man Tinker!"

32

OVERWATCH

BAKER SECURES EVERYTHING in Kelly's hotel room into a large metal strongbox on wheels, then wipes down the room for prints. For good measure, he tosses the hotel shampoos, soap, and conditioner into her things. He loads the box into the van, gets his gear on, and assembles his rifle. It's a beast of a weapon.

As part of his port security research, Baker ran recon on the shipyard last year, and has an entry plan and sniper position already mapped out. He parks his van in a lot on St. Georges Avenue in North Vancouver, then takes a ski bag with him that holds his sniper rifle. He puts one downhill ski in the bag so it keeps its shape. It's damn heavy, but anyone who takes a quick look at him in his parka, gloves, and ski gear will think he's heading home from night skiing at Mount Seymour or Cypress. He walks casually down the hill to the shipyard.

In an unlit area close to the water's edge, he puts the ski bag on his back, snaps on his night vision goggles, and slips invisibly over the yard's slat wood fence. He lands behind a pile of rubble. There is no one close by, but figures are moving near one of the large buildings, the equivalent of a city block away. Baker takes out the rifle, slings it across his back, and leaves the ski and bag by the fence. This isn't the first time he's had to scale something wearing this monster.

He gets on top of the rubble pile and reaches up for a cast-iron drainpipe. It seems strong when he pulls at it. There's a slight overhang to get past before getting onto the roof, but it looks doable. The roof has seen better days, and he can tell this is going to be tricky.

Baker works his way up the pipe and swings one foot onto the edge of the roof. Just as he's thinking that all his yoga is paying off, the pipe slowly separates from the building with a low creak. He lets go and grabs the old eaves trough, keeping one leg on the edge of the roof. The twenty-eight-pound rifle on his back isn't helping.

One of Baker's hands explores further up the roof, where he finds a rotten spot, and manages a handhold. He stretches with the second hand, barely gets two fingers into the same hole, and pulls. Some wood breaks away, but he pulls harder. His foot slips off the overhang and swings over, but Baker uses the momentum to pull up hard. It works, and he gets a knee on the edge of the roof, pulls harder, then gets his other leg up too, like a bizarre version of *child's pose*. He slams one hand higher into another rotten place, only to feel a rusty nail rip into the meaty edge of his hand below the pinky. He grits his teeth and suppresses the pain.

Baker knows from his free-climbing days that hand injuries are never as bad as the pain makes you think they are, but he can tell it's a nasty gash. He pulls himself onto the roof and allows himself a soft expletive. "Fuck me …" Baker catches his breath and listens. There's no indication that anyone knows he's there, but he lays dog for five minutes, just in case.

His view when he gets to the top of the roof is excellent. If need be, he can make his way along all the rooftops on the western side of the shipyard.

"Breadman to Tinker."

After a pause Taylor comes back. "Tinker here. We're on scrambled comms so speak freely."

"Roger that. On the roof, southwest corner. Lots of movement at Building Six. About a dozen men around the perimeter of it with AK-47s. I'll try to get a proper count. I have the entire south and west sides of the building covered, plus the main gate and approach from the north. Plus, I'm rooftop mobile on the entire west side, if need be, over."

"Roger that, Breadman. I'll cover the north and east, once we get there."

"Confirmed. Breadman out." With that, Baker unslings his rifle.

Some shooters might say using the Barrett M82 anti-materiel rifle on human targets is overkill, but Baker isn't one of them. As a former Marine sniper, he's found that a lot more power than you need is exactly the right amount of power to have.

This rifle is semi-automatic, because who wants to pull a bolt back every time you need to fire? The M82 was designed to disable vehicles, tanks, and planes, and to explode munitions from a distance. If there are targets behind walls, even brick or cement ones, the M82 cuts right through them. Rounds move through bodies like they're not even there.

After Baker left the Marines, they asked him to test a prototype of the M82, and he liked it so much he never gave it back. They took that as a compliment, and the Corps bought one hundred and twenty-five of them to get started. The weapon's weight, and the way it uses its recoil energy to cycle the action, cuts down on its kick. He had a suppressor made for his that greatly lowers the noise. In Baker's line of work, quiet is good.

He is locked and loaded with the ten-round mag with the night vision scope attached, so he takes off his goggles and looks around through the 10x scope. He ranges the most likely target areas from where he is and makes adjustments to his sights.

His gear is all matte black as are his balaclava and gloves. Taylor left him little hot packs in all the right places to keep him toasty, and other than being hungry, he is ready to rock. He feels a lump in one of the pockets and pulls out a package of beef jerky, "Tinker, you're the best."

The ten or twelve guards are staying close around Building Six, and there's no other movement. He checks the yard. The abandoned freighter is dark and quiet, as are the rest of the buildings. Baker swings over to the guard shack and finds an older Asian man in it. He scans around and sees an AK-47 hanging on the back of his chair. There's no company patch on his jacket, which confirms that he's one of the bad guys. He can also just see the feet of what must have been the overnight guard. Baker lets out a deep sigh and settles in.

◆ ◆ ◆ ◆

Kick walks over to the phone and looks at it while it rings. He looks up at Taylor, Wong, and Mustafa and says flatly, "Besides present company, Kelly's the only other person with this number." Taylor steps in, picks up the receiver, and offers it to him.

Kick takes it without hesitation. "You must be the shithead with the stupid fuckin' socks." Taylor looks down and shakes his head.

There's the hint of a laugh, then a voice says, "If you want to see Kelly alive again, come to your old shipyard in North Vancouver. You come. She goes free. All I want is you — and your stupid fuckin' head."

Kick stays ice cold. "Proof of life, asshole."

There's some scuffling, then Kelly's strained voice. "I'm all right. Sorry I didn't listen."

"Come alone," says White Socks. "You have one hour, *youling*. Then I start to chop things off."

"Wait, there's no way I can get there that fast!" Kick protests.

There is a click, and a dial tone. Kick hangs up.

"*Youling* means ghost," says Wong. Kick thinks about that.

"That's what they called you over there, right?" asks Taylor.

"Among other things. Narrows it down to my four years in 'Nam, like that helps."

Wong asks, "Why? How many kills did you have?"

"It's best we don't talk about that," Taylor says, as his radio crackles.

"Tinker, Breadman."

"Tinker here, go."

"Overwatch operational. It's a baker's dozen — excuse the pun — around Building Six. Several cars and vans. It's the only building with any activity. Perimeter surveillance looks like guard shack only at this point. Like they want him to walk right in."

Taylor looks at Kick and Wong, who are now all geared up. Wong checks her Colt AR-15 SP1 rifle, fitted with a night vision scope and silencer. "Nice gear, Taylor. I love the AR," She fills up her vest with extra twenty-round mags.

"I'm point," Kick says.

"I figured, *Achilles*." Wong laughs and tucks her blue hair under her watchman's cap.

Taylor grabs Kick's shoulder. "Don't let her fool you. She's a wrecking machine. You'll see. Baker has the eighty-two, and mine will be looking south from across the street, so we'll have you covered. I'll coordinate from there. Wong, take one of those small walkies too, in case the bad guys cheaped out, and you can listen in."

Wong says, "Wouldn't be the first time."

"Let's do this right," concludes Taylor. "We make them think you've come alone for as long as we possibly can."

Kick checks out Wong. "Okay, *Witchy*. You'll get an idea of my rhythm as we go."

"Yeah, *white boy*. You go ahead and tell me all about rhythm!" Wong laughs and heads for the kitchen. "I'm getting another slice for the road. You should take one too, sacker of cities." Wong laughs harder.

Taylor looks at Kick and shrugs. "She'll grow on you."

33

Debrief
Danang, Vietnam, 1969

KICK FLOATS INTO THE COOL SMOKY ROOM full of brass, all seated at long tables. Aides, lieutenants, and ARVN officers stand at the edges. He recognizes the ambassador and a man he knows is Colonel Rheault, the new commander of special forces in Vietnam. Colonel Campbell indicates someone at the back of the room. It's General Creighton Abrams, the commander of all US forces in Vietnam. Kick faces him, stands at attention, and snaps off a sharp salute, which is returned. Abrams doesn't look that happy. A young man in plain clothes adjusts a microphone in front of Kick and starts a reel-to-reel deck recording. A camera is rolling at the back of the room.

Kick is told to stand at ease and Colonel Campbell briefly introduces him, then comes over, shakes his hand, and whispers in his ear, "Start with the kill shot. Hold nothing back, and don't take any shit." Campbell sits down beside a hard-looking man in a dark suit.

There is a map of Vietnam, Cambodia, and Laos on the wall behind Kick, with a red pushpin in the spot where he had initially been dropped. Kick clears his throat and dives in. "I had been operational for several hours in an elevated position above the trail. If I may?" he asks, picking up a green pushpin.

"Go ahead," replies Campbell. Kick finds the correct spot, then sticks it into the map where he stationed himself on the Ho Chi Minh Trail, miles from the red pushpin.

"A contingent of fourteen cadres entered the area just before sixteen hundred hours. Dusk or early morning, tend to be the best times."

"Why is that, Sergeant Tacker?" asks a light colonel at the back.

"In the morning, cadres are well rested and fed, have had tea, and are excited about the day. They tend to be talkative, and often aren't yet focused. In the evening, they tend to be tired, hungry, and with poor concentration. Plus, the light is low at both times."

"Please continue," says Campbell.

"After several minutes, I was able to confirm the identity of the general and some suspected spies on my target-of-opportunity list. I immediately neutralized the primary target with one shot to the head. The secondary target became extremely agitated and ran around, so I took out two more cadres and continued to pick off targets until I could acquire him."

Another question comes from a different colonel at the back. "Did you just say that you took out the general first? With a single head shot?"

"Yes, sir," Kick answers. A few men at the back whisper among themselves. They have a definite special forces look to them.

"At what distance?" asks another colonel.

"Approximately eight hundred and fifty meters, sir." Somebody gives a low whistle. Kick's embarrassed by the attention.

Campbell smiles. "Outstanding. Continue, please."

Kick realizes he hasn't had a smoke since he left the firebase, and he's jonesing. He clears his throat again and carries on. "It was only a matter of time until one of them spotted my muzzle flash. A couple of them saw it and pointed, and the natural reaction was for everyone else to try and find me. They all stopped moving and stared directly at my position, including the secondary target. At that time, I neutralized him. A headshot as well."

Abrams is looking at the still dirty intelligence photos of the now deceased top two targets, plus several other pictures who have check marks on their faces. He gives no expression as he flicks away some debris from one of the pictures.

The man in the dark suit asks, "What is the greatest distance you have eliminated a target from?"

"That would be slightly over seventeen hundred meters—that's eighteen hundred yards—sir, in perfect conditions, with no wind. And with the Remington 700, sir. I would like to point out something else at this time, if I could?" The man in the suit nods to go ahead. "These cadres were carrying semi-automatic Russian-made Dragunov sniper rifles. Not a perfect weapon, but a sniper rifle just the same. In my estimation, I interrupted a sniper training mission, sir."

Dark Suit smiles as he lights a cigarette. "Thank you. Please continue."

"At this point, I considered my mission compromised and realized that, as they say here, the tiger was about to hunt me back. I had some claymore trips and traps set up, and escape and evasion maneuvers planned, but before I carried these out, I wounded two more cadres."

The man in the suit again speaks up. "Why did you do that?'

Kick can tell he already knows the answers to the questions he's asking but needs the others to appreciate the reasons for success. "Wounding them took very little time and meant two or three others would have to stay behind to treat them. I doubt they survived the night, since they were both belly wounds. That result was that the force of fourteen had been reduced to just three or four that could pursue. I had elevation and distance, plus I had the sun behind me. There was a half-moon that night too. I thought I could manage that number on the run."

There's soft chuckling from the special forces types at the back. Kick can tell he clearly has a few fans in the room. Abrams shoots them a dagger.

The man in the suit smiles as he takes note of who's laughing, then asks. "So, you effectively took out most of the snipers they were training?"

"All but two or three, yes."

Dark Suit again. "And you carried out this mission alone, correct?"

"Yes, that's correct."

"Why was that?"

"My spotter, Crawford, was KIA on the drop. Broke his back in a tree. I was careful to deny the enemy anything valuable he had on him like chow, weapons, ammo, and of course maps, plus I neutralized the field radio."

Colonel Campbell sits up. "How? And why?"

Kick is feeling like a schoolboy in front of his teachers. "There was no way I could carry it with the rest of my gear, and I couldn't leave it for the enemy. I had heard of suppressors being made from oil filters and flashlight casings, so I made one from Crawford's canteen. After I drank the contents of course. I fired rounds from my .45 through the canteen and into the radio, including the battery, sir."

No one chuckles this time. The special forces guys are smiling at the back with their arms crossed. The two opposing factions in the room are obvious. There are special forces boys and the regular military, and they are not going to be friends today.

Dark Suit asks, "You destroyed the radio knowing that you'd have no way to call for artillery, or exfiltration?"

"Yes, sir. There was no room for my Erk-10 emergency radio on this jump, so I had to decide to fish or cut bait, sir, and I felt good about my chances." There is a stony silence.

Campbell asks, "Did you return with Crawford's dog tags?"

"No, sir. We wore no tags, uniforms, or rank insignia since we were outside the normal area of operations, sir."

"Understood," says Campbell. "And where did you leave Corporal Crawford?"

"In the tree, sir, but he's not visible from the ground unless you're really looking. And there's less chance of his body being disturbed by animals there. I would be happy to lead a bright light mission to recover his body."

"We will be putting together a plan for that, but let's get back to your escape. How long did these soldiers pursue you?" asks Colonel Campbell.

"Just over two days, sir." A murmur rumbles through the room, and heads turn to catch Abrams' reaction. His face is granite.

"And what was the end result of the chase?" asks Dark Suit.

"I eventually eliminated the four targets pursuing me, along with three others who later joined them with dogs. Some of them were on my TOA list — targets of opportunity."

Campbell is beaming. "Outstanding soldiering, son. Just *outstanding*. Continue."

"From that point on, I ate what I could kill, and moved at best speed toward the western border of South Vietnam." Kick puts another pin in the map. "I got help from some 'yards.' That is, little people. No disrespect, I mean the mountain people — Montagnards, sir. They helped me find my way to the firebase at Phuoc Vinh, where the 1st Cavalry eventually contacted SOG, and here I am, sir."

No one says anything for half a minute until General Abrams stands.

The man in the dark suit says, "I could really use a cold beer. How about you, Sergeant?"

Kick answers without thinking. "Yes, sir. It's thirsty work."

The room fills with laughter and applause. Even Abrams smiles a bit. The man stops the reel-to-reel and begins rewinding it. The camera is shut off.

It will all be copied and sent via diplomatic pouch to the White House for President Nixon, with one copy secured in a top-secret location.

Abrams comes forward and shakes Kick's hand. "I look forward to hearing about your future missions, Tacker." Abrams then walks right past Colonel Campbell and Colonel Rheault without saying a word.

The ambassador gives Kick's hand a quick shake then hurries after General Abrams.

Colonel Rheault smiles broadly as he steps up to Kick and shakes his hand. "Those were some very bad men you put down." He leans in and whispers in Kick's ear. "We've got a mole in Saigon responsible for countless American deaths, and we know those sons a bitches were part of it. It's an honor to shake your hand. I'll be putting you and Crawford in for commendation." He stands back again and smiles. "And, by the way, my old man's Canadian. We should have a beer sometime."

Colonel Rheault slaps Campbell on the back, winks at the man in the suit and walks out.

The rest of the colonels file past but only the special forces crowd stop to shake Kick's hand and congratulate him. In the end, it's just Campbell, Kick, and the man in the dark suit remaining.

Dark Suit looks at Campbell. "Well, that was pretty fuckin' interesting."

"You must be starved after eating snakes," says Campbell. "Let's rustle up some steaks in the officers' mess. There's something urgent we need to discuss."

34

SHOWDOWN

WONG IS STILL EATING PIZZA, sitting beside Kick on the floor of the van. Taylor is driving.

"Breadman to Achilles."

"This is fucking Achilles, go," Kick responds.

"Right. You don't like the handle. Sorry. Listen, there's a real guard who is KIA and been replaced by an unfriendly in the guard shack. Is Buck supposed to be working tonight?" Kick hasn't had time to consider whether Buck may have been taken out. He thinks for a moment, then smiles. "Today is the lucky bastard's only night off."

"I've been wanting to make use of him for a while," Taylor says, "We have time, if he's available."

Kick scribbles a number on a scrap of paper with his tactical pen and hands it to Taylor. "There's a phone right at the bar where I guarantee he's sitting right now. Tell him to meet me ASAP in the old boiler room and say it's urgent. He's army. He'll be there. I'll need another radio to link him in, and a silenced handgun if you have one."

"You know I come loaded for bear." Taylor lights a cigarette. "Thanks for that, Breadman. We're on it."

◆ ◆ ◆ ◆

Baker swings his gaze back to Building Six. "Roger that. Give Kick's boy the call sign, 'Huntsman.' Breadman, out." Baker smiles at the inside joke.

He sees one of the guards touch his hand to one ear, then start talking. The other guards are doing the same one by one, which means they're doing a communications check. He marks the time. He takes out his secondary walkie and tucks the plug into his free ear, then cycles through the channels. He locks onto the channel they're using. Next time he'll try and get a head count and clock their check-in time. It could prove to be invaluable.

◆ ◆ ◆ ◆

Back in the van, Wong sticks an elbow into Kick. "You got ripped off with Achilles. Being a sniper, you should have been Apollo. Or something like Snowman in this fucking weather. How cold is it anyway?" Kick's not in the mood, but Wong's persistent. "You don't talk much, do you?"

"Let's keep it operational from here on."

Wong shakes her head. "You used to be fun."

Taylor has already touched base with Mustafa, who called Buck and confirmed his participation. The captured driver has sobered up to her situation, which includes a pounding headache from the drugs, but it looks like she will ultimately play the game. There's no ambiguity about how China will deal with her if they find out she squealed. There'll be prolonged torture, then death, possibly for her family too. If they do end up shooting her, the People's Republic of China will be kind enough to send a bill to the family for the cost of the bullet.

Half an hour later, Taylor is approaching the Richardson Port in North Vancouver. Kick's familiar with it since they've smuggled a few things in and out that way from time to time. It's a small but mighty terminal that ships out canola and cereal grains to the Pacific Rim. Trains a mile or two long deliver loads from the Canadian prairies. Security tends to be light since not many people want to run off with a truckload of wheat germ. Kick checks his watch. They are cutting the time close but assuming nothing goes wrong, he should make his entrance right on time.

Kick and Wong slip out of the van, hop over the guardrail, and hunker down under a stationary rail car. They don night vision goggles, and Kick leads them between two parked trains running parallel to the waterline. In less than five minutes they are a stone's throw from Pier Number One, jutting out from the eastern edge of the shipyard. There's just a chain link fence separating them. He can see Pier Two past it, and the freighter *St. Jude* moored like a lonely soul at Pier Three.

"Achilles to Breadman, Witchy and I at your two o'clock."

"Roger that, Achilles. I have visual. All clear. Witchy, be advised, target's channel on your other walkie is five, repeat, five. Haven't got a headcount yet but looks like around twelve or thirteen."

Wong responds. "Roger that, Breadman."

Taylor chimes in, having taken his position. "Tinker here. Overwatch in position across the road, north of Building Six. Clear view of the north and east sides. Three bogies on north side: one in guard shack, one bogie is moving around seven-five feet due south of guard shack, and a wild card in the far east corner. Breadman, can you see the wild card?"

"Negative, Tinker. Must be behind a building." replies Baker.

"Copy that," says Taylor. "I'm keeping wild card as my target of opportunity when the time comes."

"Copy that," confirms Baker.

"Breadman, we're heading to your building to meet Huntsman," says Kick.

"Roger that, Achilles."

Kick cuts through the fence, and they arrive at Pier Number One.

"You are good to go, Achilles," reports Baker, and they leapfrog silently past the huge Works Building, moving along the waterline past Pier Two. They get another all-clear from Baker, then scurry across the Pier Three service road and take cover against Baker's building.

"Heading inside," informs Kick.

"Roger that," responds Baker.

The night vision goggles reveal all kinds of old equipment and gear, and a very nasty-looking roof.

"Breadman, watch your step up there," Kick whispers to Baker. "Parts of your roof have fallen in."

"Copy that."

Kick leads on through piles of rubble until he gets to a room with an old rusty door. They approach it carefully, and Kick takes a quick look inside. No one is visible. He heads in with his AR-15 ready, then stops. Wong moves quietly past him and sweeps the area in front of her. After a thorough look, they determine the building is clear.

"Boiler room, clear, over," Kick reports. "Any sign of Huntsman, Breadman?"

Before Baker can answer, Wong sniffs the air, taps Kick's arm, and points her AR at a pile of debris. "Contact," she says in a hushed voice.

Kick sees nothing, but Wong takes a step forward and kicks something. It jerks a bit, then the rest of a person emerges from the heap. Kick can tell it's Buck by his belly. He's dressed in his favorite heavy plaid lumberjack shirt and watchman's hat, and you could light his breath on fire. Buck can't see anything in the dark. Wong keeps her sights on him, and asks, "What's the password?"

Buck takes a wild guess. "Gin rummy?"

Kick whispers, "That'll do. Keep your voice down, Huntsman."

Buck looks confused for a second, then whispers back, "Huntsman. Gotcha. I got here early and hid. Musta dozed off."

Kick pulls him up. "I'm Achilles. This is Witchy."

Wong takes in Buck, in all his redneck beer-belly glory, and says quietly, "It's like discovering a new species. Preserved in alcohol."

"Tinker, we have Huntsman."

"Copy that."

Kick decides that after the next comm check, Buck will approach the guard in the shack under the guise of saying hello on his way home. Once he gets close enough, he'll quietly kill the guard, then take his position in the shack.

Wong asks, "Can you repeat that back, Huntsman?"

Buck takes a second. "Gonna figure a way to snuff the guard, then pretend I'm him."

Wong shrugs, and they set Buck up with thin black gloves, a silenced Glock, and a tiny earpiece.

"Fuckin' Jesus, that's like a little bug in my ear."

Wong adjusts his earpiece. "Keep your chatter down, Huntsman, and just … do your best with all this. It'll probably get weird."

Kick tells him, "Be ready to improvise, if need be, and wait for my signal."

"No problem. Gimme a minute to get over the fence though. It's tougher than it looks." Buck disappears.

Wong heads out the door, and they slowly leapfrog up toward the corner of the building. Kick's tight against the wall, and creeping closer, when there's a pull in the pit of his stomach. His fist comes up, they stop cold, and Wong takes a knee. Even with night vision he would have missed the sentry, out of sight around the corner.

Kick is extra quiet. "Contact. Tinker, you see a bogie at my eleven, around the corner?"

After a pause, Taylor responds with, "Shit, I'm just getting a piece of his arm. Breadman, when is their next comm check?"

"Should be sixty seconds," Baker says.

"Hold, Achilles." Kick's AR goes over his shoulder, and his Ka-Bar silently slips out. He moves quietly to the corner, squats down, and waits. The arthritis in his knees is killing him. He breathes slowly and quietly.

"Movement on the bogie," reports Taylor. "He's touching his walkie."

Wong whispers, "Comm check underway. Let me get a head count."

"Agreed." Kick's knees are screaming, but he holds.

After a long moment Wong reports, "One-five bogies on the comm check, over."

Taylor orders, "Achilles, go, go, go."

Kick painfully stands up and steps around the corner. At the same time, Buck falls over on the other side of the wooden fence, making just enough noise to make Kick's target jump and look the other way. Kick can see in the dark and has the element of surprise. He covers his target's mouth and nose with one hand, cuts his throat with the other. He tightens his grip and pushes his target's face into the ground. It takes only a few seconds for him to lose enough blood to pass out. The entire process is surprisingly quiet. When his movements stop, Kick positions his knife between two vertebrae and severs his spinal cord.

He turns to find Wong covering his six. "Complete." She gives him a thumbs up behind her back. Kick realizes this girl is cold as ice.

"Roger that, Achilles. One-four to go," says Taylor.

"Plus, the leader," Kick adds.

Kick moves past Wong, crosses the roadway, and huddles behind an old shipping container.

Wong is about to follow when Baker stops her. "Hold." She freezes. "Bogie due east. You must have snuck right past on your way in."

"When's the next comm check?" Wong asks.

"They're everyone one-zero mikes, so eight mikes from now," replies Baker.

They make their way down the front of the waterline until they see the sentry they missed. He's getting ready to light a cigarette. Kick says, "Witchy …"

Wong's silenced *plink* comes before he can say the word *go*. Her target's Zippo falls, and the body drops. Kick is now officially impressed.

"One-three bogies to go." Wong says, cool as an icicle. She moves over to the dead guy, quietly closes the Zippo, and leaves it on the ground.

"Roger that, Witchy." says Taylor, with a smile in his voice. "Let's get rid of those three on the south side of Building Six. Kick, take the one on the east corner. Be dead quiet. We can't spook the one south of the gate."

"Roger that, Tinker. Witchy has the other two. Looks like she's all warmed up."

"Seven mikes before comm check," Taylor states.

Wong glides up toward the southwest side of Building Six, while Kick picks his way to the other corner. He stops cold when he sees his target. He stands six foot three and is easily two hundred and seventy-five pounds. Getting him to make a soft landing will be a challenge. Kick looks at the two small guys on Wong's side.

"Achilles, you need help with that whale?" Wong asks softly.

He considers getting Baker to take him out, but that round would continue into the building itself and ruin the whole party. "Negative."

"Tinker, I have a hippo. He's going to make noise. Adjusting Huntsman's mission."

"Lay it out, Achilles."

"Go for Huntsman," comes Buck's sloppy voice. "I'm forty feet from the guard shack."

"On my go, go up to the sidewalk and yell at the guard, like you think he's the weekend guy. Just shoot the shit real loud until we tell you to stop."

"Fuckin' right, Antilles. Will wait for your go."

"Witchy, you good?" asks Taylor.

"All good, Tinker," replies Wong.

"Breadman, if it comes to it, take target south of guard shack. I'll get the wild card, if need be," says Taylor.

"Roger that, Tinker."

"Take it away, Achilles," orders Taylor.

Kick's massive target is looking out at the water, and Wong's guys look bored and cold. "Huntsman, go, go, go."

◆ ◆ ◆ ◆

Buck has to take a mean piss, but puts duty first; he gets up to the sidewalk, then heads toward the guard. There is no one else around, and just scattered cars passing by. Buck knows it's mostly people coming from bars. Except for the car coming toward him now. Buck gives everyone a heads-up. "Cop car driving past." It slows, and the driver's window comes down.

"You okay there, Buck?" asks the cop behind the wheel.

"Hey, I thought that was you, Jerry! Keepin' busy?"

Jerry the cop laughs. "You know it, pal. Where you comin' from?"

"Wally's. Pretty good night there. Figured I could use the exercise and walk home." The cop's radio squawks. "Gotta run, Buck," Jerry says quickly. "You get home safe now." He takes off.

Taylor says, "Cop is gone. Proceed, Huntsman."

Buck spins around and looks right at the guard shack. "Manny? Holy shit, I thought you fuckin' quit!" He takes a few steps toward him.

The guard looks irritated. Buck can see the bad guy has made himself right at home in his shack. There's a bowl of Buck's instant noodle soup sitting out, and his winter coat is on the back of his chair. Fuckin' asshole's drinking out of his mug.

He can also see the bad guy to the south of the guard shack carefully moving up to see what's happening but staying in the shadows with his AK-47.

Wong is talking in his earpiece. "They're telling the guy to shoo you off, Huntsman."

"We'll see about that," Buck mumbles. He then launches into a tirade about the security company's management. Taylor mutes his comm. Everyone can hear him anyway.

◆ ◆ ◆ ◆

Kick hears Buck yacking away at the guard. His huge target has turned around to follow the commotion. He calls it. "Witchy, go, go, go." Kick moves at the same time. Wong is so small and low that her first target has no idea she's even there. *Plink, plink.* Her two rounds hit him right under the nose, and he keels over. Kick sees her pivot left to her second target, as Kick stands and puts two rounds into the back of the big guy's head. Chunks fly off, and he wobbles, but somehow doesn't fall.

Kick knows he's already dead, but there's a real danger he's going to fall like an old oak tree. He checks on Wong and her second target, who just watched the fat guy's head come apart. It looks like he's trying to say, "Oh shit …" Wong comes at him fast and puts two in the side of his head. He drops, and she turns to fat boy.

Kick doesn't have time to figure out why his unfriendly giant is still upright. He pulls his Ka-Bar and severs the tendons at the back of one knee. The leg buckles, and he crumples to the ground in a spiral just as Buck yells, "I woulda fuckin' quit too, man!" The sound of the impact is effectively muted.

There's a wisp of gun smoke hanging at eye level as Wong gives Kick a big smile and a thumbs up. She's obviously getting a real kick out of this. Tufts of blue hair are sticking out from under her cap, and he can't help but wonder how so much violence got jammed into such a tiny package. She's like walking dynamite.

"Complete," whispers Kick. "One-zero bogies to go."

◆ ◆ ◆ ◆

The guard in the shack is talking into his radio. Having heard the guards are down, Buck feigns shock and yells, "You're not fuckin' Manny! Who the in the name of …? Never mind. That's just fuckin' typical, eh?"

Buck moves back to the sidewalk and spews away about getting the union in here, and what a great guy Manny was, and how there's no loyalty anymore. The guard starts to snicker, then says something else into his walkie. When he's far enough away, Buck whips out his dick and starts a very long, satisfying leak. "I piss all over this fuckin' company." The sentry on the other side of the shack and the guard are getting a good laugh out of it all. Buck lets out a huge belch and continues his tirade.

Wong translates, "The guard's calling him something like a 'white trash country boy.'"

Taylor breaks up the party. "*Two mikes* to comm check. Ready, Breadman?"

"Target locked."

"Once Baker and I take out our two targets, Achilles and Witchy take a fast position at the northeast corner of Building Six. You will take the three on the north side, while I hit the guard shack. Baker, you watch the building in case they hear us. Buck, stay where you are for now."

"Got it," says Buck as his piss continues. He has the best seat in the house.

Taylor counts down. "Three, two, one, go, go, go!"

◆ ◆ ◆ ◆

Kick and Wong run to the south corner of Building Six as Taylor and Baker's shots hit both targets in the chest, blowing chunks the size of baseballs several feet out the exit wounds in their backs. They're thrown off their feet and skid to a stop face up. The exit wounds are facing down, so unless someone spots the bloody chunks, it looks like they were shot with a conventional gun.

Kick and Wong are around the corner before the bodies hit the ground. Their three targets are looking right at them. Wong drops low and takes the first in line, while Kick stays upright and hits the man at the far end with two in the chest. There is no time to pity the middle guy, who looks completely confused and can't get his gun up in time. They hit him with two shots each to the head. There's not much left of it. From the corner of his eye, Kick sees Buck on the sidewalk, looking on in awe. He's still taking a piss.

Kick sees movement in the guard shack as Taylor's first shot goes wide. "Bastard!" Taylor says. The guard is leaving the shack with his walkie. Taylor's second round hits the guard's arm at the elbow. It explodes and the arm is effectively amputated. Kick and Wong don't have clean shots. The guard stares in shock at his arm stump spouting blood.

"Huntsman, take him!" commands Taylor.

Buck pulls his silenced Glock, runs to the guard, and puts two in his head. "He's fuckin' dead, Stinker," is his protocol-free response. "An' fer the record, I *am* a country boy."

Wong can't suppress a quiet laugh. "That was fucking wild!"

"*Four bogies* remain, plus the leader," Taylor says, "I'm starting to like these odds."

"Reloading," says Kick, as he and Wong refresh their mags.

"Huntsman, slip into the shack and slump over like you're shot," says Taylor.

"Fuckin' pleasure, Tinky," he says as he puts some old plywood over the guard's body.

"And Huntsman, keep your gloves on. We can't have prints."

"Yup." Buck gets into the shack and stops. Stepping back out, he reaches down and carefully picks up the guard's severed arm and puts it on the floor where anyone checking will notice it. As he does, he sees the dead body of his friend Manny. He shakes his head, and puts on the guard jacket, folding one sleeve underneath to make sure he maintains the illusion of having one arm missing. He keeps his Glock hidden, and slumps forward so he can still see what's happening. Remembering something, he stands, and puts his dick back in his pants. He zips up and slumps back down. "Huntsman in position, *Tinkle*."

"Roger that," Taylor says. "Witchy, get out of sight, so you can cover Building Six and Achilles. Breadman and I will stay in position. We made it with no time to spare, folks."

"Roger that," confirms Wong. "Rest of the plan still the same, Achilles?"

Kick looks at the building, knowing Kelly is in there. "Affirmative. Hopefully these assholes still want me alive." Kick is on one knee at the east end of Building Six, in line with the main door, with his AR-15 locked and loaded on full auto.

Wong whispers to Taylor, "Comm check happening. Oh fuck — they're freakin' out."

Taylor says calmly, "Get ready, Kick."

At a volume that's barely audible Kick growls, "I have a rendezvous with death."

The big door facing Kick slowly opens and two guards look around cautiously. They carefully step out and see one of their dead comrades. Kick opens fire. One bad guy goes down right away, but the second gets off two shots before Kick can hit him. The first bullet goes wide, but the second hits Kick just above his heart and is caught by his bulletproof vest. It feels like he's been hit with a cannonball. The force knocks him back off his feet. His rifle flies out of his hands, and he lands with a painful thud on his back. As he tries to catch his breath, he hears a single *plink*, followed by the sound of the second man falling.

The last thing he hears is Wong whispering, "Two down. Two plus the leader, remaining. Achilles took a hit in the vest. He's still breathing ... I think."

35

PUSH

KICK HEARS ANGRY VOICES YELLING in Mandarin as he wakes up. He's freezing. The left side of his chest is pounding like a jackhammer. He looks down at it and sees a large crimson bruise with thick rings rippling out. The vest took most of the bullet's impact, but it still hurts like a bitch. He feels the handcuffs on his wrists. His mouth is taped, and his bare legs are taped to the legs of his chair. They have him stripped to his boxers, and all his weapons are on the floor in front of him. The AR-15, Glock, ammunition, tactical pen, and Ka-Bar are all there. His clothes and bulletproof vest are in a pile. He can feel the earpiece is still intact as he looks around.

Kelly is nowhere to be seen, but he senses someone behind him and takes a deep inhale. There's a trace of perfume. Honeysuckle, mixed with heavy fear sweat. They must have her bound in a chair, back-to-back with him. He reaches out, finds one of her quivering hands, and gives it a squeeze. She squeezes back hard and holds it. He can feel her terror. Kick can also feel the arm of her coat, which means they've been gentlemen, of sorts, and kept her clothed.

There is one guard in the room giving him a mad-dog glare. He has one arm in a sling, and Kick figures he's the one Wong shot the other night outside the van. Probably mad that his friends are all dead. Good. An older, heavy-set Chinese man stands behind him. Kick recognizes the dick-of-all-trades local crime boss, Mr. Chung. Far in the background, sitting on a crate, is a young Chinese man with one foot up, revealing a white sock.

A second guard runs into the room and starts shouting in Mandarin and pointing excitedly in different directions towards outside. When he's finished, the older fat man walks up to Kick and backhands him across the face, then again the other way. He screams at him in Mandarin. Kick maintains eye contact, as best he can. The two guards are visibly shaken, knowing they are the only ones left. The one who just came in has a scar on his cheekbone. It's the driver who took Kelly.

Taylor's soft voice is in his ear. "Achilles. Cough once for yes, twice for no. Can you hear me?" Kick coughs once, muffled by the tape on his mouth. "Good. Stand by."

Kick checks the angle of his chair against the sightlines of the bad guys and moves his hands slowly under Kelly's jacket to the waistband of her jeans.

Chung screams a question at White Socks, and he replies in English, with a touch of a Hong Kong accent. "I told you what he was capable of, but you didn't take me seriously. Did they ... *youling*?"

Kick looks right at White Socks as he silently removes a bent bobby pin and cups it in his hand. "You'll all be ghosts by sunrise," Kick says back, his voice muffled by the tape.

Chung is livid; he keeps screaming at White Socks. "Why didn't you bring *your* men? How do I explain this to their families? I've known them since they were boys! Authorities are snooping in my bank accounts now! A man was killed today in this asshole's apartment. Opened a cupboard and got a wooden stake in his eye! This man is big trouble!" Chung screams. "You are nothing but problems!" White Socks keeps smoking, completely unconcerned. "And *how*?" Chung asks. "How can *one* man do all this outside? In minutes? And we heard nothing? Not possible! Someone is helping him!"

"How?" White Socks gets up from his crate and drops his smoke. He points to Kick's weapons. "Silencers, and night vision, stupid. But to understand someone like him, you have to understand his story. His real story. Right, *David*?" Kick's eyes widen involuntarily. "We meet at last, Mr. Tacker." He turns back to Chung. "Born in Port Hardy on Vancouver Island. He killed hundreds in Southeast Asia. A real chip off the old block. His daddy did the same in the Second World War, where he found God. Later, Daddy went to Jesus by his own hand, because he couldn't handle the past."

Chung lights a cigarette and walks back and forth muttering in Mandarin, his hands shaking with rage. From the corner of Kick's eye, he sees a tiny bit of movement at the bottom of a wall to the left.

Wong comes on the comm. "Mic in position, Tinker."

"Recording is loud and clear, Witchy. Resume position. Achilles, try and get them talking, if you can."

Kick coughs once through the tape.

White Socks comes over to Chung and steals his smoke. Chung swallows his pride and lights another. "First Sergeant David Tacker — known as

Kick only to his closest friends —went berserk after his special forces buddy Hollywood dropped artillery on his own head. Talk about a metaphor! I can see the headline — *Hollywood Fantasy Dies in Vietnam*. He might as well have been John Wayne, right, Kick?"

White Socks takes a big drag on his cigarette and blows the smoke in Kick's face. "Poor David tried to take on the whole patrol but got dragged away. Living to fight another day." Rage, sadness, and embarrassment boil inside Kick, but he holds it in. "TV brought us closer together to watch America torch the global village." White Socks laughs. "Some Marshall McLuhan. You see, I was educated in America. I know its weaknesses, and I am dedicated to bringing this arrogant, self-righteous bully, with its bloated suburban soccer-mom mentality, to its fucking knees. The West is *soft*. It's complacent about its democracies, and ripe for the plucking." He believes everything he's saying.

"Oh," adds White Socks. "I'm very sorry about your dumb friend Roger who guarded the tunnel to your little hideaway. Chung's boys took care of him. Too bad." White Socks holds a baggie with two ears in it in front of Kick's face. Kick screams and tries to explode out of his chair, but he can't.

Taylor whispers, "Easy, Kick. Breathe."

He looks at the floor and slows his breathing.

White Socks laughs. "Like America, you think you're invincible. You see Mr. Chung, the legend of the *youling* was that of an invincible spirit that no one could touch. Everyone thought you were …"

Wham!

The backhand lands across Kick's face, and he sees stars.

"… bullet …"

Wham! Another backhand the other way.

"… proof. A real *super* …"

A hard punch in the gut.

"… *hero*!"

Another solid punch. Kick is woozy and almost lets go of the bobby pin, but squeezes tightly. He's reeling, but slowly sits back up straight in his chair. His captors are all laughing.

White Socks goes back to his crate and picks up his smokes. "You still with us?"

Kick takes Kelly's trembling hands and crosses them so that each is holding onto the opposite cuff.

"He went on a rampage, Mr. Chung. Nothing stopped him." White Socks lights his smoke. "The loss of his asshole buddy Hollywood made him into a monster. That's what you are, aren't you?"

White Socks rips the tape off Kick's mouth and gets a face full of spit.

Kick growls, "What I am is your worst fuckin' nightmare!"

White Socks takes a step back and laughs hard. "That's funny. Coming from a guy tied up in his underwear. Look at all the scars on him, Chung. All the times someone tried, and failed."

Kick's voice growls. "No one could touch us. We were gods of the night in black choppers. Lightning flew from our fingers." He opens Kelly's cuffs while he talks. "Deadly whispers dropped in the darkness. Corpses fell in our wake." Kelly holds her cuffs.

White Socks snorts. "Nightmare? You don't even qualify as a bad dream. You're a *mess*. A booze-soaked shell-shocked crazy piece of shit. But it is nice to finally meet you face to face. Because the wounds I give you will be your last. I am here for my revenge."

Kick gets an inkling of why he looks familiar. "You're overconfident." He remembers those eyes.

Taylor whispers in Kick's ear, "Good. Keep at him."

Kick notices the brand of cigarettes White Socks is smoking. "I thought Winstons were just for girls." Kick takes a stab in the dark. "Or did your Russian buddies give you those?"

White Socks takes a moment but moves on. "The day I saw you on Hastings, you looked like some skid row drunk. Was that just good cover? Do you still work for the CIA?"

Kick laughs. "You're funny. I was straight army. Never went near those fucking suits."

"Then who were the men in the van with you?"

Kick looks at the guard with the sling. "You were daring, kid, I'll give you that." The guard steps forward, but Chung stops him.

"Those are my biker buddies. We grow weed in Burns Bog and move it into Washington State. You thought those clowns were CIA? That's funny." He spits blood on the floor. White Socks keeps checking for bullshit. "Especially the old guy. He can't even get on his hog anymore—"

The fist hits the side of his head without warning, and stars explode again in Kick's vision. "Why did you kill our woman if you're just growing dope?" White Socks demands.

Kick spits out more blood. "Her? She was either a narc, or after my stash! Ask the old fucker behind you if bikers like getting ripped off. Looks like he's made a drug deal or two."

Chung stands up. "I will get my piece of you, round eye!"

"All you're getting is a bullet in the head, chunky." Chung starts toward Kick, but White Socks stops him.

"If I get busted or lose my stash, I have to cover the loss, or get taken out. Someone gets in the way, they get wasted. Simple."

The next fist comes from the other direction, and Kick barely hangs onto his bobby pin. He shakes his head. "You hit like a fuckin' baby."

"Okay, Kick," says White Socks. "We'll get you back to China and see what's true. Unless your biker friends are going to ride in and save you?"

Kick gives a bloody smile. "Only way you're going anywhere is in a body bag, bitch."

White Socks laughs. "I guess you didn't see the latest fashion item your girlfriend is wearing." The two guards drag Kick's chair around in front of Kelly. "We've added more incentive."

They pull him around, and there is Kelly. Face racked with terror and tears streaming down her face. She's covered in dried blood, but that's not the shocking part. A tactical vest loaded with C4 explosive is strapped to her.

White Socks takes the detonator out of his pocket. "You really seem to have bad luck with exploding girls, don't you?"

36

THE OFFER
Danang, Vietnam, 1969

DURING KICK'S LUNCH WITH COLONEL CAMPBELL and the man in the dark suit, Campbell peppers him with more operational questions. The specifics of his Canadian background are confirmed, like how he has no siblings, his father is gone, and that it's just him and his mother now, and a few scattered friends. The mess hall isn't busy, and Kick and Campbell settle into a good conversation, while Dark Suit stays mostly quiet. The meal has helped Kick get his feet back on the ground. As he's finishing his chocolate cake and ice cream, they drop their bomb.

"Your service to us in Vietnam is exemplary, David," says Colonel Campbell. "But my colleagues at the CIA have picked up disturbing intelligence. We've been trying to ferret out a leak we have somewhere in Saigon, and it's brought to light a significant issue."

Dark Suit now speaks. "My name is Richard Taylor, and I run counter-insurgency operations under the Phoenix Program on the civilian side, if you will. I've been watching your very impressive progress. You know the bounty on a LRRP soldier is one year's wages, right?"

"I've heard that," replies Kick.

"Now that you're special forces it's gone up, and it seems they found out about your little trip up the Ho Chi Minh Trail. The Chinese know who you are," Taylor says. "They know your mother's name and her address on Vancouver Island, and the names of your childhood friends."

Kick is horrified but says nothing.

"Your bounty is now ten years' wages. It's the same for your mother."

Campbell leans in. "They may have narrowed it down from the Remington slugs they've been pulling out of your targets. There are only a handful of rifles like yours in the whole theater right now, and your ammo is hard to get. What we can say for sure is that they will muster every effort to capture, torture, or kill you, and make examples of your mother and friends as well."

Taylor speaks next. "You and your family are no longer safe."

Kick feels like he's been hit by a tank. "Shit."

"We have a proposal for you to consider," Campbell says. "It's unorthodox, but Mr. Taylor has used it before with success."

"You're cutting me loose?" asks Kick.

"No, we will not abandon you," Taylor answers. "But if we rotate you home, trouble will eventually find you and your mother, no matter what. The only solution is to kill you."

Kick automatically puts his hand on his side arm.

"Easy, Tex," Taylor says softly as his hands come up. "Not *actually* kill you. You're too valuable, plus I'm not that big of a dick."

Campbell takes it from there. "We find a way to make it look like you've been killed in action. Preferably in a way that makes an NVA cadre look like a hero, and we write that up in *Stars and Stripes* and release it to the press."

Kick takes his hand off his gun. "But what about my mother? She'll be told that I'm dead?" He can feel his eyes sting as tears well up.

"She will. And for all legal purposes, you will be. The alternative is for Chinese assassins to torture and kill both of you. It could be soon, or in a few months, or years."

Kick's stomach is churning. "Any chance of some whiskey, sir?"

"Let me check." Taylor heads to the kitchen.

The colonel continues. "All we can do is ask you to think it over, David. If we had a better solution, we'd suggest it. But we don't."

The mess hall has emptied out as Taylor returns with a mickey and some glasses. "Should you accept this arrangement, your mother will receive your full military pension and death benefits. And I will welcome you to come and work for me." Taylor pours three whiskeys. The brand, ironically, is Canadian Club.

Kick looks confused. "You want me to be a spy, sir?"

"Not exactly. We'll send you to Langley for more specific training, then back here as an employee of the State Department, under my supervision. You will continue to do what you're doing now, but you'll have a new civilian identity and a substantial increase in pay. Essentially, you'll be an independent contractor."

Campbell chimes in. "I'm afraid your nickname, Kick, will have to go away."

Taylor smiles. "I'll still call you that privately if you like."

Kick nods. "Sure. And when the war's over?"

Taylor smiles. "If all goes well, you'll continue to work for us in various capacities. Work that's similar to what you're doing now, but you would carry out your duties with even more discretion."

Kick takes out a cigarette, but before he can reach for his own lighter, Taylor snaps open his Zippo and gets it. "I'm a decent guy once you get to know me. Unless you're a communist. Or a fascist. You know, one that's not on our side." He smiles.

Kick feels lightheaded. Campbell adds, "We wouldn't steer you wrong, and we will be sure to look after your mother in every way possible."

Kick takes a big drag on his Marlborough and exhales. Taylor and Campbell pick their whiskeys up and reach across to Kick. He lifts his as well, and they clink.

"Colonel Campbell and I have similar histories to yours, Kick," says Taylor. "I became a good soldier, lost friends, then got hard as granite. My best friend stepped on a mine in Korea and died right in front of me. A week later I was grazed by a bullet, and I just lost my shit. Stood up in the middle of a firefight and charged the enemy. The Koreans literally stopped shooting in complete shock. It was a miracle I didn't die right there."

Campbell adds, "People like us have traveled so far into the dark we'll never make it all the way back out. And that can be okay. You may feel damaged and unwanted back home, but there are plenty of ways to be of service to your country and fellow citizens."

Taylor adds, "There has to be a shepherd to look after the flock, and from what we've seen, you can kick the shit out of any wolf. Your skills are more advanced than ours."

"Really?" Kick asks.

"Really," answers Campbell.

"Since you'll no longer have a home, we're offering you one with us." Campbell smiles.

Kick stares at his glass and considers what they've said. "Thanks for your honesty. I'll give you an answer tomorrow morning, sirs." He stands to leave.

"We can't ask for anything more." They walk him to the front door.

Kick steps outside and puts on his sunglasses. He thinks about Hollywood, and how much he misses him, as he walks into the crowded streets of Danang. His mind is racing, and he's tired, drained, and empty. The choice is to let his mother be assassinated and have a target on his back forever, or become a hired gun for the CIA. He feels boxed in and relieved at the same time.

Kick keeps walking, and once he's a few blocks away, there's a pull in the pit of his stomach. Hollywood's voice says as clear as a bell, "Contact." He looks around. And then he sees the threat.

"Shoeshine?"

37

SHOVE

"PRETTY STUPID. A C4 vest with remote detonator so close to the harbor," Kick says. "With radio cross-chatter, who knows what might happen? Plus, if she goes, we all go, right?" Kelly screams through her gag, and Kick feels like an idiot. He's just made her feel even worse.

"We have a C4 vest with detonator, everyone," Taylor says in his ear. "Huntsman, stay in the shack. Things just got complicated. Kick, hold tight." Kick coughs once.

White Socks calls over the guard with the sling, and whispers in his ear. He leaves, and an engine starts. Kick catches Kelly's eye. "It'll be okay, Kelly."

White Socks laughs. "No, it won't! Take her!"

The other guard drags Kelly, chair and all, to the double doors on the south side. As he opens it and pulls her outside, Kick takes advantage of the noise to open his cuffs and holds them tight. A horrified and screaming Kelly gets loaded into the back of a large van.

"Kelly, I'll come for you!"

"Put her on the old freighter and come right back," White Socks tells the driver, and the van takes off. "Don't worry, Kelly," he yells after the van. "This will all be over soon!" He comes back in and drags Kick over in his chair to the open doors, so he gets a good view of the ship. Kick's tempted to pop out of his cuffs and snap this bastard's neck right there, but he respects Taylor's orders. "Something tells me your friends would be here already if they were coming," White Sock says. "Right?"

Kick's mind is racing. This is his fault. He didn't look after himself; he got lost in the bottle and got sloppy. Kelly was never going to stay put at the hotel, and if he'd been on his game, he would've seen that. Is Taylor right? Does he need a shrink? Fuck.

Chung stands gloating beside him at the door, and watches as the van pulls up to the ship. Baker must see he has two clean shots. Kick looks where he knows he must be and gives a nod.

"Tinker, I have visual on Achilles. He is bound to a chair in his skivvies in the middle of the south-facing double doors. I have clean shots on Chung and Socks. He just gave me a nod to go ahead and shoot," reports Baker. "Want me to take Chung?"

"Negative, Breadman," responds Taylor. "White Socks could trigger the bomb and bring the whole city here. We're not ready for that. We stick to the plan and let them think Achilles is alone — for now."

"Confirmed," responds Baker.

Kick lowers his head and tears drip from his eyes. His mind goes slack and he can't put thoughts together. Taylor is talking in his ear, but he can't focus. He hears himself saying, "I failed." Taylor keeps talking, but Kick drifts off. He feels someone pulling his head up and opens his eyes.

It's White Socks. "You are broken. And now, you are mine."

Then Taylor says, "Everyone got it?" All the confirmations come in, but not Kick. Taylor whispers his name, but he can't find a way to answer. Taylor keeps calling his name. "Kick?"

◆ ◆ ◆ ◆

There's a light rain blowing in, as Baker watches the van approach the *St. Jude* at Pier Three. He sneaks a look back at Building Six and sees Wong snaking quickly toward him.

"Breadman, Witchy moving into position."

"Have visual. You are clear."

Out in the harbor, there's a small craft tossing crab traps overboard. Baker lets Taylor and Wong know. The van has stopped at the ship. The two thugs haul Kelly up a makeshift gangplank onto the ship, place her in the middle of the deck, then check the line of sight to Building Six. Satisfied, they leave, and one of them says something in Mandarin. They laugh.

"Breadman, Witchy in position."

"Copy. Did you catch what they said?"

"Translates to 'Merry Christmas, bitch.' Boarding the ship." Wong slides like a shadow up the gangplank to Kelly. "At *Package Two*. She is out of her cuffs already. Working on the vest now."

Kick's falling into a dark hole in his mind and tries to find something to hang onto. He tries to focus on the voices. They're not English, but he doesn't care. Shaking his head, he looks up and sees White Socks and Chung talking excitedly. He can tell they're dropping names, since some are in English, but he can't make heads or tails of it. The van returns. He prays that Baker and Wong will step out of it, open fire, and wrap all this up. They don't. The guards return, looking smug.

Taylor's in his ear. "Stall for time, Achilles." Kick coughs once.

Kick knows Taylor has to take White Socks alive. That's number one. Kelly is secondary, and therefore expendable, but Taylor must have something up his sleeve. Kick shakes his head. He has to hold it together and try not to think about Kelly. He swears he will never get close to anyone again. Chung and White Socks stop talking and size him up.

He needs to get White Socks talking. "Who the hell are you anyway?" Kick asks.

White Socks comes over. "Who do you think I am?"

"A spoiled brat barely out of his diapers."

White Socks grabs Kick's Ka-Bar and stands behind him. "That's funny. A brat who somehow knows who you are, even after the CIA faked your death, and kept you killing for them in Vietnam. Not to mention your *freelance* career after that."

"Assuming that's all true, you'd need very good connections to know it."

"Good connections is right." White Socks moves in front of him and scrapes the tip of the blade across Kick's throat, drawing just a touch of blood. "Good *government* connections."

Kick realizes why he looked so familiar when he first saw him. He looks in his eyes and can't deny it. "Your father was the White Tiger." The knife stops moving, but the pressure increases.

He feels White Socks' respiration increase. His smokey breath hitting his face. Kick spits out blood onto the floor. "Kill me or don't but stop jacking off on my neck if you don't mind."

White Socks is taken aback. "I don't think you're in any position to boss me around."

"That's what this is about? You think I killed your daddy in the war, and you're here to get revenge? I didn't hunt down the Kraut who gave my old man a gut wound that never healed. You're just some punk-ass wannabe gangster with some cheap thugs — like fat-ass over there. Looks like he's had a bit too much roast duck."

Chung goes red in the face and runs at Kick. "No one speaks to me that way!" White Socks swings the knife toward Chung. He stops and goes back to his corner.

"Remember who is paying you, Mr. Chung!" White Socks barks, tossing the knife on the ground. Chung is right where Kick wants him to be. Out of control.

White Socks turns back to Kick. "You don't see your own hypocrisy." Kick is confused. "You don't think everything you've done was for revenge? I don't think you've been killing people all over the world just to take in the culture. Your mission has always been *payback*." White Socks sees the puzzled look on Kick's face and laughs. "You really should have invested in a good shrink, *youling*."

"We have that in common."

"Finally, a grain of truth," White Socks says. "Out of respect for that I will confirm your theory. The White Tiger was my father. His real name was General Liu Wei Zhang, descended from a long line of military leaders. I am his oldest son, Wang Lei. My father believed you had to be on the battlefield to lead, and that is where he served."

"And that is where I put a bullet in his head," Kick says coldly. White Socks stiffens.

Kick continues, "You wear those socks to remember him? Pathetic."

White Socks goes red and takes out the detonator. "You stink of dishonor. You killed like a coward in hiding, and the revenge is mine." He leans in and whispers, "Starting with your *lover*."

"You know what they say, 'when you set out for revenge, dig two graves,' but in your case, you might want to get a volume discount." Kick gets another hard backhand. His head swims for a moment, but he can still hear him talking through the haze. "Your girlfriend Kelly will be in a thousand pieces soon, smartass!"

Kick looks down at the shiny black shoes White Socks is wearing, and spits blood on them. "Bombs are for the weak. You're dishonoring your father this way. Fight me one on one!" Kick smiles at Chung. "You know all about dishonor, don't you, Chung. Fucking *lard ass*!"

Chung is steaming and asks White Socks something in Mandarin. "Why not, Mr. Chung. You've been very patient. Just don't kill him. I look forward to that honor at my father's grave."

Chung walks over to Kick, and winds up to punch him in the gut, but while he's drawing his fist back, Kick opens his cuffs, grabs him by the belt buckle, and punches him square in the nuts. Before the two guards know what's happening, Chung is doubled over with his face against Kick's. From there, Kick inverts his right hand, and clamps his thumb and forefinger hard around Chung's windpipe. He rotates his hand and pulls. Ironically, it's called *the tiger grip*, and it effectively removes Chung's windpipe. One of the guards instinctively fires a round that hits Kick in the side of his gut, and he doubles over.

"Stop!" yells White Socks.

Chung grabs his throat and careens around, completely panicked. White Socks knows he's doomed and lets him flail. Mr. Chung, the illegal arms dealer, drug runner, and human trafficker, has run out of luck and stares in horror at the face of death. His lungs fill with blood and Chung dies gasping and twitching like a bug hit by pesticide.

Kick tosses the piece of windpipe at White Socks' feet, splattering blood on the sacred white socks. "And then there were *three*," says Kick, his voice dripping venom. "Goodbye Mr. Chung," Kick says, for the benefit of Taylor. "This is why your daddy didn't stand a chance."

The guards raise their weapons but White Socks shouts, "No shooting!" Seething anger, he scoops up the tactical pen from the ground, and stabs Kick through the left foot. "Now you have a matched pair!" Kick screams in pain.

"I've lost patience with you, *youling*! Before I ship you off for the blowtorch and pliers treatment in China, I want you to see your Kelly die. Sear it into your mind. Just like Hollywood, this is the moment you lose everything you love." Kick shakes as White Socks holds the detonator in front of Kick's face. "Three, two, one." He hits it.

There is a massive explosion on the freighter that shoots high into the night sky. The *St. Jude* buckles and creaks, then lists toward the pier. Chunks of the upper structure groan and fall over. Something else on it catches fire, and flames and smoke fill the night sky. Kick stares in stunned silence as his world implodes. Kelly is gone, and it's his fault. Then he hears a distinctive sound.

Whiz, whiz. Two bullets whip past him on either side, taking out both guards. One thug has an exit wound the size of a softball. That's Baker with the M82, and the other has to be Wong. White Socks' face blanches. He's trying to process this new reality but can't believe he was wrong.

"How?" is all he can say, as he stares at Kick in disbelief. He darts for the other door, but Buck runs in with his Glock raised. Then Wong walks confidently in the double doors with a big smile on her face, tufts of blue hair sticking out everywhere. "Tinker, can I put one in his shoulder, just for fun?" she asks.

"Negative, Witchy. Wrap him up toot sweet," replies Taylor.

Wong screams in Mandarin, "On your knees, hands on your head!"

White Socks just stands there, so Buck strips him of his gun, then hits him with a kidney punch. He then grabs White Socks by the hair and takes him to the floor. White Socks screams, "You're going to be sorry you did this! I'm—" Buck bounces his forehead off the floor, silencing him. "You're fucked, Stockings!"

Wong laughs. "Tinker, you should see this. Huntsman's on fire."

Kick still has his legs taped to the chair, but he tips it over, and starts dragging himself toward White Socks. "I'm going to chew your fucking throat out!"

Wong goes to him and holds him down. "Easy. We got her. She's safe. All in one piece. Look, look!" Wong points into the harbor. The crab boat is moored at the end of Pier Three, and Kick sees Kelly sitting in it. He recognizes the big guy waving as they take off.

"It's Pharaoh. They'll meet us at the house. Sit tight." Kick is speechless. Wong binds White Socks hand and foot and tapes his mouth. She says quickly, "Primary is secure, Secondary loaded, recommend Breadman bugs out."

"Breadman, do it," snaps Taylor.

"Roger that," Baker responds.

White Socks kicks like a mule, but Wong and Buck toss him unceremoniously into his own van, and then bind his hands and ankles together behind his back like a rodeo calf. Buck frees Kick from his chair, and sees the stab wound through his foot. He takes out an old hanky and wraps it.

"I'm packed up and halfway down, Tinker," reports Baker, then stifles a yell. "Shit! My leg just went through the roof. I'm stuck." The first sirens are audible in the distance.

Before anyone can stop him, big old Buck is hustling out the door. "Got it, Twinky. I'll catch a ride with Whitebread!"

"Huntsman's on his way to Breadman, Tinker," sighs Wong.

"Roger that. Let it happen. We have a primary to deliver."

Kick's hands are shaking as he touches the bullet wound in his side. He curses, pulls on his pants, and gathers up his gear and weapons. Wong is already outside grabbing the mic she placed under the wall.

Taylor orders, "Move it. The fire department's on the way. Cops are right behind! Breadman?"

◆ ◆ ◆ ◆

Baker feels like an idiot, with his leg jammed through the roof, but his mood lightens as a wobbly ladder appears below.

"Buck's got a ladder up, Tinker," says Baker. "Got a big cut on my leg, but not bad."

Buck's big head pops up. "Drop 'er down, Doughboy!"

Baker extends the rifle as far as he can, then lets it slide toward Buck's waiting arms. If he wasn't so juiced, he probably could have handled it, but the ladder is at a steep angle, and that twenty-eight pounds is all it takes to knock Buck past the point of no return. He falls ass-over-teakettle into a dirt pile, and the rifle falls to the ground. Baker works his bleeding leg out, gets to the edge of the roof, and then shinnies down the shaky drainpipe. The sirens are closer.

Buck isn't moving, so Baker slaps his face. Nothing. Baker gives him another.

"Whoa! Shit, that fuckin' thing's heavy, eh?" Buck shakes his head and gets up.

Baker already has the rifle into his ski bag. "Huntsman, I'll boost you over. There's pizza at our place, but we have to hurry." Buck puts his foot into Baker's interlocked hands. With a good heave, he gets over the fence in a way that's far from graceful. Baker eases the ski bag over, then himself.

"Tinker, walking to my ride with Huntsman."

"Copy that, Breadman."

"Tinker, Achilles plus honored guest are through the gate," says Wong.

"Glad you're okay, Anchovies!" Buck says. The sirens close in as Buck and Baker head up the hill.

"Huntsman, radio silence. Witchy, I see you, and you are clear. Drive the speed limit, be careful, and we'll see you at base," says Taylor. "I will transit in one mike."

"Huntsman, this is going to be close. If anyone asks, I'm your nephew from Colorado. We're heading to Whistler to ski. Close your coat, so they can't see your gun, and look down."

Buck does as he's told. He's wheezing up a storm walking up the hill. Crossing Esplanade, they have to run to avoid being hit by the first fire truck. Another is coming down the hill toward them. Baker snaps, "Look down. Keep walking!" The truck passes, then a news van and two cop cars. The cops are coming from all directions now. It's getting very real, very fast. They toss the gear in the van, get in, and in a few blocks, they connect with Highway One.

"You guys got any beers to go with that pizza, Breadbox?" asks Buck.

"Fucking right, dude. Hey Tinker, Breadman, and Huntsman are Charlie Mike and mobile."

"Roger that Breadman. Well done." Baker can hear the huge grin in Taylor's voice.

◆ ◆ ◆ ◆

Taylor settles into the driver's seat of his van and turns on the radio. He grabs a fishing pole and tackle box from the back, puts them in the passenger's seat, and exchanges his watchman's cap for a trucker's hat with a fish on it. Next, he pulls the tiny tape recorder from his pocket, winds it back, and checks the sound. It's good, so he spins it back to the spot where Chung and White Socks are speaking Mandarin. Taylor leaves it cued, then clicks the radio to *JR Country*, and is delighted to hear Loretta Lynn in the middle of "Fist City." He turns it up loud, lights a smoke, and sings along.

◆ ◆ ◆ ◆

Mustafa has Kelly wrapped in a blanket on board the little Hewescraft and they are halfway across the bay into East Vancouver. "Don't worry, Kelly. You are safe now. Here — have chocolate." He hands her a KitKat bar, and she rips it open with her teeth.

"Thank you," she manages. "Aren't you the guy …?"

"Yes! I am the army driver for your cab. Very good!" Mustafa beams. "You call me Pharaoh, like Egyptian Pharaoh. Your man bought you time to get free, my friend. He must like you very much. And bad guys think you are dead now, so good! We will go to our place and take care of you. Everything okay now. We take care of everything. You are safe now!"

Kelly chews the chocolate bar and says with a full mouth, "Pharaoh, this is the best fucking thing I've ever eaten."

Mustafa laughs heartily. "Okay, I will have one too!" He rips open his KitKat and takes a bite, then starts singing "Freebird." It's terrible. "You know this one, Kelly?"

The situation is so absurd that Kelly starts to laugh and cry with her mouth full of chocolate. Tears roll down her cheeks.

◆ ◆ ◆ ◆

Wong's stolen van tools along smoothly, with only the occasional sound of struggle from White Socks in the back. There's a divider between the cab and the back of the van, so Kick pulls it shut. Wong checks her mirrors and steals a look at Kick. Blood is dripping from his gunshot wound and his foot, plus his face is bleeding from the beatings, and yet all the way through it, he kept talkin' shit right back in their faces. He reminds her of her dad. "Hey, you've gotta show me that throat thing you did on Chung. Those are some mad skills."

Kick looks at her, tries to say something, then starts laughing, and can't stop. Tension pours out of him to the point where it looks painful. Wong starts laughing too. White Socks starts kicking in the back, and it just makes things funnier. Wong yells, "Stop it! If your dad and I have to stop this car ..."

"That is one floppy fish we've got back there," Kick says between laughing fits. He wipes away sweat and sighs. "So, who the fuck are you, Witchy?" He lights two cigarettes, and hands one to her. There's blood on it.

Wong looks offended by the smoke. "Really? Isn't your body a temple?"

It takes a moment for Kick to realize she's kidding, then he starts laughing again. "Thanks, man. I'm dying for one." Wong grabs the cigarette. "You did okay, Achilles. For a boy."

"Seriously, what's your story?"

Wong takes a long drag on her smoke and blows a smoke ring. She looks back at where White Socks is, then turns on the radio so he can't hear them. "Yeah, well, my old man fought with the underground when the Japanese occupied Hong Kong in forty-one. When I was a kid, he taught me how to fight, shoot, and generally raise shit. In seventy-five, I joined the Hong Kong Police Force, and helped clean it up from the inside. It had to get straightened out or we'd never have our city back. I did a lot of stuff by the book at first, and stayed under the radar, but that was pretty slow going."

"So, you switched to the fast way?"

"Yeah. No one really saw me coming looking like this."

"I made the same mistake."

Wong laughs. "Yeah, you fuckin' did! But you didn't talk down to me, or interrupt me, and you gave me respect. I appreciate that. So, eventually, Taylor crossed my path, and he made me an offer that was pretty hard to refuse."

"You probably saved my life."

"I *definitely* saved your life." She laughs again. "You owe me, bitch!"

"Agreed. I coulda used four guys like you in 'Nam. We would've been unstoppable."

"Thanks, but I'm glad I missed that one, if you don't mind me saying so."

Kick smiles. "I don't mind at all. And how'd you get that vest off Kelly so fast?"

"Those dudes weren't military, so no trips or traps. Just took it off, and we ran. Correction — we ran like *motherfuckers*!" Wong laughs again, and Kick can't stop himself either.

"God, you're funny." He collects himself. "Seriously, thanks for saving her."

"Don't mean nothin', brother. I'm sure you'll return the favor."

"I look forward to that, Witchy," Kick says.

Wong takes a long drag on her smoke and looks wistful. "There's something wrong with Baker. You've gotta get a better fuckin' handle than Achilles next time, man. It doesn't exactly roll off the tongue during an op. I'm surprised it wasn't Rumpel-fuckin-stiltskin!"

Kick doubles over in a painful fit of laughter. "Or Cinderella …" he manages, before convulsing into more laughter.

Wong joins in. "Keep it together, man. We're almost home."

38

MOPPING UP

KICK AND WONG ARRIVE FIRST with White Socks, back in, and get the door down. Taylor asks Wong to stay with White Socks in the van. "No sweat, Tinker, but can you play the part of the recording with those two talking in Mandarin?" asks Wong.

"I'll make some notes while I'm sitting here."

"Roger that, Witchy. Here it comes." Taylor plays it over his open mic, spins it back, and plays it again. It's not much more than two minutes, but Wong scratches down a bunch of names and locations on her pad, while White Socks freaks out behind her. "Tinker, the way our boy here is jerkin' around, he is not happy we have this. I'll get a rough outline together in a few minutes."

Kick takes a peek at her notes while she writes. "Wow. That should raise some eyebrows."

Wong smiles. "Go get cleaned up. You smell disgusting."

"No argument there." He gingerly gets out of the van. Blood has seeped through the sad-looking hanky on his foot, and he's leaving a red smudge along the garage floor. He looks back at it and keeps going. Besides a bullet wound in his side and a possible broken rib from the shot to his vest, he could have severed tendons or broken bones in his foot, not to mention infection.

Once inside, Kick opens the first aid kit and deals with the gunshot in his side first. The bullet pierced what would have been one of his love handles, if he had enough fat to have them. It's through and through, and that's fine by him. The alcohol burns like napalm.

◆ ◆ ◆ ◆

Wong is still organizing the info from the recording when Baker and Buck arrive and back their light-brown van in beside her. Buck sees the blood trail, and heads inside to help Kick, while Baker quickly unloads the van, then heads back out to park it a few blocks away. Taylor arrives a few minutes later and unloads.

"When you get back, Tinker, I have something for you," Wong tells him.

"Can't wait." He takes off to park a few blocks away in the other direction.

As Mustafa arrives with Kelly, Taylor is walking back in with his fishing gear in hand.

He smiles and waves at Kelly. "Remember me?"

Kelly is bewildered for a moment. "From Dusty's. Holy shit, I didn't see that coming."

"That means I did my job. You did great, by the way. You'll find my partner Baker inside. I'll bet you could use a cold beer."

Kelly nods, and Taylor takes her inside while Mustafa heads off to park his van a few blocks away in yet another direction. White Socks is still struggling in the back of Wong's.

Taylor comes back out and switches the plates on it, then sticks his head inside. "You got it?"

She grins ear to ear and hands over three small pieces of paper. "You're going to really like this." White Socks starts bucking again, so she goes back and smacks him on the back of the head. "Can it!"

Taylor reads the pages twice and breaks into a big smile. "You're right. I really like this!" Wong beams as he tucks the papers into his pocket. She's proud of the difference she's made to this mission and knows her father would be proud. If she could tell him about it, that is. As with all covert operations, only the team members and some higher-ups in Langley will be privy to this information. It makes everyone here even more special to her.

◆ ◆ ◆ ◆

Once inside, Taylor picks up the phone and dials a sixteen-digit number, says all the magic words, and makes the necessary arrangements. He reads what Wong translated for him and listens as it's repeated back to him. "Yes, it's authentic," he answers. "I was there. The recording will have to be double checked, of course. We also have a pager from one of the consulate drivers." The line goes dead. Taylor looks around to see how his team's doing.

Baker is chatting with Kelly as he pulls medical supplies out of the first aid kit to deal with his sliced leg and punctured hand. Kelly is drinking her beer with shaky hands. Baker takes a wet wipe and turns to Kelly.

"Let me just clean you up a bit." She turns to him, and he gently takes the blood splatters off her face, neck, and hands, and tosses the bloody wipe into a bag. "There you go. How's that beer going down?"

Kelly laughs nervously. "Good. Thanks."

Baker catches Taylor's eye and nods toward Kick, who's just sat down beside Kelly.

"I'm going to grab some food for you, Kick." Taylor says. "I know they called you the ghost, but you're starting to actually look like one."

"Yeah," is all Kick can muster.

Baker tosses Kick the wipes. "You've got a little something all over your face, dude."

Kelly looks at Kick, and her face says it all. She takes the wipes and starts cleaning blood off his face.

Taylor adds, "Look after that leg, Baker. When Mustafa gets here, he'll hopefully make coffee."

"I heard that, and I am here to save you from bad American coffee!" Mustafa comes in and hugs everyone. "I am so hungry I could eat the whole horse myself! Why has no one turned on the oven for pizza?" He heads into the kitchen, snaps it on, and starts sliding the rest of the pizzas inside.

Taylor steals three pieces. "We've got people in there who need slices, Mustafa!" He evades Mustafa's playful attempt to stop him and heads back to the living room.

"Tinker Taylor, come back for your bear hug!" Mustafa says, then sets about making Egyptian-style coffee on the stove while Taylor delivers the slices to Baker, Kick, and Kelly.

Taylor asks Kelly, "How you feeling?"

"Weird."

"We're going to look after you. Don't worry. Everything is going to work out fine."

By Taylor's watch, it's after four in the morning. Everyone is drained, but there's celebration in the air, and the gang is nice and punchy.

Kick motions for Taylor to come over. "What's the story on Dusty?" he whispers.

"Cleaners report he wasn't there when they arrived, so that's good news. We're checking plane manifests and an op is heading to his apartment." Taylor can tell Kick is worried. "We'll find him."

Kick nods. "Thanks."

"Get some food into you," Taylor orders. "I'll let you know as soon as I find anything out."

Baker is inspecting his leg wound. "Hey Kick, can you help me with these stitches?"

"What've you got?"

Baker sticks out his leg to show off a long deep cut. "Holy shit!" Kick exclaims. "That's a beauty! Did Taylor tell you I was a medic at the start of my first tour?"

Kick pours rubbing alcohol onto the open wound, and Baker grits his teeth. "I'm not sure it makes me feel better ..."

Kick splashes a bit more alcohol. "And that was for calling me Achilles."

Baker holds his grimace and nods. "Tough, but fair."

"Looks like five or six stitches to me, kid," Kick says, getting out the needle. "I know I gave you a hard time, *Breadman*, but I got a lot out of that *Iliad* book."

Baker winces as more alcohol goes on. "What a tale, huh? You see any similarities?"

"Yeah," Kick says earnestly. "I did."

Kick starts weaving the needle through the skin, and Baker grits his teeth and grunts. "Oh!" Kick is enjoying himself. Kelly watches the scene with a combination of horror and admiration, as Taylor laughs.

Baker flinches again as the first knot gets tied. "I think we're gonna be friends. Ouch." Kick smiles as he starts on the second stitch.

Baker continues, "The classics give you everything, dude. You should check out Hercules. His shell shock was so bad he killed his own kids, and his music teacher. Shit — spoiler."

Kelly asks, "He played music?"

"I know. Let's stay in touch and swap books. I'd like to check out some of that cowboy stuff. I can send you *The Gunslinger* and *True Grit*. There's some great reading out there." Kick pierces his skin again.

"Jesus!" Baker yells.

"Did I just get suckered into your book club?" Kick asks.

Baker laughs through the pain. "You should be honored, bro. The membership is exclusive, although Taylor usually just reads the paper."

Taylor laughs. "Hey, I like sports."

Baker holds up his punctured hand. "I think the nails in that roof were older than Calvary. Boss, I'm gonna need a tetanus shot." Kick ties another knot.

"Roger that," responds Taylor. "I'll get that for you."

Baker adds, "And thanks for the beef jerky gift in my coat."

"What can I say," says Taylor. "*I am a river to my people.*"

Mustafa laughs from the kitchen. "Lawrence of Arabia!"

Taylor laughs. "Nailed it, Mustafa. Baker and Kick, you need to take some antibiotics while you're at it. You can wash them down with a big slug of this."

Buck walks in with a bottle of 18-year-old Macallan scotch and sets up glass tumblers on the coffee table. Mustafa joins them with hot pizza and makes a second trip to bring in a tray of cups and his coffee.

Kick smiles. "Now you're talking."

Mustafa pours the coffee and hands out cups.

Taylor takes the middle of the floor. "All right, I'm happy that we're all here right now, safe and sound. This is a night with a lot of good news. Everyone improvised well when shit went sideways, and only one asshole got shot."

Kick snorts. "Oh, we're going down this road again, are we?"

"Sorry, I meant to say shot *twice*, and *stabbed* once. I'm just saying, you do tend to get shot from time to time, and I tend not to."

"Does the term, 'in the rear with the gear' mean anything to you?" asks Baker.

Taylor laughs. "All aspects of the mission are complete, except the handoff, and we completed this mission with *style*. First of all, Kelly is safe and sound, and so is all her material." Taylor speaks to her directly now. "You showed guts and stayed strong. Want to say anything?"

Kelly's voice quivers. "I don't feel strong. I'm glad I fooled you, because I was terrified. And thanks ... for fixing my stupid mistake."

Taylor looks around the room. "Hey, with the exception of Buck, I could tell you stories about everyone here who has fucked up worse than you, so don't worry about it. I heard you were out of your cuffs and had the tape on your legs sawed off by the time Wong got there."

Kick gives her a look of congratulations, and Kelly says, "Gotta like that paracord."

Mustafa reaches out and gives her arm a squeeze. "Just let us know if you want to change to a new line of work."

Kelly waves off the thought. "No!" Kick puts his hand on her back, and the tension between them melts a little more.

Taylor goes on. "There's a separate team waiting with great anticipation for our honored guest in the van. A very special transport will be rolling in here soon. He's got a lot of questions to answer."

"Uh-oh!" There's more laughter.

Taylor goes on. "Baker was outstanding on Overwatch, as usual, and what can we say about Mustafa saving the day in a stolen fishing boat?"

"Hey! I caught some nice crabs too. A very good night!" exclaims Mustafa.

Baker holds up his cup. "Buddy, this coffee is fucking amazing!" Mustafa takes a bow.

"Okay, next we have to thank Buck. Not everyone could be yanked from their barstool, three sheets to the wind, and pressed into service on such short notice. But then again, not everyone can say they held their ground against the Chinese on Hill 677 in Korea either." Back slaps for Buck all round.

"Kapyong. That's a story that should be told too, Kelly," Kick suggests.

Buck just looks down and says nothing, so Taylor adds, "Well done, Corporal. You made the Princess Pats proud tonight. But don't fuckin' tell anyone." There are *ooooos* and more laugher. "We'll talk about that later."

Taylor holds up Wong's pieces of paper. "We also picked up some solid intelligence from conversations between White Socks and Chung." Kick reaches out to take a look, but Taylor pulls them back. "Uh-uh. Sorry, Kick. This is eyes only for way up the ladder, but if you buy me a drink later, maybe we can work something out." Kick gives him the finger, and then finishes Baker's last stitch.

The phone rings and Taylor picks it up. "Confirmed," is all he says. "*Don't open that scotch without me, and I mean it!*"

Taylor goes to the garage and lets in a black van with darkened windows and diplomatic plates. The door closes, and four serious men dressed all in black get out. Wong goes out and opens the back doors of her van, and they muscle White Socks into the black one. His tape is pulled off, and he's fitted with leg irons and cuffs and chained to a metal bench in the back in less than a minute. No one says a word. Taylor hands them the mini-tape of the Chung and White Socks recording, the driver's pager, and Wong's notes. One of the men checks the plates on Wong's van, then gets in the driver's side. The garage door opens and both vans leave, each taking a different direction. Wong's van is going to a crusher and then onto a barge going somewhere, and the one with White Socks will go to an airport, and then — somewhere else.

As they watch the doors close, Wong says, "Not exactly a chatty bunch, are they?"

"I wonder what their book club's like," Taylor says.

Wong laughs, and they both let out a sigh of relief. "Did you bring whiskey?" Taylor looks at her, stone-faced. "Aw, shit! How could you forget?" Taylor breaks into a smile, and Wong punches him in the shoulder and jumps on his back. "Just for that, you owe me a piggyback!" They head into the house.

Inside, Wong makes a triumphant entrance on Taylor's back, jumps off, and heads right for the pizza. Mustafa intercepts and gives her a big hug.

Taylor clinks the butt of his Glock on the scotch bottle to quiet everyone down. "Okay, okay. So, our guest is gone, and Wong is in the house!" There's applause and cheers. "Not only did she have to work in the shadow of a rather crusty old barnacle ... not mentioning any names." He points at Kick.

"I'm not that old."

Taylor continues, "...But she translated up a storm, took out a bunch of bad guys, neutralized a suicide vest, and helped save Kelly, then saved Kick's ass when he got *shot!*"

Wong does a victory lap and enjoys seeing Kick giving her a slow clap of appreciation. He shakes her hand and says, "*King Wong.*"

Wong loves it. "Ten times as good as a man, baby!" Then asks, "Taylor, what are you saving that scotch for?"

"All right, pour everyone a glass."

Wong grabs the bottle, cracks the seal, and pours.

Taylor continues, "Let me just correct the record. I am not fat, I'm big boned, and I can outride anyone in this room on my Harley!" The room erupts with laughter. "I also want to thank my old pal from the 'Nam days, whose real name I've actually forgotten, plus most of the other names he's had, but who's known affectionately to his close friends as Kick. He doesn't like a lot of flowery stuff, so just raise it and drink up, motherfuckers!"

Everyone drinks, and Taylor goes on, "And here's the only Shakespeare I know, thanks to Baker ..."

Wong yells, "Nerd!"

Taylor clears his throat. "'If we do meet again, we'll smile indeed. If not, 'tis true this parting was well made.'"

Baker looks proud. "*Julius Caesar.*"

"Now, in all seriousness, we need to get everyone but me, Kick, and Kelly the hell out of Dodge, ASAP. I'll get set up in the dining room with travel docs. Mustafa, you organize and pack all the weapons with Wong, and both of you come and see me in ten. Baker, you're heading to Los Angeles for R and R."

"Solid!" says Baker. "Looking forward to some surf time once this leg heals."

"Buck, bring your drink and step this way," Taylor orders. They sit at the dining room table, which is covered with travel arrangements and documents for everyone. There are also contingencies like fake passports and wigs in case things get hot and exits have to be made from other cities.

"I have a thank you gift and a little proposition for you," Taylor begins. "So, we've talked before about you helping us out on a more permanent basis, right?"

"Yeah. I'm still good with that." Buck says.

"Great. You performed exceptionally well tonight. You improvised well and didn't hesitate, even a bit. I had a clear view of you taking care of that guy in the guard shack, and it's going in my report." Taylor laughs. "Plus, you saved my bacon on that one."

"Happy to help out. Sorry I was wasted. If I'd known, I'd only have been half as drunk." They both laugh.

"Not to worry, pal. So, you just came down with a bad case of pneumonia and won't be in to work for a few months. We'll get you a doctor's report and all that. Assuming you get security clearance, I'd like to send you offshore for training, then have you as eyes and ears at the ports here when you get back. Naturally, you'll be on our payroll, along with whatever you make as a guard."

Buck is touched. "Okay. I like the sound of that."

Taylor hands Buck a fat envelope of cash. "Don't put that in the bank, ever. They'll be checking the accounts of everyone who has anything to do with the shipyard for *years*. Just use it for spending money now and then over the next while. Like a hundred or so a month. Do *not* buy a new car. Ever. We'll set up an account offshore, and you'll have retirement benefits and all that."

Buck nods and opens the envelope. He whistles in appreciation. "Generous. Thanks. Kick said you were in Korea?"

"First of the Eighth Rangers. I did a little sniper work. Nice to meet someone else who nearly froze their ass off. Hang tight for a bit, and I'll get you a cab home. Call in sick with a bad cough, and I'll have someone pick you up later tomorrow."

◆ ◆ ◆ ◆

Kick has Baker's leg all stitched up and bandaged. Baker pulls on a fresh pair of pants, then pops some antibiotics and a painkiller. "Thanks, dude. Nice work."

Mustafa has completed his work on Kick's bullet and stab wound, and he is all patched up. "Your foot looks okay but get an x-ray of your chest and make sure no rib is broken. It's going to be a beautiful bruise for you." The bull's-eye impact mark on Kick's chest is a darker red now. "Taylor might want to get a doctor here for you." He gently hugs Kick. "You are the bravest man I know, *habibi*. I will miss you, until the next time, *inshallah*."

Kick hugs him back. "*Inshallah*."

Mustafa takes Kelly's hand. "Miss Kelly, I am sorry I have to leave so fast, or I would take care of you. But Mr. Kick knows even more than me. You are in good hands. I am so glad I could help you." He hugs Kelly gently, and whispers in her ear. "You will both be fine. I know in my heart."

She hugs him back. "Thanks for the KitKat, and the best coffee I've ever had." There's a tear in Mustafa's eye as he breaks away.

"Kelly, you have any cuts, bruises, or broken bones?" Baker asks. She shakes her head no, even though her clothing is still covered with blood. "We've been in triage mode here, and no one's had time to get to you. Sorry about that."

Kick takes her hands. "Baker and Taylor will back me up on this, so please listen. You've had a severe shock. If you want, I'll help you get cleaned up and get some fresh clothes on. We've got a room set up for you. There'll be lots of time to talk through things later, but first you need some solid rest."

Baker adds, "It'll take time for all this to work itself through, and you'll need someone to talk to. We can set you up with one of ours."

"It's no small thing to see people killed, or to take a life," Kick says. "What you did in that cab was pure self-defense, and not even God will fault you for that. Okay?"

"Thanks. I appreciate that."

Taylor calls from the living room. "Okay, I need the big teddy bear and dude in here." Mustafa and Baker say their goodbyes and head over to Taylor.

Kick takes Kelly's hand and walks her down the hall to a bedroom. He hands her a robe and says, "Take everything out of your pockets, and put everything you were wearing in a pile on the floor. Blood flies everywhere, and we have to burn it all. The good news is you get first dibs on the shower."

Kelly wraps her arms around him and squeezes. "Thank you. For coming to get me."

Kick hugs her gently back. "How could I not?" He doesn't have the heart to tell her she wasn't the first consideration. "I'm just glad you're safe. Once you've cleaned up, come back out, and we'll go over what happens next. We have the holidays to decompress."

"Tomorrow's Christmas Day, isn't it?"

"Shit. It is. I'll have Taylor rustle up a turkey. He's actually a really good cook, for a fat biker." Kelly laughs, and Kick heads back to Taylor.

Wong is pocketing her new passport, and travel materials. "You know the boss likes a quick exit before the authorities clue in." She gives Kick a hug and smacks him on the ass. "Try not to get shot next time, bitch."

"Been a pleasure. Happy to kick ass with you any time, Wong. If that's your real name."

"You're one to talk. Tell Kelly to write a great story," Wong says. There's a little bit of a spark between them, then she waves on her way out the door and jumps into her cab.

Taylor watches from the window. "What was your impression?"

"Can you clone her?"

Taylor laughs. "I'll make a couple of calls and see what I can do."

"I guess I'll get all that shit ready to burn," Kick says. "And wash up after that."

Taylor lets out a big sigh and heads back to his table.

Kick is naked except for the towel around his waist. He's packed up several garbage bags and stacked them in the garage, ready for pick-up. He goes into the kitchen and pours another cup of Mustafa's coffee. Taylor's at the table looking exhausted, but happy. He's so used to seeing Kick's scars he doesn't even notice them.

Kick sits across from him, and Taylor steals his coffee and takes a sip. "Wow. He hasn't lost his touch." Kick yawns. "You need some rest, cowboy, and that's an order. I've got about five hours of shit to organize. Why don't you go to ground, then sub me off?"

Kick steals the coffee back. "Soon as I'm done my coffee. What's next for me?"

Taylor is too tired to sugarcoat it. "Your cover's blown, and we've got to get you out. Don't get me wrong, this was a great op, but we have to treat this like we've been burned to a crisp. Baker and I will never come back here either. I'm sending you to one of our sites for a medical-tune up, then we'll figure out a new place in the world for you."

"Warm and dry, please? My arthritis isn't getting any better."

"That can be arranged. You need to learn a new language or two, and it's time for you to talk to a specialist. You understand what I'm saying?"

Kick takes a hit of coffee. Taylor notes his resistance and takes a moment. "You ever see two animals fight?" he asks.

Kick nods. "Sure."

"Ever notice how after they're done, they start shaking, or get tremors?"

"Okay."

"That's their natural mechanism for clearing trauma out of their body. It's called unwinding. Humans don't do that. Sure, we get adrenaline shakes, but we mostly push our feelings down so we can get on with life, or get back into combat, and it piles up. When more stuff gets packed on top, all that pressure has to go somewhere. To simplify, it gets amplified, distorted, and eventually comes out via your mind. You know what I'm talking about."

Kick stares at the black coffee. "Nightmares and hallucinations."

"And suicide." Taylor sits back. "You clean and oil your guns, right?"

"Yeah."

"The CIA has to do the same to us. It's not like they necessarily care — we're expensive. What they used to generally call shell shock is now PTSD."

"And what the fuck does that mean?" Kick asks.

"Post-traumatic stress disorder. There are ways to treat it, and a big part of that is just talking about your shit. You know how to talk, right? Personally, I love sitting around talking about myself with someone who can't leave."

"And Kelly?"

"There's shit going down at her paper. You know I don't consider myself a liberal, but I'm no fan of fascism, so let's just say I have an interest in making sure she kicks up a good bit of shit with this. I mean, no one spit on ArmaLite, Colt, or Mattel for making the M16. *The Vancouver Telegraph* is being bought by some asshole named Lenoir. He's a spoiled billionaire who thinks people should stop thinking for themselves and start thinking like him. I didn't always like what Cronkite said, but he didn't really make anything up. This asshole does. And in this case, I prefer the truth to get out." Taylor steals some more coffee.

"Can I stay until she publishes?"

Taylor thinks it over. "I think I can swing that. You've got to heal up anyway, so I'll say it's too hot for you to move for a couple of weeks. But we lock you both down right here. I'll be staying in town to see her story through. Technically, I have diplomatic immunity here, so it's not so risky for me."

"I'll let her know."

"Until it's done, she does nothing but write that story, and neither one of you leaves this house. Got it?" Taylor asks.

"Clear." Kick checks his watch. "Shit, let's see if we made the news." He turns the TV on to the morning news in time to see a report of a freighter on fire with cops and emergency vehicles all over the place. The announcer is explaining there was some kind of gang shootout overnight at the Versatile Shipyard, ending in a massive explosion aboard an old Victory freighter. A police spokesperson comes on to say the bodies are of several known gang members, and they'll be investigating thoroughly. The news anchor dubs the event, "'The Christmas Eve Massacre.'" Taylor laughs. "I like it!"

As he goes on, they show footage of fire trucks and a news crew arriving at the scene. There, in the murky background, are two familiar shapes. Taylor and Kick get closer to the screen and see Buck and Baker with heads down, looking away from the camera, limping up the hill, Baker with his ski bag.

"Hood up and head down, just like I taught him. I always say, cover is important."

"'Cause you never know."

"Baker gets a forty-pounder of something nice for sticking to the basics."

"Hey, did you get a fix on Dusty?"

"No sign at his apartment. We have to assume he went straight to the airport. I'm sure he's good."

"You checked the morgues?"

Taylor nods. "Yeah. No sign of him. We'll keep looking but stop worrying."

"Sure."

"Just get some rest," Taylor orders.

Kick takes his coffee and heads down the hall. Peeking into the bedroom, he sees Kelly has cleaned up and changed. She's lying fully clothed on the bed, sound asleep. He pulls a duvet over her and lies down on the floor beside her bed, under a blanket. Kick stares at the ceiling, wondering what the future has in store for him.

39

SHOESHINE
Danang, Vietnam, 1969

"SHOESHINE?" the young voice asks.

One of the most important lessons that soldiers in the Vietnam War learned early was that ordinary things can kill you. Eventually, everyone knew better than to pick up anything that wasn't theirs in enemy territory, and sometimes even on base. Hollywood used to joke he wouldn't pick up a candle in the Vatican, in case it blew up.

Booby traps inflicted around ten per cent of US casualties. Sharp *punji sticks* smeared with poison or feces waited at the bottom of camouflaged pits. Grenade traps were set along trails with trip wires. *Toe-poppers* had a nail at the bottom of a bamboo tube with a bullet on top, to fire through your foot when you stepped on it. Venomous snakes waited in deep pits or in your rucksack, and spiked maces could swing down and crush your skull while you were walking on a trail.

In warfare, these things are referred to as *friction*. Kick and his men did similar things; in fact, this was how they escaped after calling in artillery, or taking a kill shot. Frosty's claymore inventions were a good example. As a result, everyone was hypersensitive about picking up captured maps, enemy flags, or weapons.

One of the Cong's favorites in urban areas was to wire a shoeshine box with C4 and shrapnel and give it to a Vietnamese kid. Like one who had lost their parents. They were told, if they got close to an American soldier to just open the box. After that they would see their parents again. Kick is looking at one of those kids right now.

"Shoeshine?" the girl asks again in English. She's barefoot, no more than ten years old, with a sad little face. The shoeshine box is almost too heavy for her thin arms.

Kick levels his Colt. "Stop! Get back! *Didi mau!*"

People stop, look, then scatter fast. Kick backs up. There's an MP half a block behind her. "It's a bomb!" Kick screams.

The MP gets on his walkie and runs back. Kick breaks out in flop sweat as he realizes he may have to do something he's dreaded since getting here. He bumps into a food stall behind him and stops. He might have a chance if she doesn't get much closer, so he fires a warning shot into the air. The girl stops. She's shaking with fear. Time slows down. Everyone is running.

The smells of the Danang market are suddenly overpowering. His pounding heart is deafening. Her face. The box. Bare feet. People screaming. Then an eerie silence.

In the distance there's a black car. Inside it, two Vietnamese men in sunglasses watch. They aren't scared. They're interested. He goes back to the girl. The food stall has a large plywood sandwich board, so Kick grabs it and holds it in front of him like a shield.

The girl is crying as she repeats what they told her to say. "Meet your ancestors."

Kid gets his head behind the sandwich board just as the lid of the shoeshine box pops open. The flash still blinds him, and the explosion is deafening. He's blown off his feet, back through the food stall, and lands on his back. The plywood is pinned to him by nails and shrapnel. Splinters dig into his legs and chest and shrapnel fragments pepper his hand where he gripped the sign. He looks at the spot where the girl was. There's nothing left but smoke, dust and one tiny bare foot, charred on the top.

The air drips with the stench of seared flesh and blood. Like burned pork. Kick's hearing is dull, except for a high-pitched squeal. There's a metal taste in his mouth from a scrap of steel jammed through his cheek. His sunglasses and beret are gone. Blown off his head. The arms of his uniform are shredded, and nails and shrapnel stick out of his arms.

He's numb, but slivers of pain are exploding in him, the largest in his right foot. He reaches down and feels something sharp sticking out of his boot. He cranes his head and sees a bloody shard of what looks like the girl's tibia that has penetrated his foot. A siren approaches, but it sounds strange. Kick's vision flutters, and he wonders if it might be angel wings. Maybe they're coming to get him. Maybe he'll meet his ancestors.

40
Go to Print

KELLY MAKES HER WAY OUT OF THE BEDROOM and heads toward the smell of roast turkey and fresh coffee. Taylor is at the stove with all the fixings in the works, wearing a bad looking Santa hat, and the same clothes he wore yesterday. Kick's in his boxers and nothing else, plopping fluffy mashed potatoes into a bowl. The coffee maker is burbling.

Taylor takes a sip of the gravy. "That's fuckin' good!" He spots Kelly. "Hey there! I'd say good morning, but it's five in the afternoon. Merry Christmas!" He looks like he hasn't slept yet, but he's right in his element.

Kick throws on a t-shirt. "Don't mind him. He's been getting his ass kissed by Langley," he chides. "Not to mention, he had a second bottle of scotch."

"And some beer," adds Taylor.

Kick pulls out a chair for Kelly, and he and Taylor make a show of serving her a big slice of the bird, while Kick slaps down the potatoes, stuffing, and carrots cooked in the pan with the turkey. They treat her like royalty.

Kelly is all smiles. "What a fantastic meal, gentlemen! Thank you. You do look pretty happy, Mr. Taylor."

"I'd have to agree with that," Taylor says, eating a crunchy piece of skin. "Oh, my god, that makes it all worth it, right there. Dig in!"

It's surreal having a meal like this after a night like they had. The boys are clearly starving and inhale their food. Eventually, they come up for air.

"And now, Kelly," Kick says, "as an encore, I'm excited to get this story out."

Taylor adds, "Needless to say, you can't include anything about the CIA, or getting kidnapped, almost blown up, and all that, but everything else is fair game. Plus, I've got some goodies on the way for you that I know you're going to like."

Kelly looks uncomfortable. "Are you sure it's a good idea right now, after last night?"

Kick and Taylor stop chewing and answer in unison, "Yeah!"

Taylor goes first. "Keep in mind no one knows you had anything to do with that. As far as the world knows, you're enjoying your Christmas vacation, and your boss thinks you're writing. You should give him a call today to check in. Make up some questions to ask, or wish him Merry Christmas, or something."

Kelly smiles. "Believe it or not, he'll be happy to deal with work today."

"The thing is, the window to get this published is closing, and we need to hustle."

Kelly takes that in. "Oh. And why is that?"

"There's going to be a change of ownership at your paper," Kick replies.

"Or rather, there already has been, but not many people know about it," Taylor adds. "Most likely, shit will go down after everyone gets back from the holidays."

"Didn't see that coming. I'll get on the phone with my editor and let him know I'll have something next week. Should I start looking for another job?"

Kick looks at Taylor. "No. I mean yes, you can, but I'm making some calls. If this story is as explosive as I think it'll be, you'll likely have your pick of news outlets."

Kelly drops her fork. "Really?"

Kick goes next. "You can call your editor from the secure phone here. Just don't speak to anyone else until this goes to press. And we'll both have to hang out here until that happens. It's not safe yet. Sorry."

Kelly digests all that. "All right. I get it. This is my job, and it's a great opportunity. Not to mention, things didn't exactly go well the last time I didn't listen to you guys."

Taylor smiles. "Don't worry about that. I'll be around to support this whole thing, so if there's anything you need, just let us know, okay?"

Kelly nods. "Yeah. Got it." She smiles at Taylor and says, "Thanks again, too. For coming to get me."

Taylor waves her off. "My pleasure. Kick, are *you* going to thank me for rescuing you?"

Kick looks up from stuffing his face. "No. You still owe me."

Taylor considers that. "Yeah, that's true."

Kelly gets up and hugs Taylor, then gives Kick a kiss on the cheek. "I'm calling my editor right now."

"You left half your plate!" Kick shouts after her.

"It's all yours, boys." She heads for the phone. "After all, I want to be able to still get on my hog."

Kick howls with laughter, as Taylor barks, "After all I did for you, Kelly?"

Kick grabs her plate. "Dibs on the stuffing."

◆ ◆ ◆ ◆

Stewart picks up the phone. "Hello?"

"Hi, Mr. Stewart, I mean Malcolm. It's Kelly O'Leary calling. Is this a good time?"

"Kelly, what a nice surprise! Are you writing furiously?" Stewart says.

"Yes, that's why I'm calling," Kelly answers. "I have a lot more information coming, and I want to make sure that's it's okay to include it. Frankly, it's explosive."

"Is it *okay*? If it's as good as the rest of the material, then hell yeah, it's okay. Make sure you source it all, but don't worry about it being too long or too many articles. We can buy more newsprint. There's a good reason to make a big splash right now. What's your ETA on the whole piece?"

"A week," Kelly replies. "I'd like it to all land the Saturday before everyone comes back to work after New Year's, if that's all right? Maybe its own section in the big weekend edition?"

Stewart clears his throat. "I think that's perfect, and now I have to tell you a few things, but you can't tell a soul, understand?"

"Agreed. What's up?"

"Kelly, the paper has been sold to a first-class asshole named Charles Lenoir, aka *Charles the Black*, aka a giant a-hole, and he's going to be rolling in after Christmas break and making major changes. It'll be a bloodbath, and no one's job is safe, especially mine. Do you understand what I'm saying?"

"Oh!" Kelly answers, faking surprise. "All right. Didn't see that coming. Well, I guess this is our last chance to raise a little hell before we get fired."

There's a moment of silence, and then Stewart explodes with laughter. "I wasn't expecting that, but I love it! You put the boots to everyone who deserves it and let the chips fall where they may. I'm so glad I hired you, O'Leary. But listen, do yourself a favor and cash out your retirement funds immediately. Ask for a check to be mailed. If they ask why, say you're buying a house or something. Lenoir will not hesitate to plunder those funds, and whatever else he can get away with. Got it?"

"Okay. Anything else?"

"Don't go back to the office. When you're ready to publish, call me and read it all to me over the phone. New Year's Eve Day would be great, because then I can sneak in the next day when no one's around and do the layout. I'll give you instructions after that as to how we sneak this in for printing. Lenoir has some little prick he calls *Darth Vader* going through the books with his staff, plus someone else who's watching what's getting printed. I'll figure out a way around it, though. Don't worry. Christ, I'll run the goddamn press myself if I have to, and don't think I don't know how!"

"Okay! This is pretty exciting, isn't it?"

"You're goddamn right it is, Kelly! The way news ought to be! This'll be my last shot getting something like this into print. Now, before my wife makes me julienne carrots for Christmas dinner, I have to get a call in to Ted Turner. I'm selling the contents of the Evil Room to him and putting that money aside for folks who get fired. Lenoir doesn't know it, but there are boxes full of juicy details about him in there. I can't remember the last time I was this excited. Godspeed, Kelly O'Leary. God fucking speed!" Stewart has hung up. Kelly puts the phone down and turns to see Kick and Taylor smiling in the doorway.

"Well, I guess I'd better get at it," Kelly says getting up. As she walks back to the bedroom, she stops and whispers in Taylor's ear, "Get Kick a cherry pie next time you're out." Taylor nods and gets his coat.

◆ ◆ ◆ ◆

It's the morning of New Year's Eve, and Kelly has been writing like a fiend for the past eight days. One reason is to meet her deadline; the other is to try and quell the images from her ordeal. Her sleep has been constantly interrupted by events looping over and over in her mind. Little five-second movies, where she keeps trying to change the outcome, but can't: Chung's men stuffing her into a car, being beaten in the back of the cab, the smell of blood from the driver she stabbed, the explosive vest, being left alone to die on the ship.

She relives Wong saving her, with her beautiful, kind eyes and blue hair, whispering, "It's all right, girlfriend. I'm good at this." And Mustafa, a bear-like man in his smelly little boat. She should write something on trauma next. She's amazed at how Kick and Taylor can deal with the amount of shit they've seen. No wonder they hardly sleep and look half dead.

Kelly wonders if people who experience trauma somehow recognize each other. It seems like she and Kick did. Is there some sort of psychological secret handshake? Maybe that's why Kick gravitates to people who've all been damaged in a similar way. Maybe they're drawn to each other. And can you really call it *damage*? I mean, isn't this the mechanism that kept our species alive? Learning from close calls so we can avoid them next time? Kick's hyper-vigilance makes him an outsider in civilian life, but it kept him alive in Vietnam. It kept primitive humans alive in the African savanna. She's been thinking about Kick a lot and knows now that she really loves him. She also knows it will never work between them, and she's pretty sure he knows that too.

Kick finishes reading the last page of her draft and looks at Kelly. "It's great. I don't think you've missed a thing. And it's so easy to read."

"Unlike Baker's books, I take it? Malcolm likes small words."

"You ready to make the call?"

Kelly looks around the room at the boxes and stacks of paper. "I'm ready." She pulls the typewriter ribbon out and hands it to Kick. "Burn this, please."

Kelly spends roughly an hour and a half on the phone, reading her pieces to Stewart, and when she hangs up, her hands are shaking, and her face is flushed. "It's good to go. Malcolm got all misty a couple of times and said it's fantastic how you and I made it work together. He called us the Sword and the Pen."

Kick smiles. "And by the weekend I'll know which one is mightier."

Kelly manages a laugh. "But I have some bad news about my co-worker Val. Malcolm says she was mugged or something on her way home from our last day of work. She has a broken arm and is pretty banged up. I'd like to see her before I take off."

"You guys spend a lot of time together lately?"

"Yeah. She's my best friend. Why?"

"I'm thinking we already took care of whoever did that to her." Kick considers things for a moment. "Let's see what Taylor can do when he gets back."

"I feel responsible."

"Don't. They must've been satisfied she didn't know anything, so good for you for keeping your mouth shut. We'll figure something out. Back to your story. What's next?"

"I have instructions for handing it off, and I'll need some help with that."

Taylor walks in with his arms full of grocery bags. "Hey, all, I thought we'd make lasagna for dinner. Got a big bottle of red to go with it." He takes one look at Kelly's flushed face and stops. "You look like you're ready to publish."

Kelly nods, and Taylor puts the bags down. "I'll go back out and get something with bubbles."

"I have to make a copy of this and get the original to my editor. He and the head of production will get a separate section ready tonight when no one's there, and it'll go out as a part of a special edition on Saturday. Most of us will be getting fired on Monday anyway, so fuck it. We have to box up all the research materials and send it to someone at *The Washington Post*, which will be picking up the story on Monday." Kelly hands Taylor a slip of paper with a name and address on it. "They're offering me a job, if I can get a work visa."

Taylor has been smiling the whole time. "A little bird told me that's ready and waiting, Kelly. And there's a reservation for you at the Jefferson Hotel in DC, until you find a place to live. Assuming you're interested in the job?"

Kelly takes a minute to collect herself. "Yes, I'm interested! What, are you kidding?"

Taylor hands over a business card. "Once we get this delivered, call this person, and work out the details. And start thinking about follow-up pieces you'd like to do, who you'd like to interview, and all that."

Kelly gives Taylor a big hug and wipes tears from her eyes. "Okay. Thanks. This is a lot." She isn't sure what to do next. "Guess I'd better start packing this up."

"I'll get this copied at the consulate, and be back in an hour," says Taylor. "I'll make sure all this gets to DC. You're going to really like my lasagna. One of my favorite spies in Italy gave me the recipe. He stole it from some famous chef there."

"Looking forward to it," Kelly says. "Thanks, again."

Kick stops Taylor. "Hey, we need to give her friend Valerie from *The Telegraph* a hand. She got roughed up by Chung's boys, and Kelly needs to say goodbye before she leaves. Plus, Val needs to find a job. Kelly typed up all her details. You got a few more tricks up your sleeve?"

"They always need good local people at the consulate, if she passes the background check. Let me see what I can do about all that." Taylor leaves.

Kick and Kelly crack a couple of beers and look at the massive amount of material they have stacked up in the living room. This could be their last private moment together, and it's awkward.

Kelly turns to him. "We don't have to know what comes next. All we can do is say goodbye for now and see what happens. And that's okay."

"Yeah. That's okay."

She takes his hand. "The work is done. So, what do you say we stop being so professional, and say a proper goodbye?" She takes his hand, and they walk to the bedroom, and close the door.

41

A NEW LIFE
Danang, Vietnam, 1969

ALL KICK CAN SEE IS WHITE. It's bright and smells so good he wonders if he's made it to heaven. As his eyes grow accustomed, he notices his hearing is dull. While he listens for signs of where he is, he smells honeysuckle. There're murmurs and shuffling, then something recognizable. It's a woman's voice. "He's awake. Call the doctor and ... that man."

"Shit. Not heaven."

"No, but at least it's not hell," the woman says. Kick tries to sit up, but he can hardly move. "You're heavily sedated. Just be still. Your friend will be here in a minute."

"What's that smell? Is it flowers?"

"Oh. It's called Rangoon Creeper. It's all over the walls outside. Smells like honeysuckle, doesn't it?"

"My mom's favorite ..."

The nurse stands over him with a big smile on her face. "We almost lost you. Can you tell me your name?"

"My name?"

"I'll take it from here," says a deep voice. "Thank you. I really appreciate you taking such good care of my friend." There's a man in a short-sleeved white shirt and tie. The nurse leaves.

"You look like a fucking Mormon."

The man smiles. "I have very little to do with God. Just take it easy, Kick."

After a few seconds, tears roll out of Kick's eyes, and he starts hyperventilating. Taylor yells, "Nurse? Another shot, please? Looks like he needs more rest."

◆ ◆ ◆ ◆

Kick is looking at the girl again, but she's moving in slow motion as her hand opens the shoeshine box. "Don't! Don't!" There is a blinding flash, and he's flying off the ground, and up into the brightness, until he sees an angel. She's so beautiful. He reaches out his hand to touch her, but she shakes her head.

"Not yet, David." Her voice is so sweet. "There's more for you to learn here."

Then he's falling and screaming. Kick bolts up in bed panting hard and pointing his hands at the wall like he's about to fire his gun.

"Wake up!"

Kick opens his eyes and sees Taylor. "I know you ..." He stares at him for almost a full minute. "Taylor. I need a smoke." Taylor offers him the one he's holding, and Kick reaches out with a bandaged hand. He looks at his hand, then takes the cigarette, and pulls hard on it.

Taylor lights himself another. "Good to have you back, Kick. What's the last thing you remember?"

Kick looks at him, and tears flow out of his eyes. "Shoeshine. Meet your ancestors."

"Yeah. You saved a lot of people by clearing out that market. And *you* didn't send her. We grabbed the guys who did and they're now at the bottom of the South China Sea. Okay?"

Kick absorbs all this information slowly. "Do they think I'm dead?"

Taylor brings a chair up beside the bed and sits. "Yeah, they do. And you actually were dead by the time the ambulance got to you. But they brought you back somehow. I guess you weren't ready to go. And here you are."

"They wanted the bounty."

"Yeah. We haven't notified your mother yet, though, since we wanted to hear from you first." Taylor's words hang in the air.

"I've already decided. I need to save her, so tell her I'm dead."

◆ ◆ ◆ ◆

Kick is on the firing range with his Remington picking off everything he chooses. It's hot as Hades, and he and the rest of the men firing with him are shirtless and sweaty. Colonel Campbell and Taylor sit in the shade a ways back and watch the targets with binoculars. Kick looks at his watch and calls it. "Finish up! Make these your last shots and make 'em *count*!"

Kick starts packing up his rifle, while Taylor comes over with a cold can of beer. "Get this into you." Kick pounds the beer, and belches. "Ahhhh. It's thirsty work."

Taylor laughs and he pulls up a chair beside him and Campbell. "That limp's not too bad," Campbell says. Kick shrugs, tosses the empty beer can, and grabs his t-shirt. His wounds have scarred over and glisten under his sweat.

Taylor hands him a fresh beer. "These clowns are not looking too bad. I see you have a couple of LRRPs in there."

Kick takes a swig. "Yeah. I want to get them off this range, and into some real field situations: wind, rain, elevation, stress."

"Us too," says Campbell. "We'd like you to do some actuals with each of them. One on one. You feel ready?"

Kick looks at his beer. "Yeah. Looking forward to it. But nothing out of bounds yet. I don't want them fucking up in the middle of Laos. Close to a firebase, and easy to exfil."

"Tomorrow night you can take your pick of the litter," Campbell says.

Taylor puts a hand on his shoulder. "And welcome back ... to your new life."

43

GONE FISHIN'

IT'S FOUR A.M., AND A BLACK CHEVY SUBURBAN with darkened windows pulls over by a *Vancouver Telegraph* news box. It's dark, and a cold rain pounds the box with the help of a sidewinder wind. Kick, wearing black winter rain gear and a ball cap under his hood, gets out and puts in the required change. He grabs five copies of the Saturday, January 2nd edition, and gets back in. "Keep the fucking change, Lenoir."

Taylor reads the headline above the fold. "'Canada Secretly Armed the US in Vietnam War — 40K Canadian Boys Volunteered.'" The byline is Kelly O'Leary, and there's a picture of two soldiers in a rice paddy firing M16s. "Ooooh," he says, as he snaps his copy open to the special section. "That gets your fuckin' attention, doesn't it?"

"Who's in the picture?" Kick asks, pointing to one of the soldiers. "He looks familiar."

"The guy on the left is Mohawk, from the Kahnawake Reserve near Montreal, and he can't wait to be interviewed. You'd like him. And the guy on the right is your old pal Frosty.

"Shit. We were so young."

"Yeah. I thought these two would make a good impression in a pic. They ended up in the same unit after you died."

"I'll be damned. Where are they now?" Kick asks with a bit of hesitation.

"They both made it home, but I'm afraid Frosty didn't last long." Taylor pulls back into the pre-dawn traffic. "Sorry."

Kick watches the rain. He thinks about his time with Frosty and his old military and high school friends. It's like it all happened to someone else. His life feels like a blur.

Kick pulls out the section Kelly wrote. There are different headlines for each aspect. Kick reads the first headline out loud to Taylor. "'America's Bitch — Johnny Canuck did Uncle Sam's Dirty Work on the Sly.'"

Taylor howls with laughter. "That's fantastic! Read the rest of 'em!"

"'What Companies Made War Materials for USA?,' 'What Did the PMs Know & When?,' 'Canada Spied for US Bombing Runs,' 'Agent Orange Tested by Unprotected Canadian Soldiers,' 'How Did Canadian Boys Volunteer?,' 'Vietnam Birthed Our Arms Industry,' 'How Complicit Was the Press?,' 'Dawn of the Surveillance State,' 'What Did We Make for Vietnam?,' 'Taxpayers Subsidized US War Production,' and 'Why Did We Do This?,'" The final headline is the most surprising. "'My Dad Was a Canadian Arms Dealer.'"

Taylor whistles. "This may not be combat, but that's fuckin' brave."

Kick reads the article about Kelly's dad first, and it's powerful. This is one she didn't share with him. She writes about her father breaking down one night while watching the news. It was a story showing Vietnamese children who'd been burned by napalm. Napalm that he had most likely sold. Because Kelly was the same age as the girl, and was in the room, he couldn't handle it. After that night, there were late-night phone calls and mysterious visitors. Then one day, he left for business overseas and never came back.

Kelly lays out that her father brokered Canadian-made napalm, artillery shells, bullets, grenades, TNT, Agent Orange, and numerous other war materials to the United States. Most of this material was made by Canadian companies — for example Bata, who made boots for the troops, and the Dorothea Knitting Mills in Toronto that made the green berets. In some cases, her dad was simply a middleman who made sure Uncle Sam got what it wanted from wherever he could find it. She admits that she has a trust fund left to her by her father and will eventually inherit an enormous amount of money from his estate, once she reaches a certain age.

The last part of the article is the most potent. She writes about the guilt she feels, her feelings of helplessness, and promises to use her wealth for positive purposes. More importantly, she aims to devote her career to holding powerful institutions accountable for their actions. Her father, like her home country, and many Canadian companies, betrayed the trust of Canadian citizens, to simply gain wealth, and for that they should be exposed. If exploiting Canadian taxpayers to help fund an arms industry was such a good idea, then why did they work so hard to keep it a secret? And when you catch your own government hiding things like this, it makes you wonder what else they have tucked out of sight.

Kick reads the articles out loud all the way to the Tsawwassen Ferry Terminal, where they get in line and wait for the ferry to Nanaimo on Vancouver Island.

Taylor runs inside to the parking lot coffee shop and comes back grinning with two cups of joe. "Everyone inside is talking about the article. I fucking love democracy." He puts on a new fishing hat he bought inside, then notices Kick's cloudy face. "Hey, we don't have to do this, you know."

"We made a deal. You helped me with this, and now we go fishing. I keep my word. Thanks for the coffee." He takes a sip. "It's going to be tough though. Being back in my hometown. You still think it's okay?"

"Yeah. And I think it's necessary too. Don't worry, I get it." They read in silence for a while as they wait for the ferry.

"I don't want to see any puking while we're out there," Taylor warns. "Once we're fishing, we don't come back in until we have at least a couple of good ones each."

"Hey, I'm good. First, I fished here all the time, and second, jumping into Laos during the wet season is a hell of a lot worse."

"Okay. In other news, we have a call to make tomorrow. I had to send out operatives, but I think I finally tracked him down. Dusty really knows how to disappear."

"Yeah, I guess he would."

The announcement comes for their ferry to load, and they drive on and are directed to a lower deck. Kick stays in the truck to sleep, while Taylor heads up for breakfast.

"Bring me one of those breakfast wrap things, will you?" Kick asks. Taylor nods and heads out.

Kick is still coming down from the past few weeks. He drifts off thinking about the dark place he was in, wanting to kill himself, and all the events that led up to the newspaper now sitting on his lap. Before he knows it, the door opens and Taylor drops something warm in his lap.

"Eat up. The line up was intense, and all anyone is talking about is Kelly's section," Taylor reports. "She's lucky she flew out last night, because she'd be swamped. *The Washington Post* has interviews lined up for her on the Sunday shows, and more starting Monday. It's going to be fucking *wild*, man." Kick unwraps his breakfast wrap. "You okay?"

Kick nods and takes a bite. "I hope she does great."

"Did you guys leave on good terms?"

"Yeah. There was no way it could go any further." If he'd continued the thought, he would have had to talk about things like his hyper-vigilance, how he couldn't sleep in the same room with her, and all the rest of his PTSD baggage. "We managed to find each other and share something great for a while. And now we move on."

Taylor looks over at him. "That's a good way to look at it, brother. And unlike a lot of special people we've shared great times with, she's still alive. Chances are you'll see her again."

"You never know."

They sit in silence for a while, and then Taylor changes the subject. "So, after I show you how to catch salmon today, we are heading to DC to figure out your next steps. From what I've heard so far, I think you're going to like it. And you'll be happy to know, I got you onto the sniper range with some fancy new shit."

Kick brightens up. "Thanks, Tinker."

◆ ◆ ◆ ◆

Taylor and Kick roar out of the ferry just after seven am and end up in Port Hardy a bit after noon, thanks to Taylor's choice to ignore the speed limit. They drive out to a tiny cemetery at the top of a hill on the edge of town. The town lies below, still socked in by fog. It's the kind of morning that makes Kick wonder if the sun even bothered to come up. A cold rain is pelting down. Taylor wanders off, while Kick places his flowers on the joint headstone for his parents. He feels at once like a lost little boy and a grown stranger. Warm tears seep from his eyes, mix with the rain, and drip into the grave.

He turns to the right and reads the next marker. It's his. He reads the lies carved into it and feels sick for the pain it must have caused. Kick stands caught in this surreal moment, until he notices that Taylor is standing one row over. He wipes his eyes and walks over.

The grave is for Michael 'Hollywood' McCormick. Kick takes out a mickey of rye whiskey and pours half of it over the headstone and grave. "God, I miss him the most," Kick says. He and Taylor take turns drinking the rest of the booze.

"I'll never get back to the way I was, will I?" Kick asks.

"No. We've been changed all the way into our cell structure. It's been proven that human brains literally change shape with combat trauma. But the Buddha said that every morning we are born again, so it's what we do today that matters most. Peace lives in the now. Remember that."

"Jesus, you've been reading Baker's books," Kick teases.

"Guilty. There's another guy you should read. He's badass."

"Ghandhi?"

"No. I'm paraphrasing badly, but he wrote, 'Life isn't a journey to the grave in hopes of getting there safe and looking all pretty. It's better to skid in sideways in a big cloud of smoke, all used up, totally beat to shit, and yelling, "Wow, what a ride!'"

Kick chuckles. "Hollywood would have loved that guy."

Taylor laughs. "Hunter S. Thompson. And yeah, they would've partied."

Kick takes a moment. "Don't you feel like you're kind of like …" Kick can't find the right words.

"A Charlie in the Box in the Land of Misfit Toys?" finishes Taylor.

"That wasn't at all what I was going to say, but yeah."

"Sure. But if it wasn't for the misfits, who'd jump out of planes and take out bad guys? Who'd protect what's important? We're better suited for conflict now than a desk. Just embrace it. Seeing this shrink will help you manage your shit. Turn your pain into purpose. So don't worry; it's going to be fine. Take a six-pack in with you. It takes the edge off. Your quote was Alan Seeger."

"What?"

"'I have a rendezvous with death.' Before they came out of the building to shoot you. That's Alan Seeger, the World War One poet. Baker was proud."

Kick nods and lets the cold rain hit him in the face for a while. "Let's go fishing, bitch."

"Good fucking idea." They walk back to the truck, leaning in against the rain. "I brought extra beer for the boat. I promised the captain a little refreshment."

Kick stops and turns back, like he's expecting to see someone, or hear a voice. There's nothing. Nothing but a warm, comfortable feeling. "I'm glad we did this, Taylor."

Taylor yells back, "Me too. Now come on. Those fish won't catch themselves!"

Out on the boat, Taylor surprises Kick by sparking up a joint. The beer has been flowing freely since they got out there, and the old captain is enjoying these two American import-export executives on a short break from their conference in Vancouver. "Nice weed, Captain!" Taylor yells over the engine noise.

The captain smiles. "Grew it myself." He takes a couple of hits. He looks like he has absolutely no problem overcharging them for a day on the water.

Kick catches the captain staring at him like he's trying to remember his face. Taylor's pole doubles over just in time, and he gives it a hard yank. "Fish on!"

After Taylor lands a thirty-two-pound spring salmon, the captain congratulates him on joining the Tyee Club. Kick explains that *tyee* is a coastal indigenous word meaning *chief*, and any Chinook salmon, also known as a spring, over thirty pounds qualifies. Taylor's tickled pink.

"I'm in the Tyee Club!"

"Technically, these are out of season," the captain says. "But I happen to know the Fishery guy's on vacation, so it'll be our little secret." He gives Kick another look, and asks, "Have I taken you fishing before? You look awful familiar."

Kick shakes his head, and Taylor replies, "He's got one of those faces. Like Bruce Willis." The captain thinks that's hilarious.

Kick lands the next one, also well over thirty pounds, and by the end of the day they have two big ones each.

"God, so much for daylight," Taylor moans.

The captain laughs. "We're out of beer anyway. I'll help you guys get 'em cleaned."

"I'm going to need a picture of these babies too," Taylor says beaming.

Once they're on the dock, the captain snaps off a few pictures on Taylor's camera. The best one has them both holding one each by the tail and pushing them toward the camera to make them look bigger. Finally, Kick breaks a smile.

"That one's getting framed!"

The captain helps clean them and shares some tall tales about fish that got away, how halibut cheeks are a delicacy around here, and a couple of awesome Sasquatch sightings he had. They hunker down for the night at nearby Bear Cove, in separate cabins, in case one of them wakes up with a flashback. Taylor finds that pretty amusing.

"We should have a sign on the door that reads 'Do not disturb. Violent sons-a-bitches.'"

Alone in his room, Kick stares out the window into the dark and picks through everything he's feeling. He thinks about the terrible people he's killed, and wonders how they got that way. Some of them probably thought they were doing the right thing; some may have just taken a wrong turn in life. Many times, he has stood at his own crossroads and could easily have taken a different path. His mind is spinning again, and the bull's-eye bruise on his chest throbs. Why has he been so lucky, and others not?

He tries to take Taylor's advice and stay in the moment. The sound of the rain falling in his hometown is soothing as he lies down on the bed, shuts off the light, and follows his breathing to a fairly sound sleep.

44

The Broadcast

THE NEXT MORNING KICK IS SHAVING when an excited Taylor comes to the door. "You got the TV on?" he asks.

Kick has it on ABC already, and the coffee is ready. They spike it with rye and turn up the volume on *This Week with David Brinkley*. Brinkley is teeing up his next interview, which will be with Kelly, right after the commercial break.

Kick can't help but be impressed. "I've gotta say, Taylor, this is fucking cool."

Taylor is in his glory. He has his feet up on the bed, and is smoking a Marlboro and sipping his whiskey coffee. "She's going to be great." And she is.

Kelly and Brinkley hit it off immediately, and over two segments they cover the Canadian companies and US branch plants based in Canada that produced munitions for the Vietnam War. She also gets into the grants and forgivable loans they were awarded by the Canadian government. Then Brinkley digs into more interesting items like the manufacturing of the green berets, how Canadian hospitals became instruments of the US war machine, and the three billion dollars of war material Canada quietly sold to the US over the term of the war. How Pierre Trudeau had time to meet with John Lennon and Yoko, but no time for Claire Culhane, who was a nurse in Vietnam, and one of the most vocal Canadians to speak out against Canada's war machine, based on her firsthand experience there.

Segment two covers Canadian napalm made by Dow Chemical in Sarnia, Ontario; Agent Orange, tested at CFB Gagetown; and how the chemical wasn't even banned in Canada until 1985. They discuss the involvement of Canadian ICC officials in Vietnam and how forty thousand Canadian volunteers were magically processed into the US military, even though they were not legally allowed to fight under the Canadian Foreign Enlistment Act of 1937. The button on the interview comes when Brinkley asks why all this is so important to know right now.

Kelly's response is concise and effective. "Well, David, the short answer is that when a democratic nation starts lying to its citizens, it's the birth of a monster. It doesn't matter if it's Canada lying about Vietnam, or the US getting caught with *The Pentagon Papers*. The government works for the people, not the other way around. In this case, the Canadian government started taking its marching orders from America rather than its own people. And the funny thing is, America didn't even ask Canada to do it. The government volunteered because they smelled jobs and money."

Brinkley is about to interject, but Kelly motors on. "Consider this. Our cash-based society is being replaced by plastic cards that will track everything we buy, and where we buy it. So, it won't be long until companies, law enforcement agencies, and governments will want to store this information. They may find ways to track us through future technology. How will they use it? Something like a surveillance state is just around the corner, unless we start setting up guardrails."

Brinkley finally shoehorns in a question. "But doesn't that beg the question, Kelly, that if you're not doing anything wrong, what's the problem with the government knowing what you're up to?"

"So, just because you don't have anything to say, does that mean the government can take away your free speech? It's the same principle. I believe I have a right to my privacy. Don't you?"

Brinkley tries to interject, but again Kelly marches on. "If you don't vote every time, should they be able to take away your right to vote? Our rights and freedoms are forever, aren't they? What if suddenly Jews, atheists, or environmentalists are made to look like bad guys, and they have their rights taken away? Consider the shameful example of Americans of Japanese descent being imprisoned during World War Two. What if a women's right to vote is taken away? Or the right to control her own body?"

Kelly doesn't wait for Brinkley to answer. "As you know from history, most government takeovers are bloodless, and most fascists were democratically elected. They removed people's rights and freedoms by rewriting laws.

"Let's say some popular guy with fascist ideals becomes president. By the way, *fascist* is just a fancy word for someone who is power hungry and will do anything to get it and hold on to it. A bully on the grandest scale. Maybe they're funny, or irreverent. Call themselves an outsider, a person of the people. Whatever. But fascists could care less if they get there through the party of the Left or the Right, because their only real politics is *power. Power for the sake of power*.

"Once fascists are in place, they stack the courts, place their own people, friends, and family members in key positions of power. Then let's say there's an election, and even if this fascist loses, they refuse to go, or say the election was rigged. They could have a private army that helps take control of Congress or have a powerful branch of the media behind them, like a TV network. They can take power and have your personal information, collected by the banks, at their disposal. Maybe they don't like Catholics, or maybe they hate gay people, people of color, or anyone who just disagrees with them. They can use your personal information, and even edit it, to make you look guilty of whatever they want."

Brinkley chuckles. "This sounds like a Robert Ludlum paperback. I don't think anyone really believes that can happen here, do you?"

"No one thought Pearl Harbor could happen." Brinkley's smile drops. "No one talks about it much, but there were many turning points in World War Two where it could have gone the other way. If British pilots had lost the Battle of Britain, the Nazis would have landed ground forces and taken the country. If one Waffen-SS division hadn't stopped to cleanse a few villages on the way to Normandy, that may have turned the tide on D-Day. Imagine how different our world would be."

Brinkley tries to speak, but Kelly's just hitting her stride. "America is still smarting from leaving Vietnam, a war that superior technology was supposed to win. It's great to be confident and strive to be the best, but we must also plan for the worst and safeguard the principles America was founded on. Principles I'm a fan of. Democracy is not a spectator sport. It must be vigorously defended, which is what I'm doing here."

Brinkley interjects. "All right, but let's say …"

Kelly rolls on. "The very process I just laid out has happened in countries all over the world. A process we are very quick to criticize when it happens somewhere else. The founders knew all this and put bulwarks in place. But let one fascist in who can remove those defenses, and they will have the greatest military in the world at their fingertips. And money. America is not bulletproof, and it *absolutely* could happen here. And that would make me mad, David, because I really *hate* fascists."

Mr. Brinkley is chuckling at Kelly's steamroller approach and knows a good line to get out on. "You've given us a *lot* to think about, Kelly O'Leary, and I understand you're taking up a new position with *The Washington Post* tomorrow. I'm looking forward to watching you keep everyone on their toes around here." He shakes her hand. "And for the record, Kelly, I hate fascists too."

Kick and Taylor jump to their feet and applaud in the cabin.
Taylor proclaims, "There is no substitute for victory!"
"I know that! MacArthur!"
They top up their coffees with rye, and drink.

◆ ◆ ◆ ◆

Baker is at Millie's Café on Sunset Boulevard, looking very LA in his t-shirt, old jeans, and flips-flops. His injured leg is sticking straight out under his table as a server brings him a steaming cup. He applauds the TV as Brinkley wraps it up. Baker sips his Oolong tea, and says quietly, "If people only knew, dude."

◆ ◆ ◆ ◆

It's late afternoon, of what is technically the next day, in Hong Kong. The noisy city is flying past Wong as she stands in front of her favorite sidewalk newsstand. Her hair is back to jet black and cut shorter. She's holding a copy of *The Washington Post*. She reads all the way to the end, not moving from her spot on the busy sidewalk, then puts the paper down. A torrent of Mandarin pours out of her that roughly translates to, "Holy fuck! This is some awesome shit!"

◆ ◆ ◆ ◆

Further around the globe in Cairo, it's late at night, and Mustafa is trying to get his bouncing children to bed. The TV is loud in the apartment, his wife is talking to him, and the entire household sounds like a riot, which is normal. One of the neighbor kids comes running in with a newspaper and hands it to him. Mustafa lets the kid keep the change and looks at the paper. He's excited, but tucks it under his arm and yells to his wife that he is going to the roof to smoke cigarettes. Once up there, with the green lights of the city's mosques lit up around him, he sits cross-legged and smokes, reading it all again, and again. Mustafa then prays that Kelly and all his friends will stay safe and gives thanks for the chance to help her when she was in need.

◆ ◆ ◆ ◆

In Vancouver, a bulbous Charles Lenoir is in Stewart's office having a different kind of experience. "Who in the name of Christ is this fucking bitch? Find her and fire her right fucking now!" he screams at the accountant known as Darth

Vader. He throws copies of *The Telegraph* and *The Washington Post* around Stewart's office. "And where the fuck is that editor? I want him standing in front of me within the hour!" On the huge window behind Lenoir, the former editor has spray-painted a giant peace sign, a sixties-looking flower, and the words *Hippies Rule!*

◆ ◆ ◆ ◆

Malcolm Stewart will not be standing in front of Charles Lenoir within the hour. That's because he and his wife are on a stunning tropical patio in Turks and Caicos. They've been watching Kelly's ABC interview with glee. Stewart jumps to his feet applauding and spills his piña colada. He then holds up a copy of *The Vancouver Telegraph* that he had flown in and yells to anyone who cares to listen, "That's my girl right there! I did that! Take that Lenoir, you fascist prick! I went out on top! I went out on top!" His wife applauds loudly as several early-bird strollers on the beach stop to look at the spectacle. Stewart then invites them all in for drinks and breakfast, and they graciously accept.

◆ ◆ ◆ ◆

Back in Port Hardy, Kick drops his bag on the floor. Taylor holds out a slip of paper and says, "This is the number." Kick sits down and dials.

A voice with a beautiful Costa Rican accent says, "Front desk."

"Can I speak with Mr. Patrick 'Dusty' Tucker, please."

"Mr. Dusty. Yes, sir."

Kick laughs. "She called him Mr. Dusty." Taylor snorts.

A few seconds later a sleepy voice picks up. "Whoever this is, it better be important. I'm on vacation!"

Kick plants his newly buffed cowboy boots on the table. "If you still know how to read, pick up a copy of *The Washington Post*."

"You *motherfucker* ... I should have known it'd be you messing up my sleep with ... Wait, what?"

"You've heard of Washington, DC, right? They have a newspaper there called *The Post*. Find a way to get today's copy and fucking read it, dumbass."

"I just woke up, fucker. Don't be condescending all over me after I closed down the pool bar last night!"

Taylor is laughing on the bed. "Tell him why."

"Kelly's story broke yesterday in *The Vancouver Telegraph* and *The Washington Post* just picked it up. She starts work there tomorrow."

Dusty howls with laughter. "Why the fuck didn't you say so? Am I supposed to guess what the hell you're talkin' about with all your cryptic shit? Like I'm a fuckin' mind reader? It is good to hear your stupid voice though. Where you at?"

"On the island fishing with Taylor. We're catching a flight to DC. You'll have to come and visit me there, Dust. I won't be back."

"Ooooo, that bad, huh? I guess I'll hear all about it when I get back in three weeks. That's right I said *three weeks*! That's how much more vacation I'm taking!"

Kick holds up the phone so Taylor can hear Dusty laughing.

"All right, motherfucker, you and Mr. Badass have a good flight," Dusty continues. "I'll catch you as soon as I can, and I can't wait to find out what all y'all troublemakers did to get in so much shit."

"Semper Fi." Kick says. Dusty is still laughing as Kick clicks the phone on the cradle.

Taylor picks up his copy of *The Vancouver Telegraph* and notices the catch phrase 'The Truth Will Set You Free' under the banner. "Is that new?"

Kick takes a look. "I'll be damned. Stewart must have added that, the sly old dog."

"I can tell you, as a lifelong, card-carrying intelligence officer, that is true. The truth *will* set you free."

Kick tops up traveler cups for them. "Who said that anyway? Aristotle?"

"No." Taylor thinks for a moment. "Gordon Lightfoot."

Kick nods in agreement, then drains the last of the rye from the bottle. They head out the door. Taylor fires up the truck and puts it in drive.

"Put your seatbelt on, man. I'm in the mood for a wild ride."

As they crest the top of the hill on their way out of town, the sun breaks through the clouds and streams into the truck. The boys put on their sunglasses. Kick feels good driving into the dawn of a new day, but he can still feel the long, dark trail of blood behind him. His eyes moisten as he watches the sunrise.

Taylor looks over at him. "What's up?"

"Looks like a badass mother of a day."

Acknowledgements

SPECIAL THANKS TO MY WIFE Helenna Santos for literally everything great in my life, Tara Avery for setting me on the right path as a novelist, Colleen Littledale for all the proofreads, Jen McIntyre for her wonderful editorial notes and for wrangling all my errant commas, Andrea Schwartz for the final final pass, and Phil, Vince, and James at Double Dagger Books for getting this story from my mind to yours. Special thanks as well to all members of the military, law enforcement, and all of those who keep the wolf from the door and protect our freedoms.

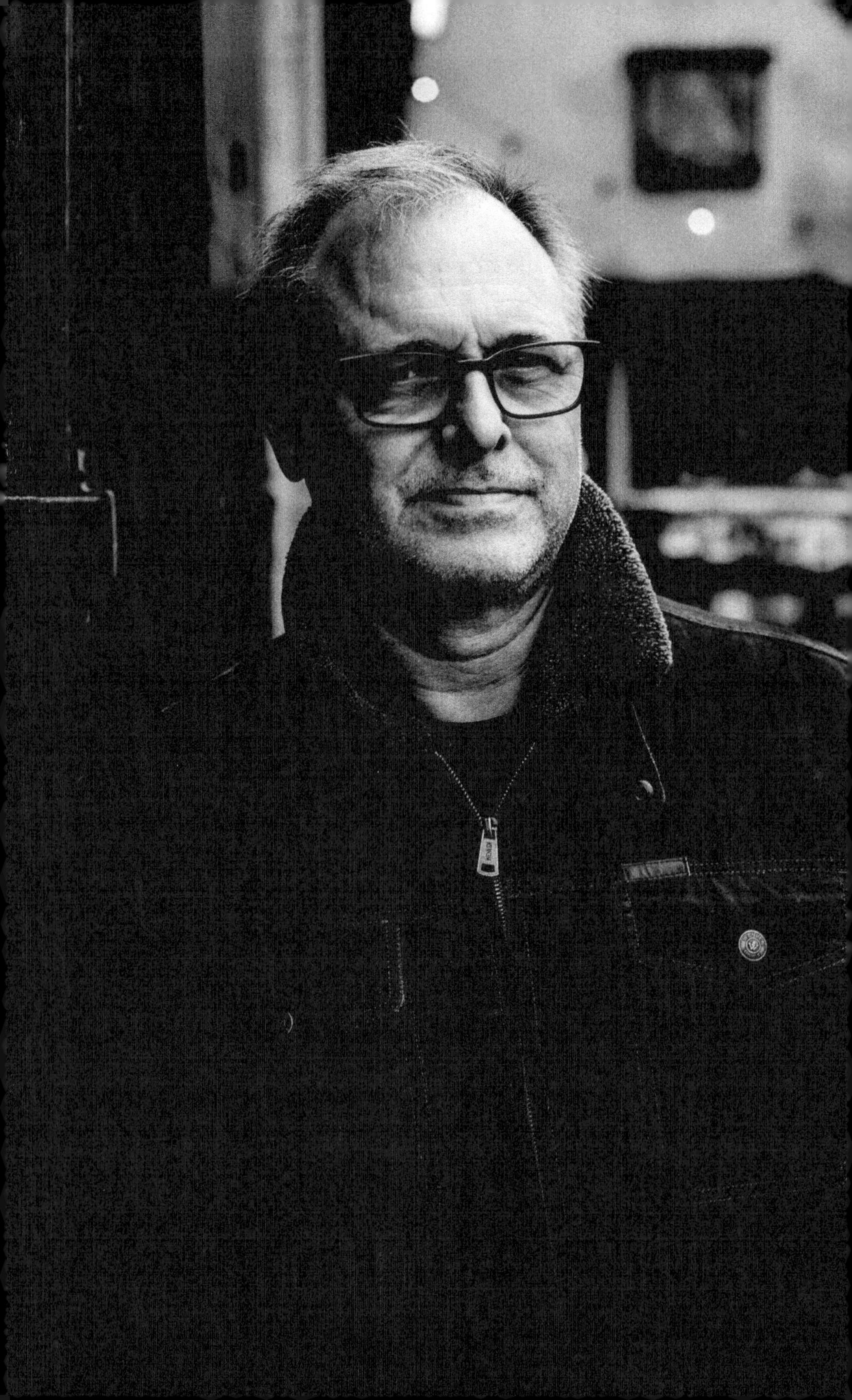

About the Author

Barry W. Levy is an award-winning actor, filmmaker, and screenwriter.

He holds a Fine Arts degree from The University of British Columbia's Department of Theatre, Film, and Creative Writing, (1991). His two feature films, 'Spook' and 'The Shasta Triangle', both of which he wrote and directed, have won many international festival awards, as have his numerous short films.

Besides being a former radio broadcaster, he has also worked as a professional film and television actor in Canada and Los Angeles for over 30 years, and has several screenplays in development.

Barry makes his home between Vancouver, BC, and Los Angeles with his wife, Helenna Santos, and dog Ella who are constantly entertained with his attempts to make pickles.

THE WAR MACHINE is his debut novel.

DOUBLE ‡ DAGGER
— www.doubledagger.ca —

DOUBLE DAGGER BOOKS is Canada's only military-focused publisher. Conflict and warfare have shaped human history since before we began to record it. The earliest stories that we know of, passed on as oral tradition, speak of war, and more importantly, the essential elements of the human condition that are revealed under its pressure.

We are dedicated to publishing material that, while rooted in conflict, transcend the idea of "war" as merely a genre. Fiction, non-fiction, and stuff that defies categorization, we want to read it all.

Because if you want peace, study war.

Printed in Great Britain
by Amazon